8
NIGHTS

ABBY GREEN
LYNN RAYE HARRIS
NATALIE ANDERSON

Three glamorous, smouldering-hot affairs!

NIGHTS COLLECTION

July 2013

August 2013

September 2013

October 2013

Exotic
NIGHTS

ABBY GREEN
LYNN RAYE HARRIS
NATALIE ANDERSON

MILLS & BOON

THE VIRGIN'S SECRET

ABBY GREEN

Abby Green got hooked on Mills & Boon® romances while still in her teens, when she stumbled across one belonging to her grandmother in the west of Ireland. After many years of reading them voraciously, she sat down one day and gave it a go herself. Happily, after a few failed attempts, Mills & Boon bought her first manuscript.

Abby works freelance in the film and TV industry, but thankfully the four a.m. starts and the stresses of dealing with recalcitrant actors are becoming more and more infrequent, leaving her more time to write!

She loves to hear from readers and you can contact her through her website at www.abby-green.com. She lives and works in Dublin.

This is for my lovely editor, Meg,
who shines a torchlight into the dark corners
where I've tied myself into knots and helps me
unravel it all again into something coherent.
Thanks for everything—you're a star.

I'd also like to dedicate this book with special
thanks to Anne Mary Luttrell, whose waiting
room is a magical place where many a plot
has been incubated.

Thanks for your healing hands (needles) and words.

PROLOGUE

LEONIDAS PARNASSUS looked out of the window of his private plane. They'd just landed at Athens airport. To his utter consternation his chest felt tight and constricted—a sensation he didn't welcome. He was curiously reluctant to move from his seat, even though the cabin staff were preparing to open the door, even though sitting still and not moving was anathema to him. He told himself it was because he was still chafing at the reality that he'd acquiesced to his father's demand that he come to Athens for 'talks'.

Leo Parnassus did not carve out time for anything or anyone he deemed a waste of his resources and energy. Not a business venture, a lover, nor a father who had put building up the family fortune and clearing their shamed name before a relationship with his son. Leo grimaced slightly, his face so harsh that the steward who had been approaching him stopped abruptly and hovered uncertainly. Leo saw nothing though but the heat haze on the tarmac outside and the darkness of his own thoughts.

He was Greek through and through, and yet he'd never set foot on Greek soil. His family had been exiled from their ancestral home before he was born, but his father had returned triumphantly just a few years ago; finally realising a lifelong dream to clear their name of a terrible crime and to glory in their new-found status and inestimable wealth.

Bitter anger rose when Leo remembered his beloved *ya ya*'s lined and worn face. The sadness that had grooved deep lines around her mouth and shadowed her eyes. It had been too late for *her* to return home. She'd died in an alien country she'd never grown to love. Even though his grandmother had urged him to return as soon as he'd had the chance, he'd condemned Athens on her behalf for breaking her heart. He'd always sworn that he wouldn't return to the place that had spurned his family so easily.

Athens was still home to the Kassianides family who had been responsible for all that pain and sadness, and who were suffering far too belatedly and minutely for what they had done. They had cast a long shadow over his childhood which had been indelibly marked by their actions, in so many ways.

And yet, despite all that…here he was. Because something in his father's voice, an unmistakable weakness had called to him, in spite of everything that had happened. It had touched him on some level. In short, he'd felt *compelled* to come. Perhaps he wanted to prove to himself that he was not at the mercy of his emotions?

The very thought of that made him go cold; at the tender age of eight he'd made an inarticulate vow never to let any intensity of emotion overwhelm him, because that's what had killed his mother. Surely he could handle looking his ancestral home in the face and turn his back on it once and for all? Of course he could.

But first he had to deal with the fact that his father wanted him to take over the Parnassus shipping business. Leo had denied his inheritance a long time ago; he'd embraced the entrepreneurial American spirit, and now ran a diverse subsidiary business that encompassed finance, acquisitions, and real estate, recently snapping up an entire block of buildings in New York's Lower East Side for redevelopment.

His sole input to his father's business had been a couple of years before when they'd tightened the noose of revenge around the neck of Tito Kassianides, the last remaining patriarch of the Kassianides family. It was the one thing that had joined father and son: a united desire to seek vengeance.

Leo had taken singular pleasure in making sure that the Kassianides' demise was ensured, thanks to a huge merger his father had orchestrated with Aristotle Levakis, one of Greece's titans of industry. That victory now, though, when he was faced with the reality of touching down in Greece, felt curiously empty. He couldn't help but think of his grandmother, how much she'd longed for this moment and never got a chance to see it.

A discreet cough sounded, 'I'm sorry, sir?'

Leo looked up, intensely irritated to have been observed in a private moment. He saw the steward was gesturing to the now open cabin door. Leo's chest clenched tightly again, and he had the childishly bizarre urge to tell them to slam the door shut and take off, back to New York. It was almost as if something outside that door lay in wait for him. Such a mix of emotions was rising to the surface, and it was so unwelcome that he stood up jerkily from his seat as if he could shake them off.

He walked to the cabin door, very aware of the eyes of his staff on him. Normally it didn't bother him, he was used to people looking at him for his reaction, but now it scraped over his skin like sandpaper.

The heat hit him first, dry and searing. Strangely familiar. He breathed in the Athens air for the first time in his life and felt his heart hit hard with the intensifying of that absurd feeling of familiarity. He'd always felt that coming here would feel like betraying his grandmother's memory, but now it was as if she was behind him, gently pushing him forward. For a man who lived by cool logic and intellect, it was an alien and deeply disturbing sensation.

He concealed his eyes behind dark shades as an ominous prickling skated over his skin. He had the very unwelcome sensation that everything in his life was about to change.

At the same moment on the other side of Athens.

'Delphi, just take a deep breath and tell me what's wrong— I can't help you until I know what it is.'

That just provoked more weeping. Angel grabbed another tissue, a trickle of unease going down her spine now. Her younger half-sister said brokenly, 'I don't do this kind of thing, Angel, I'm a law student!'

Angel smoothed her pretty sister's fall of mahogany hair behind one ear and said soothingly, 'I know, sweetie. Look, it can't be that bad, whatever it is, so just tell me and then we can deal with it.'

Angel was absolutely confident when she said this. Delphi was introverted, too quiet. She always had been, and even more so since a tragic accident had killed her twin sister about six years ago. Ever since then she'd buried herself in books and studies, so when she said quietly, after a little sniffly hiccup, '*I'm pregnant...*' the words simply didn't register in Angel's head.

They didn't register until Delphi spoke again, with a catch in her voice.

'Angel—did you hear me? I'm pregnant. That's what... that's what's wrong.'

Angel's hands tightened reflexively around her half-sister's and she looked into her dark brown eyes—so different from her own light blue ones, even though they both shared the same father.

Angel tried not to let the shock suck her under. 'Delph, how did it happen?' She grimaced. 'I mean, I know *how*…but…'

Her sister looked down guiltily, a flush staining her cheeks red. 'Well…you know Stavros and I have been getting more serious…' Delphi looked up again, and Angel's heart melted at the turmoil she saw on her sister's face.

'We both wanted to, Angel. We felt the time was right and we wanted it to be with someone we loved…'

Angel's heart constricted. That was exactly what she had wanted too, right up until— Her sister continued, cutting through Angel's painful memory.

'And we were careful, we used protection, but it…' She blushed again, obviously mortified to have to be talking about this at all. 'It split. We decided to wait until we knew there was something to worry about…and now there is.'

'Does Stavros know?'

Delphi nodded miserably and looked sheepish. 'I never told you this, but on my birthday last month Stavros asked me to marry him.'

Angel wasn't that surprised; she'd suspected something like this might happen with the two of them. They'd been sweethearts for ever. 'Has he spoken to his parents?'

Delphi nodded, but fresh tears welled. 'His father has told him that if we marry he'll be disinherited. You know they've never liked us…'

Angel winced inwardly for her sister. Stavros came from one of the oldest and most established families in Greece, and his parents were inveterate snobs. But before she could say anything Delphi was continuing in a choked voice.

'…and now it's worse, because the Parnassus family are

home, and everyone knows what happened, and with Father going bankrupt...' she trailed off miserably.

A familiar feeling of shame gripped Angel at the mention of that name: *Parnassus*. Many years before, her family had committed a terrible crime against the much poorer Parnassus family, falsely accusing them of a horrific murder. It was only recently that they had atoned for that transgression. When her great-uncle Costas, who had actually committed the crime, had confessed all in a suicide note, the Parnassus family, who were now phenomenally successful and wealthy, had seen their chance for revenge, and had returned to Athens from America on a wave of glory. The consequent scandal and shake-up in power meant that her father, Tito Kassianides, had started haemorrhaging business and money, to the point that they now faced certain bankruptcy. Parnassus had made certain that everyone now knew how the Kassianides family had wilfully abused their power in the most heinous way.

'Stavros wants us to elope—'

Angel's focus came back, and she immediately went to interject, but Delphi put up a hand, her pale face streaked with tears. 'But I won't allow him to do that.'

Angel shut her mouth again.

'I won't be responsible for him being cut off and disinherited—not when I know how important it is to him that he gets into politics some day. This could ruin all his chances.'

Angel marvelled at her sweet sister's selflessness. She took her hands again and said gently, 'And what about you, Delph? You deserve some happiness too, and you deserve a father for your baby.'

A door slammed downstairs and they both flinched minutely.

'He's home...' Delphi breathed, a mixture of fear and loathing in her voice as the inarticulate roars of their father's drunken rage drifted up the stairs. More tears welled in her red-rimmed eyes, and suddenly Angel was extremely aware of the fact that her baby sister was now pregnant and needed at all costs to be protected from the potential pain of dealing with any scandal or losing Stavros. She took her gently by the shoulders and forced her to look into her eyes.

'Sweetheart, you did the right thing telling me. Just act as if everything is normal and we'll work something out. It'll be fine—'

Delphi's voice took on a hysterical edge. 'But Father is getting more and more out of control, and mother is unravelling at the seams—'

'Shh. Look, haven't I always been there for you?'

Angel winced inwardly. She *hadn't* been there when Delphi had needed her most, after Damia, her twin's death, and that was why she'd made the promise to stay at home until Delphi gained her own independence, her twin's death having affected her profoundly. Now her sister just nodded tearily, biting her lip, and looked at Angel with such nakedly trusting eyes that Angel had to batten down the almost overwhelming feeling of panic. She caught a lone tear falling down Delphi's face and wiped it away gently with a thumb.

'You've got exams coming up in a few months, and enough to be thinking about now. Just leave everything to me.'

Her sister flung skinny arms around Angel's neck, hugging her tight. Angel hugged her back, emotion coursing through her to think that in a few months her sister's belly would be swollen with a baby. She had to make sure she and Stavros got married. Delphi wasn't hardy and cocky, as her twin had been. Where one had been effervescent and exuberant, the other had always been the more quiet foil. And as for their father—if he found out—

Delphi pulled back and spoke Angel's thoughts out loud. 'What if Father—?'

Angel cut her off. 'He won't. I promise. Now, why don't you go to bed and get some sleep? And don't worry, I'll handle it.'

CHAPTER ONE

I'LL handle it. Those fatalistic words still reverberated in Angel's head a week later. She'd gone to speak with Stavros' father herself, to try and remonstrate with him, but he hadn't even deigned to see her. It couldn't have been made clearer that they were social outcasts.

'*Kassianides!*'

Abruptly Angel was pulled out of her spiralling black thoughts when her boss called her name. It must have been the second or third time, judging by the impatience on his face.

'When you can join us back on earth, go down to the pool and make sure it's completely clear and that the tea lights are set out on the tables.'

She stuttered an apology and fled. In all honesty Angel's preoccupation had been distracting her from something much more panic-inducing and stressful. Almost too stressful to contemplate.

She was here at the Parnassus villa, high in the hills of Athens, to waitress at a party that was being thrown for Leonidas Parnassus, the son of Georgios Parnassus. Everyone was buzzing about the fact that he might be about to take over the family business and what a coup it would be, Leo Parnassus having become a multimillionaire entrepreneur in his own right.

It hit her again as she hurried down the steps that were expertly overgrown with extravagantly flowering bougainvillea. *She was in the Parnassus villa, the home of the family who hated hers with a passion.*

For a second she stopped in her tracks, a hand going to her breast as an intense pain tightened in her chest. This was the absolute worst place she could be in the world. For a second she felt hysteria rising at the irony of it. She, Angel Kassianides, was about to serve drinks to the *crème de la crème* of Athens, right under the Parnassuses nose. The thought of what her father would do if he could see her now made her break out in a cold sweat.

She bit her lip and forced herself to go on, breathing a sigh of relief when she had a quick look around the pool area and saw no one. The guests hadn't started to arrive yet and, though there were some staying at the villa, Angel knew that they'd be getting ready. There was no reason for anyone to be by the pool, but still…an uneasy prickling skated over her skin.

She hadn't been able to avoid coming here tonight. She and her waiter colleagues had been halfway to their secret destination in a packed minibus before it had been revealed, for 'security reasons'. Angel knew well that if she'd bailed out of this evening her boss would have sacked her on the spot. He'd sacked people for less in his prestigious catering company. She couldn't afford for that to happen—not when her income was the only thing helping put her sister through college and keeping food on their table.

She tried to reassure herself: her boss was English, recently moved to Athens with his English/Greek wife. He knew

nothing of the significance of who Angel was, nor her scan-
dalous connection to the Parnassus family. She busied herself
placing out the tea lights in their antique silver holders in the
middle of the white damask-covered tables, and sent up
fervent thanks that, tonight of all nights, not one of the other
staff were local. Things were so busy at the moment that her
boss had had to call in their part-time workers, and they were
all either foreign or from outside Athens.

Her only fear now was that someone at the party might recognise her. But, knowing these people as she did, she'd no doubt
that in her uniform of black skirt and white shirt they'd not take
a second look at her. She worried her lip again. Perhaps she could
just stay in the kitchen and get the trays together and avoid—

Angel started suddenly when she heard the splash of water
coming from nearby. *Someone was in the pool.* Carefully she
placed the last candle down and made to slip away, back up to
the kitchen. As if she'd been subliminally aware of it but had
blocked it out, she realised that someone must have been in the
pool all along—but not swimming, so she hadn't noticed them.

The sky was a dusky violet colour, so perhaps that was also
why she hadn't—Angel glanced quickly to her right as a flash
of movement caught her eye, and her legs stopped functioning
when the sight before her registered on her retina and in her
brain.

An olive-skinned Greek god was hauling himself in one
powerfully sleek move out of the water, droplets of water cas-
cading off taut muscles. Everything seemed to go into slow
motion as the sheer height and breadth of him was revealed.
Angel shook her head stupidly, but it felt as if it had been
stuffed with cotton wool. Greek gods didn't exist. This was
a man, a flesh-and-blood man. And the minute she registered
that she was standing transfixed, staring at him, she panicked.

But her body wouldn't obey her order to move, or it would, but her limbs all moved in independent directions, and to her utter horror she found herself backing into a poolside chair and almost toppling over it. And she would have, if the man hadn't moved like lightning and grabbed her, so that instead of falling back she fell forward into his chest, with his hands around her upper arms.

For a long moment Angel tried to tell herself that this wasn't happening. That she wasn't breathing in an intoxicating mix of spice and earthiness. That she wasn't all but plastered against a bare, *wet* chest which felt as hard as steel, her lips just a breath away from pressing against skin covered in a light dusting of intensely masculine hair.

Angel tried to break away, and pulled back, forcing his hands to drop. Heat scorched upwards over her cheeks as she finally stood upright again and found her eyes level with hard, flat brown nipples. She looked up, swallowing, and her gaze skittered up and past broad shoulders to his face.

'I'm so sorry. I just…got startled. The light… I didn't see…'

The man quirked an ebony brow. Angel swallowed again. Lord, but his face was as beautiful as the rest of him. Not beautiful, she amended, that was too girly a word. He was devastating. Thick black hair lay sleek against his head, and high cheekbones offset an impossibly hard jaw. His mouth was forbidding, but held a promise of sensuality that resonated deep in her body.

Suddenly that mouth stopped being forbidding and quirked. She nearly had to put out a hand again to steady herself. A thin scar ran from his upper lip to his nose, making her fight the absurd urge to reach up and trace it. Making her wonder how he'd got it—this complete stranger!

'Are you okay?'

Angel nodded vaguely. He sounded American; perhaps he was a business colleague, a guest who was staying over. Although somehow, in her muddled brain, that didn't fit either. He was *someone*. She struggled to remember where she was, what she was here to do. *Who* she was.

She nodded. 'I'm...I'm fine.'

He frowned slightly, seemingly completely at ease with his lack of dress. 'You're not Greek?'

Angel alternately shook and nodded her head. 'I am Greek. But I'm also half-Irish. I spent a lot of time in boarding school there...so my accent is more neutral.' She clamped her mouth shut. What was she blathering on about?

The man frowned a little deeper, his glance up and down taking in her uniform. 'And yet you're waitressing here?'

The incredulity in his tone made Angel's sanity rush back. Only girls from privileged backgrounds in Greece went abroad for schooling. Immediately she felt vulnerable. She was meant to be fading into the background, not engaging in conversation with the guests of the hosts.

She backed away, looking somewhere in the region of his shoulder. 'Please excuse me. I have to get back to work.'

She was about to turn when she heard him drawl laconically, 'You might want to dry off before you start handing out champagne.'

Angel followed his gaze down to where it rested on her chest. On her breasts. She gasped when she saw that she was indeed drenched, her shirt opaque and her plain white bra clearly visible, along with two very pointedly hard nipples. How long had she been plastered against him like some mindless groupie?

With a strangled gasp of mortification Angel scrambled backwards, nearly tripping over a chair again and only just righting it and herself before there could be a repeat rescue performance. All she heard as she fled back up the steps was a mocking, deep-throated chuckle.

A little later, Leonidas Parnassus looked around the thronged salon and tried to stifle his irritation when he couldn't see the waitress. It had made him uncomfortable, how urgent his need to see her again had been as soon as he'd walked into the main reception room. It had also made him uncomfortable how vividly her image had come back to him in his recent shower, forcing him to turn the temperature to cold.

And now her image surged back again, mocking his attempts to thrust it aside. He recalled how she'd looked, with a dark flush on her cheeks, those intensely light blue eyes wide and ringed with thick black lashes, staring at him like a startled fawn. As if she'd never seen a man before.

She had a tiny beauty spot just on the edge of a full lower lip, and he grimaced when he felt the effect remembering that had on his lower body. He hated having such an arbitrary response. But when he'd seen her arrive by the pool and do her work, with quick, economic movements, her glossy light brown hair pulled into a high topknot, something about her had stirred him. Something about her intense preoccupation, for patently she hadn't noticed him in the pool. And Leo was not a man who was used to going unnoticed.

When he'd caught her against him in that completely instinctive move tendrils of her hair had come free and framed her face and the defined line of her jaw, making him want to slip his hand into the glossy strands and cause it to fall down around her shoulders. He could almost feel it over his hands now, the heavy silky weight.

Irritation spiked again. Where was she? Had she been a

figment of his imagination? His father approached then, with a colleague, and Leo forced a benign smile to his mouth, hating the fact that he was in thrall to a nameless waitress.

Distracting him momentarily was the reality he now faced of just how frail his father had become, even since he'd seen him last. As if something within him had shifted subtly but profoundly. He felt a deep-seated sense of inevitability steal over him, he was needed here, his own empire notwithstanding. But *was* his place really here? He tried out the word now: *home*. His heart beat fast.

He thought of his sterile, yet state-of-the-art penthouse apartment in New York; the steel and silver skyscrapers of the world he inhabited. He thought of his impeccably groomed and very experienced blonde mistress; he thought of what it might be like to walk away from all of that—and he felt...nothing.

Athens, being here for the past week, had confounded his every expectation. He'd thought he'd feel nothing. On the contrary, he felt as though he'd been plugged into something deeply primal within his soul. Something had been brought to life, and wouldn't be pushed back to some dim and distant recess.

Just then, as if to compound this feeling, he caught sight of something in the far corner of the room. Glossy hair piled high, a long neck. A familiar slim back. Leo's heart started to thud, this time to a very different beat.

Angel was trying to keep her head down and not meet anyone's eye. She'd done her best to stay in the kitchen, preparing the trays, but her boss had eventually sent her up to the main salon as she was his most experienced staff member.

At that moment she caught a pointed frowning look from Aristotle Levakis across the room—he was business partner

to Parnassus, and her stomach quivered with renewed panic.
This was a disaster in the making. Aristotle Levakis knew her,
because their fathers had been friendly before Aristotle's
father had died. Angel could remember that Aristotle had
been to one or two parties at her father's house over the years.

In the act of offering some red wine to a small group of
people, she had to keep going, but then she got accidentally
jostled by another waiter. The tray tipped off balance, and
with mounting horror Angel watched four glasses full of red
wine disgorge their contents all over a beautiful woman's
pristine and very white designer dress.

For a second nothing happened. The woman was just
looking down at her dress, aghast. And then it came, her
voice so shrill that Angel winced. Conversely, at the same
time, an awful silence seemed to descend.

'You stupid, stupid girl—'

But then, just as suddenly, a huge dark shape appeared at
Angel's side, and she barely had time to take in a breath
before she registered that it was the man from the pool. Her
heart skipped a beat, before starting again erratically. He sent
her a quick wink before taking the gasping woman aside to
speak to her in low, hushed tones, and Angel saw her boss
hurry forward to take the matter in hand.

Her boss and the woman were summarily dispatched, and
then the man turned around to face Angel. Words dropped into
her head but made no sense. He was so downright intimidating in an exquisite tuxedo that shock was rendering her
speechless, breathless and motionless.

He calmly took the now empty tray from her hand and
passed it to another waiter. The mess from the fallen drinks
was already being cleared up. Angel would have protested
that she should look after it, if she could have spoken.

Everyone else in the immediate vicinity seemed to melt away, and with a light, yet commanding touch from his hand on her arm Angel felt herself being manoeuvred across the room, until they'd walked through a set of open patio doors and out to the blessed quiet of the grand terrace.

The cool and fragrant evening air curled around Angel like a caress, but she felt hot, right down to her very core. Hot from embarrassment and hot from where this man's big hand was curled around her upper arm. They came to a stop beside a low wall, beyond which a pristine lawn sloped gently downwards and off into the distance.

Silence surrounded them, thick and heavy, the muted sounds of the party coming from behind the closed patio doors. *Had he closed the doors?* The thought of him doing that to give them privacy made her shiver. She looked up, and with a disconcerting amount of effort pulled her arm free from his light, yet devastating grip. He smiled down at her, putting his hands in his pockets, and he looked so rakishly handsome that Angel felt weak all over again. Hair that had been slicked back with water was now thick and glossy, a little over-long.

'So...we meet again.'

Angel forced her brain to retain a small sliver of sanity, but no matter how much she wanted it to, she feared her voice wouldn't come out as cool as she hoped for. 'I'm sorry...you must think me an awful klutz. I'm not normally so clumsy. Thank you for...' She gestured to the room, thinking of the red stain spreading over the woman's white dress again and feeling sick. 'For defusing the situation, but I don't think my boss will forgive me for it. That dress looked like it was worth about a year's worth of my wages.'

He took a hand out of his pocket and waved it nonchalantly. 'Consider it taken care of. I saw what happened, it was an accident.'

Angel gasped. 'I can't let you do a thing like that. I don't even know you.' His insouciance and casual display of wealth made something cold lodge in her chest. It was a rejection from deep within her of this whole social scene. She'd grown up with it and it reminded her too much of the darkness in her own family.

His eyes glinted with something dangerous. 'On the contrary, I'd say that we're well on the way to becoming…acquainted.'

An electric current seemed to spring into action in that moment. The man moved closer to Angel, closing the small distance between them, and the breath lodged in her throat. She couldn't think, couldn't speak. His eyes held hers, and for the second time that day she noted the way they seemed to burn with a golden light.

He lifted a hand and trailed his finger down one cheek to the delicate line of her jaw. It left a line of tingling fire in its wake.

'I haven't been able to stop thinking about you.'

The something cold that had lodged in Angel's chest melted. 'You…haven't?'

He shook his head. 'Or your mouth.'

'My mouth…' Angel repeated stupidly. Her gaze dropped to *his* mouth then, and she saw once again the jagged line of the scar extending from his upper lip. She had the strongest desire to reach up and trace it with a finger, so strong that she shook.

'Are you thinking about what it would feel like if my mouth was to touch yours right now?'

Angel's gaze flew up and clashed with pure molten golden

heat. An answering heat invaded her lower body. She felt the urge to clamp her legs together, as if that might calm the disturbing ache building up there.

Before she could answer, or articulate a response, his hand had cupped her jaw and cheek, and suddenly there was no distance between them, only him, so tall and close that he blocked out the sky, and his head was descending, coming nearer and nearer.

He smelt musky and *hot*. It was something so earthy that Angel could feel the response being tugged from down low in her belly, as if she recognised it on some primitive level. Dimly she wondered if this was what people meant when they talked about animal attraction.

Desperately trying to cling onto something, *anything* rational, Angel brought a hand up to cover his, to pull it down, to stop him, to say no… But then his mouth was so close that she could feel his breath feather there, mingling with hers. Her mouth tingled. She wanted…she wanted—

'Sir?'

Angel wanted his mouth on hers so badly that she made a telling move closer–

'Mr Parnassus…sir?'

Angel's eyes had been fluttering closed, but suddenly flew open again. Their mouths were just about touching. If Angel was to put out her tongue she'd be able to explore his lips, their shape and texture. And then the name that had just been uttered exploded into her consciousness properly.

Mr Parnassus.

Reality slammed back, and the cacophony of the party rushed out to meet them through open doors. Angel was barely aware of pulling his hand down and moving back. Shock was starting to spread through her entire body.

Someone else came out to the patio then. The butler who had been standing there—*for how long?*—melted away discreetly. The new arrival was the host's wife, Olympia Parnassus. Angel knew this because she'd given all the waiting staff a pep talk in the kitchen earlier.

'Leo, darling, your father is looking for you, it's almost time for the speech.'

In a smooth move, Angel realised that she'd been effectively shielded from view. She felt more than heard the deep rumble of response.

'Give me two minutes here, Olympia.'

His tone was implacable. Clearly he was someone used to giving commands and having them met. He was *Leonidas Parnassus*.

Angel barely heard the older woman make some comment before she turned and clipped her way back into the party in her high heels, pulling the doors shut again. Shock was gathering force, and Angel started to react. She had to get out of here.

She knew that Leonidas Parnassus had turned back to face her, but she couldn't look at him. A warm hand tipped her chin up and she felt sick. She couldn't avoid his eyes unless she closed her own, and the thought of doing that made panic rise. He smiled a sexy smile.

'Please forgive the interruption. I'll have to go in a minute, but…where were we?'

Angel had to get out of here right *now*. She'd just been about to kiss Leonidas Parnassus, the very man who must be gloating over her family's very public ruination. A sudden spurt of anger bloomed. They were in dire straits, and it was all because of *his* family and their lust for revenge. She thought of Delphi, who was so vulnerable now; she and her sister didn't deserve to be paying for something that had happened decades before.

Angel pulled down his hand and forced frost into her voice. 'Look, I don't know what you're playing at. I have to get back to work. if my boss saw me out here with you I'd be sacked on the spot, which is obviously something that hasn't occurred to you.'

Leonidas Parnassus looked at her for a long moment before straightening to his full intimidating height and moving back a pace. Gone was the sexily teasing man of just moments before and in his place now stood the son and heir of a vast fortune. The man who was already a self-made millionaire. No wonder she'd had that feeling earlier that he *was someone*.

Arrogant confidence oozed from every pore, and Angel had to repress a shiver at the cold of his eyes—not tawny gold any more, but almost black, like flint.

'Forgive me.' His voice was frigid. 'I would never have attempted to kiss you if I'd known you found the prospect so repugnant.'

His demeanour made a mockery of his words. He was completely unrepentant. At that moment he reached out and cupped her jaw again. Her heart hammered against her ribs, she felt herself flushing.

Any pretence of remorse was gone, or charm. 'Who do you think you're kidding, sweetheart? Don't ever fool yourself like that again. I know the signs of desire, and you're practically panting for me right now, just like you were by the pool.'

Angel ripped his hand down again, panic surging in earnest. If he had even an *inkling* of who she was… 'Don't be ridiculous. I am not. I want you to get out of my way, please, so I can get back to work.'

'I will,' he bit out. 'But not before we've proved your words to be a lie.'

Before Angel could take a breath he'd cupped her face in both his hands, stepped right up to her body, and his mouth was crashing down onto her shocked open one with all the force of a huge wave. Her hands covered his in a hazy attempt to remove them, and she struggled against the onslaught, but it felt like going against the strongest current.

Her open mouth had provided an unwitting invitation to his, and his tongue stabbed deep and plundered, seeking hers, sucking it deep. To be kissed so intimately shook her to her core.

Her body had stiffened with the shock of his action, but a spreading, melting sensation was quickly taking over. The urge to fight was becoming more and more distant. All Angel could feel was the sinewy strength of those hands. They were so big that he was cradling her entire head, long fingers threading through her hair, massaging her scalp. And all the while his mouth and tongue were sucking her down into a deep spiral of the unknown.

When she stopped trying to pull his hands away she would never know. Nor would she be able to say when she moved her own hands and arms to wind their way up and over his shoulders.

She only knew that all reality had ceased to exist as they kissed and kissed with furious intensity. Their bodies were tight together and she pressed against the long, lean hardness of him. The thundering beating of their hearts was drowning out voices, concerns. She strained against him, on tiptoe to get even closer…could feel the unmistakable signs of his burgeoning arousal, and when she felt that her brain melted completely.

And then all of a sudden it was over, and he was stepping back from her. Angel made an awfully betraying move towards him, as if loath to let him go, her hands still outstretched from where they'd been wrapped like clinging vines around his shoulders. It was only then that she noticed her hands were held in his….and the awful suspicion arose. Had he had to forcibly take them down? Mortification flooded Angel even as she tried to assess the situation, gather her scattered nerves. Her heart still hammered. She was mute. Dizzy.

Leonidas Parnassus just looked at her, his face flushed… with anger? Or satisfaction that he'd proved himself right? Angel's mortification rose to a new level.

A discreet cough came from close by, and then a voice.

'Sir? If you could join your father inside now…*please*?'

Leonidas just looked at Angel, nothing given away on his face. It held a steely imperviousness that she would never have guessed the teasing man she'd met earlier to possess.

'I'll be right in.' Leonidas pitched his voice to reach the hovering staff member, but his eyes never left hers. He seemed to be utterly in control, apart from that betraying colour in his cheeks. She felt as if she was unravelling at the seams.

'I—' Angel began ineffectually.

He cut her off with an autocratic, 'Wait for me here. I'm not done with you yet.'

And with that he turned on his heel, and Angel watched him stride powerfully back into the thronged room, raking a hand through his hair as he did so. His back was huge and broad in the black of his tuxedo.

She couldn't believe what had just happened.

In shock she put a finger to her mouth, where her lips felt plump and bruised. Thoroughly kissed. In a fresh rush of embarrassment and disgust Angel could remember wantonly arching her body even closer to his…almost as if she'd wanted to climb into his skin. Not even in the most passionate moment of her relationship with Achilles had she felt that intensity of desire, every thought wiped clean from her mind. But then, she recalled bitterly, that had been part of the problem...

Angel felt raw and exposed, and painful memories were surging back, as if it wasn't awful enough to deal with what had just happened.

She heard a hush descend on the crowd in the salon, and searched for some means of escape. Finally, growing desperate, she spotted where some steps led down from the patio to the lower levels, and presumably back around to the kitchen. Hurrying down, she knew that she could forget about her job. The incident with the wine would have sealed her fate anyway; her disappearance with the guest of honour would have merely ensured it.

If her boss hadn't known the significance of who she was, he soon would, and she didn't want to be around to witness that.

Down in the kitchen she grabbed her things, and then crept out and headed down the drive, away from the glittering villa, not looking back once.

Leo stood and listened to his father's unashamedly emotional speech, Georgios Parnassus made no secret of the fact that he was ready to hand over the reins of power to Leo. The prospect of a shift in power had been evident in the room instantaneously. Again, Leo felt that welling of some ancient pride, that sense of right to be here. While he wasn't going to give the old man the satisfaction of capitulating so easily, he couldn't deny the sense of needing to stake his own claim to his birthright, the birthright that had been stolen from him.

His old man was no fool. No doubt he'd banked on exactly this by asking him to come to Greece, but Leo was not about to let him see that he might have won so soon.

Even while Leo was able to function and articulate his thoughts and intentions as the rapturous applause died away after his father's speech and the din of conversation rose again, his body still hummed with desire for the woman he'd left outside on the patio. He flicked a glance to the doors, once again open, but couldn't see her. Irritation prickled to think she might have moved. He'd told her to wait for him. He was trapped now, though, by the usual sycophants, all vying to get a slice of him.

He chafed to leave, to get back outside, finish what they'd started, and that irked him. Here he was at the potential forking of the road in his life, a huge moment, and all he could think about was a sexy waitress who'd had the temerity to blow hot and cold and then hot again. Anger gripped him, surprising him. He'd never encountered that before. He'd had women play hard to get in an effort to snag his interest and it never worked. He didn't indulge in games. The women in his life were experienced, mature…and knew the score. No emotional entanglement and no game-playing.

But when *she* had looked at him as if he'd been some callow youth trying to maul her…he'd seen red. He'd never felt that singular desire before to prove someone wrong, to imprint himself on a woman. He'd never felt such a ruthless need to kiss anyone like that…and then, when he'd felt her initial struggle fade, when he'd felt her grow hot and wanton in his arms, kissing him back almost as if her life—

'Georgios couldn't have been more obvious—so, are you ready to take the bait, Parnassus?'

Leo was so helplessly deep in his thoughts that it took a

second for his brain to function and come back into the room. The fawning crowd surrounding him was gone. He blinked and saw that Aristotle Levakis, his father's business partner, was looking at him expectantly. Leo liked Ari Levakis; they'd worked closely together at the time of the merger, albeit with Leo based in New York. But, much to his chagrin now, he had to force himself to remember what Ari had just said.

He couldn't shake the building tension, wanting to get back out to *her*. What if she'd gone? He didn't even know her name. He forced himself to smile and joked, 'You think I'm going to discuss it with you and have any decision I make all over Athens by morning?'

Ari tutted good-naturedly. Leo tried to concentrate on their conversation even as he looked for glossy brown hair piled high, exposing a delicate jaw and neck.

He missed something Ari said then, and cursed himself. 'I'm sorry, what did you say?'

'That I was surprised to see *her* here. I saw you taking her outside—did you ask her to leave?' Ari was shaking his head. 'I'll admit she has some nerve…'

Leo went very still. *'Her?'*

'Angel Kassianides. Tito's eldest daughter. She was here working as a waitress… She spilt wine over Pia Kyriapoulos and you took her outside. I think everyone presumed that you were telling her where to go.' Ari looked around for a moment. 'And I haven't seen her since, so whatever you said worked.'

Leo had an instant reaction to hearing the Kassianides name mentioned. It was the name of their enemy; a name that represented *loss, pain, humiliation, and unbelievable heart-ache.* He frowned, trying to understand. 'Angel Kassianides… *She's* a Kassianides?'

Ari looked back and nodded, frowning when he saw Leo's face. 'You didn't know?'

Leo shook his head, his brain struggling to take in this information. Why would he know what Tito Kassianides' children looked like? They'd not dealt directly with the Kassianides family during the merger. The merger itself had been all that was needed to precipitate their downfall. It had been a clean and sterile revenge, but it felt curiously insufficient now, when he'd been faced by one of them here tonight. *When he'd kissed one of them.*

He felt acutely vulnerable; if Ari had recognised her, then who was to say that others hadn't? He remembered how he'd led her outside with one thought in mind: getting her alone so he could explore his attraction, with no clue as to her identity. He let anger dispel the unwelcome feeling of vulnerability. Had she been planning some sort of incident? What the hell had she been playing at with him? Seducing him with those huge blue eyes and then trying to pretend she didn't desire him? She'd been toying with him from that moment by the pool. Those widening eyes must have held recognition of who he was, not the mutual flash of attraction he'd believed it to be. The thought made bile rise. He hadn't felt so exposed...*ever*.

Had her father sent her, like some sort of pawn? Had the whole thing been an act? Leo's entire body stiffened in rejection of that thought. Just then he saw his own father approaching, with a delegation of other men. He had no time to process this now, and for the rest of the evening Leo would have to act and smile and pretend that he didn't want to rip off his bow tie, throw his jacket down and go and find Angel Kassianides and get her to answer some very pertinent questions.

A week later, New York

Leo stood at the huge window in his office that looked out over downtown Manhattan. The view was familiar, but he didn't see it. All he could see, and all he had seen every time he closed his eyes since Athens, was Angel Kassianides' angelic face, tipped up to his, eyelids fluttering closed, just before he'd kissed her. He laughed caustically to himself. *Angel.* Whoever had named her had named her well.

He wrenched his mind away from Angel and thought of Athens. Not that he'd admit it to anyone yet, and certainly not his father, but Athens had changed something fundamental inside him. New York was spread out below him and he felt nothing. It was as if even though he'd been born and brought up here it had never claimed him. It didn't resonate within him the way it once had. Now it was just a fast-living jumble of towering buildings.

He'd even rung his mistress that morning, after avoiding her all week, *which was not like him*, and broken it off. Her histrionics still rang in his ear. But he hadn't even felt a twinge of conscience. He'd felt relief.

Angel. It irritated him how easily she kept inserting herself into his consciousness. He hadn't been able to indulge in seeking her out and asking her just what the hell she'd been playing at in his father's villa due to a crisis erupting here in his head office. A crisis that looked set to continue for at least a few weeks, much to his irritation. Not that it was serving to take his mind off her. He wasn't used to women distracting his attention, and certainly not ones he hadn't even slept with.

Anger bubbled low within him. The feeling that he'd been made a fool of was a novel one, and not something he was prepared to allow for a moment longer. Angel Kassianides was playing with fire if she thought she could make a fool out of a Parnassus. Out of him. How dared she? After everything her family had done to his? On the very night of his public introduction to Athens society?

Her sheer audacity struck him again. Evidently the Kassianides family weren't content to let the past be the past. Did they want to rake up old enmity or worse, to fight to the death until they reined supreme again?

Leo frowned. Perhaps they had the support of some of the old Athens elite? Perhaps the threat was something to be concerned about…? And then, he chastised himself. Maybe it was all nothing. A pure coincidence that Angel had been there that night.

A small voice mocked: *was it a coincidence that out of all the people there, she was the one you noticed*? Leo's hands fisted in his pockets. He was not going to let her get away with this.

He turned around and picked up his phone and made a call. His conversation with the person on the other end was short and succinct. When he was finished he turned back to the view. Leo had just made a momentous announcement with the minimum of fuss: he was going to return to Athens and take over Parnassus Shipping. A tingling anticipation skated over his skin, made his blood hum.

The thought of facing Angel Kassianides again and forcing her to explain herself made the blood fizz and jump in Leo's veins. His jaw tightened as he fought the sudden surge of extreme impatience, a demand in his body that he act on his decision and go *right now*. He had things to do, his business in New York to sort out; a crisis at hand. He would bide his time and prepare, drive down this almost animalistic urge to leave. He assured himself that Angel Kassianides was not the catalyst behind his decision; but she was going to be one of his first ports of call.

CHAPTER TWO

A month later

ANGEL'S heart hammered painfully. She felt a cold sweat break out all over her body. For the second time in just weeks she was in the worst place in the world: the Parnassus villa. She felt sick when she remembered what had happened out on the terrace. She closed her eyes and breathed deep. She could not be thinking of that now. Of Leo Parnassus. Of how he'd made her feel just before she'd found out exactly who he was. Of how it had been so hard to forget him.

She opened her eyes again and tried to make out the rooms in the dim light. To her intense relief the place appeared to be empty, and she sent up silent thanks that for once the newspaper reports had been right. She'd read about Georgios Parnassus' ailing health, and how he was taking a rest on a recently acquired Greek island. She felt the reassuring bulk of the document in the inside pocket of her jacket. This was why she was here. She was doing the right thing.

Ever since it had been announced in the press just a few days ago that Leo Parnassus was taking over the reins of the

Parnassus shipping fleet, and leaving New York to come back
to Athens permanently, Angel had grown more skittish and
her father more and more bitter and vitriolic, seeing any
chance of redeeming himself diminish. A young, vibrant head
of the Parnassus Corporation was a much bigger threat than
the ailing father had been, despite their success.

Angel had returned home from her new job yesterday to
find her father cackling drunkenly over a thick document.
He'd spotted her creeping through the hall and called her into
the drawing room. Reluctantly she'd obeyed, knowing better
than to annoy him.

He'd gestured to the document. 'D'you know what this is?'

Angel had shaken her head. Of course she didn't know.

'This, dear daughter, is my ticket out of bankruptcy.'
He'd waved the sheaf of pages. 'Do you realise what I'm
holding here?'

Angel had shaken her head again, an awful sick feeling
creeping up her spine.

Her father had slurred, 'What I'm holding is the deepest,
darkest secrets of the Parnassus family and their fate.
Georgios Parnassus' final will and testament. I now know everything. About all their assets, exactly how much they're
worth, and how he plans on distributing it all. I also know that
his first wife killed herself. They must have hushed that up.
Can you imagine what would happen if this was leaked to the
right people? I can take them down with this.'

I can take them down with this. Nausea had risen from
Angel's gut to think that after all these years, and after what
the Parnassus family had been through, her father still wanted
to fuel the feud. He was so blinded by bitterness that he
couldn't see that doing something like this would make him
and *his family* look even worse. Not to mention cause untold

pain to the Parnassus family in revealing family secrets, if
what he said about the suicide was true.

'How did you get it?'

Her father had waved a dismissive hand. 'Doesn't matter.'

Familiar cold disgust had made Angel bite out, 'You sent
one of your goons to the villa to steal it.'

Her father's face had grown mottled, confirming what
she'd said, or at least the fact that he had stolen it. She'd no
idea how he had actually done it, but some slavishly loyal men
still surrounded her father.

Her father had become belligerent, clearly done with her.
'What if I did? Now, get out of here. You make me sick every
time I look at you and am reminded of your whore of a mother.'

Angel was so used to her father speaking to her like that
she hadn't even flinched. He'd always blamed her for the fact
that her glamorous Irish mother had walked out on them
when Angel had been just two years old. She'd left the room,
then waited for a while and gone back. Sure enough her father
had passed out in his chair, one hand clutching the thick
document, the other clutching an empty bottle of whisky to
his chest. He'd been snoring loudly. It had been easy to slide
the sheaf of pages out from his loosened fingers and creep
back out.

Early that morning she'd gone straight to work, taking the
will with her, knowing that her father would still be passed
out cold. And then, late that evening, she'd taken the journey
up to the Parnassus villa, but had panicked momentarily when
faced with a security guard and the enormity of what she had
to do. She'd blurted out something about being at the function
some weeks before and leaving something valuable behind.

To her intense relief, after the unsmiling guard had consulted with someone, she'd been let in. To her further relief,

when she'd reached the kitchens, she'd found no one and had crept up through the silent house, praying that she'd find the study. She'd leave the papers in a drawer and slip away again.

She was not going to let her father create more bad feeling between the families. That was the last thing they needed, the last thing Delphi needed. Every day now Stavros was begging Delphi to elope, but she was standing strong and refusing, determined not to ruin Stavros' prospects and be responsible for tearing his family apart.

The flaring up of their old feud with the most powerful family in Athens would make any prospect of marriage between them even more impossible. Angel heard her sister sobbing herself to sleep every night, and knew that a very real rift could break the young lovers apart for ever if something didn't happen soon. On top of everything else, Delphi had important law exams to think about.

The enormity of it all threatened to swamp Angel for a moment.

She emerged into the huge reception hall and stood for a moment, trying to calm her nerves, to stop her mind from spiralling into despair. Her breath was coming fast and shallow. She felt a prickling across the back of her neck and chastised herself. There was no one there. *Just get on with it*!

Seeing a half-open door across the expanse of marbled floor, she held her breath and tiptoed across. Gingerly pushing the door open a little more fully, she breathed a sigh of relief once more when she saw that it was the study. Moonlight was the only illumination, and it cast the room in dark shadows.

Angel could make out a desk and went over, feeling for a drawer. Her fingers snagged a catch and she pulled it out, while reaching her hand into her pocket for the will at the same time. She'd just pulled it free and was about to place it into the drawer when the lights blazed on, with such suddenness and ferocity that Angel jumped back in fright.

Leonidas Parnassus stood in the doorway, arms folded, eyes so dark and forbidding that they effectively froze Angel from feeling anything but numb. And then he said quietly, but with ice dripping from his tone, 'Just what the hell do you think you're doing?'

Angel blinked in the intense light. She heard a roaring in her ears and had to fight against the very real need to faint. She couldn't faint. But she couldn't speak. Her brain and body were going into meltdown at being confronted with Leo Parnassus, standing just a few feet away, dressed in dark trousers and a plain light blue shirt, looking dark and intimidatingly gorgeous. Looking like the man who had invaded her dreams for the past seven weeks.

She opened her mouth, but nothing came out.

With a few quick strides Leo had crossed the room, moving so fast and with such lethal grace that Angel just watched in disbelief when he effortlessly whipped the will out of her white-knuckle grip.

'Well, Kassianides, let's see what you came for.'

Angel watched dumbly as he unfolded the document. She heard his indrawn breath when he registered what it was.

He looked at her, his dark gaze like black ice. 'My father's will? You came here to steal my father's will? Or just whatever you could get your dirty little hands on?'

Angel shook her head, registering that he'd called her Kassianides. It distracted her. 'You…you know who I am?'

His jaw tightened. Angel saw the movement and felt a flutter in her belly. He threw the will down on the table and reached out, taking her arm in a punishing grip. Angel bit back a cry at his touch, more of shock than pain.

He unceremoniously hauled her from behind the desk and led her over to a chair in the corner. He all but thrust her into it.

'I should have guessed after your last stunt that you obviously don't have any qualms about trespassing where you're not welcome.'

He didn't answer her redundant question. Patently he now knew exactly who she was, and she realised that someone at the party must have told him after they'd seen him take her outside.

She knew it was probably futile, but she said it anyway. 'If I'd known for a second where I would be working that night I wouldn't have been here, I found out when it was too late.'

He all but sneered, towering over her now, arms crossed again over his broad chest. 'Please, give me some credit. You might be able to distract other people with that seductively innocent face, but after what I've just seen I know that you're rotten to your core. Your whole family are.'

Angel went to stand up on a fierce wave of anger. It was not fair to assume that she was like her ancestors, or her father, but before she could get a word out Leo had easily pushed her back down, not even using much force. Angel felt as weak as a rag doll, shaky all over. Once again the reality of his touch was more shocking than his action.

She clenched her fists and welcomed the rush of energy that anger brought. 'You have it all wrong. I'm not here to steal anything. If you must know—'

Leo slashed a hand through the air, silencing her. Angel stopped abruptly. As much as she held no love for her father, she realised in that moment the futility of landing the blame at his door. Leo Parnassus would just laugh in her face. She'd quite literally been caught with her hand in the cookie jar, and could blame no one but herself.

She watched as he paced back and forth, his hands on his hips. The fingers were long and lean, and a sprinkling of dark hair dusted the backs of his hands. Suddenly an image of him hauling himself out of the pool that evening in one sleek movement caused heat to explode low in her pelvis.

In a moment of blind panic, feeling intensely vulnerable, Angel sprang up again and stood behind the high-backed chair. As if that could offer protection! Leo stopped and turned around to face her, surveying her coolly.

Angel asked huskily, 'What…what are you going to do? Are you going to call the police?'

He ignored her question and walked over to a sideboard, where he poured himself a measure of whisky. He downed the drink in one swallow, the strong bronzed column of his throat working, making Angel feel even more weak and trembly.

Leo's eyes snared hers again, and she saw something flame in the dark depths, revealing golden lights.

'Did your father send you here that night? Was it a recce for tonight? Or is this your own ingenuity?'

Angel's hands clenched on the back of the chair; she could feel her ponytail coming loose. 'I told you. The night of the party I had no idea where we were going. I worked for that catering company, they didn't tell us until we were on the way for security reasons.'

He all but laughed out loud. 'And once you and your father knew that Georgios was away, you took advantage of the opportunity. The only thing you didn't factor in was my return.'

'Th…there was nothing in the press.'

Leo glowered, and Angel quailed even more. Now she'd made it sound even worse. No way could she reveal that she'd been helplessly drawn to scanning the papers every day to read about his movements.

'I came a week early, hoping to surprise a few people. We're very aware—' his mouth tightened '—more so now we're in transition of power, that people will believe we're an easy target to take over.'

Angel had a nauseating realisation. 'You saw me arrive. The security guard checked with *you*…'

Leo indicated to Angel's right-hand side, and she looked over to see an ante-room off the study, the door through which he had appeared. In it, she could clearly make out a glowing wall of cameras, showing flickering black and white images. CCTV cameras. One of which looked directly over the main gate. He'd watched nearly every step of her progress. She felt sick when she thought of how she'd crept through the house. Her naivety mocked her. Of course she'd never have got near this place if he hadn't been here. She looked back.

Leo's face was so harsh that Angel felt a jolt of pure fear go through her. This man was a million miles from the seductive stranger she'd met that night.

'Your audacity is truly astonishing. Clearly you have the confidence born of your position in society, even if you don't hold that position any longer.'

Angel could have laughed if she'd had the wherewithal. Tito might have been wealthy once, but he was a despot and had controlled all their lives with a tight fist. It hadn't been audacity that had led her to that gate; it had been sheer fear and a desire to right a wrong.

'I wasn't coming to steal anything, I swear.'

Leo gestured back to the will sitting on the table and completely ignored her statement. 'What were you hoping to glean from it?' He laughed harshly. 'That's a stupid question. No doubt your father was hoping to use inside information on my father's estate to undermine him in some way. Or were you going to use the information to do a bit of honey-trapping, maybe? You'd have enough information to try and winkle out some more? Take advantage of the kiss we shared that night?'

Angel flushed hotly when she thought of that kiss, and then remembered her father's gloating talk last night. That was exactly how her father would think. Too late, she saw the hard, unforgiving look come into Leo's eyes, his jaw tense. Clearly he was misinterpreting her misplaced guilt.

Once again she knew that it would be futile to tell the truth. Leo Parnassus would be more likely to believe in Santa Claus than in her innocence, especially when the circumstantial evidence was so damning. All she knew was that she needed to get out of there. She was feeling increasingly hot and bothered under his intense and concentrated regard.

Tentatively she came from around the chair. She reassured herself that he was an urbane man of the world. An American. She had to be able to appeal to some rational part of him.

'Look. You have the will. I'm sorry for trespassing where I'm not welcome. I promise if you let me go that you'll never see or hear from me again.' Angel ignored the way her heart gave a funny little clench when she said that. She couldn't even begin to contemplate her father's reaction to what she'd done, and of course she couldn't promise that he wouldn't do something stupid again, but she kept her mouth shut.

Leo put down the glass silently on the table. Angel followed the movement warily. A strange charge came into the air between them and she found her eyes being helplessly drawn back to his. They were glowing with gold in their depths again, reminding her of how he'd looked at her just before he'd kissed her that night on the terrace. His eyes dropped then, insolently sweeping down her body, taking in her worn jeans, black top and jacket. Sneakers. And suddenly it was as if she was breaking out into little fires all over her skin.

Her heart started thumping. In a blind panic, to negate her reaction, she moved again, telling herself that he wouldn't stop her if she just walked out. After all, it wasn't as if she'd actually broken into the villa.

But just as she was about to pass him she felt her arm being gripped, and she was swung around so fast that she lost her balance and fell against him. All the breath seemed to leave her body.

In an instant he'd loosened her already unravelling hair, and it fell around her shoulders. His hand held her head, tilting her face up to him. His other arm was like a steel band around her back. Angel was afraid to move or breathe, because that would invite a contact that would scatter what remained of any coherent thought. As it was, she was barely clinging onto a shred of sanity.

'Do you know that you've actually done me a favour, Kassianides?'

Angel winced inwardly at his use of her surname, hating the fact that it bothered her.

'You've saved me a trip. Because I was going to confront you about why you'd come here that night. You couldn't possibly have believed you'd get away with it, could you?'

It was a rhetorical question. Angel said nothing, too scared of the burgeoning feelings and sensations running through her body. When Leo spoke again his chest rumbled against hers.

'I was also curious to know if perhaps I'd been too harsh

in my first assessment as to why you'd been waitressing at our party. After all, just because you're Tito's daughter, perhaps it wasn't entirely fair to assume the worst.'

Angel couldn't believe it. She saw a glimmer of hope and started to nod her head. She opened her mouth, but he wasn't giving her an opportunity to speak. His voice became harder and harsher.

'But your actions here tonight have damned you completely. The minute you saw the opportunity you were back, and this time to steal something of real value that could be used in an effort to harm our family. That will has information about my own estate, so it's not just my father you've committed a crime against, it's me.'

Cold horror trickled through Angel. This was so much worse than she'd thought.

Leo continued, 'It's almost cute, how naive you were to think you could be so blatant. Do you really think if I hadn't been here that it would have been so easy to get access to this villa?'

Angel's fragile hopes died there and then. She tried to summon her strength and pull free, and regretted it immediately when it merely gave Leo more room to hold her even tighter against him. Her breasts were crushed against his chest. They were pressed together, torso to torso, hip to hip. His breath feathered near her mouth—when had his head moved so close?

She tried to pull back and his fingers tightened in her hair. She winced, even though he wasn't really hurting her. His mocking smile sliced through her defences.

'You can't be so naive as to believe you're getting away that easily, Kassianides, can you?'

Cold fear trickled through Angel. For a second she was distracted enough to ask, 'What do you mean?'

'There was another reason I was going to come for you.'

Angel shivered inwardly, he sounded so implacable. 'There was?'

He nodded, his face so close now that she felt as if she was drowning in the dark golden depths of his eyes. Her hands were between them, resting on his chest, where they'd gone in an instinctive move to steady herself. She could feel his heart beating steadily underneath them and it made her want to move her hips. She stayed rigid.

'You've kept me awake for weeks.' He grimaced. 'I tried to deny it, ignore it. But this desire wouldn't abate. I'm not in the habit of denying myself anything, or anyone I want. As much as I despise myself for feeling this…I want you, Angel.'

Angel's brain couldn't compute the significance of what he was saying, and certainly couldn't compute the tumult of emotions that had threatened to swamp her when he'd called her *Angel*. All those nights she'd woken sweating from torrid dreams…he'd been thinking of her too?

She tried to push back again, but Leo held her effortlessly. His head bent closer and Angel twisted hers away in desperation. He whispered near her ear with deadly silkiness, 'You came here that night to humiliate my family, and you tried to humiliate me. And you came here tonight to steal from us. You won't get away with it, Angel. You can't expect to keep playing with fire and not get burnt.'

Angel turned her head back, seriously panicked now. She'd never stolen anything in her life! 'But I wasn't. I—'

But the rest of her words were silenced under the devastating crush of Leo's mouth to hers. He was ruthless, *he was angry*, and he plundered and took until Angel felt weak tears smart at the back of her eyes and her hands were fists trying to beat ineffectually against his rock-hard chest.

A weak moan of pleading came from deep in her throat. Finally Leo pulled away, and she felt his chest moving against hers with his harsh breaths. It should have disgusted her, *scared her*, made her recoil when she saw the heated look in his eyes, but it didn't.

It made her quiver deep down inside, somewhere very vulnerable. As if she'd been waiting for this. As if, despite everything, this somehow felt right. In that moment Leo's hand gentled on her head, his fingers massaged her skull, and the movement weakened her further. She couldn't cope with tenderness, gentleness. She felt a thumb move across her cheek, and only realised then that a tear must have crept out.

Leo smiled, but it was tight. 'The tears are a nice touch, Angel, but unnecessary—along with trying to pretend that you don't want me.'

He shifted slightly, so that Angel fell more into the cradle of his lap, and she gasped when she felt the hard evidence of his arousal against her belly. The shocking reality of it made moisture gather between her legs in a very earthy recognition of a mate. She couldn't believe she was having this reaction, and yet from the moment she'd seen him emerge from the pool...

She was caught by his eyes as if hypnotised. Everything melted away: who she was and why she was there.

When Leo bent his head again, this time he wasn't cruel and harsh. His touch was firm and seductive. His mouth settled over hers and caused a deep sigh to move through her.

With an expertise she dimly acknowledged Leo forced her mouth to open to him, touching his tongue to hers and causing a flash flood of liquid heat to her groin. Angel moved instinctively, barely aware of what she was doing, just sensing that she wanted...more.

Leo hauled her even closer, growling something in his

throat as his mouth continued its dark magic on hers. Angel was vaguely aware that her hands had unfurled and had climbed up over those impossibly broad shoulders. She was now clinging to his neck, arching her body into his, fingers tangling in the surprisingly silky strands of his hair.

When Leo took his mouth from hers she gave a little mewl of despair. She opened heavy eyes to see him smile with sinful sexiness and her heart turned over. A lock of glossy black hair had fallen forward onto his forehead and Angel pushed it back with a trembling hand, barely aware of what she was doing, just following some deeply felt instinct.

Leo's hand settled at the waist of her jeans, and after a heart-stopping moment snaked under her top. The feel of him touching her bare skin made her pulse rocket skywards. His hand crept higher and higher, to where she could feel her breast grow tight and heavy, until after an excruciatingly slow moment he cupped the soft mound and pulled the cup of her bra down.

Angel bit her lip. She was seriously out of her depth, and she felt as if a part of her was standing apart and watching with mounting horror as she let him touch her so freely. But she was caught in the grip of something so powerful she couldn't move.

Leo moved his thumb back and forth over the tight puckered tip, and then with a brusque movement he thrust up her top to bare her breast to his gaze. To see him looking down at her breast made Angel feel faint with a rush of desire. And then, when he bent his head… Her mind was screaming at her to pull away…but she couldn't. When he flicked out a tongue and then sucked that peak into the hot, swirling cavern of his mouth Angel's head fell back. Her hands gripped his shoulders tightly.

She was fast being transported to a place of no return. The

pleasure was so intense that she was afraid she'd burst. Leo brought a hand between her legs, forcing them apart to cup between her thighs, and she was lost completely. She'd never felt this out of control of her own body before.

He caressed her through her jeans, the material acting as a paltry barrier to his expert touch. He knew exactly where she ached, and all the while he suckled mercilessly on her breast. Angel cried out in desperation: for him to stop and for him never to stop. The sensation of her jeans and his hand moving remorselessly against her was excruciatingly exquisite.

Angel felt her body tensing. She'd lost any hope of regaining control by now. The world had ceased to exist. *This* was her reality.

With a husky whisper she entreated him, hardly knowing what she was looking for. '*Leo…*'

Everything went very still. But Angel hardly even noticed until, with sudden ruthlessness that almost bordered on cruelty, Leo stopped what he was doing and thrust her back from him with two hands on her shoulders.

For a long moment Angel stood in shock, breathing swiftly as the earth righted itself again. Her heart thumped painfully and a light sweat had broken out all over her body. He rearranged her top and bra so she was covered again, with an abruptness that made Angel wince. The material chafed against her still sensitive nipple.

She just couldn't believe— Her thoughts ground to a halt when she realised her hands were glued to his chest, fingers curled and clinging to the material of his shirt. Hurriedly she dropped them as though burnt. Angel also realised then that her legs were incapable of holding her up, and she nearly collapsed in a humiliating heap at Leo's feet before he cursed and picked her up, bringing her back over to the chair and sitting her down.

Angel let her hair fall around her face. She couldn't find a word to articulate how awfully raw and exposed she felt. Leo had set out to humiliate her and it had taken a nanosecond before she'd turned into a groaning wanton in his arms. How he must be laughing at her. He'd accused her of stealing just seconds before he'd kissed her, and she'd all but lain down and given herself to him.

Her cheeks burned so hot they felt on fire. She could remember the way she'd said *Leo*, breathlessly, huskily, just as her whole body had been about to tip over the edge into an experience she'd never had, an experience that her jangling nerves craved to know even now. She'd thought she'd been in love with her boyfriend at college, and he hadn't even managed— She gulped. Yet here, with someone who clearly despised her… Mortification twisted her insides into hard knots.

'Angel—'

His voice was suddenly too close, and Angel jumped up in a reflexive surge of horrified anger at how she'd reacted. Too late she saw that Leo had been holding out a glass of what looked like brandy, and she could only watch dumbly as it was knocked out of his hand with the force of her jerky movement, spinning away to crash into the corner of the room, glass shattering, alcohol staining the parquet floor.

She looked at Leo in shock. 'I'm so—'

He cut her off, his face all sharp angles and forbidding lines. Jaw tense. 'You could have just refused, Angel. There was two of us involved in what happened just now, so don't try the outraged virgin act.'

If only he knew! His words fell like tiny cuts all over her skin. Angel quivered with a rush of contradicting and mixed emotions. Right then she was glad the glass had smashed, and yet she also wanted to rush to clean it up. She wanted to smack Leo across the face, when she'd never hit a soul in her life, but she also wanted to throw herself into his arms and beg him to kiss her again. Her body still tingled and burned.

She made a monumental struggle and tipped up her chin. 'I didn't see the glass. I'm sorry.'

His eyes flashed in response. In a bid to put space between them Angel went on jelly legs to where the glass had smashed and started to pick up the bigger pieces. She heard something inarticulate behind her, and gasped as she was pulled up, a hand under her arm.

'Leave it. I'll get someone to look after it.'

They were very close again, and all of Angel's recent humiliation rushed back. Something caught Leo's eye and he looked down at her hands, saying harshly, 'You're bleeding.'

Angel looked down stupidly. She hadn't felt a thing, but saw that her finger *was* bleeding from a nasty-looking gash. Leo expertly took the glass out of her hands and put it on the table behind them. Then, holding that hand carefully in his, he picked up the phone, dialled a number and bit out terse instructions in accentless Greek.

Angel would have been impressed if she'd been able to think clearly. All she could do was follow Leo when he led her from the room and up the main staircase, her hand held in front of him so she had to hurry to keep up with his much longer strides.

He brought her into a huge bathroom, switched on the light, and rummaged around for something in a cupboard. Angel could see that it was a first aid kit, and blustered, 'Oh, no, don't. Let me—'

'Sit down and be quiet.'

Angel was forced to sit down on the closed toilet seat, and she watched incredulously as Leo knelt before her and inspected the cut. And then he brought her finger to his mouth and sucked it deeply.

Angel's breath stopped. She tried to pull back, but he was too strong. Finally he let her finger go and said tersely, while inspecting it again, 'I want to make sure there's no glass in it. It's a deep cut, but I don't think you need stitches.'

Thoroughly bemused, and feeling as if reality as she knew it had morphed out of all existence, Angel watched as Leo expertly and gently cleaned the cut and placed a tight plaster around the top of her finger.

Then, just as perfunctorily, he led the way back downstairs, this time into a drawing room adjacent to the other side of the hall. She saw someone scurrying out of the study with a dustpan and brush. Leo let go of her hand and Angel scooted over beside a couch, sitting gingerly on the edge because she didn't think she could stand.

Leo poured a measure of something dark and golden—*like his eyes*—into a glass and brought it over. His mouth was set in a grim line. Angel accepted it with both hands, while avoiding his eyes. She didn't drink much alcohol at all, but right now she welcomed the prospect of its numbing quality.

CHAPTER THREE

LEO watched Angel take the glass in both hands, a curiously child-like gesture that made something in his chest twist. He wanted to wring her pretty neck. But he also wanted to flatten her back against the couch and finish what they'd started in the study. He could still remember how it had felt to roll his tongue over her small tight nipple, the way she'd arched into him, and he had to use iron will right now to control the rush of response.

He had *not* meant to ravish Angel standing in the study like that. The impulse to kiss her had been born out of his inarticulate rage that she had such a visceral effect on him, especially when he knew exactly who and what she was. But the kiss had got out of control very quickly. He couldn't remember the last time he'd been so consumed, to the extent that he'd shut out every clamouring voice in his head. Until she'd said *Leo* with that husky catch, and her hips had jerked against his hand, and he'd emerged from what had felt like a trance.

He'd touched down in Athens barely three hours ago and was still reeling slightly at facing the reality that he'd willingly upended his life. Feeling acutely vulnerable *again*, Leo turned and strode back to the sideboard, to pour himself a drink and try and gather his scattered thoughts. They'd scattered as soon as he'd taken the call from the security guard and seen who was at the gate. For a disturbing second he'd almost believed he was imagining her.

And yet he couldn't deny that he'd felt a rush of pure sensual excitement at seeing Angel approaching the house. It had eclipsed the disappointment he'd felt that her effect on him hadn't grown less in the interim.

Her guilt had been obvious from the moment she'd gone straight to the kitchen entrance rather than come to the main door. And then, when he'd seen her creeping through the house like the little thief she was, something hard had solidified in his chest.

He hated to admit it but he *had* thought that perhaps he'd judged her too swiftly. Seeing the evidence of her avarice in front of his eyes tonight had made a fool of him *again*. She was no innocent. Hadn't years of witnessing hardened New York socialites in action taught him anything?

As he poured himself a drink now, and threw it back in one gulp, he told himself that his decision to come home and the speed with which it had been expedited had absolutely nothing to do with the woman sitting on the couch behind him. He knew exactly how he was going to deal with her and get her out of his system, so that he could get on with his new life here in Athens.

Angel sat on the couch, cradling her glass, and felt as if she was waiting to hear a sentence pronounced. Leo kept his broad back turned to her for long moments, and the tension in her body was beginning to ratchet up, despite the calming effects of the alcohol.

Eventually he turned around, and Angel almost breathed a sigh of relief. Leo's face was stark, unreadable. Not once had he cracked a smile, shown a glimmer of humanity…*apart from when he'd tended her cut.* Angel remembered the way he'd sucked her finger into his mouth and quivered deep in her belly.

She swallowed. She thought of how his lazy, easy American accent had made her assume he was just one of the guests at the villa that night… She'd never have suspected she'd ever hear the steel running underneath the velvet caress of that voice. But he was Leonidas Parnassus. Practically the uncrowned King of Athens. And she was his bitter enemy. Even more so now.

There was a final reckoning to be had between their families, and Angel was very afraid this was going to be it. She tried to force the fear down—after all, what else could happen to them now? She thought of Delphi then, and felt slightly sick.

Leo came over and took a seat on the couch opposite Angel. He sat back and crossed one ankle over one knee. He spread a hand out across the back of the seat, making the material of his shirt stretch enticingly across his chest. It was a dominantly masculine pose. Angel could feel her face heat up and willed it down.

'Why did you come here the night of the party?'

Angel couldn't believe it. Weariness tinged her voice. 'I already told you. I had no idea where we were headed. I couldn't have just walked out; I would have lost my job on the spot.'

'But you lost that job anyway,' he pointed out silkily.

Angel held in a gasp. How did he know that? Not that it would have taken a rocket scientist to deduce that her behaviour that night might result in that. Did he know that she'd been working as a chambermaid in the plush Grand Bretagne Hotel since then, and was doing regular double shifts? No doubt he'd love to know that she'd felt compelled to find jobs in areas where her name would require the minimum amount of investigation. She'd been conscious of Delphi still being in college, and had not wanted to draw any potential press attention by going for something more high-profile, only to get knocked back because of their name. Humiliation was becoming annoyingly familiar in this man's presence.

Leo took a sip of the drink he'd carried over. 'My picture was splashed all over the papers here the week I arrived. Your father has been scrabbling around like a rat in a sinking ship looking for someone to rescue him—and you expect me to believe that you saw me at the pool-side that night and had *no idea* who I was?'

She shook her head. She truly hadn't known, having instinctively shied away from reading anything about the Parnassus family and their triumphant return. It had been too close to the bone on so many different levels. Also, she'd been preoccupied with her sister's news.

Angel sat forward, hands clenched around the glass. From somewhere deep and protecting came a dart of anger at his high-handed arrogance, at how threatened he made her feel. 'Believe it or not, I had no idea. Aren't you satisfied that your family has done its level best to ruin mine?'

Leo let out a short, sharp laugh, making Angel flinch. 'I fail to see where the satisfaction comes when it's clear, based on the evidence tonight—which, I might add, is recorded on CCTV—that you are intent on re-igniting this feud. No doubt you have something to gain from it—most people would have moved on from the drama of the Parnassus family coming home.'

He sat forward then too, his eyes flashing sparks. Angel

wanted to cower back, but held strong and cursed herself for provoking him. For a moment she'd forgotten all about why she was here in the first place. He scrambled her brain that much.

His tone was withering. 'And do you really want to play the game of apportioning blame?'

Angel felt something cold trickle down her spine when Leo's eyes turned dark and deadly.

'We have done nothing to affect your family directly. Your father's greed and ineptitude has seen to the demise of the Kassianides shipping fleet. All we had to do was merge with Levakis Enterprises, and that in itself highlighted the inherent weakness of your father's position.'

Angel swallowed. Everything he said was true. She couldn't really blame him or his father for having done anything concrete. Her father had done it all by himself.

'However,' Leo continued, sitting back like a lord surveying his subject, 'it leaves me with an interesting dilemma.'

Angel said nothing. She'd no doubt that Leo was about to enlighten her.

'While we've managed to get our due revenge in seeing the Kassianides fortune reduced to nothing, lower than even we were ourselves seventy years ago, I must admit that it feels somehow…empty. Since seeing the extent of your sheer boldness, I find myself desiring something of a more… tangible nature.'

Panic struck Angel. She felt as if an invisible noose was tightening around her neck. Desperation tinged her voice. 'I'd call going bankrupt pretty tangible.'

Leo leant forward again, utterly cold, utterly ruthless. 'The bankruptcy is for your father, not you. No, I'm talking about something as tangible as my great-uncle being accused of raping and then murdering a pregnant woman from one of the wealthiest families in Athens. As tangible as an entire family forced into exile from their homeland because of the threat of a criminal investigation they couldn't afford, and the possibility of my great-uncle facing the death penalty. Not to mention the scandal that would linger for years.'

'Stop,' begged Angel weakly. She knew the story and it always sickened her.

But he didn't. Leo just looked at her. 'Did you know that my great-uncle never got over the slur of being accused of that murder and eventually killed himself?'

Angel shook her head. She felt sick. This went far deeper than she'd ever imagined. 'I didn't know.'

'My great-uncle loved your great-aunt.' Leo's mouth twisted. 'More fool him. And because your family couldn't bear to see one of their own darlings slum it with a mere ship worker, they did their best to thwart the romance.'

'I know what happened,' Angel said quietly, her insides roiling.

Leo laughed harshly, 'Yes, everyone does now—thanks to a drunken old fool who couldn't live with the guilt any more, because *he'd* been the one who committed the crime and covered it up, had it paid for by your great-grandfather.'

Her own family had murdered one of their own and covered it up like cowards.

Angel forced herself to meet the censure in Leo's eyes even though she wanted to curl up with the shame. 'I'm not to blame for what they did.'

'Neither am I. Yet I paid for it all my life, I was born on another continent, into a community in exile, learning English as my first language when it should have been Greek. I saw my grandmother wither away a little more each year, knowing that she'd never return to her home.'

Angel wanted to beg him to stop, but the words wouldn't come out.

Leo wasn't finished. 'My father was so consumed it cost us our relationship. And it cost him his first wife. I grew up too fast and too young, aware of a terrible sense of injustice and a need to put things right. So while you were going to school, making friends, *living* your life here in your home, I was on the other side of the world, wondering how things might have been if my father and grandmother hadn't been forced out of their own country. Wondering if I might then have had a father who was present, not absent. Wondering what we had done to deserve this awful slur on our name. Do you have any idea what it's like to grow up being reminded that you don't belong somewhere every single day by your own family? Like you've no right to put down roots?'

Angel shook her head. She didn't think he'd appreciate hearing about how lonely she'd felt when her father had sent her to a remote and ultra-conservative catholic boarding school in the wilds of the west of Ireland. Somehow she didn't think that even the worst of her experiences there would come close to what Leo had described.

She felt hollow inside. 'Please, will you just tell me what it is you want or let me go?'

Leo sat forward, elbows on his knees, glass held casually between long fingers. Supremely at ease, as if he hadn't just related what he had.

'It's quite simple, really. I wanted you the moment I saw you, and I want you now.' His lip curled. 'Despite knowing who you are.'

Angel could feel her mouth opening and closing like an ineffectual fish. 'You don't. You can't.'

In a flooding of panic, Angel stood up. She carefully placed the glass down on a nearby table and hoped Leo wouldn't notice how badly her hand was trembling.

Leo stood too, and they faced each other across the expanse of a few feet.

'Sit down, Angel, we're not finished yet.'

Angel shook her head mutely, feeling the world start to constrict around her. Leo shrugged as if he didn't care. She tried desperately to block out the way he looked so intimidatingly huge opposite her.

'You're going to pay me back for everything you've done to me, and you will do it in my bed. As my mistress.'

Angel nearly burst out laughing, the need to release some of her pent-up panic almost emerging as hysteria. It faded, though, when she saw the look on his face. Her belly quivered.

'You're serious.'

'Of course I'm serious. I don't joke about things like this.'

A pulse beat in his jaw, making Angel's belly clench.

'Do you think I'm so naive as to assume your father is just going to roll over and take what's coming to him? I want you, and I want to keep you close, where I can see you—*away* from your father and his machinations. If that heat between us is anything to go by, I don't imagine it'll be unpleasant for either of us.'

Angel's belly quivered even more strongly and she felt slightly faint.

'You want to sleep with me?'

His mouth quirked dangerously. 'Among other things.'

'But…'

'But nothing. Everyone saw you and I at that party. I am not about to let you capitalise on that now that I'm back. Not to mention tonight's fiasco. You're a danger and a threat. You've had the audacity to come into my home twice, and now you'll pay for it.'

'But my father—' She stopped. *He will kill me,* Angel thought, with a mounting dread that had been born long, long ago.

Leo waved a hand in an abrupt gesture of insult. 'Your father I don't much care about. I'm hoping it'll cause him the maximum amount of humiliation when he sees his precious eldest daughter taken as mistress by his enemy. Everyone will know exactly why you are with me—warming my bed until I'm ready to move on, perhaps even settle down. Whatever you and he had planned, this will play out on my terms. And you can tell him that taking you as my mistress will afford him no honey-trap favours. Things still stand as they are. We certainly won't be bailing him out.'

Angel just looked at him, barely believing the direction their conversation had taken. She didn't see the point in revealing the reality of her dismal relationship with her father. He'd believe that as quickly as he'd believe her intentions had been honourable this evening.

So many things were impacting upon Angel at once, not least Leonidas Parnassus' cold and calculating words. She wanted to shout out that she didn't want him, that she didn't desire him, but her mouth wouldn't formulate the words. And in all honesty she was afraid of his reaction if she did say that. She was still smarting from what had happened in the study. She was far too vulnerable to him.

Feeling so cornered and impotent finally woke her from the stasis that had gripped her. He couldn't force her to do this.

'I'll gain nothing from this liaison because I won't do it. You couldn't *pay* me to be your mistress.'

Feeling panic escalate, right then Angel thought that even if he called the police and they charged her with trespass it had to be a better option than facing what he spoke of.

He looked at her steadily from under hooded lids. A flash of cynicism twisted his features for a moment. 'You're absolutely right. I wouldn't pay you. But you'll do it because you can't *not*. The desire between us is unfortunate, but tangible. You went up in flames in my arms just now, and you owe me after this stunt tonight.'

Derision laced his voice. 'Despite your words, as soon as you're in my bed you'll try and seduce as much out of me as you can. Playing hard to get might be a part of your repertoire, but I don't do games, Angel, so you're wasting your time.'

All Angel could feel was mortified heat enveloping her at remembering how she had come apart in his arms, literally. She made a jerky move towards the door, praying that he wouldn't touch her. She stopped when she felt safer. Leo hadn't made a move to stop her, but it didn't make her feel reassured. She turned back to face him and tipped up her chin.

'I won't be doing it because you're the last man on earth I'd willingly sleep with.'

She turned around, but just when she was about to put her hand on the doorknob she heard him drawl from behind her, 'Do you really think I'm about to let you walk out of here?'

Angel hated herself for not just turning the knob and walking out. She turned around again and tried to inject confidence into her voice. 'You can't stop me.'

Leo stood tall, legs spread, hands in pockets. He smiled, but it was feral.

'Yes, I can.'

Angel felt hysteria rising. She backed up to the door and felt for the knob in her hands behind her back, ready to run.

'What are you going to do? Kidnap me? Lock me away?'

Leo made a disparaging face. 'You've been watching too many Greek soap operas.'

He walked towards her then, and Angel gripped the doorknob even tighter, her whole body tense. He stopped a few feet away.

'Quite apart from the fact that I caught you in the act of stealing, and could call the police in for that alone, I will let it go—because I don't want our relationship to be mired in any more controversy than it's already likely to be when the press finds out.'

Angel blurted out, 'But we won't *have* a relationship, and I wasn't—' She stopped abruptly. Obviously Leo hadn't watched long enough to see her take the will *out* of her pocket. Which would mean that she'd have to explain how she'd got it. So either way it was still theft, albeit not by her. She was back to square one: damned by the actions of her father and her own impetuous desire to rectify matters.

Angel longed to toss her head and tell Leo she'd prefer to see the police, but she realised that she couldn't do that. It would cause the whole thing to explode in the press and she couldn't do that to Delphi. The noose was tightening.

Leo merely stood there and rocked back on his heels for a moment before saying, 'We do have a relationship, Angel, it started the evening of the party. And since then I've found out quite a wealth of information about you.'

Angel's hands were gripping the doorknob, shock still reverberating through her. 'What kind of information?'

'Well,' Leo started almost conversationally, 'I found out

that you went to art college and studied jewellery design. And yet at no point since leaving college have you made any attempt to leave home, which can only point to a close relationship with your father.'

Angel bit back the explanation. It was her sister she was close to, her sister she cared for, and her sister she had tried to create a stable environment for, because they'd never got it from their parents. After Damia's death, when Angel had come home from school in Ireland, she and Delphi had turned to each other for support.

A look of mock sympathy came over his harsh features. 'But since the collapse of Tito's business you've had to make ends meet by working for that catering company, and now working as a chamber maid for the Grand Bretagne. Tell me,' he said musingly, 'it must be hard, changing the sheets for people who were once your peers... I did wonder why someone as educated as you had resorted to menial work, but then I realised that you obviously want to avoid any unnecessary investigation into your disgraced name. No doubt you figured that you'd re-emerge on the social scene and find yourself a rich husband once the Kassianides name had lost some of its notoriety.'

Angel could feel the colour draining from her face at having it confirmed that he knew where she worked, and why she'd taken those jobs, albeit not quite for all the reasons he'd so cynically outlined. She thought of her dreams to set up a jewellery-making studio as soon as she had enough money. She thought of the aching disappointment she'd had to keep to herself every day that she hadn't yet been able to realise that dream.

'You have it all wrong. So wrong.'

He ignored her, and she could have had no warning for what he was to say next.

'Most interesting of all, perhaps, is that I also know that Stavros Eugenides and your sister are so-called sweethearts and want to marry, but his father won't let them.'

Angel's legs nearly gave way. 'How do you know that?'

He ignored her question. 'I will ask you this—is it important to you that your sister marries Stavros Eugenides?'

Angel felt sick inside. Her brain clicked into high gear and she shrugged minutely, trying not to let it show how hard her heart was thumping. She knew instinctively that if Leo guessed for a second just how important it was he'd go out of his way to not let it happen.

She tried to smile cynically, but it felt all wrong. 'They're young and in love. Personally I think it's too soon. But, yes, they want to marry.'

'I think you're lying, Angel. I think it's of the utmost importance to you and her that they get married. After all, why would you have gone to speak on their behalf with Dimitri Eugenides otherwise?'

Angel found herself starting to tremble violently. How on earth did he know this? Was he a magician?

'I—' But she got no further.

'I think that your sister is looking to get herself a rich husband just before you lose everything. If she can get engaged before the truly pathetic state of your father's affairs becomes public then she'll be safe. And you, by proxy, will be taken care of too.'

Angel shook her head, as much in negation of what he said than anything else.

Leo grimaced. 'In some ways I can't blame you. You're two poor little rich girls, just trying to survive. Unfortunately you don't seem to be aware that most of the world has to work to make a living to get through life.'

Angel shot into action and launched herself at Leo, her two hands aiming for his chest, but before she could hit him he'd caught them in the tight grip of his own hands.

Angel glared up, incensed to be feeling so weak and ineffectual. 'You have no right to say those things. You know nothing about us. *Nothing*—do you hear me?'

Leo looked down at Angel for a long moment, slightly stunned by the passion throbbing in her voice. He could see the twin thrusts of her high breasts against the thin material of her top. Immediately his body responded. Who was he kidding? His body hadn't cooled down one bit since the study. And yet how dared she stand there and speak to him as if he'd just insulted her grievously?

With ruthless intent, he drew her in closer to his body. There were two twin flags of colour high in Angel's cheeks. Leo caught both her hands in one of his and caught her neck with his other hand, drawing her close. The tension spiked between them. He lowered his head, his mouth close to hers, and had to bite back a groan. She smelt so…so clean, and pure. With a hint of enticing musk. Just enough to make his body throb with need. This woman, she knew exactly what she was doing.

'I haven't finished with you, Angel.'

'Yes, we have finished. I'd like to go now.'

Leo could hear the tremor in her voice. Her breath tantalised him. He longed to crush her sweet, soft mouth under his again, but something made him hold back.

'We haven't finished because I'm not done telling you what I know. I can offer you something that despite your lofty protestations I don't think you'll be able to refuse.'

Angel finally jerked away from Leo's hands and stepped back, crossing her arms over her chest. The fact that he knew so much and could turn her upside down with just a touch was devastating. 'There's nothing you could say that I want to hear—'

'I can persuade Dimitri Eugenides to give his blessing to a wedding between his son and your sister.'

Angel's mouth was still open. She shut it again abruptly. She hated what she was giving away, but she had to ask, 'What…what do you mean?'

'Ah,' Leo mocked. 'Not so sure now that they're too young to marry?' A look of unmistakable triumph came into his eyes.

He was right, damn him, but for all the wrong reasons.

'Just tell me what you mean,' Angel bit out, vulnerability clawing through her.

'It's very simple. Dimitri wants to do business with me. The last time I was here he told me about the romance between his son and your sister, and thought he'd please me by telling me how much he disapproved, knowing of the history between the families. It had little significance for me at the time. Now, though, it has become…more significant. I can guarantee that as soon as it becomes apparent you're my mistress he'll be tripping over himself to make amends, terrified that I'll remember his less than favourable remarks. I can make it a condition of that business that he allows Stavros to marry your sister.'

Angel shook her head even as her heart fluttered with hope. 'He won't allow it, he hates our family.'

Leo waved aside her concern and said arrogantly, 'He'll do whatever I ask, believe me. The man is desperate to enlist my favour.'

Without really thinking, Angel found a chair nearby and sank into it. Her brain was buzzing. With a click of his fingers

Leo had honed in on the one thing that Angel wanted most in the world—to be able to make things right for Delphi. She looked up at Leo, standing there like a marauding warrior, legs planted wide apart.

She didn't care what he thought; she just knew she had to do whatever it took. She stood up again. 'I presume your condition for doing this is to make me agree to become your mistress?'

Leo's mouth thinned, and a hint of anger came into his eyes. 'Don't try and dress this up into you being the unfortunate victim. We both want each other, Angel, you just seem determined to deny it.'

'But essentially you won't help Stavros and Delphi unless I agree to go to you?'

Leo shrugged insouciantly. 'Let's just say that then I would care even less what happens to them than I do right now. Why would I put myself out like that unless I was getting something in return?'

'Me,' Angel said flatly, but with an awful telltale quiver of physical response in her belly. She couldn't even tell herself that she was immune to or disgusted by Leo's offer, and she hated herself for it. Her conscience pricked her. *How* could she walk away from this opportunity for her sister and Stavros to be happy, no matter how it was coming about?

Angel's mind became very clear as she saw all her options dwindle away. Delphi was the best part of three months pregnant, and wouldn't want the ignominy of everyone knowing that on her wedding day.

'If I agree to this, I have a condition of my own.'

Leo's eyes flashed a warning. 'Go on.'

'I want Delphi and Stavros to be married as soon as it can be arranged.'

That look of cynicism that Angel was beginning to recognise all too easily crossed Leo's face again.

'Don't think that by having them marry as soon as possible it'll indicate the end of our affair, Angel. I won't let you go until I'm good and ready.'

Angel's belly quivered again. How would he react when he discovered she was a virgin? He didn't strike her as the kind of man to entertain novices in his bed.

Leo was looking at her assessingly. 'But I don't see why I can't fulfil that request. Not when you're mine from this moment on.'

Angel felt the colour drain from her face.

Leo didn't like the way Angel had just paled so visibly. He strode over to where she stood and snaked out a quick hand to caress the back of her neck again. He felt the silken fall of her hair over his skin, and it made his voice rough with suppressed desire. 'There's no time like the present. I'll have my car take you home, so you can pack some things and be brought straight back here to me.'

Just like that.

CHAPTER FOUR

LESS than three hours later, Angel stood in the hall of her own house, a suitcase at her feet. When she'd finally left the Parnassus villa she'd been aghast to see that dawn had been breaking, it had made her feel acutely disorientated. By some miracle her father wasn't at home; Angel's more and more harried looking stepmother informed her that her father had left the previous evening for London, to try and beg a loan from his cousins. Angel had been dreading the inevitable showdown with him, for undoubtedly he'd know that she'd taken the will.

She'd gone into her sister's room and woken her up and told her what was happening, while omitting the real reason why Leo was asking her to move in with him. Delphi had been understandably concerned. 'But, Angel, they *hate* us. They must do. What do you mean, you just happened to meet him and he swept you off your feet? It's all so fast and you never said anything…'

Angel hated lying to her sister. She'd smiled tightly and explained how they'd met at the party, and how she hadn't wanted to say anything in case their father found out. 'Delph, I didn't want you to be worried. I wasn't sure what to expect myself, wasn't even sure if he'd come back to Athens. But he has…' Here Angel had flushed hotly, remembering his kiss in the study. 'And he wants me to move in…I know it all seems weird and too fast and unlikely…but just trust me, please? I know what I'm doing.'

Delphi had completely misread Angel's acute embarrassment as being infatuation, but even so it had only been after more grilling that she'd finally seemed satisfied with Angel's answers.

When Angel had taken a deep breath and told Delphi about Leo's link to Stavros' father, and what he'd promised to do for them, and seen her ecstatic reaction, she'd known then that she had no choice but to follow her fate.

As if she'd had a choice anyway. Leo could still call the police and accuse her of stealing. No court in the world would believe her over him, with the evidence he had. But, apart from that, she couldn't jeopardise Delphi and Stavros' happiness now—their bid for independence and the future security of their baby.

For the first time Delphi had sounded grown up. 'Angel, you don't have to be responsible for everything, you know. Just doing this for us is enough. I'll be fine here, I promise. It's time you got to live your own life.'

Angel might have laughed at that if she hadn't known that she would be in danger of it turning to tears. She wouldn't be free to live her life now until Leo had decided he'd had enough of her. Her only hope was that her woeful inexperience would be enough of a turn-off for him that he would be content to use her like some kind of trophy mistress until he deemed she'd paid her dues.

But why, when she thought of that, did her womb contract with what felt like disappointment? Angel quashed that thought down ruthlessly. Her mind was just playing tricks.

She'd just made a call to the hotel where she'd worked and resigned her job; there was nothing left to do. She took a deep breath and picked up her small case. It was time to go.

'Won't your father be here at the villa too?'

Leo had led Angel into a palatial bedroom, the sheer under-stated luxury of which had made her eyes goggle. Her father's taste had always been seriously lacking, he being the kind of person who believed trappings like gold taps were the sign of a rich man.

Leo was in the act of showing Angel where a door con-nected with his room, and she'd blurted out the question as much to disguise her panic as anything else. Now he turned and leaned nonchalantly against the doorjamb.

In the few hours since she'd left the villa and returned, she was disgusted to see that Leo looked as if he'd had a full night's sleep and was as rested and vibrant as anyone had a right to be. She felt sticky all over, with gritty eyes, and still dazed from everything that had happened.

The rumble of his voice brought her back. 'My father is staying on the island indefinitely. His doctors have advised no stress, and Athens means stress because he's incapable of staying away from work. Even now.'

Angel winced at the bitter edge to Leo's voice, and was reminded uncomfortably of what he'd revealed about their re-lationship. Irrational guilt assailed her. She could say nothing to that; any murmur of sympathy or empathy would be shot down in an instant. Anyway, Leo was ignoring her, revealing another room.

Angel had seen the *en-suite* bathroom, as big as her bedroom at home, and now Leo was pointing to an empty walk-in wardrobe. She came closer and looked in warily.

Leo sent a cursory look up and down her body and Angel fought not to cringe. She was still in the same clothes.

'I'll have a stylist come to consult with you tomorrow, and sort out a full wardrobe. We can't have you looking anything less than a bought woman from now on, can we?'

Angel caught a flash of the huge bed she'd been ignoring in her peripheral vision and it scared her silly, making her say flippantly, 'Knock yourself out. Fill that wardrobe and I'll be only too happy to act out the part.'

He pushed himself off the door, coming close enough to have Angel's panic and pulse zoom skywards. He smiled lazily. Cynically.

'I don't think it'll take too much acting. Your Skittishness is intriguing me. I would have expected you to be ecstatic that I've chosen you as my mistress. You forget that I come from New York…the natural habitat of the mercenary, gold-digging socialite. Your black soul won't surprise me, really.'

Angel searched for words, but to her chagrin couldn't get them out in time. To her consternation, Leo merely looked at his watch then, and said crisply, 'I have to go to the office. Why don't you get some rest? You look tired.'

And then he was gone, and she was alone. Angel walked into the bathroom and looked at herself in the mirror. She didn't just look tired. She looked shell-shocked. Feeling incredibly weary, and more than a little numb, she stripped off and stood under a steaming hot shower for a long time.

And then she got out, dried her hair, shut the curtains, crawled into the softest bed she'd ever felt, and fell into a deep dreamless sleep.

The first thing Angel knew was a gentle rocking. And then a voice. A deep, soulful voice that she found herself instinctively turning to. She smiled. The rocking became more forceful, and so did the voice.

'*Angel.*'

She wasn't dreaming. In an instant she was awake. Wide awake. Looking up with big eyes at Leonidas Parnassus, who was far too close to her, sitting on the bed, his face inscrutable. It all rushed back. She wasn't in her own bed; she was in his home and had agreed to become his mistress.

Angel grabbed for the sheet and pulled it up, even though she was dressed in pants and a vest. She scrabbled back as far as she could go, away from him. She felt exposed at having been caught sleeping. How long had he been there?

Leo stood up from the bed and Angel asked huskily, 'What time is it?'

He consulted his watch. 'It's 8:00 p.m.'

Angel sat up in shock, still holding the sheet. 'I've been asleep *all day*?'

Leo nodded and went over to pull the curtains back, so Angel could see the sun starting to set in the sky. She felt completely disorientated—jet-lagged, almost. Leo started to walk out of the room, barely glancing at Angel now. 'Dinner will be served in twenty minutes. I'll wait for you downstairs.'

While he waited for Angel, Leo stood at the huge French windows of the less formal dining room. The doors were opened out onto the terrace—the same terrace he'd brought Angel out to on the night of the party. He could scarcely fathom that he'd been in Athens for barely twenty-four hours and already had Angel in his home. Yet bizarrely it felt right.

Just now, when he'd woken her, he'd seen something that had reminded him of that first evening they'd met. For a moment before she'd woken she'd almost turned to him, with a soft smile around her mouth, and that enticing beauty spot at the corner of her lip had made him want to bend down and kiss it. Made him want to do so much more. When she'd opened her eyes, though, he'd noticed slight shadows still lingering.

Her hair had been sleep-mussed, tangled over one bare shoulder, where the strap of her vest had fallen down. She'd looked incredibly sexy, yet unbelievably vulnerable, and he had felt a niggle of unease at how quickly things had progressed from him finding her creeping through the villa. He'd pushed the unease aside. Even those three hours waiting for her to return had been torturous. He'd actually been nervous that she wouldn't return. That, despite everything he had on her, she would defy him. Leo noticed his hands had gone into fists now, just thinking about it. He forced them to uncurl.

He thought of how she'd looked when she'd returned, with shadows like bruises under her eyes...

She'd come into his family home to steal from them.

With more effort than he liked to admit, Leo pushed down the concern. A tight coil of desire held him in its grip. Tonight he'd have her, and he'd no doubt that within a very short space of time she'd prove to be as dismayingly predictable as every other woman he'd ever met, ultimately using emotion arising from intimacy, thinking that she could manipulate him.

He heard a noise at the door and turned around slowly. It was time for Angel to face the consequences of her actions.

Angel's skin prickled when she was shown into a dining room by a smiling housekeeper and saw Leo standing with his back to her. The windows were open and the curtains fluttered on the breeze. She had no idea how to act in this situation. No idea what was expected of her. She felt acutely lonely all of a sudden.

Leo turned around slowly, and the impact on her senses was nothing short of cataclysmic. She'd not really noticed what he was wearing in her room; she'd been too shocked and groggy. But now she saw that he was dressed in a pair of lovingly worn and faded jeans, which clung to him like a second skin. The material stretched over powerful thighs and long, long legs.

A black polo shirt made the brown of his eyes seem even darker, his skin seem even more olive. His shoulders were almost too broad for the material, and huge biceps bulged from beneath the short sleeves.

'Come and see the view, Angel.'

I'm already looking at it, she felt like blurting out slightly hysterically.

Knowing she was in a situation she couldn't get out of, her fate sealed by her own stupidly impetuous actions and her wanting to make everything all right for Delphi, Angel walked over to Leo, very self-conscious in her plain black shift dress. Hair pulled back. She coloured when she saw his gaze drop. She'd viewed him on Google him in a moment of weakness and seen exactly the kind of woman he went for: invariably tall, blonde, soignée. *Experienced*. A million miles from herself.

'Very demure,' he murmured when she came close.

'If I'd known casual was okay I would have worn jeans too,' she said stiffly, her gaze resolutely fixed on the view of Athens spread out below them. Not even that spectacular vista could distract her from the man beside her.

'I like to be casual at home, Angel, so here you can wear what you want…even go naked if you wish,' he finished softly.

Angel coloured even more at his mocking tone, wondering what on earth he saw in her. 'I don't think so.'

'Pity.'

She heard him pour some wine into a glass, and then he was offering it to her. She took it—anything to try and give her some courage.

'What do you think of the view—it's amazing, no?'

Angel snuck a quick look up; Leo was staring out, his profile to her, showing that he had a slight bump in his nose, and she could see the faint raised line of the scar over his lip. Hurriedly she looked back, afraid to be caught staring.

'Yes, it's truly beautiful.' Amidst everything, she thought of something else, and looked at her watch to check the time. 'Actually, any minute now...yes, there. Look—' Angel lifted her hand to point to where the evening lights were coming on to illuminate the Acropolis, far below in the distance.

She heard Leo's intake of breath and couldn't look at him, for some reason afraid of what she might see. It was always a magical sight, and one that took her breath away too. Was it having the same effect on him? She felt a lurch to think that she'd grown up seeing it as an everyday occurrence but he hadn't.

'I've seen the lights before, but never the moment when they come on like that.'

Angel murmured something inarticulate feeling unaccountably guilty. She turned with more than a little relief when the housekeeper bustled in with their food, and Leo turned too, indicating for her to precede him to the table.

Leo watched Angel walk in front of him, took in the glossy hair tied back in a low, careless bun, the long, elegant neck. And looked down to where her bare legs were slender, yet shapely enough to make his heart kick and his pulse throb.

Her palpable air of nervousness had caught him unawares as

she'd stood beside him. He had to question why she was feigning it *now,* when they both knew where they stood. She'd been nervous before, in the study, but that had no doubt been because she'd no idea how he'd react to catching her red-handed.

He'd certainly not been prepared to have her point out a sight she must have seen a thousand times before, which must be wholly unremarkable to her but had taken his breath away, seeing it for the first time. In any other instance he would have considered it a sweetly considerate gesture.

She wasn't acting the way he'd imagined she'd act in this situation. He'd expected a certain initial belligerence, or even defiance at having been caught and manipulated so spectacularly. Or he'd imagined that she'd want to make the most of the situation and take advantage of becoming his mistress. Leo had yet to meet a woman who didn't see the advantage in becoming his mistress, so for her to be feigning this nervous skittishness was going to get her nowhere fast.

They sat down. Leo looked at Angel darkly, but she was avoiding his eyes. Straightening her cutlery, her napkin. She was up to something. She had to be. Trying to disarm him for some reason. He reminded himself that she'd been home earlier, and of course she must have taken advice from her father. Leo cursed himself. The fact that he didn't trust Angel was not in question, so why was he trying to decipher her behaviour? The only behaviour that concerned him was her good behaviour as his mistress, on his arm and in his bed. Anything above and beyond that was of no interest to him.

Angel was doing her best to eat the deliciously prepared dinner, but it tasted like sawdust in her mouth. All she could see, all she could think about, was the man eating his dinner at the head of the table to her left. Her eyes kept being drawn to his hands, how powerful they looked. The tension mounted and mounted, especially when she thought of those hands in other places. On her.

Leo, however, seemed happy to concentrate on his food. Angel had countless questions bubbling on her lips: did he expect to sleep with her tonight? What would he do when he discovered how inexperienced she was? Would he reject her outright, as Achilles had? And why did that thought hurt so much? Why was she so consumed with him when he was all but blackmailing her into his bed?

Angel had never felt more confused, and very, very vulnerable. The silence, she was sure, was Leo's way of unsettling her, reminding her she was here for just one purpose. A purpose she was woefully ill prepared for. He wasn't even attempting small talk. When she felt something brush against her bare legs under the table she let out a startled cry, and dropped her knife to the floor with a clatter.

Just then the housekeeper came back in—Leo had introduced her to Angel earlier as Calista—and Angel saw that it had just been a cat. Her cat. After profuse apologies, and her knife being replaced, they were alone in the room again.

Leo put down his knife and fork and Angel jumped minutely.

'Why so tense, Angel?'

She looked warily at Leo. His eyes were dark, like mysterious pools. He was all hard angles and shadows. A dark line shadowed his jaw after a day's growth.

'I…' She couldn't articulate a word. Something dense was in the air around them all of a sudden, something tangible and electric. *Was this desire?*

'No appetite?' he asked then innocuously, with a raised brow.

Angel just shook her head and watched, dry-mouthed, as

his gaze fixated on her mouth. It tingled. God, why couldn't she be immune to him and stand up in disgust and tell him if he touched her she'd call the police? Because then he'd probably call the police himself, send her away, and Delphi and Stavros would be back to square one. Worse, with the ensuing media storm.

However, those very good reasons aside, with the heavy weight of inevitability, the real reason sank into her head: she wanted him to touch her. The truth was shocking when she acknowledged it. Despite everything, she *wanted* him to touch her. Had done from the moment she'd seen him emerge from the pool…and from the moment he'd kissed her on the terrace. Since that night she'd had dreams, when she'd woken in sweaty tangled sheets, aching… And it killed her to admit it. Especially when she'd all but written sex off after her first experience.

Her hormones had turned traitor and were in league with this man.

Leo suddenly pushed his plate away and stood up, towering over her. His eyes glittered with a dark promise. A muscle popped in his jaw. 'I find that my appetite for food has gone, too.'

There was something rough in his voice that resonated deep within her. When he held out a hand, Angel hesitated for a second before putting her hand in his. She told herself this was just part of the agreement. She was securing Delphi's freedom and happiness. He wasn't throwing her to the police with accusations of theft. All she had to do…all she had to do… She stumbled as Leo led her from the room. They encountered Calista on the way, and Leo explained in rapid Greek that they were both tired and going to bed.

Angel's cheeks burned as Leo led her up the stairs. She was

mortified. She tried to tug her hand back, panic making her voice high. 'She's going to know exactly what we're doing.'

Leo's voice was hard. 'You're my mistress. I should hope so. And if the gossip here is anything like in New York, it'll already be halfway round Athens by morning that I have taken Angel Kassianides into my bed.'

CHAPTER FIVE

His stark words rendered Angel mute. She felt she had no choice as Leo led her into his bedroom. She chastised herself; there was always a choice. But her choice to retain her dignity and walk away would have an effect on the person closest to her.

And she found as Leo kicked the door shut with one foot and led Angel further in, close to his massive bed, that the desire to walk away was disturbingly elusive. She hated to admit it to herself, but was she using Delphi in some way to justify this?

Disgusted with herself, because that was a very real possibility, Angel wrenched her hand free from Leo's. The very pertinent fact of her virginity had also been easy to push down to somewhere she didn't want to explore. But now it was rising again. How could it not, when it was about to become an issue?

Angel backed a few feet away from Leo and stood tall. 'I'm not going to just fall into your bed like some concubine.'

His mouth tightened. 'No, there's a more modern word: mistress. You'll fall into my bed like the mistress you are. I'm sure you've done it for countless others, Angel, no need to be shy.' He smiled, and it was cruelly mocking. 'It's lucky I caught you between lovers.'

'How...?' Angel asked shakily, the wind taken out of her sails. 'How do you know I don't have a lover?'

Leo walked over to where she stood. 'Because I've had you followed since I left Athens and your every move reported back to me. So you see, Angel—' here Leo reached out and tucked some wayward hair behind her ear '—I know that you must be dying to get a taste of the life you've undoubtedly been missing, thanks to your father's excessive greed.'

He lifted up her hands, which were dry and a little rough from all the cleaning she'd been doing. Each time she'd had to scrub a toilet she'd imagined the day when she'd be polishing the white gold of one of her jewellery designs.

With no clue as to what was in her head, Leo brought her hands up to his mouth and kissed them one by one, making Angel's heart speed up even as delayed shock made her useless. *He'd had her followed?*

'You can't deny that you aren't craving the easy life again, Angel, and I can provide that for you.'

Bitterness that he had so little idea of who she really was made Angel say, 'Just temporarily, though.' She knew saying that would most likely give him the impression that she was greedy, and she hated that she cared.

He quirked a brow and dropped her hands, but kept hold of them. 'It's up to you, Angel. It depends on how much you please me in bed...'

Bed. Panic exploded in her gut. He thought she was experienced, really experienced. And, to give him his due, most of the girls in her peer group were. She and Delphi, they were a breed apart—always had been, thanks to Tito's excessively controlling nature, and the fact that he'd had Angel all but locked away in a remote school for most of her teenage years. It was why their sister Damia had rebelled and come to such a tragic end.

'Leo, I don't think you understand—'

He came even closer and snaked a hand around her neck, drawing her mouth up to meet his. 'There's nothing to understand, Angel except *this*.'

Leo tipped her chin up, and before she could react his mouth was on hers for the second time in just twenty-four hours. So much had happened in so little time that Angel's head reeled, but it was all being washed away as Leo's mouth moved seductively against hers, eliciting a response that she couldn't deny.

With a muted groan of despair at her own helpless reaction, Angel let her hands find their way to Leo's chest, where they clung to his shirt. She had to hang on or she'd fall down in a heap. She could not understand how this man had such an instantaneous effect on her, but he did.

His tongue sought hers and made her insides melt into a pool of lust, just by stroking it. Their mouths clung. Angel remembered the study and her awfully wanton response, how he'd left her so unsatisfied. But she didn't have time now to feel humiliated; all she could feel was that new-found ache, growing again.

Leo's hands were on the back of her dress; the zip was being drawn down. Angel pulled away and looked up. Her chest rose and fell rapidly, and her heart was thumping so hard she felt faint. Her mouth felt bruised and swollen. She could only stand there as she felt a cool breeze whistle over her skin as the zip descended. All the while Leo was holding her gaze and not letting her look away.

When the zip was all the way down, to just above her buttocks, Leo pulled Angel in close again and smoothed his hands up and down her naked back. Electric shocks of sensation made her shudder; the tips of her breasts tingled. She felt him undo the clasp of her bra. Things were moving quickly…too quickly.

Jerkily Angel pulled away from Leo's caressing, distracting hands. The dress gaped forward slightly, and she put up her hands to stop it falling. She knew now that she'd blocked out the reality of what it would mean to do this.

But just when she went to open her mouth to say something Leo started pulling off his own clothes. Her eyes grew huge, and between her legs she throbbed when he stood before her naked, like a proud warrior. His broad, superbly muscled chest and shoulders had been awe-inspiring when she'd seen them, but when her gaze dropped Angel's breath stopped altogether.

A taut, flat belly led down to a thatch of dark hair from which sprang a truly intimidating erection. Angel had only ever seen one man in this state, and that would never have prepared her for *this*. Leo stood proud, legs apart, thighs heavily muscled, cradling his impressive masculinity.

There was a blur of movement and Angel felt her dress being pulled away and down her arms. Suddenly it lay in a pool of black at her feet. She gave a squeal of protest but Leo was remorseless, and somehow, with an economy and efficiency of movement that took her breath away, she stood before him in just her panties. Her hair fell about her shoulders. She put an arm across her breasts and a hand down to cover between her legs.

Leo chuckled darkly, 'There's really no need to act the innocent…'

'But I'm not—'

'Enough talking,' he growled, and stopped her words with his mouth again, his naked body coming into hot and immediate contact with hers. Angel's brain went into meltdown. He took her arm away from her breasts, and Angel's brain nearly short-circuited when she came into contact with that turgid erection.

Despite the wild excitement that flared through her body she wasn't ready for this. She'd never be ready for this. She'd had some dim and distant hope that perhaps she could pretend, that her virginity might not be glaringly obvious, but that hope laughed in her face now.

Leo was backing her towards the bed, pushing her down. Things were moving too fast. She had to stop him, even though knowing that he was naked and feeling his smooth olive skin next to hers was turning her thoughts to mush.

Angel couldn't bear for them to get to the point she'd reached before with Achilles and have Leo look at her with the same awful dawning horror on his face when he found out she was a virgin. Angel could remember the excruciating pain, the awful humiliation when Achilles hadn't been able to penetrate her. He'd shouted at her, told her she was frigid, that no one would want to sleep with her because she was a virgin.

. And even though Angel felt in her body instinctively that *this* was different, that the same outcome wasn't assured, her brain was warning her of the pain and humiliation to come. And she knew that, however bad it had been with Achilles, to face the same from Leo would wound her so much more deeply, and that knowledge alone was enough for her to call a halt.

With a mammoth move, Angel pushed at Leo's chest. One of his hands was travelling up her leg, and already she could feel herself weakening, moistening. Her body wasn't hers any more.

She shoved again, and knocked his hand away with enough

violence to make it sound like a slap, 'No!' The sound echoed in the room.

Leo's movements stilled over her.

She looked up at him and bit her lip. All she could see were the strong planes of his face. He too was breathing harshly.

'I…I have to tell you something.'

After a long moment Leo pulled back and reached over to put on a lamp beside the bed; it cast out a warm pool of low light. Abruptly he plucked his jeans off the floor and pulled them on roughly, standing up.

Angel felt very exposed and sat up, grabbing the sheet and pulling it around her.

Leo stood with hands on his hips, jeans undone. She could see the bulge of his arousal. He oozed such potent virility in that moment that Angel knew she was right to stop this now; she was no match for him. He needed a woman with experience, a woman to equal him, a woman like the women she'd seen on the internet. She felt sick.

'Well, Angel? This had better be good.'

Angel would have stood, but the sheet was tucked into the bed so she sat awkwardly, holding it against her. She looked down for a moment, gathering her courage, and felt the welcome curtain of her hair around her face.

She looked up finally, and spoke at the same time as Leo.

'Angel—'

'I'm a virgin.'

They both stopped. Leo looked at her. A strange stillness seemed to come into his body, and the air grew thick with atmosphere around them.

'What did you say?'

Angel gulped. 'I said that I'm a virgin.'

Leo shook his head. 'No, it's impossible.'

Angel felt the cold trickle of humiliation come into her body. This was going to be so much worse than she'd envisaged. On an impulse to cover up properly she scooted quickly from the bed and plucked her dress off the floor, stepping into it and pulling it up over her chest, clutching it there with her hands.

She looked at Leo and fought to stay standing in the face of his obvious disbelief. 'I'm afraid it is possible. I'm not what you…' She bit her lip. 'I've never been anyone's mistress.'

Leo's hand came out in a slashing movement; anger throbbed in his voice. 'You're lying. This is some game you're playing. I've told you, Angel, I don't play games.'

'Neither do I,' she said miserably. 'And believe what you want, Leo, but I don't think it would take long to prove you wrong.'

Leo just stared at her, his hands bunched into fists on his hips. It was as if he was trying to see inside her very soul.

Angel couldn't take the intensity of his regard. She looked down and stupidly felt she had to apologise. She quashed the impulse. 'We didn't…there hasn't exactly been the opportunity to discuss…' She stopped. Mortified.

Leo's tone had gone from angry to icy. 'You could have informed me when I told you I was going to take you as my mistress.'

Angel looked up, stung, anger rising. To think that she was going through this humiliation *again*. 'How? Was I supposed to just come out with it?'

Leo just glared at her, a muscle popping in his jaw. Angel felt deflated all of a sudden. She backed away. Leo didn't let her escape his blistering gaze. 'Dammit, Angel you should have told me.'

He stilled then, and instinctively Angel grew wary. He

asked silkily, 'Did you come back here to sleep with me after discussing your options with your father? Like some kind of sacrificial virgin?'

Horror rose from Angel's gut. She shook her head. 'No. *No*. How could you think such a thing? My father isn't even here, he's gone to London.'

Leo raked a hand through his hair, making it flop with unruly sexiness onto his forehead. Angel's belly clenched even now. She was aware of a pervading sense of hollow disappointment. Evidently he wasn't willing to sleep with her, to take her innocence. Suddenly she couldn't bear to be so vulnerable in front of him for a moment longer.

'I'm going to go back to my room.'

After a long moment Leo just nodded, and said darkly, 'I think that's a good idea.'

Leo watched Angel walk out of the room, the gaping dress showing the slender length of her smooth back in a curiously vulnerable way. He felt pole-axed. Winded. *She was a virgin*. Or was she? He cursed himself. As she'd said herself, it wouldn't take much to find out, and if he took her now, as he was aching to do, and she was telling the truth...he'd hurt her.

So if she was telling the truth she hadn't had countless lovers, hadn't been mistress to other men. It meant that his belief in one aspect of her behaviour had to be amended. For a second he again had the sickening suspicion that this was all part of some plan concocted with her father. Lead him on and drop the bombshell. But then he remembered the look of abject horror mixed with disgust on her face when he'd suggested that. It had been too real to ignore. She'd said her father hadn't even been there, and that would be easy enough to prove. Something uncomfortable lodged in Leo's chest.

He sat down on the edge of his bed and dropped his head

for a moment. How the hell did someone like her remain a virgin till the age of twenty-four? For some reason he wasn't prepared to look too closely at why that might be.

He suddenly remembered when they'd been in the study the previous evening. He'd brought her to certain orgasm, or very close. He'd been disgusted to find himself so out of control in that moment. Bringing a fully-clothed woman to orgasm—a woman who had just been caught stealing from his family! At the time he'd dismissed her reaction, not believing it, thinking she was acting. But if her reaction had been genuine it would explain the shocked look on her face, her embarrassment.

Hadn't he felt compelled to pour her that drink? And then her agitation had led her to knock the glass out of his hand… Leo looked up again at the door she'd just walked through. The certainty hit him that she was telling the truth. You couldn't fake that kind of innocence.

He was angry—angry with himself for not noticing the signs. He was a connoisseur of women, and yet he'd kissed and held an innocent in his arms and hadn't even noticed. Because he'd been too inflamed. That was the truth. The minute he came within a foot of Angel his brain started to melt and hormones took over. Out of control. He grimaced. As evidenced by everything leading up to this moment.

When she'd stopped him it had taken more strength than he'd known he possessed to pull back from her lithe, firm body. He'd nearly exploded just seeing her breasts revealed, two beautifully shaped firm mounds, tipped with those small, hard nipples, enticing him to lick and explore.

Already the fire was building in his body again. And something else. The realisation that no other man had discovered the intimate secrets of Angel's body. A curious bubbling feeling made Leo's chest expand.

Leo realised that every other man they encountered in Athens might want Angel, but he would know that they hadn't been her lover... She was a virgin, and she was his. He had the power in his hands to make her uniquely his. Something deeply primitive within him thrilled at the sound of those words, at their implication...

To Angel's horror, as soon as she stepped under the spray of her shower, weak hot tears started falling down her cheeks, followed by gut-wrenching sobs. She pressed her hands to her face. She couldn't believe she was feeling this way. She couldn't believe that Leo, a man she barely knew, was so far under her skin that he had the power to hurt her like this, when she had every reason to hate him. How could she *want* someone like him to want her? Why wasn't she happy she'd scored a point? Even she had seen that she'd dented his insufferable confidence for one moment. Stopped him in his tracks...

Angel eventually turned off the shower and stepped out, shivering slightly despite the heat. She roughly towel-dried her hair and pulled on a voluminous robe that was hanging on the back of the door, not even drying herself properly.

She felt flat and empty. Achilles had turned away from her in disgust when he'd discovered her virginity, when he'd known that she couldn't please him. But Achilles had been a boy. Leo Parnassus was a man. She'd been right to worry; it was so obvious now that he would want nothing to do with a novice.

Angel felt nauseous. Had he been so repulsed? But why else would he have stopped? For a man as virile as him to stop making love just because she was a virgin had to be because he had no interest in being her first lover... Angel couldn't contemplate for a second that it might have been because she'd genuinely caught him off guard. That there might have been an honourable intention behind it. To indulge in that line of thinking made all sorts of feelings emerge in Angel's belly; much easier to think of Leo being cruel, single-minded.

She had no idea how things would work now. Perhaps Leo would take lovers on the side while he paraded her in public as his mistress? Angel's heart constricted. No doubt that might be a further humiliation he'd appreciate when he came to consider it.

But the stark evidence that no man wanted to sleep with her...*that Leo didn't want to sleep with her*...sapped her confidence totally—no matter how much she might try and pretend otherwise. Somehow the reason why she was here, the fact that this all stemmed from Leo's desire for revenge, seemed of little consequence right now.

She stepped out of her bathroom, turning the light off as she did so. For a moment she didn't notice anyone else in the dimly lit bedroom. Then she heard a muted sound and looked up, suddenly tense.

Leo stood there, just a few feet away, still in his jeans, the top button open, giving a tantalising glimpse of the dark hair which led—Angel gulped. Was she dreaming? Was she so pathetic?

Leo put out a hand. 'Come here, Angel.'

It was him. On numb legs, trying to ignore the renewed zinging of energy through her veins, Angel walked forward. She stopped a couple of feet away, still needing to protect herself. Just because he was here, it didn't mean anything.

But in that moment Leo closed the distance, stepped right up to Angel, took her face in his hands and kissed her. Her mouth opened on a shocked gasp and Leo took devastating advantage, tongue stabbing deep, stroking along hers, until Angel's legs felt weak and her hands went to Leo's waist to hold on. It was a sensual onslaught that impacted every cell in her body.

The feel of his hot satiny skin under her hands made them stretch out, trying to feel as much as she could. She couldn't begin to explain what had just happened; she was only capable of feeling. And, like a coward, she shut out the cacophony of voices in her head.

Eventually Leo pulled back, but not much. With a gesture that was almost tender he stroked Angel's damp hair behind one ear. And then, his eyes on hers, glittering darkly, he said, 'You're mine now, Angel, no one else's.'

Angel looked up and couldn't speak. The moment was too huge. Leo's hands came to the belt of her robe and pulled it open. She kept looking at him, drawing confidence from the way his eyes fell and flared when he took in her naked body. He pushed the robe off her shoulders and it fell at her feet with a quiet thump. Moisture pooled between her legs and she fought not to squirm.

And then Angel watched with a palpitating heart as Leo removed his jeans, *again*. He was as magnificent as she remembered. She suddenly wanted to reach out and touch him. As if reading her mind, Leo said throatily, 'Go on. Touch me, Angel.'

Hesitantly she put out her hand and, with her heart in her mouth, encircled it around his erection. She heard his swift intake of breath. It felt amazing to her, hot and silky, but with a steel core. Experimentally she moved her hand up and down, shocked when she felt him harden and swell even more in her hand. Leo expelled a long hiss of breath and Angel looked up. His face was tight, eyes black, cheekbones slashed with dark colour. The thought of him embedding himself *in her* was nearly too much to imagine.

He put his hand on hers and gently removed it. For a

second Angel felt bewildered. She was doing it wrong. And then he said, 'If you keep touching me like that this will be over very quickly for both of us.'

Angel blushed and felt an absurd burst of relief. Leo took her by the hand and led her to the bed, gently pushed her down. She watched as he came over her, huge and dark and powerful. When he'd done this just a short while before she'd felt out of her depth and overwhelmed, but now…something had shifted. There was a gentleness about Leo that was desperately seductive.

As he took her mouth with his Angel arched herself into him, arms and hands searching to touch him, hold him. Their tongues collided feverishly, teeth nipping and biting. Angel could feel herself writhing underneath him, as if to try and feel every part of him.

Leo took his mouth away, and Angel gave a mewl of distress which quickly turned into a groan when she felt him cup one breast and bring the aching, tingling tip into the hot cavern of his mouth. Angel's back arched. Her hand stabbed into his hair.

His other hand was travelling up her leg, caressing, smoothing, feeling, until he spanned one thigh. Angel's legs fell open. He traced a path from her inner thigh to the juncture of her legs and she squirmed with intense pleasure.

His mouth moved to her other breast as his hand and fingers found that secret sweet spot between her legs, and she had to bite back a groan when she felt him stroke along plump and moistened folds. She was so wet.

Leo started to press hot kisses down her belly. Angel lifted her head, dizzy with desire and lust and an achy need for fulfilment. 'Leo…please…' She was not even sure what she was asking for.

'What, Angel?' He looked up, his voice sounding unbelievably husky, rough. 'What do you want?'

His fingers continued to tease, stroking her, making her hips twitch. And then, with a determined look in his eyes, he inserted two fingers inside her, going deeper, harder, and Angel gasped out loud. The feeling was so…intimate. Leo kept his hand where it was and moved up, his mouth hovering for a long moment just inches away from Angel's breast, where a nipple pouted wantonly towards him.

Feeling emboldened, Angel arched her back, offering herself up, and with a feral smile Leo bent his head and flicked out his tongue, teasing that hard tip until it stood tight and erect. Angel's head fell back. His hand was between her legs, his tongue on her breast… The tightening, building deliciousness she'd felt before was happening again and she couldn't stop it, didn't want to.

Just when she hovered on the edge, about to tumble down, Leo took his hand from between her legs and moved away slightly. Angel let out a faint moan of despair. She heard the rustle of a package. A condom.

Then Leo was back and hovering over her. Broad and powerful. She could feel his body move between her legs.

'Open up more for me, Angel…'

Angel parted her legs, allowing Leo into the cradle of her hips. Holding himself in one hand, he allowed the tip of his sex to move along the wet heat of her arousal to see how ready she was. She felt a pulse throb down there and groaned. Her head went back. She could feel that smooth head, teasing along her slick folds, being moistened with her juices.

Her hips started to buck towards Leo; she wanted him to impale her, but he drew back for a moment. His voice sounded rough. 'Patience, Angel…'

He bent down and covered her body with his, his chest crushing her breasts. Her nipples were like knife-points against him. Angel felt like sobbing out her frustration, but just then she felt Leo slide into her, his mouth coming over hers in as if to swallow her pain.

She gasped open-mouthed against him. The sting of pain was there, but not as she'd felt it before. He pulled back and looked down at her. 'Okay?'

Angel nodded.

She felt him push in a little further and winced. She could feel that she was so tight around him, but the awful dreaded pain wasn't lingering. It was slightly uncomfortable, yes, but very quickly that was being overtaken with something that felt amazing.

Angel's heart sang, and she said breathily, 'It's fine, Leo…it feels fine.'

In that moment Angel got a sense of how much Leo was holding back. She could see his shoulders shake slightly and his brow was beaded with sweat. With a deep groan Leo thrust all the way into her, and Angel gasped, her back arching on an instinct.

She couldn't speak. She felt so full, so *right*. So she spoke with her eyes and her hands, urging him to go on, to take up the rhythm, without even really knowing what she was doing or asking.

Leo pulled back and then thrust again, taking it slow and easy for the first few times, allowing Angel to get used to him. But then she felt an urgency build up within her. She wanted him to go harder, faster. She craved it. She was answering some deeply ancient call of the most feminine part of her. 'Please, Leo…'

'Yes, Angel, yes…stay with me.'

Leo answered her incoherent plea. With their bodies slick with sweat, he started to thrust into her, exactly as she craved with every atom of her being. Her hips jerked to meet his, to try and wring every drop out of him with each cataclysmic penetration of her body.

Then the pinnacle of every sensation she'd ever known was reached and transcended. She stopped breathing, her eyes on Leo's—did he know what was happening to her? He smiled as if he knew exactly what was happening, and with one powerful surge of his body into hers Angel was flung into another universe. A universe filled with exploding stars and a sweet, sweet oblivion.

Leo lay on his back, Angel tucked into his side, his arm around her. One long, smooth leg was thrown over his. He could feel her breasts pressing into him, those sweet, soft mounds tipped with those small, hard nipples. Even now he could still taste them on his tongue, their sweet muskiness.

Even though he'd taken her just a short time ago his body was ready for more. In fact he'd never been kept in such a state of arousal after making love. He could feel the unsteady beat of Angel's heart, slowly coming back to normal, and her breath was a little uneven. He knew that she'd fallen into a sleep of sorts.

Leo reeled. He'd had sex. Lots of sex. But nothing had come close to what he'd just experienced. He tried desperately to rationalise it: It had to be because she'd been a virgin. It had to be. Because if it wasn't—Angel moved. Leo's heart stopped; anticipation coiled deep inside him.

Angel was aware of consciousness returning slowly, trickling back. She was tucked into Leo's body, his arm tight around her, and everything rushed back in glorious Technicolor. She was a woman now. Leo hadn't rejected her.

Immediately she could feel moist heat between her legs, readying her for him again.

Angel's hand moved down over Leo's chest, exploring the play of his powerful muscles underneath that exquisitely golden olive skin, the brush of hair that made her tingle all over. She could feel tension come into the muscles under her hand and smiled against his skin. She didn't want words, she couldn't speak; she just wanted him.

When her seeking hand found what she was looking for a fiercely feminine exultation ran through her at finding him so hard and ready. She lifted her head and Leo turned to face her. He looked serious, and a little shiver of something snaked down Angel's spine, but she quashed it. He put his hand over hers, stopping her movements.

'Angel…you're bound to be sore.'

She came up and shook her head, putting her finger to his lips. She did ache, but it was an ache that cried out for fulfilment, not an ache of pain. She took her other hand from him and guided his hand to the juncture between her legs where he could feel for himself how ready she was.

Leo said something that sounded guttural and then moved fast, so that Angel was on her back and he was looming over her, already moving between her legs. The ache was building at her core, and if Angel could have stopped and slowed time in that moment, she would have.

'Yes, Leo…this is what I want…please.'

He bent his head said close to her mouth, 'Well, since you ask so nicely…'

When Angel woke again, the curtains were open and sunlight flooded her room. For a second everything was a blank. And then she became aware of certain *aches* and sensations in her body that weren't usual. As her consciousness returned fully everything came back in glorious Technicolor, and her heart tripped before starting up again at double speed. She knew that Leo wasn't in the bed; she'd somehow known that immediately.

It stunned her slightly to know how quickly her life had changed one hundred and eighty degrees. This time yesterday *she'd still been a virgin.*

Last night Leo had made her a woman. He'd taken her to a paradise she'd never dreamed existed. Heat suffused Angel from head to toe. And yet she couldn't stop a smile from breaking across her face. It was impossible to ignore the fact that her body felt as if it had been awoken from a deep, cold sleep...

But just as quickly her smile faded again, when the enormity of it all sank in. How could she be feeling like this for someone who had so coldly set out to take her because he wanted her and wanted to punish her? She frowned minutely, staring at the ceiling. She felt confused; Leo had taken her innocence with such devastating generosity that she reeled. Several times she'd seen the strain of his efforts to hold back, as if he was afraid he'd hurt her.

Angel lifted the sheet and looked into the bed, ignoring the signs of having been seriously seduced on her body, the faint bruises and reddish marks. There was no blood. Angel let the sheet drop; she knew rationally that there wasn't always necessarily blood, but there was a stinging between her legs that spoke of the potential of it if Leo hadn't been so gentle. And yet she could remember the desperation with which she'd urged him on, even when he'd tried to hold back for her sake.

With a burgeoning feeling of something huge in her chest Angel got out of bed and pulled on the robe which still lay on the floor. To think of how Leo had pushed it off her shoulders with such singular intent made Angel blush all over again.

Without really thinking of what she was doing, Angel went to the door that connected their rooms. After hesitating for the merest moment, she turned the handle and went in.

She stumbled to a halt when she saw Leo standing at the mirror of his wardrobe, knotting a tie. His eyes merely flicked to her through the mirror and then back to his task, with no change in expression. She hadn't been sure what to expect, but it hadn't been that. Angel was immediately tongue-tied. Leo looked so distant and intimidating in a dark suit, white shirt and tie. He looked like the phenomenally successful businessman he was. And nothing like the tender lover of last night. She suddenly knew she'd been an abject fool.

His eyes flicked to Angel again, and she felt heat rise in her face when she registered how cool they were. One dark brow rose quizzically. 'Was there something you wanted, Angel?'

Was there something you wanted, Angel? Angel balked and died a tiny death in that moment. Was this the same man? Acting as if the most cataclysmic thing on the earth hadn't just happened? But then, she realised in sick horror, it hadn't—not for him. If anything, last night for him must have been excruciatingly banal. How could it not have been, with a complete innocent?

She shook her head vaguely. 'I just…' *I just what?* she mocked herself bitterly, cursing her impulse to come in here. How could she have disregarded everything that lay between them, forgotten why she was there?

A lot of things were impacting upon Angel, all at the same time. Leo turned from the mirror, his tie perfectly knotted, his shoulders broad and awesome in the jacket, hair smoothed back, jaw clean shaven. Aloof.

Very quickly Angel assessed the situation, her brain working overtime. She brought her hands to her robe and tightened it, barely registering the way Leo's eyes dropped there for a split second. She tipped up her chin, forcing her voice to be cool. 'I was just wondering what time the stylist will be here? You did say that you'd have someone come today?'

Leo's jaw clenched and he strolled nonchalantly towards Angel, barely leashed power in every step. A flash of memory—those muscular thighs between hers last night—made a light sweat break out over Angel's top lip. She fought not to retreat, not to show that she was barely holding it together in the face of his obvious distance. He stopped a few feet away, his gaze sweeping up and down in a blistering moment that nearly scuppered Angel's precious composure.

'You were an eager student last night, Angel. I can see our time together being most...enjoyable.'

Angel burned inside. With humiliation and, more treacherously, with hurt, in response to his whole demeanour and his calling her *eager*. She had been desperately, awfully eager. She had fallen into his bed more easily than a ripe apple falling from a tree. She wanted to lash back, and hitched her chin a mite higher.

'I wouldn't know, as I have so little experience to compare it to. But for what it's worth last night was...pleasant enough.'

Leo laughed out loud, a big burst of sound that made Angel flinch. When he looked at her his eyes flashed a warning, and a mocking smile played around his sensual mouth. Angel had to fight against the pull in her belly, the desire to just stop and look at it. She dragged her gaze back up to his.

He stepped even closer and put out a hand, touching her jaw. Angel clenched it.

'Sweetheart, I know exactly how it was for you. I felt every ripple of every one of your orgasms, so don't pretend that it was anything less than *pleasant*.'

Angel knocked his hand away, dying somewhere inside. 'Like I said, you'd know so much more than me. I'm sure the novelty won't last long.'

Leo calmly replaced his hand, taking a firmer grip on Angel's jaw. 'On the contrary,' he drawled, 'I don't see this novelty fading for some time. You're all fire underneath that angelic exterior, and I'm looking forward to seeing a lot more of it. This is only the beginning.'

With that, he dropped his hand and stepped back. Angel thought for a split second that she saw some chink in his composure, and it had her heart beat hard in response. But then he looked at his watch and said crisply, 'The stylist will be here at noon, followed by someone to give you some beauty treatments. We've got our first public outing tonight, Angel—a ball to celebrate my taking over Parnassus Shipping as CEO. It should be fun for you. It's at the Grand Bretagne, where you're more intimately acquainted with the dirty sheets. I'll be back later. Wear something appropriate for your first viewing as my mistress.'

He ran a finger down her hot cheek. 'I'm looking forward to stirring things up with you by my side.'

CHAPTER SIX

As Leo sat in a meeting in his new boardroom later that day, to his utter chagrin he found he wasn't concentrating on the discussion—which didn't disturb him too much; he was already two steps ahead of everyone else in the room. All he could think about was Angel and last night. And how she'd looked this morning when she'd come into his room, the lurch he'd felt in his chest when he'd seen her hesitation. How hard it had been to stand there and see her softly flushed face, those huge blue eyes, and not rip her robe from her body and spread her underneath him again.

His body was tight with arousal even now—*not* a state he welcomed in the middle of the day, surrounded by work colleagues, and with Ari Levakis looking at him with a small frown. Leo smiled.

But it was futile. He kept getting flashes of moments: when he'd thrust into her for the first time and heard that telltale indrawn gasp, how tight she'd clamped around him, how sweetly she'd opened up for him, allowing him to sink deeper and deeper. How her skin had tasted, like sweet musk and crushed roses.

Like sweet musk and crushed roses? Leo gave himself an inner shake. He had to get it together. Angel Kassianides was a piece of work.

For a moment that morning he'd thought that he'd seen something achingly vulnerable in her face, and it had made him close up inside. Close up against the inevitable attempt of a woman to turn intimacy into something emotional. But then, when he'd walked over to her, she'd been composed and cool. So much so that he knew he'd be a fool if he trusted any of her reactions for a moment.

She was his mistress, she was *his*, and the thought of the evening to come, when he could parade her in public and know that he was her only lover, was tantalising in the extreme.

Angel sat beside Leo in the back of his car later that evening. Her throat ached with a huge lump. She hated the fact that she was so raw about what had happened. All day she'd not been able to get out of her head the coolness Leo had subjected her to that morning. Right now, she didn't think she could ever let him touch her again, but just then, as if to mock her assertion, she felt a big hand close over hers, where it lay on her leg, and her blood started to speed up.

'You look beautiful tonight.'

Angel exerted iron control over her emotions and turned slowly to face Leo, not a hint of her inner turmoil showing on her face. She smiled and it felt brittle. 'Well, you paid enough for it.'

Leo's eyes were dark, with those golden lights lurking in their depths, already undoing some of Angel's rigid control. She left her hand lax in his, even though she wanted desperately to pull away. His dark tuxedo elevated his appeal to another level. And he just said, softly now, while shaking his head, 'Money has nothing to do with true beauty. And you are, Angel, truly beautiful.'

Leo found that he was saying the words with a reverent sincerity that he couldn't help. When he'd walked into her room earlier he hadn't known what to expect. His heart had beaten a curious tattoo, and he'd found that his chest had been tight with anticipation. She'd been standing at her window, slender back to him. He'd seen many women, in many beautiful gowns for his pleasure, but none he'd ever seen had taken his breath away before they'd even turned around.

The dress was floor length, and a deeply turquoise colour. Silk. Apart from that Leo hadn't known much, because he'd felt dizzy with lust. It draped and fell in such a way as to turn her into some sort of goddess creature. Her hair was twisted up and held in place by a flower of a similar colour to the dress.

Disgusted with his reaction, he'd had to call her name to get her to turn around, and she'd done so, so slowly it had had the effect of a striptease on his body, even when she was fully clothed!

Her breasts were lovingly caressed by the silk of the dress, the deep V between them a shadow of promise. Her head had been high, chin tipped up in a gesture that had seemed almost defiant. It had been all Leo could do to stand still and extend an autocratic hand, gesturing her to come to him. And when she'd walked, and the soft silk had swirled around her body—

Leo came back to the present and shifted uncomfortably in the back of the car.

For a second the cool and controlled woman suddenly looked slightly unsure. And Leo reacted. What was he doing, all but drooling over her like this? His hand tightened on hers for a second, and he felt the small delicate bones, the slight roughness of her skin that hinted at the work she'd been doing, and his chest tightened again for a second.

He thrust aside all the nebulous feelings he didn't under-stand, and asked, 'How do you think your father will react to seeing us together when he gets the papers tomorrow? Because this is going to be all over the world, Angel…'

Angel shivered and tried to pull her hand away, but Leo held it tight. She hated him in that moment. Really hated him. The only thing stopping her from trying to jump out of the car as it idled at a set of lights was the memory of the ecstatic phone call she'd had from Delphi earlier, telling her that she would be marrying Stavros in a month's time. And also the surprise that Angel had felt at Leo acting on his word so soon.

Her voice was unaccountably husky, with all the confusing emotions rushing through her. 'I think you know very well how he'll react. He'll be apoplectic. He'll be utterly humiliated.'

Leo lifted a brow, speculation all over his face. 'Will he, though, Angel? Or have you and he planned exactly this all along?'

Hating feeling so cornered and mistrusted, Angel hit back. 'What if we have? You'll never know, will you?'

Leo moved close and Angel arched back, but it was no good. Leo's hand came out and caressed the back of her neck. His other hand came up and cupped her silk-covered breast. She hadn't been able to wear a bra, and she was horrified to feel her nipple peak and thrust against the silk. His thumb moved lazily against her nipple and Angel bit back a moan. *How* could he have this effect on her?

'I'll know, Angel, because from now on, until I'm bored with you, I'll know every move you make. So any plans you and he have cooked up will be futile.'

'But we don't—'

Her words were crushed under Leo's mouth and everything disappeared into a haze of urgent desire. Since he'd come into her room earlier, when she'd not even been able to turn around to face him until he'd called her name, finally doing so with her heart beating so loud he had to have heard it, Angel had, in some deep and traitorous place wanted to feel his mouth on hers again.

And now it was, and she was being sucked under all over again. Mindlessly helpless to fight him. She wasn't aware of the car drawing to a halt, or the driver clearing his throat. She was only aware of Leo pulling back, and her gasping in of breath when she opened her eyes and tried to focus. Her body felt jittery and on fire. Leo just smiled at her, triumph in his gaze, and Angel could only watch as his eyes travelled down and took in the obvious state of her arousal, her nipples as hard as berries, standing out starkly against the unforgiving silk.

'Perfect.'

And before Angel knew what he meant Leo was out of the car, coming around to open her door and pulling her out. She still felt dizzy, spaced out, and then there was nothing but Leo's hand around hers and a barrage of lights and questions. She'd just become Leo's very public property.

Later, Angel sat in her chair and felt thoroughly out of place. She'd been away at boarding school for so long, and then at college, so that she'd never really integrated into Athens society. Her mouth twisted. Well, not the way Leo believed, anyway. Despite that, she did know people in the room, and she saw their looks and their whispering and she hated that it affected her. She'd gone to the bathroom earlier, and heard two women talking by the sinks.

'Can you *believe* he came with her?'

'I know. I mean, no one would be surprised if he crossed to the other side of the street to ignore her and that awful family after what they did...'

The other woman had laughed nastily. 'Can't you just imagine her buffoon of a father's face if he saw them together? I wouldn't be surprised if Leo Parnassus is only taking her as some sort of revenge. He's practically ignored her all evening…'

The other woman had sighed lustily then, and said, 'I wouldn't mind him taking me for revenge… Obviously he sees something in her too-innocent-to-be-true face.'

The stinging words came back to Angel now, and she held her head up high and gritted her teeth. This was all part of Leo's plan. Ritual humiliation.

Just then Angel saw Lucy Levakis return to the table where they'd been seated. She was the English wife of Aristotle Levakis, Leo's business partner, and the only person who'd been genuinely sweet to Angel—no doubt because she didn't know of the history. Ari Levakis, though, had been sending her dark speculative looks all night, clearly of the same mind as Leo, and suspicious of her motives. After all, he'd been one of the people she'd recognised at that party in the villa all those weeks ago. Angel felt sick. Did he know about Leo's revenge?

Lucy sat down and said chattily, 'You looked lonely over here, so I thought I'd come and join you. Honestly, *men*—they get so wrapped up in themselves.'

Angel smiled tightly. She didn't want to taint this nice woman with her dubious reputation. 'Really, I don't mind if you want to go back. I'm fine here.'

Lucy shook her head, and just then Angel noticed something and felt her heart lift for the first time in days. She'd obviously not noticed before, too preoccupied with everything. She sat forward and asked shyly, 'That necklace you're wearing, where did you get it?'

Lucy beamed and told Angel all about how Ari had known

how much she loved it and had proposed to her with it. 'To this day I don't own an engagement ring.' She touched the necklace reverently. 'This is my engagement ring.'

Angel smiled, blushing with pride. 'I designed that necklace.'

Lucy gasped. 'You *what*?'

Angel nodded. 'I did jewellery design at college, and that was the only piece I sold from my graduation show. I gave the rest of the collection to my sister and some friends as gifts.'

Lucy gasped again, 'But you could have made a fortune!'

Angel was aware of the irony. It had been shortly after her graduating that their personal circumstances had changed so dramatically. She hadn't known that she'd have to turn her back on her dream profession so soon, otherwise she might have kept her collection intact. She smiled now, ruefully. 'I preferred to give it away.'

Lucy said something incoherent, and before she knew it Angel's hand had been grabbed and she was being dragged in the taller woman's wake over to the men. She tried to remonstrate with her but to no avail.

Angel heard her interrupt them excitedly and explain what Angel had just revealed. Angel looked up to see Ari's *very* speculative gaze and then, gulping, looked at Leo. His eyes showed no emotion. No doubt he thought she might be lying. Lucy gave a groan then, when she realised the time, and said she'd have to go home to relieve their nanny. Angel had learned that they had two small children.

Her heart clenched when she saw Ari's attention go back to his wife and he pulled her close, making his excuses too, despite Lucy's insistence that he stay. Clearly the man couldn't wait to be alone with his wife, and Angel's heart clenched even harder.

They made their goodbyes, Lucy still excited to have discovered Angel's secret, and then they were gone. Angel expected Leo to make an excuse and leave her alone again, and she had even started walking back to the table when Leo caught her hand and pulled her back.

She looked up at him.

'Where do you think you're going?'

'I…' Angel faltered, and cursed herself for being so weak. She felt a fire of rebellion start to build. 'I was going back to the table to sit alone again, so that everyone can see how you ignore me. But actually, now that the speeches are over, the dais is so much more public. Why don't I just go up and sit there? I could even put a sign around my neck if you wish—'

'Stop it.'

Angel couldn't, too hurt. 'Why, Leo? Isn't this exactly what you planned? A round of public appearances with your mistress of revenge, making it perfectly obvious that your only interest in me is completely superficial? Making sure there is maximum speculation, maximum humiliation?'

Angel bit her lip. The words had spilled out before she could stop them. 'Well, if it's any consolation, the gossip in the powder room is already rife, and let's just say I don't come off well.'

Leo frowned. 'What did you hear?'

Angel shook her head, aghast at having revealed so much. 'It doesn't matter.'

Because the awful thing was, he might be humiliating her in public, but he'd be taking her to bed at night, and once in his bed the last thing she felt was humiliated.

Leo opened his mouth to speak, but just then someone came to interrupt them. Much to Angel's surprise, he didn't let go of her hand; he kept her close, introducing her to the other man. And, while he didn't go out of his way to include her in the conversation, he didn't let her out of his sight for the rest of the evening, making Angel's emotions see-saw even more.

In the car on the way home, Angel rotated her head to try and ease out the kinks. She was exhausted.

'Did you really design Lucy's necklace?'

Angel stopped rotating her head and looked at Leo warily. 'Of course. I wouldn't lie about something like that. What would be the point?'

Her simple assertion struck him somewhere deep. Leo just looked at her for a long moment. 'It's a beautiful piece.'

Angel shrugged awkwardly. He sounded surprised, as if he hadn't meant to give her a compliment. 'Thank you.'

'You haven't been making jewellery since you left college because…?'

Angel jumped in. This was a very tender point for her. 'I haven't been making jewellery because I don't have the facilities.'

Leo shook his head. 'But you've been working, surely it's possible to rent a workspace?'

'The equipment and the raw materials I need are too expensive.'

Leo sat back. 'You must really resent having had to resort to menial work.'

Angel blinked. In that moment she realised that she'd never resented having to work; she'd only missed the fact that she'd had to put off her dream. It had been very simple: she'd had to be there for Delphi. Necessitating that they stay at home to cut down on living costs. She shook her head. 'I had no choice.'

Leo found himself wondering uncomfortably why Angel

hadn't just resorted to hanging out on the vibrant Athenian social scene in order to try and seduce a rich husband from her own social sphere. Evidently her sister had done just that… But then just as quickly he found himself quashing the curiosity when he found it inevitably led to wondering how she'd remained a virgin. A virgin didn't go out to seduce rich husbands.

She wasn't a virgin any more; she was *his*. Something deeply primitive and possessive moved through him. Ruthlessly he pulled Angel over until she sat in his lap. She resisted him, but he caressed her back through the flimsy silk. He'd seen her sitting alone at their dinner table earlier, and had had to restrain himself from going over and claiming her. The only thing that had stopped him had been the weakness he'd felt that would show, especially when Ari Levakis had been quizzing him as to why on earth he'd taken her as his mistress. So he'd let her sit there, but had been burningly aware of her every second, of the proud way she'd held her head—defiant, almost.

It hadn't sat well with him, and when Angel had said those things to him he'd felt shame clawing upwards. Not an emotion he was used to when it came to women.

No matter why he was with Angel, he'd had no conscious intention of ignoring her in public. His plan had been humiliation, yes, but that would come when he had had enough of her and ejected her from his life, making it very clear she'd been just a temporary addition. It would come from knowing that Tito Kassianides would be confronted with pictures splashed all over the tabloids tomorrow of his daughter in bed with the enemy.

In truth, he'd been shocked to hear her say that she'd already been the subject of gossip; clearly Athens was in a league with New York and its wildfire gossip circuit.

Angel still resisted him on his lap, looking resolutely out
of the window. He stroked her back and pressed an open-
mouthed kiss against her arm. He felt the first tiny signs of
her relaxing and smiled. His caressing hand pulled her in
closer, until she fell against him, yet still she was tense. His
other hand rested on her thigh and then started to move to
where her legs were pressed tightly together.

With gentle force he pressed his hand against her *mons*.
He could feel heat coming through the silk, and the inevitable hardening of his own arousal. He moved subtly
and heard Angel's indrawn breath as she felt him push
against the thin barrier of her dress, against the globes of
her bottom.

He reached up and pulled her chin around to face him. He
didn't like the look in her eyes: it was too *naked*. Too full of
things he didn't want to know. So he pulled her head down
and kissed her, hard, and with a deep groan of triumph felt
her sink into him completely, her lithe body pressing into his,
enflaming him so much that by the time they reached the villa
he was aching to bury himself inside her.

By the end of that first week the whole world knew that Leo
Parnassus had taken Angel as his mistress. Paparazzi were
camped at the gates to the villa. Every night they'd gone out,
either to a function or just for dinner, and the response had
been a growing hysteria.

Headlines screamed out of newsstands: *'Parnassus and
Kassianides bury seventy years of enmity between the sheets.'*
And other headlines, more snide, with suggestions of Leo
Parnassus being paid *in kind*. It was awful. It was exactly what
Leo had planned.

One morning, when Angel had gone down to breakfast and

had been surprised to see Leo there, she'd asked nervously, 'What about your father—won't this hurt him?'

Leo had looked at her sharply, and then with a hard look had said, 'My father is aware of the situation, but he has no say in who I choose as my lover.'

Angel had swallowed nervously, unaccountably concerned for the much elder man she could remember seeing at the party in the villa; he'd looked so *frail*. 'But still, it can't be easy, when he's spent his whole life wanting to avenge his family name.'

Leo had just replied with silken emphasis, 'Which is exactly what I'm doing. My father, above all things, is a strategist. If he knew for a second what you'd done, what a threat you are, he would endorse my methods wholeheartedly.'

Angel had still felt miserable to think of how his father might be feeling, and had been reminded again that whenever Leo spoke of him it was clear that little love was lost.

And then Leo had asked casually, 'Have you spoken to *your* father yet?'

Angel had blanched and shaken her head. She knew from Delphi that her father was home and in a near constant state of violent inebriation, cursing her volubly. His trip to London had been spectacularly unsuccessful. Angel knew a lot of his bluster was just that. And she wasn't scared for Delphi's safety. Her father had only ever lashed out at her, Angel, with his fists, in those moments when she reminded him too much of her mother.

She'd shaken her head again. 'No, we haven't spoken.' Angel sent up a silent prayer. At least when Delphi was married she'd be moving in with Stavros and Angel would be free to live elsewhere. And lick her wounds from the fall-out of her association with Leo.

Leo had looked suspicious. Angel had done her best to
ignore him.

Now, Angel sighed as she looked in the full-length mirror
of her dressing room. She was tired. And she had to admit that
she was still shell-shocked. She felt as though from the
moment she'd met Leo again, that fateful night in the study,
she'd not had a chance to draw breath.

He consumed her utterly. In the nights he taught her body
how it could respond so powerfully to his; but she was still
shy, still mortified at her reaction to him. And her days were
filled with vivid flashbacks to moments that took her breath
away, making her body heat up and melt all over again.

She quite literally could not remember what it had been
like not to know this man, not to know his hard features, the
faint line of the scar above his mouth which still tantalised her.

She tried to clear her mind of him and twisted in front of
the mirror. The dress she wore was the most daring one yet.
It was strapless and mostly gold, ending a few inches above
her knees, where the gold tapered off into silver. Her waist
was cinched in with a gold belt, and gold hoop earrings and
strappy sandals completed the outfit.

Something defiant had made her pick it out of the myriad
clothes that now filled the walk-in closet, along with a glittering array of stunning jewellery. When she'd seen the jewellery her heart had twisted. How she longed to make her own
again. She'd always found the designs of others too garish for
her tastes, preferring delicate chains and subtle designs. Like
Lucy's butterfly necklace.

She heard a sound, and whirled around to see Leo, leaning
nonchalantly against her door, already dressed and ready to
go. She felt vulnerable at having been observed. This was how
it seemed to be going. He'd be gone every day to work when

she awoke, her body heavy after the rigours of a long night of lovemaking. Then he'd come home and get ready, only coming to fetch her when she too was ready. Minimal conversation. Minimal emotional involvement.

She'd noticed Leo tensing beside her last night, at an art gallery opening, when a couple had started a passionate and very public row. When Angel had glanced up at him in response to his hand tightening on hers, she'd been surprised to see him looking slightly mesmerised, and yet grey underneath his tan. Eventually he'd turned from the scene, with disgust etched all over his face. Angel hadn't been able to understand his reaction; it had seemed totally disproportionate to what was really just a domestic fight.

She found that the memory and the concern she'd felt now made her feel even more vulnerable. She didn't care about what made Leo tick. She only cared that he was facilitating her sister's happiness.

She drew on all the confidence she could and put a hand on her hip, cocking her head. 'Well? Is it suitably mistressy for you?'

Leo's jaw clenched, and Angel's belly quivered.

'Don't push me, Angel.' His eyes dropped then insultingly, lingering and assessing. He looked at her again, and all her bravado had melted.

He just said cuttingly, 'Yes, it's perfect. Exactly the kind of thing the press will be expecting you to wear. Let's go.'

CHAPTER SEVEN

In the car on the way down to Athens, Leo fought back waves of anger and irritation. The sight of Angel's smooth thighs out of the corner of his eye was nearly too much.

When he'd first seen her in the dress he'd wanted to march in and rip it off her. To find something much more suitable, something that might cover her from head to toe. To his utter shock and ignominy, it had only been when she'd turned around and been so provocatively cocky that he'd realised his desire to change it stemmed from somewhere very ambiguous.

He'd suddenly been uncomfortable with the idea of her going out and looking so obviously like his mistress. When that was exactly what he wanted. The fact that he'd had to remind himself of that fact struck hard now. Also, more worryingly, sleeping with Angel for the past week had done nothing to diminish her effect on him. Every time he slept with her, thrust into her lissom body, his desire increased exponentially. He'd also been growing acutely aware of the attention Angel garnered from other men, attention she *appeared* not to notice, but he didn't trust her for a second.

He was embarking on a new path, taking up residence in

his ancestral home, not to mention taking control of a multi-million-dollar organisation while keeping track of his own business concerns in New York. He had a million and two things to occupy his time and energy, not least of which was being vigilant and mindful of the vulnerabilities of his company in its time of transition.

He couldn't help feeling, with the space that Angel took up in his every waking moment, that he was being incredibly stupid. Willingly taking his enemy into his bed, where she was fast proving to have more control over him than he cared to admit.

The only way Leo knew to counter these doubts was to exert his own control, and right now he only wanted control of one thing: Angel. With a growl he ordered the driver to put up the privacy partition, and turned to reach for Angel in the exact moment that she turned to him with a question in her eyes.

The minute she saw him a delicate flush bloomed in her cheeks. He saw her eyes dilate and, without speaking a word, he pulled her over to straddle his lap. He pushed her short dress up over her thighs so that her legs could move more freely.

Leo gripped her waist then, moving her strategically, so that she could feel where he ached most. He was rewarded with a gasp, but Angel's eyes were curiously unemotional, as if she had locked herself away somewhere. To his utter consternation Leo found that thought repulsive. How dared she try and hide herself from him? She was *his*—mind, body and soul.

What ensued was a battle of wills more than an act of love-making, although it was that too. Explosively, with ruthless intent, Leo drew down his zip and pulled Angel's panties aside, and surged up into her moist heat.

He wouldn't let her look away. Every time she turned her face he ruthlessly brought it back. She closed her eyes, but he ground out, 'Open your eyes, Angel, *look* at me.'

And she did. With defiance blazing. It only served to make their lovemaking even more intense. Eyes locked. Angel clearly knew that Leo wanted something of her, and she was determined not to give it. Finally the moment came, and Leo could bear it no more. His body was screaming for release, Angel's moans had got more and more fractured, and he could feel the start of the spasms of her orgasm. He knew as soon as he felt it that he couldn't last. And he didn't.

For a long moment in the aftermath Leo's head rested on Angel's still covered breast. Their bodies intimately joined. He felt every last pulsating clench of her body around his. But it was only when he felt her hesitate for a second and then bring her hand up to stroke his hair that he realised he'd won that particular round. Curiously, though, he felt no sense of victory.

That night, at yet another function—Angel wondered desperately how much anyone could endure of this endless posturing and preening and networking—she was trying desperately not to give in to the temptation to tug her dress down over her legs, feeling exposed and angry with herself for choosing it now. She'd been too angry to change when Leo had declared that it was *perfect*.

What had happened in the car on the way there… She still burned at knowing she'd just let Leo do that. She'd done her best to remain aloof. But that was near impossible.

She'd learnt her lesson that first morning after they'd slept together. When he'd been so cold. Each night since then he'd come to her bed and they'd made love, but within minutes of finishing he'd get up and walk, naked, back to his own room.

No hanging around. No nice words. No cuddles or, God forbid, tenderness. No whispers in the night, talking of inane things, which was how she'd always imagined it might be with a lover.

'You're a million miles away, Angel.'

Angel's focus came back into the packed ballroom of one of Athens' plushest hotels. Lucy Levakis was looking at her with a teasing smile.

'Not that I blame you, of course,' she whispered then, with a pointed glance in the direction of the two men who conversed nearby, both tall and both commanding lots of attention—mostly female.

Lucy sighed indulgently as she looked at her husband. 'I can remember what it's like…' she said, and then, dryly, 'Who am I kidding? He still makes the rest of the room fade away.'

Angel smiled tightly. Ari had greeted her with more warmth tonight, as if she'd passed some silent test. Angel had fleetingly and far too wistfully wondered what it might take to break through Leo's wall of mistrust. She thought of how he'd caught her red-handed in his office, and had to concede it would take a lot. A belief that she could possibly be innocent when he had no reason whatsoever to believe otherwise, and zero interest.

Angel forced her thoughts away from that now, stung that she was feeling so vulnerable. She forced herself to smile more widely at Lucy. 'Anyone would think you two were still on your honeymoon, not going home to two small children.'

Just then Lucy got pulled aside by an acquaintance, so Angel was left on her own again, with Lucy sending back an apologetic grimace. Immediately, though, Leo turned his head where he stood with Ari a few feet away and held out a hand. With an awful lurching in her chest Angel reached out and took it, feeling as if something slightly momentous had just occurred. Which was ridiculous. But she realised in that moment that Leo hadn't once left her on her own since that first function. While he'd not exactly been demonstrative, he'd been solicitous and attentive.

But to be faced with Leo and Ari was nearly too much. They both packed a punch, even if Leo was the only one who made Angel's pulse race and her legs turn to jelly. She tried to ignore him and smiled at Ari, shyly asking about his and Lucy's children.

Ari rolled his eyes and groaned, 'Zoe is walking as of this week, so with her and Cosmo underfoot it's like an assault course. Just getting through the day and keeping them both alive is a feat in itself. Running a shipping fleet is a piece of cake in comparison.'

Angel smiled, inordinately relieved to see that Ari seemed to have definitely thawed towards her. She wondered if it was Lucy's influence.

Ari looked at Leo briefly, and then back to Angel, 'Actually, I have a favour to ask of you.'

Angel nodded. 'Sure, anything.'

'I'd like to commission you to make a set of jewellery for Lucy. Our anniversary is in a couple of months, and since she's found out that you designed the necklace I gave her I know she'd love a complete set. I was thinking of a bracelet, and perhaps earrings to match?'

Angel felt a dart of pure pleasure go through her, and she blushed. 'Well, I'm honoured that you'd ask… I'd love to do something…'

But then, just as suddenly, her spirits dropped like a stone when she realised that she had no way of being able to take on such a commission. 'But unfortunately I'm not

really in a position at the moment to make anything new...
I don't have the—'

'I'll make sure she has everything she might need.'

Angel's mouth opened and closed and she looked up at
Leo, genuinely stymied.

Ari was already responding. 'Great. Angel, can you come
to my office tomorrow morning and we can discuss the
designs?'

Angel looked back to Ari, feeling as if the wind had just
been knocked out of her. 'Yes, of course.'

Lucy returned then, and reminded him that they'd
promised to be home by a certain time. As they left, Ari gave
Angel a discreet wink. When they'd gone, Angel looked up
at Leo and said stiffly, 'You shouldn't have promised Ari that
I could take the commission. You've no idea how expensive
it might be to make what he wants, especially if he wants it
so soon. Plus, I've no workspace.'

Leo pulled her into him, and that little move set off a host
of butterflies in Angel's chest. Apart from holding her hand,
Leo rarely touched her more intimately in public. 'The villa
has a million empty rooms, and I've no intention of denying
my friend what he wants.'

Why did her heart ache when his easy generosity to his
friend was so apparent?

Angel stood at the door of the room, which had been found
at the very back of the villa, and shook her head wryly. This
was what untold limitless wealth did: it gave you a state-of-
the-art jewellery-making workshop within days.

She walked in and touched the wooden table reverently,
seeing the myriad tools and expensive metals and stones she'd
listed for Leo all laid out. She hadn't had access to facilities

and equipment so fine even in college. It gave her a pain in her heart to know that just as quickly Leo would have it ripped out and replaced by the generic room it had once been when the time came. She sighed deeply.

'Don't you like it?'

Angel whirled around, her hand going to her chest. 'You scared me half to death, creeping up on me like that!' But, even so, her treacherous body was already responding to the way Leo lounged so nonchalantly against the door, hands in the pockets of his trousers, shirt open at his throat.

'You look as if someone has just died, so the only thing I can deduce is that you hate your workshop.'

Angel shook her head, aghast that he'd seen her turmoil so easily. 'No, I love it.' She turned away, so he wouldn't see how vulnerable she felt to be caught like this. 'You must have spent a fortune on it.'

She turned back then, feeling more in control, and saw Leo shrug. 'I just told them to install the best.'

Angel smiled, feeling hurt at his nonchalance. 'Well, you got the best. I just hope it won't cost too much to rip it all out again.'

For a long moment he said nothing, and then, 'You don't have to concern yourself with that.'

Leo felt a surge of something rip through him at her casual words. She just stood there, in jeans and a T-shirt, looking so effortlessly sexy that he felt weak inside. He heard himself say harshly, 'Don't get any ideas about Ari Levakis, he's a happily married man.'

The look of sheer incomprehension on Angel's face made Leo want to alternately shake her for acting and kick himself for being so obvious. But something about the way Ari had visibly warmed towards Angel, evident in the fact that he'd

asked her for this commission, had sent something ominously
dark into Leo's belly the other night.

He could remember the look of pure happiness on Angel's
face when she'd returned from meeting Ari at his office to
discuss the designs. For some reason Leo had decided to stay
at home to work that day, and he'd walked into the hall when
he'd heard her return. She'd been humming. But the minute
she'd seen him her face had changed to wariness. She'd
stopped humming.

Leo had walked over to her and all but dragged her into
his study, where a passion like nothing he'd ever experienced
before had made him take her on the edge of his desk like a
hormonal teenager.

Now she just looked at him, her mouth looking bruised.
Her eyes looking bruised. With *hurt*?

'I am well aware that Ari is a happily married man, and I
can assure you that even if I had designs on the man, which
I do not, he'd be about as likely to look at me twice as you
will ever believe I'm innocent of trying to steal from you.'

Leo's chest tightened. 'Which is impossible.'

She hitched in a little breath, barely perceptible, but he'd
heard it. 'Exactly' was all she said, but with a curious resig-
nation in her voice. Almost defeated.

Later, when they returned from the opening night of a new restaurant, exhaustion was creeping over Angel in earnest. That
little exchange in the jewellery workshop earlier had taken
more out of her than she cared to admit. She was caught in
such a bind. Apart from the fact that if she was ever to defend
herself to Leo about that night in the study he'd have to trust
her word, at this stage she was all too aware of Delphi's
wedding looming on the horizon, and how important it was

that nothing jeopardise it. Defending herself was futile. She was angry with herself for even wanting to be able to do so. For even feeling the need. As if Leo would ever show her another side of himself. She was damned because of who she was, no matter what.

She trailed Leo up the main staircase, hardly able to lift her head. She even bumped into him at the top of the stairs and gave out a yelp of fear when she felt herself falling backwards into thin air.

In a second Leo had turned and caught her, hauling her into his body. He looked down at her, frowning. 'What is the matter with you?'

Angel shook her head. Despite the aching tiredness, she could already feel the predictable response heating up in her body. Stirring it to life. 'Nothing, I'm just…a little tired.'

Leo continued to look down at her, until Angel started to squirm uncomfortably in his arms. Abruptly he let her go and backed away. Angel felt curiously bereft, and nearly fell down in shock when Leo just said, 'Go to bed, Angel. I have some calls to make to New York. I'll be on the phone for a couple of hours.'

Angel nodded, and tried not to acknowledge the stab of disappointment low down in her belly. Just before she turned away she stopped and said, 'I'm going to be out all day tomorrow with my sister. We're shopping for our dresses.'

And then she said hesitantly, 'I never said thank you for making sure Delphi's wedding could be organised so quickly.'

Leo's face was cast in shadow, so Angel couldn't see his expression, and all he said was 'It was part of our agreement, remember?'

Angel's mouth felt numb. 'Of course.' And she turned and went into her bedroom.

* * *

Leo knew he should be making his calls—they were important, and an entire boardroom was in New York right now, waiting for him to contact them—but…he couldn't get Angel's face out of his head. And the dark shadows of tiredness he'd seen under her eyes. He couldn't get the roller coaster of the past days and nights out of his head, when everything as he knew it had been turned upside down and inside out. When only one thing seemed to make sense: Angel Kassianides in his bed.

It was as if the fog and haze that had clouded his brain since he'd caught Angel in the study was clearing slightly, and the extent to which he'd become consumed by her shocked him. The anatomy of their relationship was so utterly different from any other he'd known. And he still couldn't get a handle on Angel. She was an enigma. A dangerous enigma.

He couldn't get out of his head the way she'd just thanked him for organising her sister's wedding. When she had been so quick to jump on it and use it as a bargaining tool—no doubt ensuring her own future as well as her sister's. There had been something about it that niggled at him now.

Leo knew that she'd had plenty of opportunity to speak with her father, and yet she hadn't. On the few occasions she'd gone out it had been to meet her sister. She'd gone nowhere near her own home. So that pointed to her father not being involved. But Leo knew he would be a fool to let go his suspicions entirely.

One thing he knew: the more time he spent with Angel, in bed or out, the less logical he became. Maybe it was time to start pulling back, getting some perspective on things.

He finally picked up the phone, and spent the next couple of hours doing his best to forget all about the woman asleep upstairs.

* * *

A week later Angel lay in bed. Alone. It was late. Leo had rung earlier to say that he had to work late and that she should eat at home. It wasn't the first night in the past week that this had happened, and, rather than making Angel feel relieved at having a reprieve of sorts, it made her feel slightly nervous.

Leo had been so all-encompassing, so passionate since the moment they'd met, that it was a shock to see this more distant side to him. She heard a noise then: the unmistakable sound of Leo moving around his room. She held her breath, but as the minutes ticked by he didn't come in.

Angel turned over and stared into the dark. She hated the fact that she couldn't feel relieved he wasn't coming in. Hated the fact that her body throbbed with need. She closed her eyes, but opened them again quickly when lurid images filled her mind. She'd never thought that sex could be so...so... *exciting*. And addictive. She felt like some kind of sex addict; the minute she saw Leo her hormones seemed to go into overdrive and she had zero will-power when it came to resisting him. He only had to look at her and she caught on fire.

Angel couldn't help but suspect that this had to be part of his plan of revenge. After all, he was so much more experienced than her.

She tried her best to sleep, but even after everything had gone silent next door sleep still eluded her, so she gave up and sat up, swinging her legs out of bed. She'd get some water from the kitchen...

Padding down through the quiet villa, Angel felt a jolt, thinking back to the party that night, all those weeks before. Never in a million years would she have imagined that she'd be here, ensconced as Leo Parnassus' mistress.

Too late, just as she was pushing open the kitchen door, she realised that she wasn't the only night visitor. Leo sat at the island in the middle of the kitchen, illuminated under a circle of low light from overhead. He looked up as she came in. He was eating something. Angel instinctively started backing away, feeling as if she was intruding on a private moment. 'Sorry. I didn't realise you were up.'

Leo waved a hand, gesturing for her to come in. 'You couldn't sleep?'

Angel hovered awkwardly and shook her head, 'No.' She felt self-conscious in loose pyjama bottoms and a skimpily clinging vest top, but knew it was silly to feel self conscious when this man seemed to know more about her own body than she did. Not that he seemed inclined to be all that interested any more. Insecurity lanced her. 'I just wanted to get some water.'

It would be ridiculous if she left now, so she went to the fridge in the corner and busied herself getting out a bottle, trying to ignore the way her pulse had rocketed. She hated to think that he might see something of how much she craved him.

Out of the corner of her eye she saw that Leo was wearing a T-shirt and jeans. Angel glanced at him surreptitiously. He might have been working late in the study after he'd come home. She noticed that he had faint smudges of colour under his eyes and felt a spike of concern. Something else caught her eye then, distracting her. Despite herself she moved closer to where Leo sat at the gleaming counter, clutching the bottle of water to her chest.

'Is that peanut butter and *jam*?'

Leo nodded and finished eating a mouthful of sandwich. Angel must have looked bemused, because Leo wiped his mouth with a napkin and said dryly, 'What?'

She shook her head and moved closer to the stool opposite Leo, unconsciously resting against it for a moment. 'I just…I wouldn't have expected…' she said inanely, feeling like a complete idiot. But there was just something so disarming about finding Leo like this that her stomach had turned to mush. Without realising what she was doing, she sat on the stool opposite him.

'Want one?' he offered, with a quirk of his mouth.

Angel shook her head, slightly transfixed.

Leo started putting lids back on the jars. 'My *ya ya* was the one who introduced me to it. She used to say that peanut butter and Jell-O was the only thing that made living in the States bearable. We'd sneak down to the kitchen at night, and she'd make sandwiches and tell me all about Greece.'

Angel felt a strange ache in her chest. 'Sounds like she was a lovely lady.'

'She was. And strong. She gave birth to my youngest uncle when they were a day away from Ellis Island on the boat from Greece. They both nearly died.'

Angel didn't know what to say. The ache grew bigger. She started hesitantly, 'I was close to my *ya ya* too. But she didn't live with us. Father and she didn't get on, so she only visited infrequently. But as we grew up Delphi, Damia and I would go and see her as much as we could. She taught us all about plants and herbs…cooking traditional Greek dishes—everything Irini, my stepmother, wasn't interested in.'

Leo frowned. 'Damia?'

'Damia was our sister. Delphi's twin.' Familiar pain lanced Angel.

'Was?'

She nodded. 'She died when she was fifteen, in a car accident on one of the roads down into Athens from the hills.' Angel grimaced. 'She was a bit wild, going through a rebellious phase. And I wasn't here to…' She stopped. Why was she blathering about all of this now? Leo wouldn't be remotely interested in her life story.

But nevertheless he asked, 'Why weren't you here?'

Angel sent him a quick look. He seemed genuinely interested, and there was something very easy about talking to him like this. She decided to trust it. 'Father sent me to a boarding school in the west of Ireland from the time I was twelve until I finished my schooling, so I could learn about the Irish part of my heritage and see my mother.' Angel conveniently left out the part about how her father had basically wanted her gone.

She looked down for a moment, picking at the label on her bottle of water. 'The worst bit was leaving the girls and *ya ya*. She died my first term there. It was too far for me to come home in time for the funeral.'

Angel looked up again, and pushed down the emotion threatening to rise when she thought of how she'd not been allowed home for Damia's funeral either—hence Delphi's subsequent clinginess and their intense connection.

Leo just sat there, arms relaxed, and then asked quietly, 'Why did your mother leave?'

Immediately Angel bristled. She never talked about her mother to anyone. Not even Delphi. She felt so many conflicting emotions, and yet Leo wasn't being pushy. Wasn't cajoling. They were making bizarre late-night conversation. So with a deep breath Angel told him. 'She left when I was two. She was a beautiful model from Dublin, and I think she found the reality of being married to a Greek man and living a domestic life in Athens too much for her.'

'She didn't take you with her?'

Angel fought against flinching. She shook her head. 'No. I think the reality of a small toddler was also too much for her to bear. She went home, and back to her glamorous jet-setting life. I saw her a couple of times while I was at school in the west of Ireland…but that was it.'

It sounded so pathetic now that Angel told it. Her own mother hadn't deemed her worth keeping. If it hadn't been for the birth of the twins, their instantaneous bond, Angel didn't know how she would have coped.

Leo, seemingly not content with that, asked, 'What was the school like?'

Angel had the strangest sensation of the earth shifting beneath her feet. She quirked a small smile. 'It's in Connemara, one of the most stunning parts of Ireland, but very remote. It's an old abbey, and it looms across a choppy lake like something out of a Gothic nightmare fantasy. When I went that first September it was raining and grey, and it was just…' Angel couldn't help a shudder running through her.

'A million miles from here?'

Angel nodded, surprised that Leo seemed to understand. 'Yes.'

Silence fell, and Angel felt awkward. She'd just told Leo more than she'd ever willingly shared with another person. When he got up to put away the jam and peanut butter she felt a question of her own bubbling up inside her. It was something her father had mentioned that fateful night she'd found him with the will. Afraid to ask, but emboldened after what she'd shared with him, as he came back she said, 'What happened to your mother?'

Leo stopped in his tracks and put his hands on his hips. The temperature in the air around them dropped a few degrees. But Angel was determined not to be intimidated; she was only asking him what he'd asked her.

'Why do you ask?' he said sharply.

Angel gulped. She couldn't lie. 'Is it true that she committed suicide?'

Leo went even more still. 'And where did you pick up that nugget of information?'

Angel had to say it, even though she knew that it would damn her to hell for ever in his eyes. 'The will.'

His body had gone taut, his eyes to obsidian black. No gold. He seemed distant, as if he wasn't even really aware that Angel was there any more. And then he laughed curtly. 'The will. Of course. How could I have forgotten? Yes, I do believe that my mother's suicide is mentioned there—while omitting the gory details, of course.'

Angel wanted to put out a hand and tell Leo to stop; he was looking at her but not *seeing her*.

'I saw her. Everyone thinks to this day that I didn't see her, but I did. She'd hung herself with a torn sheet from one of the banister railings at the top of the stairs.'

Horror and sorrow filled Angel's heart. But instinctively she kept quiet.

'My parents' marriage was an arranged one. The only problem was that my mother loved my father, but he loved building up the business and reclaiming our home in Greece more than her—or me. My mother couldn't cope with being sidelined, so she got more and more manipulative, more and more extreme in trying to get his attention. She started with emotional outbursts, but that just turned my father in on himself. The more tears, the less he'd react. Then she started self-harming and claiming that she'd been mugged. When that didn't work, she took the ultimate step.'

Angel had gone cold inside. What a hideous, hideous thing to have borne. She knew from reading between his words that Leo had seen a lot more than anyone had believed. Not just the suicide. She remembered his reaction to seeing that couple arguing in public, how disgusted he'd looked.

She stood up from the stool. 'Leo, I…' She shook her head. What could she say that wasn't going to sound inept, ridiculous?

Leo finally looked at her properly, as if coming to, and a shiver went down Angel's spine. She'd no doubt that he'd resent having told her this.

'"Leo, I…" *what*?' he asked, his voice harsh.

Angel stood tall. She knew that he hurt, but it wasn't her fault. 'There's nothing I can say that won't sound like a worthless platitude…except that I'm sorry you went through that. No child should have to see something so awful.'

Angel's lack of crocodile tears and her simple yet sincere-sounding statement did something to Leo. It broke something apart inside him. He felt a nameless emotion welling upwards, and knew the only way to push it down would be to find release. A release he'd been denying himself in the belief that he was regaining control, when control was the last thing he seemed to have in his possession.

He was done with denying himself what he wanted and what he needed. But damned if he was going to let Angel know how badly he needed her. She was going to admit her hunger for *him*.

CHAPTER EIGHT

LEO was looking at her so intensely that Angel quivered. And then he just said, in a hard voice, 'We're not here to chat and swap life stories, Angel, charming as this has been. I'm done with talking. What I'd like right now is for you to show me what you've learnt and seduce me.'

Angel just looked at him, hurt slicing through her at the way he was dismissing what they'd just shared and closing himself off again. She could deduce that he wanted to punish her in some way for having encouraged him to talk, but for her to seduce *him*? Show him what she'd learnt? She still had no idea what she was doing in bed—no conscious thought anyway. The minute Leo touched her she forgot time and space, everything but the building fire in her body, and now he wanted…

He said it again, as if he could hear her inner dialogue. 'I want you to seduce me. You're my mistress, that's what mistresses do.'

More hurt sliced through Angel. She was his mistress, and she'd forgotten for a tiny moment. The last days when he'd not come to her bed had left her feeling on edge. She hated to admit it now, especially when he was being so cold, but a part of her *thrilled* at the thought of being free to touch Leo any way she wished.

She told herself that when he pushed her back like this it should make it easier to cut out her emotions...but she caught his eyes and in a flash something glimmered in their depths. Something indefinable. She didn't believe it for a second, but Leo looked almost vulnerable. It made her make her mind up. Along with the way her pulse had jumped to think he was inviting her to take the initiative.

She put the bottle of water down on the island behind her and then turned back. She stepped up to Leo and stood in front of him for a long moment. He was so much taller than her, and so broad that she could see nothing behind him.

From here she looked up, to see Leo looking down from under hooded lids. He wasn't moving a muscle. But Angel could see the golden lights in his eyes again, and curiously that comforted her. She brought her hands to his chest and took a deep breath, spreading them out, moving them up over his pectorals, which she could feel under the material of his soft T-shirt.

She moved her hands under the collar of his T-shirt and on tiptoe, spread them out and around his neck. She tried to bring his head down to her level, so she could kiss him, but he wasn't budging. Angel bit back a retort. Determination fired her blood: he wasn't going to make this easy.

She manoeuvred him over to the stool, pushing him down onto it so he was more on her level, and she thought she caught a glint in his eye but couldn't be sure. His feet were on the ground, the height of the stool no hindrance to him.

Angel moved his legs apart with her body and stepped right up between them. She stopped for a minute and looked at the scar above his mouth. She put out a finger and traced it, before bending forward and pressing her lips there, above his top lip.

He still wasn't moving. Just looking at her as dispassion-ately as if she were speaking Chinese in a tedious lecture. For an excruciating moment uncertainty rose up within Angel and she had a flash of all the women he had been with. All those blonde scary-looking women who would no doubt know exactly what to do, who'd be bringing him to the edge of his control already, not leaving him looking as if he was about to fall asleep.

Angel stopped, and her hands fell to his thighs. She felt stupid. Kissing his scar as if she could kiss away whatever had put it there. She hung her head. 'Leo, I don't think I can do—'

'Keep going.' His voice was rough.

She looked up again. Leo's eyes weren't as clear as she'd thought. They burned gold. Angel's heart started to thump er-ratically. Her hands were still on his thighs and she started to move them experimentally up his legs, until they rested near his crotch. Her thumbs were close to where the fabric of his jeans was slightly bulging out.

Angel looked at Leo and moved one hand, so that it cupped him intimately. To her intense joy she could feel the evidence of his arousal and see the way his eyes flared. It gave her a heady confidence. She moved her hand up and down, stroking, caress-ing through the material. She could see Leo's fists clench out of the corner of her eye, and he made a slight move. Immediately she moved back out from between his legs and away.

She shook her head. 'No touching.'

Leo's jaw clenched, but he nodded. Angel moved back and placed her hand on him again. He was even bigger now, and she started to tingle all over, anticipation coiling through her like a live wire.

With one hand on him, and the other around his neck, she

leant into him fully and pressed her mouth to his. In keeping with his letting her do the work, Leo didn't respond to the kiss at first. Angel had to entice and cajole. At one stage she nearly screamed her frustration; despite his obvious arousal, she felt as if *she* was on the way to exploding, not him.

Her breasts were pressed against his chest, and the tips ached so badly that she rubbed against him. She wanted to press herself against his erection, to feel the slide of it against her body.

But his mouth...first she had to get him to kiss her. She flicked out her tongue and traced lightly along the seam of his lips, biting gently and then smoothing over the bites. When she tugged on his lower lip he opened them slightly, and Angel brought both hands to his head, holding him so that she could plunder and stroke her tongue against his exactly the way he did to her. His tongue duelled with hers, teeth nipping, biting her lower lip, making it sting deliciously.

She was in danger of being sucked down into the familiar pool of pleasure—until she noticed that Leo was still restraining himself, even though he was kissing her back. Although when she pulled back slightly she could see a slight sheen of sweat on his forehead. It helped her regain her composure. She tried to control her breathing, stood back and held out her hand. Leo took it and stood up, and Angel silently led him from the kitchen and up the stairs to his bedroom.

It was all at once incredibly intimidating and incredibly arousing to have Leo just say nothing, be passive. When his bedroom door closed behind them Angel turned to Leo and tugged the bottom of his T-shirt up. He lifted his arms and Angel pulled it off all the way.

Then she led him over to the bed and sat him down on the edge. She stepped back a few paces and bit her lip for a second, feeling nervous again. She reached up and pulled at the band that was holding her hair up haphazardly, and felt the mass fall down around her shoulders.

Then she put her hands to the bottom of her flimsy vest and pulled it up slowly, more out of intense nervousness than an attempt to be erotic. She could see a muscle pop in Leo's jaw, and his eyes had darkened. As he lounged back he put his hands behind him in an utterly nonchalant yet effortlessly sexy pose.

For a second Angel's eyes fell to his crotch and she saw the distinctive bulge. Her throat went dry, and she realised she'd stalled, baring her belly. With a deep breath she pulled her vest up and off completely, trying not to feel embarrassed. She let it drop to the ground. Her breasts felt tight and achy, the tips puckering under Leo's hot gaze.

Angel brought her hands to her pyjama bottoms and she undid the tiny bow holding them up. She pulled it loose and the bottoms sagged around her hips. With a little wiggle, she let them fall off.

Angel stepped out of them, and now she stood before Leo in nothing but her tiny panties. He filled her vision. He was like a marauding pirate, inspecting her for his delectation.

Angel walked over to him and pushed his legs apart, coming between them. She brought her hands to the fastening of his jeans and undid the button, slowly dragged down the zip. Her eyes followed the dark silky line of hair that disappeared under the top of his briefs. She saw him wince as her knuckles brushed his erection.

When his jeans were open she put her hands around his back to encourage him to tip his hips up so she could slide them down. Her sensitised breasts brushed enticingly against his belly, and Angel nearly moaned out loud before sinking to her knees to pull them off completely.

With shaking hands, she threw them behind her. She

reached up again and tugged at the sides of his briefs. Leo's face was tense, the lines stark. His eyes glittered, and Angel wasn't sure how she was still operating.

She pulled his boxers down, releasing him from confinement. And then, with her heart nearly leaping out of her throat, she looked at Leo and took him in her hand, slowly slipping it up and down over the thickness, feeling him swell and harden even more.

Acting on instinct, wanting to taste every bit of him, she leant forward. But Leo stopped her, with his voice sounding tight. 'No, Angel, you don't have to—'

'No talking.' Her voice was husky and wound around his every sense, pulling tight. Leo couldn't believe it. Angel was shielding those incredible blue eyes by lowering her lashes and taking him into her mouth, surrounding him with sweet, moist warmth. Caressing him with such innocent eroticism that he knew he wouldn't last—not when he'd nearly exploded just at the touch of her hand on him through his jeans downstairs.

Seeing her take off her clothes just now—first that skimpy vest which had shown all too readily the curve of her firm breasts with their hard tips, then the way she'd dropped her bottoms to the floor and stepped out of them. And then she had walked towards him and stripped *him*. He'd actually been afraid to touch her, afraid he'd scare her with the strength of the passion running through him, but he knew she'd pushed him to the edge now, and he wouldn't be able to contain it any longer.

Angel felt Leo's hips jerk, and then suddenly she was being gently pulled away and he was hauling her up.

'Enough,' he growled. 'I'm seduced.' With quick hands he tugged and pulled down her panties, and then, in a move so

fast he made her dizzy, she was flat on her back on the bed
and Leo was rolling a condom onto his penis.

He pushed her legs apart with a hand, stroking up her thigh
as he did so, delving into where the ache was building to screaming pitch. She nearly bucked off the bed she was so aroused. Leo
slid into her and then thrust harder and harder, taking her with
him, putting a hand under her buttocks, lifting her into him even
more. Angel wrapped a leg around his back and clung on. She
couldn't breathe, couldn't think, could only move in tandem with
Leo until everything was obliterated and shattered around them.

The next morning when Angel woke she was on her front,
with one leg lifted up and her arms sprawled out wide. She
felt utterly replete at a very deep level, and heavy—as if she
could sink all the way to Middle Earth.

She heard a muted sound, and opened one eye to see Leo
standing at the mirror of his wardrobe, knotting his tie. It was
the same image as that first morning, and she was awake instantly, pulling a sheet over her nakedness, coming up on one
arm, wary. She hadn't woken in his bed before.

Leo looked at her, and Angel steeled herself. 'You're still
here. And I'm in your bed.'

Leo's mouth quirked and his attention went back to his tie.
'You're very good at stating the obvious.'

Angel bit her lip when she remembered last night. The con-
flagration that had blown up around them. What had led up
to it.

'Do you ever wake up with a woman you've slept with?'
she heard herself asking, as if someone had taken control
of her mouth.

Leo's hands stilled. Angel could see that the glimmer of
warmth in his eyes was rapidly cooling.

Leo tried not to look at Angel, but he didn't have to. Her image was burned onto his retina. She lay there, just feet away, in such tousled and innocently sexy splendour that she hit him right between the eyes. But her question... The very impertinence of it went through him like a gunshot. His immediate reaction had been a vociferous *no*! Because waking up with a woman in his arms was anathema to him on so many levels.

It implied a level of trust he just did not have. For him, trust meant emotion, and emotion meant instability, *fear, and, quite literally, death*. His primary female role model, his mother, had been dangerously unstable. He'd only told Angel the half of it last night—and why the hell had he said anything?

Irritation snaked through him now. He'd come dangerously close to waking up wrapped around Angel like a vine as it was. With her body curled trustingly into his. And that was bad enough.

Angel knew Leo wouldn't answer her. She couldn't believe she'd asked the question. She sat up and wrapped the sheet around her as she got up to look for her discarded clothes, blushing when she bent down to pick up her knickers from where Leo had flung them in his haste last night.

She was almost at her own door when she heard his cool, 'We're going out tonight. I'll be home by eight.'

Angel stopped and just nodded her head, keeping her back to him. She couldn't bear to see that same image again, those cool eyes in the mirror. She slipped into her room and shut the door behind her.

Back to square one. Back in her place. Delphi's wedding was only a week away now. Perhaps Leo saw that as the end of Angel's penance and he'd turn around the morning after and let her go. He'd replace all the beautiful clothes in the walk-in wardrobe with a different size for a new and improved mistress. One who didn't come with messy ties and revenge.

Angel resolutely went straight into her shower and stood under steaming hot jets of water. At least she had something to look forward to apart from Delphi's wedding: her jewellery commission for Ari and Lucy Levakis. Just thinking of that and anticipating what she'd start with that day helped to clear her mind of far too disturbing thoughts, like how disarming it had been to see a totally different side to Leo last night.

The day of Delphi's wedding dawned, and Angel was getting ready at the villa. She'd agreed with Delphi that it would be best to avoid her father at all costs. At least they were fairly certain he'd not make a scene at the church, would be too conscious of his peers watching his every move. Leo had gone to the office and was going to go to the church separately, as Angel would be preoccupied with Delphi.

Butterflies erupted in Angel's chest. This was it. The culmination of what she'd agreed with Leo that night just over a month ago. To become his mistress in exchange for arranging Delphi's wedding. Why was she feeling butterflies of trepidation? Because this could be it? Here alone in her room she had to admit that she wasn't prepared for this to be it, no matter how masochistic she knew that made her. It would be Leo's ultimate revenge. Reel Angel in, show her a taste of paradise and then discard her like trash.

And Angel knew well that the paradise she spoke of had nothing to do with the 'luxuries' Leo no doubt expected she enjoyed. It was a paradise of another kind: the paradise of becoming a woman, of discovering her sensuality. The paradise of such exquisite lovemaking that Angel knew no other man would ever have the same effect on her.

She looked at herself in the mirror. Big blue eyes stared back at her, shining, glittering. Her cheeks were flushed.

Since that night in the kitchen nearly a week ago Angel had been battling her feelings. Trying to tell herself that what she felt was only akin to a victim falling for their kidnapper. She frowned. There was a name for that condition…*yes, love*, crowed a little mocking voice.

Angel paled visibly in the mirror. How could she possibly have fallen in love with Leo Parnassus, when he'd shown her nothing but cold calculation? Because, she reasoned, he'd been perfectly justified in believing that she'd come to steal from him. *She* wouldn't have believed her either. Not with all the history that lay between their families. It was perfectly conceivable that Angel had been out to try and save her family by any means possible. And yet Leo had kept so admirably to his side of the equation that any minute now a car was coming to pick her up to bring her to the church where her pregnant sister would get married to her childhood sweetheart and all would be well for them.

And that was all that mattered, right? Even without all the obstacles between Angel and Leo, there could be no future. The man wasn't even used to sharing a whole night with a woman in his bed, never mind his life…

A sound came from Angel's bedroom door and she turned, expecting to see Calista to tell her the car had arrived. But it was Leo, stunning in a steel-grey suit, white shirt and tie.

Angel's heart tripped; her hands went clammy. 'What are you doing here?'

Leo mocked, 'So pleased to see me? I must surprise you more often.'

Angel blushed fiercely. She knew what had just been going

through her mind, and here he was, *unsettling her*, or… Her heart stopped. Perhaps he was here to tell her—

'I thought I'd come for you myself, that's all. You'd better get a move on.'

Angel broke out of the stasis she was in and quickly checked her reflection again, seriously flustered now. Her bridesmaid's dress was a dark dusky pink, strapless and to the knee. Her hair was up in a chignon and she wore a flower in her hair the same colour as the dress.

Grabbing her wrap, she tottered out unsteadily in high heels, hoping that Leo hadn't seen anything of the naked emotions on her face before she'd hidden them.

Angel thankfully managed to have as little to do with her father as possible during the wedding, but she felt his malevolent stare on her periodically. When she watched Stavros and Delphi walk around the altar three times, with the stefana crowns on their heads, she had to fight back tears, feeling inordinately weepy. She studiously avoided Leo's eye throughout the ceremony, terrified again that he'd see her emotions bubbling so close to the surface. For she who had a somewhat jaded view of marriage to be so moved had scared her slightly.

Before they left for the reception Stavros took her aside and told her how thankful he and Delphi were to her, for helping their wedding to happen, and especially before the pregnancy became common knowledge. Those words alone, and seeing the unmitigated joy on Delphi's face, made everything worthwhile.

Leo was waiting for her at the entrance of the church, to take her to the reception, and to her relief her father didn't seem to be inclined to make a scene—no doubt very well aware that Leo was being courted and feted by everyone almost as if *he* was the one getting married.

Dimitri Stephanides, Stavros's father, had put on a lavish display in a top Athens hotel—no doubt also to impress Leo. Everyone was there. Angel became slowly aware that things had changed subtly in the time that she'd been with Leo. There were fewer of the snide whispers and furtive looks, and the headlines in the newspapers had all but disappeared. She realised that people had grown used to seeing them together…

'Dance?'

Angel looked up from her preoccupation to see Leo standing there, holding out a hand. She stood up and let him lead her to the dance floor, where Delphi and Stavros had just had their first dance to much raucous applause.

A slow, swoony song came on and Leo pulled Angel close. Feeling raw, she tried to resist the pull to just lean against him, but his hand on her bare back, above the top of her dress, urged her close. She gave in and moved and swayed with Leo, content to let her head fall into his shoulder. It felt like sheer indulgence.

'Your sister is not what I expected.'

Angel tensed, but Leo's hand on her back, moving in slow, sensual circles, forced her to relax again. She lifted her head and looked up. Leo's face was far too close for comfort.

'What do you mean?' she asked, half forgetting what he'd said.

He shrugged minutely, one broad shoulder moving under his shirt. He'd taken off his jacket and tie, so his shirt was open to reveal the strong, bronzed column of his throat.

'She seems…' Leo grimaced. 'Sweet. If I didn't know better, I'd say that she and Stavros are genuinely in love.'

Angel really tensed then, and tried to pull away, but Leo was like a steel wall around her, not letting her go anywhere.

She whispered up at him fiercely, 'They *are* in love, and have been for ever. They were childhood sweethearts.'

'Cute,' Leo said, clearly not impressed.

Angel hesitated, and then said in a rush, 'The reason they needed to get married so quickly is because Delphi is nearly four months pregnant. Stavros's family were never going to sanction a marriage with a Kassianides. Stavros wanted to elope with Delphi, but she wouldn't let him do that.'

Leo quirked a brow. Angel bit her lip. She'd gone too far now to turn back.

'His family would have disinherited him and cut him off.'

Angel saw the cynical gleam come into Leo's eye and colour bloomed in her cheeks as she asserted passionately, 'It's not like that. Delphi couldn't care less about Stavros's inheritance, but he wants to get into politics and she didn't want to be responsible for causing a rift in his family.'

'And yet now, no matter what you say, she—and you by proxy—will be fine, secure in the wealth of her new husband.'

Angel finally managed to pull away from Leo with a violent tug, disappointed at how hurt she was at this evidence of his bitter cynicism. 'Believe what you want, Leo. Someone like you will never know that kind of pure love.'

And before he could grab her back she'd spun on her spindly heels and was threading through the couples on the dance floor and out to the lobby. Leo raked a hand through his hair, aware of eyes on him. Aware of the way females were starting to circle, sensing an opening. Beyond irritated, and not even sure why, he pushed through the crowd and went to the bar—but not before he glanced to his right and saw the happy couple.

They were sitting apart from everyone else, in a corner, smiling. Stavros had his hand on Delphi's belly and her hand was over his, and they shared a look of such private intensity that Leo's step almost faltered. Right now they looked nothing

like what he'd just described; he felt guilty—as if he'd tar-
nished something.

Delphi was like Angel only in height and build; the younger
sister had obviously inherited her father's stronger features and
dark eyes, while Angel must have inherited her Irish mother's
more delicate features and colouring.

Leo thought then of what it must have been like to lose
their sister, Delphi's twin... At that moment he saw Ari and
Lucy Levakis approach and smile a greeting, and for once he
was glad of the distraction. Seeing Angel's family was
throwing up far too many contradictions.

When Angel felt composed enough she came back into the
ballroom, and was surprised to see Leo dancing a traditional
Greek dance with the rest of the men. She was still burningly
angry with him, but she melted inside when she saw the wide
grin on his face. He looked so powerfully sensual doing the
dance movements that she couldn't help smile. Just then her
arm was grabbed in a punishing grip, and she let out a gasp
of pain. *Her father.*

'We need to have a little chat. I've missed you, daughter,
and you've been very busy since I saw you last.'

Alcohol fumes wafted over Angel, making her feel sick.
She tried to wrench her arm away but her father held on. 'No,
we don't. There was no way I was going to let you get away
with stealing that man's will.'

Her father sneered. 'So you ran straight to lover-boy and
handed it back. Don't think you're going to get away with this,
Angel, I'm not finished with—'

Just then Delphi came up and pulled her away. Angel sent
her sister a relieved glance as they left their father swaying
drunkenly, looking after them murderously. Now that Delphi

would be living with Stavros Angel knew she'd never have
to see her father again if she didn't want to. The relief was
immense, and she gave Delphi a quick, impetuous kiss.

It was the turn of the women now, and the men sat and
watched as they all lined up and danced. Angel had taken off
her shoes, and was laughing as she bumped into Delphi. She
caught Leo's eyes as he watched from the sidelines. She
found she couldn't look away, the intensity on his face
holding her captive as she made the steps that she knew by
heart. That every Greek person knew by heart.

It felt like the most primitive of mating rituals. When the
music died away and the DJ started again, Delphi whispered to Angel, saying cheekily, 'If those looks are
anything to go by, Leo won't be letting you wait around to
say goodbye…'

Angel knew her sister was heading off on honeymoon the
next day, so she wouldn't see her for at least a few weeks. She
felt very bereft after looking out for her for so long. She also
felt uncharacteristically sad for herself; her mother had abandoned her at such an early age, her father had always resented
her, and any day now Leo would be turning around and telling
her he'd had enough. She felt a little like a piece of flotsam and
jetsam, about to be rushed downstream by an oncoming
current.

But Leo was standing in front of her. She saw he was
holding his jacket. 'Ready to go?'

Angel nodded, feeling incredibly weary all of a sudden.
She did not want another run-in with her father, so she got
her shoes and let Leo take her hand to lead her out.

Two days after the wedding Leo walked into the villa and,
after putting his briefcase in the study, strode across the hall,

heading for the room Angel used as a workshop. Anticipation was fizzing in his blood. He'd come home early the day before and stood watching her for a long time before she'd noticed his presence.

Once again he'd found himself reacting helplessly to her, his eyes devouring her slim figure in a white vest and battered loose dungarees folded at the waist. Intent on her task, with her hair in a high knot and big protective glasses on, she shouldn't have been so alluring, but she had been. The fact that his control around her was as woeful as ever had made him feel vulnerable.

All sorts of contradictory feelings were running through Leo now. He'd seen her talking to her father at the wedding; well, to be more accurate, he'd seen her father talking to her, and it had looked extremely intense. It had made him suspect that perhaps they'd known that that would be their only chance to meet, hence the fervour. And then he'd seen her conspiratorial looks and smiles with her sister. No matter that he'd revised his opinion of his sister's motives for getting married, suddenly he doubted himself again.

The facts were still stark: he'd caught her in the act of theft. A detail which seemed to be getting conveniently forgotten far too often. Something hardened inside Leo.

Just then Calista came out of another room nearby. She stopped him in his tracks and asked with a worried look on her face, 'Have you seen Angel?'

He shook his head, feeling irrationally self-conscious. 'No, not yet.'

Calista pointed back to the main part of the house. 'She's in the kitchen.'

Calista bustled off and Leo just stared after her. What was going on? And what was Angel doing in the kitchen?

Leo strode towards the kitchen, irritation spiking. He found that all the doubts that had begun to assail him had got stronger and stronger. The feeling that perhaps he'd been even more of a monumental fool than he'd thought. Angel and Delphi had got the wedding they'd wanted; he'd taken Angel into his bed. Were she and her father plotting right now to do something—? He stopped at the kitchen door when he saw Angel at the counter by the sink.

Her back was to him, but there was a set to her shoulders that seemed awfully fragile. She was dressed in a T-shirt and tracksuit bottoms. He glanced at his watch. They were due to go out to a film premiere in less than an hour, but Angel was nowhere near ready. Though he had to concede she got ready more quickly than any woman he'd ever known; she never played silly games and kept him waiting for the grand entrance.

He walked in and saw her shoulders tense. Her hair was down and she didn't turn around. In light of his recent thoughts he felt anger start to bubble down low. He wasn't used to being so sceptical of his decisions. He remembered that night in the kitchen, telling her all about his mother.

It made his voice harsh now as he came round and saw her profile, saw that she was making some kind of meatballs. That domesticity rankled. 'We're going out this evening.'

Angel didn't turn to look at him; she just said in a quiet voice, 'If you don't mind I'd like to stay in tonight. I'm tired. But you go out.'

Something about her was so intensely vulnerable that it made the hardness swell in Leo's chest. If she thought she was going to start playing games with him now… 'Angel, we have an agreement. Just because your sister got the wedding she wanted it does not mean your job as my mistress is finished.'

Angel flinched minutely, as if stung. She sent Leo a quick glance without really looking at him. 'Look, it's just for this evening. I really am tired.'

Something about the tenseness of her stance struck him then, and the tightness in her voice. *Something was wrong.* Instinctively Leo put out a hand and wrapped it around Angel's arm. She tensed, so rigid that he frowned. 'Angel... what—?'

He had to exert pressure to get her to turn around and face him. He put two hands on her arms now, exasperation lacing his voice. 'Angel, what's got into you?'

She was looking down, hair covering her face. Leo put a finger under her chin and tipped her face up. Something caught his eye, and for a second he couldn't believe what he was seeing. Then something primal exploded out of him. 'What the *hell* is that?'

CHAPTER NINE

ANGEL felt Leo put a hand to her face, tipping it to him slightly, and she closed her eyes. She hadn't wanted him to see her like this; she'd wanted him to just say, 'Okay, fine, I'll go without you.' But he hadn't. She knew what he was looking at: her swollen jaw covered with a livid bruise.

Angel tried to pull free, but Leo wasn't budging. He pushed her hair back behind her ear to have a better look. His voice was grim. 'Have you put ice on this?'

Angel looked into his eyes for the first time. 'It'll hurt.'

Leo shook his head. 'Only for the first few seconds.' And then very gently he probed and felt her jaw. Angel winced and sucked in a breath. Leo swore softly. 'It's not broken, but maybe we should get it checked out at the hospital.'

Angel shook her head. 'No, no hospital. It's just sore.'

Leo looked at her until she couldn't bear it and tore her eyes away. Emotion was welling up from deep down and she was afraid she couldn't contain it. He led her over to a stool and made her sit down, lifting her onto it. Then he went to the fridge and got some ice, wrapping it in a towel. He brought it back and ever so gently laid it against her jaw, soothing Angel when she moved to pull away instinctively. The pain made spots dance before her eyes for a second, and then the coolness was beautifully numbing.

To her abject horror she could feel hot tears welling, and before she could stop them they were overflowing and falling down her cheeks. She gave a dry sob. 'I'm sorry, I just—'

Shock was starting to set in too; she'd been holding it back since it had happened. But now she could feel her teeth start to chatter, her limbs shaking uncontrollably. Leo said something rapid in Greek over her head. Angel dimly guessed it had to be to Calista. Calista who had wanted to ring Leo earlier, but Angel hadn't let her.

In moments Calista was back, and tutting, and handing a glass of what looked like brandy to Leo. Leo dismissed the other woman and made Angel take a sip of the amber liquid. It had an immediate effect. Leo gently wiped at the tears caught on her cheeks.

After a few minutes of letting the drink have its effect, Leo took the ice from Angel and gently led her off the stool and out of the kitchen. He said something else to Calista, who was hovering nearby—something about ringing his PA to tell her he was unavailable for the evening.

He was leading Angel into the informal living room when she started to protest. 'No, you should go out. You have that premiere…'

Leo sat Angel down and brought the ice back up to her face. He looked at her steadily. 'Do you really think I'm going to sit through two hours of American inanity while you're here like this?'

Leo took the ice down, placing it on a nearby tray, and inspected her jaw again. And then his eyes speared hers: *no escape.*

'So, are you going to tell me who punched you in the jaw?'

Angel bit her lip. She couldn't lie. Calista knew anyway, and she'd tell Leo in a second. As if reading her mind, Leo said easily, 'Don't even think of trying to defend whoever did this, Angel.'

Angel could feel the colour draining from her face, and Leo cursed softly again, making her sip more brandy.

Eventually, after a long silence, he just raised a brow. He wasn't budging until she told him. 'I…my father came to visit me today.'

She looked down, shamed by her own father. And shamed by how hurt she was after all these years that his lack of love still had the power to hurt. Leo gently tipped her face up to him again.

'Your father did this?'

Angel nodded. 'He had been drinking. He came to tell me how I'd disrespected our family name. Normally I can avoid him, but…he just caught me unawares. I wasn't fast enough. I never expected him to come here.'

Leo's voice was blistering. 'He's done this *before*?'

Angel nodded, more shame coursing through her. She felt so weak. 'Never this bad, though. When I was smaller he'd lash out at me—he's always resented me for reminding him of the humiliation of my mother deserting him…us. I learnt to avoid him. Just today…' Angel wasn't about to reveal that she'd been preoccupied with defending Leo when her father had lashed out with unexpected accuracy.

A lot of pieces started to fall into place in Leo's head. What he'd seen at the wedding; the fact that Angel had been sent to a remote boarding school. 'That's why you haven't been home once since you came here.'

Angel nodded slowly.

Through a granite-like weight in his chest, Leo asked, 'He

really didn't send you here to the villa, did he? The night of the party or the night I found you in the study?'

Angel shook her head. Her heart had leapt into her mouth and was beating so hard she felt a little faint.

'Why were you here that night, then, Angel?'

'The night of the party was exactly as I told you. I had no idea where we were going and then it was too late. I tried to stay in the kitchen, but my boss sent me upstairs...' She blushed. 'I truly didn't know who you were at the pool, or on the terrace. I'd avoided reading anything about your family coming home. I was too ashamed.'

She stopped. She couldn't believe that Leo was listening to her. She willed him to believe what she said. 'And that next night...I wasn't stealing the will. I was trying to return it.'

Leo frowned. 'Return it?'

'I'd come home from work the previous evening and found my father crowing over it...that's how I knew about your mother. He'd sent some of his goons to steal it. To be honest, I'm not sure how he did it, or even if it had been taken from the villa. I just assumed... And when I could, I took it from him and brought it back, thinking I could just leave it in a drawer, or something.'

She looked away for a second, and then back. 'I felt so bad about your family, what you'd been through, and I didn't want him to be responsible for causing more trouble. But then you came in...'

'And the rest is history,' Leo said without humour. Angel had never seen him look so grim.

He shook his head, his eyes dark with something indefinable. Something that made Angel's heart trip unsteadily. 'Angel, I—'

She spoke quickly. 'Leo, I know exactly how it looked. *I*

wouldn't have believed me. That's why I didn't even try and defend myself. I knew there was no point. The whole situation was completely damning.'

'No.' A muscle popped in Leo's jaw. 'Your father had to knock you about before I'd see the truth.'

Angel shook her head. 'Leo, don't, please. I brought this on myself.'

Leo was fierce. 'Not like this, Angel, never like this. If I'd thought for a second that your father was capable of this…' Waves of anger vibrated off Leo.

He touched Angel's cheek and said huskily, 'You must be exhausted.'

Angel nodded. 'I am a little.' But she thought of going to sleep, and all the images waiting to crowd her mind: her father's mottled face, the way his hand had come out of nowhere and stunned her so badly that she'd blacked out for a minute, only to come to and see him rifling through the drawers of the study. Thankfully Calista had had the sense to be nearby, and had called the security guard up from the gate. He'd escorted Angel's father from the villa, but not until Angel had insisted that his pockets be searched. Luckily he hadn't found anything worth stealing.

'But I don't want to go to bed…' Her voice was more fierce than she'd intended, and she saw Leo wince.

'Angel, you must know that I wouldn't expect—'

She covered her hand with his, inordinately touched. 'No, I don't mean that. I just mean I don't really want to go to sleep—not just yet anyway. I don't want to think about… what happened.'

Leo nodded. Within minutes Angel was sitting on a comfortable couch in the TV den, with a blanket over her, while Leo went to get some food from Calista. Then he was back and fussing over Angel like a mother hen, making her take some soup, because it would hurt too much for her to have to chew anything.

It felt as if the most delicate chain of silver stretched between them now, connecting them, and Angel clung onto it greedily.

Leo switched on the TV without asking any more questions, and seemed content to watch inane TV, sensing Angel's need to get lost in something. She let the ribald movie wash over her like a balm, and relished Leo's protective arm around her like a guilty secret.

Angel's body had turned into a dead weight against Leo. He looked down at the glossy head that lay against his chest. The hand so trustingly curled against him. So many questions bubbled up inside him, so much recrimination, and underneath it all a fierce, primal anger. He could still see the livid swelling, and wanted to go and find Tito Kassianides and beat him to a pulp. Leo had to consciously calm himself. His heart-rate was already zooming skywards just when he thought of that man.

But, as if in league with his earlier thoughts, an insidious voice mocked him. What if this was all a set-up? What if this was part of a plan—a ruse to arouse his sympathy, his trust in Angel? Leo felt sick at the thought. It couldn't be. *It couldn't be.* She'd been a virgin, for heaven's sake. His body still thrilled with a deep-seated male satisfaction at knowing that he'd been her only lover.

Too much had fallen into place when Angel had explained everything earlier. Leo was disgusted with himself. Was he so jaded, so cynical after witnessing what he had as a child, that he'd believed someone would go to the lengths that Angel had in order to manipulate him?

Grimly, he knew he didn't have to answer that question. Leo flicked off the TV and without disturbing Angel stood from the couch, lifting her into his arms. He took her up to his bed and, after settling her, took off his clothes and got in beside her, pulling her close.

Angel woke when the dawn was a faint light coming into the room from outside. She registered that she was in Leo's bed, in her panties and T-shirt. She went hot. He must have taken off her tracksuit bottoms when she'd fallen asleep on him downstairs. She was on her side, and Leo was tucked around her, his arm a heavy weight over her waist, his hand close to cupping her breast. He was naked. Despite everything her blood stirred and her body started to hum.

She had a premonition of Leo waking to find that she was still in his bed, and went to move. She heard a deep growl. 'Stay where you are.'

Angel stopped moving, but couldn't pretend she could sleep again—not when she felt Leo's body hardening and firming against hers, making her want to push her bottom against him in clear provocation. Her breathing had grown short and shallow. She lifted her head minutely, to ease a slight ache, and sucked in a breath when pain shot through her jaw, reminding her all too clearly of yesterday's events.

Instantly Leo moved and hovered over Angel, his jaw dark with stubble. With a gentle hand he turned her face so he could see. His eyes and his low curse told her how bad it looked. It felt as if it had turned into the size of a football.

She winced. 'Is it very bad?'

Leo quirked a wry smile. 'It's a glorious shade of blueish purple, and about as big as my fist.' Then he got serious. 'We're going to the hospital today, Angel, I don't care what you say.'

Angel knew better than to argue. She lay there and looked up at Leo, and felt her chest and heart swell. With the impenetrable wall of mistrust between them gone, she realized that she loved him. She really loved him. Without thinking, she reached up and traced the scar above his lip with a finger. 'How did you get that?'

Leo caught her finger and kissed it. 'I'd like to be able to say that I got it while defending a younger kid from being bullied.'

'You didn't?'

He shook his head mock-mournfully. 'No, I got it when I fell off my training bike onto the sidewalk when I was three.'

Angel's heart lurched, and she fell a little bit more in love. She would have smiled if it hadn't hurt, but Leo was tucking himself around her again and saying, 'Go back to sleep, Angel, you need it.'

Angel felt the waves of tiredness coming over her again and said sleepily, 'Okay, but wake me up and I'll go back to my own bed in a bit…'

Angel didn't see the spasm of pain cross Leo's face. Leo lay awake, staring into the dim morning light for a long time.

Two weeks later Angel looked at the finished set of jewellery for Ari and Lucy. She looked at it but didn't really see it. Experimentally she moved her jaw and touched it gingerly. The swelling had gone down completely, and all that remained of the bruise was a faint yellowish tinge that could be covered by make-up.

Leo had taken Angel to a private clinic the day after it had happened and they'd ruled out a fracture; it was just a very severe bruise. Since that night Leo had been amazingly attentive, eschewing all public engagements to stay at home with

Angel despite her protestations. From going out practically every night, now they ate in, and Leo had surprised her one night by dismissing Calista and serving up a delicious home-cooked dinner. He was doing absolutely nothing to help her stop falling deeper and deeper in love with him, and she knew that he would not welcome it.

Clearly Leo was feeling guilty at having misjudged her, despite her assurances that she had been as much to blame by coming here in the first place. He'd insisted that Angel sleep with him every night, but he'd been careful not to touch her. Last night Angel had turned to him in the bed, frustration clawing through her body. She knew Leo was aroused, she felt it every night, but he was making the same protestations. Treating her as if she was made out of china and might break.

Angel had put her hand around him intimately and said, 'I'm better, Leo, *please*…' She cringed now to think of it, of how ardently she'd responded when he'd finally groaned deep in his throat and drawn her on top of him, lifting her vest away, helping her out of her pants. She'd felt as if she'd been starved of water in the desert for a month. But she'd been the one to initiate it, not Leo.

Angel shook her head, and then started violently when she heard a noise come from the door. Leo stood there, nonchalantly leaning against the frame. Her heart turned over as it always did. She smiled shyly. 'Hi.'

Leo smiled too and, slightly mesmerised, Angel thought again that when he smiled he looked a million miles away from the tough tycoon. From the man who had coldly black-mailed her.

He strolled in and looked at Angel's handiwork; she took in his expression nervously, valuing his opinion. He picked up the bracelet and then the earrings, turning them this way and that. Finally he put them down and said, 'You're really good—you do know that?'

Angel half shrugged, embarrassed. 'It's what I love to do, so if I can make a living out of it then I'll be happy.'

Leo put out a hand and trailed a finger gently down her injured jaw. 'It's almost healed.'

Angel nodded. 'I can put some make-up on it for tomorrow night, when we go to Lucy and Ari's for dinner.'

He nodded and then backed away, but for a second Angel could have sworn he'd wanted to say something. She forgot about it, though, when they settled down to eat dinner, after which Leo went into his study to work for a while, and Angel went to her workshop to do some last-minute checks on the jewellery for Lucy. Tomorrow she'd go into town and buy some boxes to package them before they went for dinner.

The following day Leo stood at the window of his office in Athens, looking out at the view, but not registering it. He was consumed with one thing, one person: *Angel*. She was turning him upside down and inside out. For someone who broke out in a rash at the thought of waking up in a bed with a woman, now he couldn't relax properly unless he knew Angel was going to be the first thing he saw every morning.

The guilt of how his behaviour had put her in danger still made him feel nauseous, and yet she'd begged him not to do anything to her father, reminding him that her father would capitalise on the slightest hint of enmity to fuel their feud. The best form of revenge was ignoring Tito, even though it killed Leo to do so.

In the days after she'd been hit it had been easy to restrain himself from touching her sexually. His concern had overridden his desire, and he had also felt something else more disturbing: the knowledge that his making love to Angel had become imbued with something much more ambiguous than revenge. Something that came with silken ties binding around him tightly. Silken ties that reminded him of a time when he'd vowed never to allow someone to get close enough to arouse this awful welling of emotion and feeling.

He shook his head. He hated being introspective, so when his thoughts were cut abruptly short by a soft knock he welcomed it, saying, 'Come in.'

His PA opened the door. 'Ari Levakis is here to see you.'

'Thanks, Thalia, send him in.'

He smiled when he saw Ari walk in, and greeted him heartily. They sat down to discuss the business at hand, neither one needing to stand on ceremony, both trusting each other as only men of a similar standing could.

After an hour of intense discussion Ari sat back with a coffee cup in hand and looked at Leo. Unaccountably Leo felt the hair tighten on the back of his neck.

'I spoke to Angel yesterday. She says she'll have the jewellery ready for this evening when you come to dinner. I hope she hasn't been under too much pressure to get it done.' Ari frowned. 'We haven't seen either of you out lately, so I hope you haven't been slave-driving her.'

Leo smiled tightly and fought the image of coming home every evening that week and finding Angel immersed in her task, covered in the fine dust of the precious metals and stones she'd been working with, dressed in the ubiquitous vest tops and battered dungarees, which always had an instantaneous effect on his arousal levels.

Leo realised he still hadn't answered Ari; he'd got so caught up in his own memory. He flushed, and probably sounded harsher than he'd intended. 'Not at all… We've both been happy to take a break from the social scene. She has been working hard at it, but she's enjoyed doing it.'

That was true. She'd been oblivious to him several evenings, until he'd come in and taken the headphones of her iPod out of her ears, and then she'd turned to him and smiled…

'When I first heard you were seeing her I had my doubts. After all…she is who she is, and she'd turned up like that at your father's house.'

Leo looked at Ari, and something must have shown on his face because Ari spread his hands in a gesture and said, 'What? You can't blame me, Leo. Everyone was thinking the same thing. Athens is full of beautiful women and you went for the most unlikely one—some would have said the most unsuitable one. No one would have blamed you if you'd ignored that whole family in the street.'

Ari only knew the half of it. What would he say if Leo told him what else had happened? Would Ari have jumped to the same conclusion, damning Angel before she'd had a chance to defend herself? Would he have used his knowledge to blackmail her into becoming his mistress? Leo got up, suddenly feeling agitated. Would Angel have ever become his mistress of her own volition?

Leo struggled to articulate some platitude, feeling like a fraud, and not liking his defensiveness. 'Our shared history is our business…there is a certain…synchronicity to how we came together.'

When he said those words Leo had a disturbingly vivid memory of how Angel had felt that first time he'd taken her, how she'd arched beneath him and entreated him to keep going, and how it had taken all of his skill and restraint not to hurt her. Sweat broke out on his brow. He was feeling seriously cornered.

Angel knocked on the outer door of Leo's office. His PA Thalia looked up and smiled warmly. The two had met when Thalia had come to the villa one night to work late with Leo.

'Hi, Angel. He's with Ari Levakis, but they should be done soon. I'm going out for lunch now.' The other woman started to get up from behind her desk, 'He knows I'm going out, but just in case he's forgotten could you remind him I'll be back at two?'

Angel smiled. 'No problem. I just brought him some lunch.'

She watched Thalia leave and then put the small brown paper bag on the desk and walked around the anteroom. It and the whole building screamed wealth and prestige. She'd been on her way home from picking up boxes for the jewellery, and while she was out had decided to make a visit. Angel hadn't been to Leo's office before, and butterflies were beating a symphony in her chest.

She looked at the paper bag and grimaced. She'd bought him a peanut butter and jelly sandwich. Was this the most stupidly transparent thing she'd ever done?

She jumped when the doorknob rattled and the door opened slightly. Leo's meeting must be over. She held her breath, but no one came out. With the door ajar, she could hear the deep rumble of Ari's voice.

'Lucy and I really like her.'

Angel's heart stopped cold, and her breath with it, as she listened. Leo's voice came, deep and strong.

'I know you do.' He said nothing else for a moment, and Angel could imagine him raking a hand through his hair.

Even without seeing him she could sense that he was irritated, and wondered why.

'Look, Angel and I...it's just a temporary thing. I have no desire to settle down with the first woman who crosses my path in Athens.'

Ari's voice was dry, and further from the door. He must have moved back into the room. 'I appreciate that she mightn't be the most...*appropriate*...wife material.'

Angel winced, and felt as if a knife were skewering her insides. Leo laughed then, and the knife sank a little deeper.

'Angel becoming a permanent fixture in my life might be taking my father's tolerance levels a little too far, and Athens is still reeling with our association as it is.'

Ari laughed briefly. 'You certainly know how to stir it up, Parnassus...but does Angel know this?'

The temperature in Leo's voice went down a few hundred degrees. 'Angel knows exactly what to expect from this relationship.'

The tone of Ari's voice told Leo that he wasn't intimidated. 'Like I said, Lucy and I really like her. I just hope she *does* know what to expect, we'd hate to see her get hurt...'

A dangerous quality came into Leo's softly spoken words. 'Is that a warning, Levakis?'

Ari was undeterred. 'Take it how you want, Leo... I just don't think Angel is like the other hardened socialites of our circles. Once I might have assumed it, but after getting to know her...'

Leo's voice was hard. 'You don't have to worry. Angel and I know exactly where we stand.'

Ari laughed briefly. 'Lucy sent me here with a flea in my ear...so we'll see you and Angel later. I'm looking forward to seeing the finished pieces.'

Angel didn't wait to hear the rest. On legs that were numb, and feeling as if every ounce of blood had drained from her body, she stumbled back out of the anteroom and all but ran to the lift.

It was only when she was descending that she remembered leaving the brown bag behind. Dread struck her to think that Leo might find it, but she had no intention of going back. She could only stumble out of the lift, into the street, and get away from Leo's office as quickly as she could.

A little later, as Angel polished and finished off the pieces she'd made for Lucy, she bitterly castigated herself. What had she expected, truly…? That Leo had somehow miraculously come to have feelings for her? She was his mistress; he'd taken her because he desired her, because he'd had the power to give Delphi her wedding and because he'd believed Angel guilty of a crime. Since Leo had learnt what had really happened the lines might have got a little blurred for Angel, but after hearing that conversation evidently Leo hadn't felt the same way.

She was the naive fool who had allowed herself to believe that the tenderness he'd displayed in recent weeks had meant something.

Angel's hand went to her belly and she bit her lip. The other night when Angel had all but begged Leo to make love to her they hadn't used contraception. Angel had assured Leo that she was at a safe place in her cycle, but now she wasn't so sure.

The thought that she might get pregnant made her go cold all over—especially after hearing Leo's stark words to Ari today. One thing was crystal-clear: this relationship was heading for closure, and sooner rather than later. Angel knew that Leo would not appreciate being forced into fatherhood by a Kassianides, and what if he thought she'd done it on purpose? She had an awful feeling that he still didn't trust her entirely.

The phone rang then, making her jump, and Angel reached for it. Leo had insisted on getting a phone installed in her workroom.

'Hello?'

'Why didn't you stay?'

Angel's heart tripped, and she gripped the phone with two suddenly slippery hands. *The sandwich*—he must be mortified.

'I…had to get back to package up the pieces. I only dropped in to say hello, but you were busy.'

He said nothing for a moment, and Angel could imagine him sitting in his palatial office.

'Thank you for my lunch.'

Angel laughed, and it sounded false to her ears. 'Oh, God, *that*. I don't know what—'

'It was sweet.'

Angel was glad she was alone, because a raging fire of humiliation was burning her up from her toes to her head.

'I'll be home at seven. See you then.'

And the connection was terminated. Angel's heart was thumping out of control; she felt shaky and clammy all over. She was a mess. She was in love. And she was doomed. The Parnassus family were going to have the last laugh after all.

CHAPTER TEN

THAT evening, after they returned from dinner, Angel felt like a limp rag. For once in her life her joy of making jewellery had been eclipsed by something else, *Leo*, and protecting herself around him. She marvelled at how men could have no feelings invested in a relationship and yet make you feel as if you were the only woman in the world.

All evening Leo had been solicitous. Angel had told herself it was just for show, but when Lucy and Ari had briefly left the room to tend to their children Leo had turned to Angel and taken her face in his hands, pressing a hard kiss to her mouth almost as though he couldn't help it, as though he *needed* it, and her body, traitor that it was, had responded.

It had only been when they'd heard a teasing, 'You know, there are some spare rooms upstairs if you like…' that they'd broken apart. Angel had felt unbelievably raw and shaken.

'Penny for them?'

Angel looked sharply at Leo from where she was taking off her shoes inside the door of the villa. She looked down and shrugged minutely, feeling the intense need to self-protect.

'Nothing, really—just that I hope Lucy likes the earrings

and bracelet. It's the first time I've done something in a while and—'

Leo was close, and when Angel stood he tipped her chin up with a finger, making her burn inside.

'She'll love them. Ari loved them. You're extremely talented.'

Angel blushed and could have kicked herself. Why, oh, why couldn't she pull off the whole insouciant thing?

He came too close then, and took her arm just above the elbow. She trembled and tried to pull away. His eyes flashed a little.

'A nightcap?'

Angel answered on instinct, needing to get away, 'Leo, I'm really—'

'Please?'

Something in his face made Angel stop. Her heart beat faster. She shrugged minutely. 'Okay, I guess...'

She followed Leo into the palatial drawing room, a little perplexed. If she didn't know better she'd imagine that he wanted to talk to her about something.

He asked her what she wanted, then poured a Bailey's for her and a whisky for himself. He handed her the drink.

After a long moment that seemed to stretch taut between them he said, 'Angel, I think we both know that any *arrangement* we had is out of the window. I won't and can't stop you if you want to leave.'

Angel's heart clenched so tight she thought she might faint for a second. Her hands unconsciously clenched around her glass, and she was glad she was sitting down. 'I—' she started to say, but Leo was still talking.

'But I don't want you to go, Angel.'

Her heart started to beat again. 'You don't?' she croaked.

He shook his head. 'We're not finished yet. I still want you.'

We're not finished yet. I still want you. Nothing about love or feelings. But, like earlier, she reminded herself: what did she expect after overhearing his conversation with Ari?

'The jewellery workspace is yours, Angel—yours for as long as we're together. After this commission from Ari, and with a little advertising, you're going to be inundated with commissions. This could be the start of a real career for you.'

He wasn't even asking her to stay just because she might want to. She couldn't let him see that she was hurting so much inside.

She smiled, but it felt tight. 'So you're saying that if I stay with you, until such time as you or I grow bored, you'll help launch my career? And what if I don't want to stay?'

Leo's eyes turned very black; his jaw tensed. 'I don't think you'll have any problem setting up on your own, Angel, but you can't deny that this is a launching pad that would put you at a whole other level.'

Angel felt sick. What he was doing was so cruel, and yet… he was also handing her the moon, sun and stars. He was right. With patronage from him, her career would be assured. Could she do that, though? Share his bed knowing that some day in the future he'd be letting her go, albeit leaving her with a glittering career as a token prize?

Suddenly all the ambition that Angel had always harboured felt very flat. She knew if she had the choice that she'd take Leo's love over the launching of a successful career. A career could always be pursued—but true love? Clearly love was not a word in his vocabulary, and if he ever did come to settle down it would be with someone eminently more suitable than her.

Angel felt as if she was breaking into little pieces inside, but she took a studied sip of her drink and then looked up. 'Do you know the only reason I didn't leave my home before now?' She laughed briefly. 'No doubt you must have wondered what on earth I was doing there when my father so evidently hated my guts.' She looked away, and then back again. 'I stayed for Delphi. Because after Damia's death she was lost, went in on herself. Irini, her mother, is next to useless, my father is cut off from human emotion…and poor Delphi was there all on her own. So I promised that no matter what I'd stay with her until she was ready to leave. I was hoping after college I'd persuade her to move out with me, but then father's business started to unravel and we just didn't have the money. Delphi's studying law. I worked to help her get through college, but it meant we couldn't leave home.'

Leo was as silent and still as a statue.

'I've been waiting for a long time for my freedom, Leo. Now that Delphi is married to Stavros I can finally go and live my own life.'

Leo's jaw twitched. 'And that's what you want? Despite what I can offer you?'

Angel nodded and forced a brittle smile. 'Getting the commission from Ari is more than I could have ever hoped for in the first place. And I think you must have realised by now that I was never proper mistress material.'

Leo stood tall and dark and dominant. Unmoving. No emotion flickering across his impassive face. Finally he said, 'I have to go to New York tomorrow on business. I'll be gone for about two weeks. I would just ask that you think about what I've said and then decide. I won't push you for a decision now.'

Angel nodded slowly, feeling as though she was being impaled. 'Very well.'

And that was it. Angel got up and put her glass on the drinks board. She turned and said, 'I'm tired. I'm going to bed.'

'Goodnight, Angel.'

And she walked out of the room, knowing that it would be the last time she saw Leo Parnassus.

Leo walked into the villa two weeks later and knew instantly that Angel was gone. He had never, ever faced this prospect: a woman walking away from him. In his supreme arrogance he'd not contemplated that she might go. And yet he hadn't called or made contact because something superstitious had stopped him—almost as if he didn't know, she wouldn't have left. But she had.

He walked to her workspace and opened the door. Everything was cleaned away, all the tools and leftover metals and gems in neat piles and rows. She'd left it all, and a note.

> *Dear Leo, I've left everything out so that it'll be easy to take away and dismantle. I know it might seem a little weird to say this after everything that happened, and all the circumstances, but thank you for everything. All the best, Angel.*

Leo crumpled up the note and stood for a long moment with his head downbent. And then, with an inarticulate roar of rage, he swept an arm along the top of the workbench, sending tools and metals and gems flying. Tiny diamonds winked up at him mockingly from the floor.

Three months later

Angel's lower back ached. She put her two hands there and stretched, arching backwards. She was pregnant, and just beginning to show. The growing thickness of her middle had become a little bump practically overnight. The day after her final conversation with Leo she'd had some spotting, which she'd believed to be her period when in fact it hadn't been. It was only when she'd missed her next period that she'd got worried and had her pregnancy confirmed.

'You should sit down, lovey—take the weight off your feet.'

Angel smiled at Mary, the woman she worked with in the little tourist café in the grounds of the abbey of her old school in the west of Ireland. 'I'm not about to go into labour because of a little lower back pain.'

The older woman, whom Angel had known since she'd started at the school all those years before, when Mary had been the cook there, smiled fondly. 'No. Maybe not. Well, in that case you can see to the latest arrival—some man on his own. I'd say that's it for the day, then. The last tour are pulling out of the car park now.'

Angel picked up her notepad, and a tray to clear off any dirty tables while she was out. She was looking forward to getting back to the tiny house she shared with a niece of Mary's and having a long hot bath. As she walked out into the dining area the evening sun glinted for a moment, so she couldn't see anything.

When she emerged more fully she had the impression of someone tall and dark standing up, a chair scraping back on the floor just before she saw him properly. But she didn't have to see him. She *knew*.

Leo. Tall and imposing and dark and gorgeous. *Leo*.

Angel felt faint. Her blood was draining downwards in a rush and everything tilted alarmingly.

In a second she was in a chair. Leo was crouching down, looking up at her, and Mary was there too, fussing. 'Are you all right, Angela? I knew you shouldn't be on your feet for all that time. Honestly, you're so stubborn.'

Angel had a moment of panic, afraid Mary would say too much, and put out a hand. 'Mary, I'm fine, honestly. I just got a shock, that's all. I know this man…he's an old friend of mine.'

The astute Irishwoman looked from Angel to Leo and summed the whole thing up in an instant. Angel saw the cogs whirring behind the bright blue eyes.

Mary directed her questions at Angel. 'Are you sure you're okay? Do you want me to leave you alone?'

Angel nodded, even though she felt like clinging onto Mary and begging her to stay. She couldn't. She had to face the father of her child.

'I'm fine, Mary, really. You should get home.'

'But what will you do? You've no car, and your bike is at home.'

'I'll take care of her getting home.'

Leo spoke for the first time, and the effect on Angel was nothing short of cataclysmic. Mary left with much huffing and dark looks directed at Leo, but finally they were alone. Leo stood up. He was dressed in jeans and a dark top, dark coat.

Every part of her tingled, as if she'd been frozen numb for a long time and was being brought slowly back to life. She was glad of the voluminous apron, which covered her tiny bump and her secret.

He whirled around then, and those dark flashing golden eyes that haunted her dreams made her breath catch.

'Angela?'

Angel explained, because it was easier than letting her mind implode. 'When I came here to school the nuns didn't think Angel was a suitable name, so they insisted on calling me Angela. Mary worked there, at the abbey, so she calls me Angela too.'

'You have a bike? You cycle to work here on those roads?'

Angel nodded again, noticing that there were lines of strain around Leo's mouth. That couldn't possibly be—

She answered quickly, to stop her mind going down dangerous avenues. Indulgent avenues. 'Yes. I know they're a bit intimidating, but once you're used to them—'

'Intimidating? Those roads are downright suicidal!'

The look on his face, all at once censorious and something else, made Angel stand up. The shock of seeing him here was finally beginning to wear off. How could he come in here and talk about banal things, as if nothing had happened?

'Leo, you're hardly here to discuss the Irish roads. How did you find me?' *Why did you come looking for me?*

He raked a hand through his hair, and Angel noticed that it had grown longer. In fact he looked altogether more dishevelled. He swung away and then back, his eyes intense on hers. 'It took nearly a month of constant badgering to persuade your sister to tell me where you were.'

Angel sat down again, her legs turning to jelly. She'd stayed in Athens for about a month after leaving the villa, and when Leo had made no effort to come after her it had killed something inside her, despite all her best intentions. Despite knowing it was completely irrational to have hoped for that, because she'd left, basically telling him she wasn't interested.

She bit her lip and looked up. 'I...hadn't planned on coming here, but once I found out—' She stopped. It was too bald to just come out with the most monumental thing that had happened to her. She'd always planned on telling Leo she was pregnant with his baby, but once she'd got some distance, got her wits together, and had decided the best way forward. She hadn't expected to face him so soon. But how would he take the news when she'd heard him say what he had to Ari? That conversation was still etched into her brain.

She turned her head away. It hurt to look at him and acknowledge him being here.

Leo came down in front of her and turned her face back to him. There was a tortured expression in his eyes. It made Angel's insides quiver dangerously.

With a sinking feeling Angel knew that now was the time. Distance hadn't healed her hurt or clarified things; it had made it worse.

'Found out what, Angel?'

She felt a delicate fluttering, as if their baby was already siding with its father, demanding she tell the truth.

'I'm pregnant, Leo.'

For a long moment nothing happened. Neither one of them moved. And then Leo did the last thing Angel had expected. She wasn't sure what she'd expected, but it had something to do with a horrorstruck expression or disbelief.

He reached around behind her neck and pulled the apron over her head. Then he pulled her forward and opened the apron at the back. His big hands on her made Angel's pulse quicken, her breathing catch.

'Leo, what are you—?'

But he just stopped for a moment and put a finger to her mouth. 'Shh.'

Then he pulled the apron away, and her bump was bared in all its tiny proud glory, revealed in her figure-hugging black stretchy top. Leo put his hands over it, fingers stretching out around the sides. Angel held her breath, her eyes widening at seeing him like this, prostrate at her feet.

The feel of his hands on her belly was bringing up so many emotions. Angel looked at Leo, and she could see a look of wonder come over his face. She shut down the impulse to indulge in a dangerous fantasy.

'Leo, why did you come here?'

He shook his head, his hands still on her belly. 'How can you ask that? You should have told me, Angel.'

Shame lanced Angel. Leo being disappointed was so much worse than Leo being all arrogant and demanding. She hung her head. 'I didn't know until about two months ago, and then when I found out…'

The moment she'd found out about the pregnancy hormones had taken over, and the thought of bumping into him, or seeing him with a new woman, had been too much to bear. So, like a coward, she'd run to the farthest place she'd known.

Angel lifted her head, feeling some fire come back. She couldn't think with Leo looking at her so closely, touching her. She stood up with effort, dislodging his hands, and stepped away. Instantly she felt bereft.

'Look, Leo, our relationship was never about a happy-ever-after, even if you did want me to stay on as your mistress. I overheard your conversation with Ari Levakis in your office.' Angel waved her hand in agitation, aghast she'd let that slip out so easily. 'What I heard doesn't matter. The thing is, I knew that things would come to an end eventually.'

Her eyes flicked to him, but he looked stonily impenetrable. Angel was so emotional at the moment the smallest thing could set her off. 'Look, Leo, if you've come just to ask me to be your mistress again—'

He crossed his arms and sent a pointed look to her belly. 'I think that we've gone beyond that point now, don't you?'

She reacted from a deep desire to self-protect. 'Leo, I won't have you think that just because I'm pregnant I'm going to submit to some sort of marriage of convenience. I know from what I heard you tell Ari that you'd no plans of settling down with me—I can only imagine how the thought of having to settle down with a Kassianides must turn your—'

'Angel, stop talking.'

Angel stopped. Emotion wasn't far away. Leo's arms dropped and he came closer. Angel would have backed away, but a table was behind her. She put up a hand. 'Leo, please don't…'

'Don't what, Angel? Touch you? I can't help it if we're in the same room. What else? Don't come after you? I can't help that either. I would have gone to the ends of the earth to find you.' His voice was rough.

Angel's heart started beating very rapidly. 'Leo, stop this. Don't think you're going to get the package now, just because you've found me and I'm pregnant and it's all convenient. That's exactly what I don't want.'

Leo seemed to ignore what she'd said, and reached out to loosen the pin holding her hair up. She hadn't had it cut in months and it had grown longer, falling heavily around her shoulders.

'You seem to be doing enough thinking for the both of us.'

He was twining a piece of her hair around his finger, and Angel felt curiously paralysed. He came closer, until she could feel her belly touching him. A fire started down low, preparing her body for him in a way that she hadn't felt for long weeks.

'When you left me, Angel Kassianides, I went to a dark place.'

Angel looked up, mesmerised despite herself. 'You did?'

Leo nodded and grimaced. 'I came home from New York, found your note and you gone. I trashed the jewellery workshop and promptly flew back to New York for a month, where I spent far too much time in a dingy Irish bar.'

He laughed again mirthlessly. 'Then, even though I couldn't even look at another woman, I thought I was over you, I came back to Athens and proceeded to be such an ogre that I made Calista cry, fired countless employees, and currently Ari and Lucy aren't talking to me.'

Angel gasped. 'They're not?'

Leo shook his head, still twirling Angel's hair around his finger. 'It was only after those two torturous months that I finally allowed myself to admit to my hurt that you'd chosen to walk away rather than stay with me. And then I had to convince your sister to tell me where you were.'

Angel took a breath, feeling as if she was stepping into a void. 'But, Leo, you weren't asking me to stay. You were telling me what you'd give me if I'd stay. It was conditional.'

Leo stopped playing with her hair and looked at her properly, and for the first time Angel saw the vulnerability in his eyes. 'I didn't have the guts to ask you to stay just because you wanted to. I was too terrified of you saying no, because I'd never given you a choice in the first place. I thought my only option was to try and force you into it.'

Angel shook her head; something very fragile was beginning to bloom in her heart. 'To be honest, I probably still would have walked away.' Angel could see the effect of her words on Leo, the tightening and closing of his face, the dimming in his eyes, but before he could retreat into some protective shell completely she took his hand and held it to her breast, under which her heart beat fast.

'*Not* because I didn't want to stay. Because I wanted to stay too much.' She shook her head and felt tears well. She didn't care any more. She couldn't keep it in. Not with their baby growing in her belly. 'I love you, Leo. I fell in love with you so hard that it knocked me for six. I couldn't bear the thought of staying with you only until you grew bored and decided to take a new mistress, or a wife.'

Leo gave a groan that sounded like a man on death row being given a reprieve. He reached out and pulled Angel into him, wrapping his arms tight around her. A great big sob was coming up from deep down inside Angel, and the enormity of it all was hitting her. Leo pulled back, and was blurry in her eyes, and she felt his hands come to her face, thumbs already catching the tears that were falling.

'Oh, Angel, my sweet Angel, don't cry—please don't cry. You can't cry, because I need to hear you say what you just said again.'

Through her gulping sobs Angel got out, 'I…love…you… Have done for ages…' She ended on a wail. 'And I'm really happy I'm pregnant with your baby.'

Leo wrapped his arms tight around her again, and all he said was, 'So am I…so am I…'

When her crying turned to hiccups Leo led her back to a chair and knelt down before her again, and made sure she'd taken a drink of water. Angel felt raw and open. As if her beating heart was lying there between them, telling him how vulnerable she was. He'd said all sorts of things, and patently he wasn't upset about her being pregnant, but he hadn't said that he *cared* for her…

'Angel, what you heard that day outside the office—' Leo grimaced and looked shamefaced '—was me being an absolute coward. The truth is that the moment I saw you by the pool that night I wanted you. And then afterwards, when I found out who you were, and then saw you sneak into the house…'

He tried to explain. 'I'd just decided to come home to Athens, and the enormity of what our family had been put through was still so fresh in my head...and suddenly you were the enemy. It changed everything.'

He shook his head. 'It's no excuse at all, but when I thought you were about to walk away I remembered Dimitri Stephanides. I was determined to use anything I could to bind you to me. So I used Delphi and Stavros's marriage, completely misunderstanding the reason why it was so important to you.'

Leo caught her hand and kissed it. 'When Ari confronted me that day about you he caught a raw nerve. I was just realising that what I felt for you went so much deeper than desire. My whole life I've blocked out emotions, avoided intimacy, terrified of my world falling apart the way it did when I was a kid. I couldn't articulate any of that to him, and when he was all protective of you I lashed out, because I was jealous. Jealous of him feeling like he had some right to protect you from me...'

Leo put his hands back around Angel's belly, and she covered his hands with hers. He looked up, his eyes blazing.

'My childhood fears were nothing compared to what it was like to contemplate trying to live without you. Angel, I love you, and I love this baby. And I want you to come home with me and marry me and be my wife.'

She opened her mouth but he stopped her, as if anticipating something.

'And it's not just because you're pregnant.' He bent his head and pressed a kiss to her belly. He looked up. 'It's because I can't live without you, and if you don't come back home with me then I'm going to move here to be with you, because I'm not leaving your side ever again.'

Angel bent forward and took Leo's face in her hands. Her

heart was so full she felt it could burst. 'The evening you stepped out of that pool you stole my heart, and I haven't been the same since. Ask me again.'

'Only if you kiss me first… God, Angel, I've missed you so much.'

With her heart in her mouth, Angel bent forward and kissed Leo sweetly, tenderly, until he wrapped one hand around the back of her head and pulled her closer, and the kiss quickly developed into something else much hotter.

Breathless, Angel pulled back. 'Ask me again.'

Leo's eyes burned, and his hand on her belly was like a brand. 'Angel, will you marry me? Because I love you more than life itself and quite simply can't function without you.'

'Yes, Leo, I will, and I want to go home with you.' Angel thought of something then, a dark cloud on the horizon. She bit her lip and Leo, immediately concerned, said, 'What is it?'

Angel's hands tightened on Leo's. 'Your father…he must hate me. He can't possibly welcome this.'

Leo smiled. 'Do you know that I always assumed my father had chosen Olympia to be his bride out of logic and respect, a reaction to my mother's histrionics? It was the one thing I admired him for, and the reason I always thought I'd be able to stay away from messy emotions. But I was wrong. He loves Olympia, he never loved my mother, and that was the problem. I never saw that, though, until recently. He's an old man, he's got his lifelong wish to be at home. He's quite happy to bury any ill feeling between our families, and certainly doesn't hold you responsible.'

Relief burst through Angel, but even so she said, 'You're not just saying that?'

Leo smiled. 'No, I'm not just saying that. Now, can we get out of here and go home?'

'Yes, please.' Angel stood up and let Leo help her into her coat. The Irish early autumn weather was making itself felt, with rain starting to spatter and grey clouds rolling overhead when they walked outside.

Angel tugged on Leo's hand and pointed over to where the gothic abbey sat. She glanced at him shyly, and Leo felt his heart expand so much he nearly couldn't contain it.

'When I was at school here I used to imagine that a handsome prince would come and rescue me and take me home.'

Leo turned Angel to face him and wrapped his coat around her, pulling her in close. Her head was tipped back and he could feel the burgeoning swell of her belly digging into him. *Their baby.* They were a family now.

Leo's voice was husky. 'Well, if you don't mind your prince coming a little late, and still kicking the clay off his feet, I'd like to rescue you and take you home.'

Angel smiled tremulously. 'I wouldn't settle for anyone else.'

THE DEVIL'S HEART

LYNN RAYE HARRIS

Lynn Raye Harris read her first Mills & Boon® romance when her grandmother carted home a box from a yard sale. She didn't know she wanted to be a writer then, but she definitely knew she wanted to marry a sheikh or a prince and live the glamorous life she read about in the pages. Instead, she married a military man and moved around the world. These days she makes her home in North Alabama, with her handsome husband and two crazy cats. Writing for Mills & Boon is a dream come true. You can visit her at www.lynnrayeharris.com.

To my agent, Karen Solem, whose awesome
advice and unwavering support are
so very much appreciated.
Thanks for everything.

PROLOGUE

Centuries-Old Missing Treasure Resurfaces

Washington, D.C.—Last night onboard his yacht anchored in the National Harbor, Massimo d'Oro hosted a party for his daughter. Francesca, the youngest child of the Italian businessman, celebrated her eighteenth birthday in a style to which lesser mortals can only dream. The party was attended by many of Washington's social elite, and the birthday girl's dress was rumored to have been custom designed by the House of Versace. The party is said to have cost Mr. d'Oro over one hundred thousand dollars.

Most spectacular of all was the gift Mr. d'Oro bestowed upon his daughter: a ninety-carat diamond necklace, the centerpiece of which is the fifty-five carat flawless yellow diamond known as *El Corazón del Diablo* (The Devil's Heart). This gem, once belonging to the Kings and Queens of Spain, was last known to have been in the possession of the Navarre family of Argentina; it has been lost since the 1980s.

CHAPTER ONE

Eight years later...

"I BEG YOUR pardon?" Marcos Navarre stared at the slight figure dressed in dark clothes. The gun pointed at his heart never wavered.

"I said *move*."

This time the voice was less gruff. Marcos stepped away from the hotel room door, hands up just enough so this intruder wouldn't think he was about to do something crazy.

Like lunge for the gun.

If he could get close enough, he would do just that. This wasn't the first time he'd been on the business end of a weapon, and fear was not what motivated his seeming compliance. He'd become inured to violence during the years he'd spent living in South American jungles with a guerilla army. He knew without doubt there was always an opportunity, in situations like this, to gain the upper hand. So long as his hands were free, there was a chance.

No, fear was not at all what he felt. Rage was the word he was looking for. Bone deep rage.

The person facing him was small, though he knew

better than to mistake small for weak. Darkness shrouded the room and he couldn't make out any details about his visitor. But Marcos had several inches of height, and many more stones of weight to his advantage.

The moment he had an opportunity, he would act. The key was to remain free, and to keep his senses on high alert. He refused to consider what he would do should this intruder attempt to restrain him in any way. Memories flashed into his mind: a dark room, the sharp odor of sweat and rage, and the feel of his own blood dripping down his wrists.

No. Focus.

"You are wasting your time," Marcos said mildly. "I am not in the habit of keeping large amounts of cash in my room."

"Shut up."

Marcos blinked. The gruffness in his intruder's voice was gone. The person holding a gun on him so coolly was most definitely a woman. He relaxed infinitesimally.

Dios mío.

Who had he offended this time? Which of his ex-lovers was so incensed as to carry her desperation this far? Fiona? Cara? Leanne?

He was generous with his mistresses, yet there were those who refused to accept his decision to end the relationship when the time came. Was this a jilted lover— and why couldn't he place her immediately? He was not so callous as to ever forget a feminine body or voice when they gave him such pleasure.

No, not a jilted lover then. Unless he was growing forgetful. Marcos frowned. It did not seem likely. He'd had a lot on his mind lately, yes, but surely not so much as to render him incapable of remembering a woman he'd been intimate with.

He kept his hands in her sight, moving carefully into the middle of the room to await instruction. She shrank back when he passed by, then righted herself boldly as if irritated she had done so.

Several moments passed in complete silence but for the whisper of the ceiling fan overhead.

"Retrieve the jewel," she said, all pretence of being a man gone from her voice now. So she'd made a decision to give up that deception, had she?

Bueno. It would make it easier for him to learn her identity.

"I'm afraid I don't know what you're talking about."

She growled impatiently. The gun gleamed bluish in the moonlight shafting into the room. He noted that she'd added a silencer. The thought did not give him comfort.

"You know very well what I mean. The Corazón del Diablo. Bring it to me if you wish to live."

Ah, so now it made sense. He should have ignored the ridiculous claims of the d'Oros and refused to bring the jewel back to America. But his business interests here could suffer if he did not put an end to their fraudulent claims. The courts in Argentina had already ruled in his favor. He did not need an American court's approval to keep what was rightfully his. What he'd paid for in blood.

Had this woman been sent by the d'Oros? Was the lawsuit merely a ploy to get the stone back into the United States so they could steal it? The old man was dead, but the girls were still alive. He shoved aside the pang of regret he felt when he thought of the youngest d'Oro girl.

Why he should still feel regret, when she'd manipulated him as much as any of them, was a mystery.

Part of him insisted she was innocent—and part of him knew the dark depths to which the human soul could travel. Innocence was often a façade for treachery.

"If you shoot me, *querida*, you will never have the jewel."

"Maybe I'll have something far better," she spat in a low voice.

All of Marcos's senses went on high alert. Something about that voice…

Something he'd forgotten…

"I'll take that jewel now," she continued. "It's in the safe. Open it."

Fury began to uncoil within him. Who was this slip of a woman and how dare she try to rob him of his family birthright? She was not the first to attempt it, but she would not succeed.

It was after the jewel had been stolen, when he was only a boy, that the military *junta* imprisoned his parents. They never returned. They were, like so many thousands of others, among the *disappeared*, those souls who were taken away by the ruling party and killed before democracy was restored in later years.

He blamed his uncle far more than he did the diamond. If not for Federico Navarre's ambition and greed, life would have been far different. But the Corazón del Diablo was all he had left of his family, and he would allow no one to take it from him ever again.

"Apparently you have failed to think this through, little one."

She took a step forward, the gun rock-solid in her grip. And then, as if thinking better of it, she stopped, shook her head so slightly he wondered if he'd imagined the movement. "Shut up and open the safe. Now."

He stood stiffly for only a moment. "Very well."

If he were lucky, she'd get too close.

Marcos strode toward the wall that housed the safe. Sliding the wooden panel aside, he flipped the dial in annoyance. Right, left, right. The tumblers clicked into place and the door opened.

"Frankie," a voice hissed. *"Hurry."*

Marcos stilled, straining to pinpoint the source. It had sounded oddly small and disembodied.

"Frankie," it said again, louder this time.

"Shut up," the girl said. "I'm working on it."

Ah, a radio. She was using a two-way radio to communicate with someone outside this room. Odd—and a rather inept choice for a skilled thief. Yet another puzzle piece to consider.

"Step away from the safe," she ordered, the gun glinting as she used it to motion him away. "And keep your hands where I can see them."

Marcos backed away carefully, hands at shoulder height. The girl waited until he was nearly against the opposite wall before she moved. A flashlight blazed into life. She swept the interior of the safe, then spun toward him.

"It's not here," she said in disbelief. "Where is it?"

He almost felt sorry for her. Almost, but not quite. "There are plenty of other jewels. Take them instead."

Her voice shook. "The Corazón del Diablo. Where is it?"

"It's not here," he repeated.

"That's impossible. I was assured—" The gun was

leveled at him again, her voice full of purpose. "Where have you hidden it?"

"Forget it, *Frankie*," he said smoothly, emphasizing the name the voice had called her. She had been assured? By whom? "You've failed. Now take what's there and go."

"You aren't the one in control here, Navarre. You will not tell me what to do. Not ever again," she added so quietly he wasn't certain he'd heard her right. *Never again?*

"Who are you?" he demanded, blazing hot anger sizzling through him like a living flame.

Before she could answer—or tell him to shut up, most likely—he reached over and flicked the light switch.

"Bastard," she cried, blinking against the light that flooded the room. Yet still the gun was firmly pointed at him.

He didn't care. The girl, this Frankie, was compelling—and he'd never seen her before in his life. Sun-streaked hair was pulled into a tight knot at the base of her neck, its thickness indicating long length when her hair was down. Her skin was pale with a hint of golden color. Her eyes glared at him hot and dark. She was dressed in a workman's black coveralls, but the garment was a size too small because it clung to her generous curves like a protective sleeve.

She looked furious, determined—but then she bit down on her plump lower lip and he recognized it for what it was: a crack in her armor. A current of desire arced through him at that single display of vulnerability.

Dios, now was not the time to be attracted to a woman. Especially not a woman with a gun pointed at his heart. Marcos clamped down on his wayward libido and tried to memorize everything about her. Should she get away, should she not shoot him in the process, he needed to remember what she looked like.

Because—female or not, vulnerable or not—he was going to hunt her down. He would find her and he would make her pay for thinking she could rob him of his birthright.

"Who are you, Frankie, and why do you want my necklace?"

Her eyes widened briefly before narrowing again. The gun shook in her grip. Odd when she'd been so controlled only moments before.

"You really don't know, do you?" Her laugh was strangled. "God, of course you don't. Because you're selfish, Marcos Navarre. Selfish and cruel."

Some little bit of knowledge buzzed at his mind like an annoying mosquito. He brushed it aside impatiently. He had no time to puzzle out what it was. He simply needed to remember this woman—and possibly disarm and capture her—before she could get away. "The Corazón del Diablo is mine. You will not steal it from me this night, so either take what's there and go, or shoot me and be done with it."

"I would like to," she said, her voice dripping with menace and fury. "Believe me I would. But I want that jewel, Navarre. One way or the other, you are going to give it to me."

Francesca forced down the bile in her throat. When he'd flipped the light on, she'd thought she would die. If he'd looked at her with pity, or shook his head sadly, she'd have crumbled like a house of cards. Her will and determination would have evaporated like an early morning mist, leaving her vulnerable and exposed.

But there'd been no flicker of recognition in his eyes, no stiffening of his form, nothing to indicate he had the slightest clue who she was.

And it hurt. Hurt like bloody hell that he hadn't known her. After all, she'd been the one to give him the Corazón del Diablo in the first place. Like a love struck imbecile, she'd handed it over just the same as she'd handed him her heart.

What happened next had been inevitable to all but the most blind of souls. He'd kept the jewel and discarded her love. Discarded her. She'd learned the truth too late. He'd conned her out of the diamond just like he'd conned her into believing he cared.

The Devil's Heart was aptly named. She'd given it to the devil and it had cost her nothing but heartache.

And now he stood here so haughty and handsome in his custom tuxedo, looking down his fine nose at her as if she were a bug. Her traitorous heart thumped painfully.

He was still so damn gorgeous. Tall, broad-shouldered, and as handsome as any movie star. He had a silver-edged scar that zigzagged from one corner of his mouth, a reminder of a long ago accident, she imagined. Far from ruining his dark male beauty, it only made it seem more potent. He had the kind of Latin good looks that made women prostrate themselves at his feet.

Just like she'd done. *Idiot.*

Her life had been ruined by that single act of falling for Marcos Navarre's smooth lies and sensual body. For thinking she had a future with him if only she gave him what he wanted. She'd been stupid. How could a man like him ever be interested in a chubby, shy, ugly girl like her?

He couldn't. Her sister had tried to warn her, but she hadn't listened. She'd believed Livia to be jealous. Livia, the beautiful one. The one who *should* have been the object of Marcos's attention. But Francesca hadn't wanted to accept the truth and she'd tumbled them into ruin with her need to be loved.

He'd fooled them all, she reminded herself. Charmed them all.

Didn't matter. It was *her* fault the Navarres destroyed d'Oro Shipping. Her fault that her father shot himself, that her mother clung to the remnants of her wealth in a drafty old house in Upstate New York, and that her sister barely ever spoke to her.

She'd made poor choices, choices that had cost her much more than hurt pride in the end.

She was through letting life beat her up and take away the people she loved. Her grip on the warm metal hardened.

Jacques was not going to die, not if she could help it. The old man had taken her in when she'd fled after her father's death, had given her a job and taught her everything he knew about the jewelry business. He'd also nursed her through the darkest moments of her life when she'd wanted to die, along with the child she'd never gotten to hold. After Marcos's betrayal, it had taken years to let a man into her life. Robert hadn't thrilled her the way Marcos had, but she'd told herself it was simply her youthful longings making Marcos seem so much bigger than life in her imagination.

Getting pregnant was an accident, but she'd wanted her baby as soon as she found out. Robert hadn't, though he'd stuck around for a few months, had even gone through with an engagement as if he were prepared to be a husband and father. Until she started to show. That's when he walked out.

When she lost the child so brutally, Jacques was the only one who cared, the only one who was there for her.

She loved Jacques and she owed him.

"The necklace, Marcos," she said firmly, leveling the gun at his heart once more. "I'll take it now."

"It's not here, *querida*. You waste your time."

Francesca lowered the gun to point at his groin. "Killing you would be too good. Perhaps I will simply have to deprive the female world of your ability to make love ever again. I am quite a good shot, I assure you."

She'd learned out of necessity. And though she never wanted to harm another human being, she had no compunction about making this man think she would do so if it meant she could save Jacques.

His voice dropped to a growl. A hateful, angry growl. "You won't get away with this. Whoever you are, *Frankie,* I will find you. I will find you and make you wish you'd never met me."

Her heart flipped in her chest. She ignored it. "I already wish that. Now give me the jewel before you lose the ability to ever have children."

Bitterness twisted inside her as she said those words. How ironic to threaten someone with something she would never wish on another soul. But she had to be hard, cold, ruthless—just like he was.

He stared at her in impotent fury, his jaw grinding, his beautiful black eyes flashing daggers at her. Very slowly, he reached up with one hand and slipped his bowtie free of its knot. Then he jerked it loose and let it fall.

Francesca forced herself to breathe normally as he undid the stud at his neck and his shirt fell open to reveal the hollow at the base of his throat.

"What are you doing? This is no time to attempt a seduction, Navarre," she said icily.

His fingers dipped into his snowy white shirt and came up with a silver chain. He tugged it upward, slipping it over his head and tossing it at her. Francesca caught it smoothly, though her heart thundered. She wasn't sure how she'd caught it when she'd barely seen him throw it.

The chain was warm from his skin, yet it burned into her as if it were on fire. She clenched it tightly, only realizing there was a key at the end of the chain when she felt it in her palm.

"What am I supposed to do with this?"

"There is a strongbox under the bed. The necklace is inside."

Too easy. He's up to something.

No, he simply cared about his balls more than he did the necklace. Typical. And exactly what she'd been counting on when she made the threat.

Francesca waved the gun. "Get it for me."

Marcos shrugged, then moved off toward the bedroom as if he hadn't a care in the world. She followed at a distance that kept her out of his reach if he were to turn suddenly. She put nothing past him. She hadn't known him well at all, still didn't, but she knew he was a dangerous man.

A devil wrapped in a beautiful package.

It's what had drawn her to him in the first place, the

danger of all that sharp, sensual, broody masculinity that hid the kind of dark secrets she hadn't begun to guess at in her sheltered life. That and the way he'd seemed to smile only for her.

Francesca suppressed a snort of disgust.

That naïve girl she'd been was gone. Buried in the past. The woman she was now knew all about secrets and pain.

She stopped in the doorway as Marcos moved toward the giant king-size bed that dominated the room. Silk sheets were turned down in anticipation of his arrival, and a silver bucket of champagne gleamed with sweat on the night table. Two crystal glasses sat beside the bucket.

Francesca clamped down on the rush of heat that flooded her limbs. Her ears grew hot. Of course he was expecting a woman. Wasn't he always expecting a woman?

She needed to get the necklace and get out before his paramour arrived. Another person would complicate matters. Perhaps that was what he was counting on—the arrival of a lover and the inevitable confusion that would follow.

"Hurry up," she said as he knelt beside the bed. "And don't try anything funny. I *will* shoot you, I swear."

He looked at her evenly. "Are you trying to convince me or yourself?"

Francesca gripped the gun harder. "Don't try me, Marcos. One handed," she added when he began to reach beneath the bed.

He kept one hand on the floor where she could see it and reached under the bed with the other. She heard the scrape of metal against the tile and then he emerged with a long black box.

"Now shove it over here and get on the bed," she said.

He stood to his full height and kicked the box with a vicious jab that sent it flying toward her. She stuck her foot out to stop it, wincing as it slammed into her.

"You can leave now," he said, his voice cold and deadly. "Leave the box and go, and I will not come after you."

"On the bed," she commanded.

One corner of his mouth suddenly crooked in a sensual grin. She didn't fool herself that he was anything other than angry. He was as alert as a panther, constantly looking for a way to catch her off guard.

"And here I thought you only wanted me for my jewels."

"On the bed, Marcos. Hurry."

"As you wish," he said. "Shall I strip first?"

When she didn't answer, he sat on the bed and eased back against the headboard. Francesca swallowed. God, he looked like a banquet of sinful delights as he leaned back casually, one knee bent. When he slipped open another stud, his shirt fell apart to reveal smooth, tanned skin that she'd once ached to kiss.

She'd never gotten to do so, but she'd wanted to desperately. And still he had no idea who she was. Incredible. She'd lost weight, but she hadn't changed that much. She was still Francesca d'Oro, as awkward and ungraceful as ever.

His inability to recognize her was yet another slice of proof, as if she needed more, that he'd never really been interested in *her*.

"Like what you see, *querida*?"

Francesca gave herself a mental shake, then reached into her pocket and withdrew a set of handcuffs. She tossed them at him. He caught them one handed, all pretense of seduction gone. His eyes gleamed with poorly disguised hatred.

And something else.

Was it fear she saw in the depths of his gaze? A tremor rolled over her, but she couldn't stop. She couldn't leave this room safely if he wasn't restrained. She tightened her grip on the gun, her sweaty palms making it harder to hold with each passing second. She had to get this done and get out.

"Cuff yourself to the bed. And make sure I hear the snap."

His grip on the stainless cuffs was white knuckled. "You really need to shoot me," he said evenly. "Because I will find you. And what I do to you when that happens will make your worst nightmare seem like a pleasant dream."

"Don't tempt me," she muttered. "Now do it."

He glared at her a moment longer, his chest rising and falling a little too quickly. But then he snapped one cuff to the bedpost. He fitted his wrist into the other cuff, his eyes hard on hers. She would almost swear his lips were white around the edges. But no, Marcos Navarre was afraid of nothing, certainly not of being handcuffed to a luxurious bed in a posh hotel. In fact, she would bet he'd been cuffed to beds before—though for infinitely more pleasurable reasons.

The cuff snapped in the stillness. For good measure, he jerked his arm against the restraints; they held fast and Francesca let out her breath.

Until he spoke.

"I will find you, Frankie. You will pay for this in ways you cannot imagine. I will start by binding you like a dog—"

"Shut up," she bit out, the gun wavering as she pointed it at him. But her heart pounded so hard it made her head feel light. He had no idea that she'd already suffered her worst nightmare. Nothing this man could do would ever equal what had been done to her when those thugs had beaten her half to death and killed her unborn child. "I don't want to hurt you, Marcos. But I will, I swear to God, if you force me to do so."

"Then open the box and retrieve your spoils," he said coldly. "Because I assure you we will meet again."

She bent to retrieve the strongbox at her feet, fumbling with the key as she did so. Adrenaline pumped into her veins, the rush of it heady and swift. Soon, she would have the Corazón del Diablo in her possession. Life would go back to normal again. Jacques would get well and keep making beautiful jewelry. She would continue running the small shop where they sold his creations.

A stab of fear pierced her. What if Marcos found her? But no, she couldn't worry about that possibility. Even if he did somehow remember who she was, and track her down, the necklace would be gone and Jacques would be getting the care he needed.

Not for the first time, doubt and guilt reared their ugly heads. Was it right to do this? But, oh God, what choice did she have? Marcos had wealth to spare. He would be fine without this necklace. Besides, he'd taken the diamond from her under false pretenses.

Do you promise to love, honor, and cherish....

A noise in the other room brought her head up.

"Darling, where are you?" a woman called, her soft voice accented with wealth and culture.

Francesca froze, her breath shortening in her chest. She'd had those things once upon a time. Things she'd lost, thanks to him.

No.

She'd never been happy in that life. In spite of all the culture and deportment lessons, she'd never been the kind of daughter her mother had wanted her to be. She wasn't perfect like Livia. Everything she'd ever touched, ever tried to do, crumbled apart like last winter's rotten leaves. Escaping had been a relief.

For a brief time, anyway. Until a new nightmare had nearly robbed her of her sanity.

"Darling?" the woman called again.

Francesca swung the gun up and motioned for Marcos to be quiet. Amazingly, he obeyed. She had no time to puzzle out why. She hefted the box and backed into the shadows of the open balcony. The last thing she saw as went over the side was Marcos Navarre's eyes.

They glittered hard and cold, promising retribution.

CHAPTER TWO

JACQUES LAY IN his bed, blankets pulled high, his frail body lost in the mass of covers. His eyes were closed, his breathing labored and shallow. Francesca swallowed a hard knot of pain. Her throat ached. She so badly wanted to tell Jacques about the jewel, wanted his help and advice.

But she couldn't. He would worry if he knew what she'd done. Across the bed from her, Jacques's nephew, Gilles, met her gaze. His eyes were shadowed. He'd helped her break into Marcos's room, and she'd felt the guilt of involving him each moment since.

And each moment since she'd left Marcos handcuffed to his bed, she'd felt tight inside, as if her skin were being stretched over a massive drum.

From the instant she'd seen the newspaper article that Marcos was bringing the Corazón del Diablo to New York, she'd thought of nothing else but regaining the stone. But now that she had, everything felt wrong. Though he'd stolen it from her in the first place, she couldn't stop thinking that she'd been dishonest in reclaiming the necklace the way she had.

Maybe she should have called Marcos, asked for a

meeting. Told him flat out it was hers and she wanted it back.

As if he would have listened! No, time was running out. For Jacques and for her. Livia and her mother had filed a suit claiming ownership. If they somehow won, or if the courts demanded Marcos turn the necklace over, she'd never see a cent.

She didn't have time to fight them all, nor did she have the money to do so. Perhaps she'd been wrong to steal it back, but she'd had no choice. Jacques was more important to her than a collection of polished carbon rocks and platinum.

She'd tried everything she could think of to get the money for his cancer treatments. No one would insure him with a pre-existing condition. She'd even called her mother to beg for money, though she should have known better. Penny Jameson d'Oro was no longer the fabulously wealthy socialite she'd once been. She had money, but to her it wasn't enough. She wouldn't part with a dime, and certainly not to the daughter she blamed for casting her into her current state of *poverty*—her word, not Francesca's—in the first place.

"Let me know when he wakes," Francesca said. Gilles nodded.

Francesca turned and made her way down the stairs to the shop. Thank God Gilles was here. The two of them took turns sitting with Jacques, and that enabled them to keep the shop going. Every bit of money they brought in was crucial.

She knew that if she wanted, Gilles would become more than just a friend. He was her age, strong and energetic, and he had a string of girlfriends he dated from time to time, though none seriously.

But she didn't want to cross that line with him, not really, even if she sometimes felt so empty and alone. Memories of Marcos sliding his shirt open and fishing for that key made heat curl in her veins.

Unwelcome heat.

She pushed the image away. Romance wasn't for her, and now was not the time to think about sexy Argentinians. She had to unload the Corazón del Diablo. Her stomach twisted.

You've come this far, she told herself. *Too late getting a conscience now.*

As soon as she opened the shop, she would make a few discreet calls.

The morning was gray and gloomy as she unlocked the doors. The air was beginning to turn brisk with the promise of winter. Yesterday, she hadn't seen her breath. This morning, it frosted and made her think about long ago days at her family's estate, when the leaves turned golden and the apple cider tasted spicy and sweet on her tongue.

She rarely thought of her life before, but seeing Marcos again dredged up memories of her past. She'd once daydreamed about what a life with him would be like, but he'd crushed her dreams beneath his custom soles. Life itself had dealt the final blow. She had no dreams left.

She went to the small kitchenette off the main showroom and poured a cup of coffee. The bell dinged in the shop, letting her know someone had come inside.

Cup in hand, smile fixed, she returned to the shop to help the first customer of the day.

A tall man stood with his back to her as he bent over a case. Outside the door, two more men stood with arms folded across massive chests. The hair on the back of her neck prickled in warning. The old horror threatened to consume her, but she wouldn't allow it.

Francesca set the coffee down quietly and slid her fingers toward the gun beneath the counter. They hadn't had a robbery attempt in months now, but she was taking no chances. Memories of pain and blood, of the fear she'd had for her baby as her assailant had kicked and punched her, flooded in as her fingers touched the cool metal. She'd learned to defend herself in the aftermath of that dark time, learned that she could be cold and calculating if lives depended on it.

"I wouldn't do that if I were you." The man turned toward her and all the breath left her lungs. She had an impression of cold, cruel strength. Of a strong jaw, tanned skin, and thick black hair.

And then he spoke again.

"*Buenos días*, Frankie. Or should I say Francesca?"

Marcos Navarre did not like being made a fool of by anyone. And a fool was what she'd tried to play him for. The woman looking back at him was nothing like the sweet, shy girl he'd once thought her to be. This woman was cold, hard, and ruthless. No wonder he hadn't recognized her.

At the moment she looked stunned, however. And maybe a touch vulnerable, though he dismissed the thought as fancifulness on his part. His protective instincts were too finely tuned, too accustomed to reacting to others' fear and pain. That's what a childhood in the streets of Buenos Aires did for a man.

He'd learned the hard way that he couldn't save everyone. Francesca d'Oro least of all. Oh yes, he'd had some misguided notion of rescuing her several years ago—when in fact she hadn't needed rescuing at all.

As she'd proved to him again just a few hours past.

He'd felt sorry for her once, had resented her a bit later—now, he hated her for what she'd done. She'd stolen the Corazón del Diablo from him, and she'd forced him to endure the kind of captivity he'd never thought to endure again. He hadn't spent long chained to the bed, but even a second was more than he cared to endure. He'd had to remember his darkest days, the blood and pain and fear as he'd been kept chained in a dark room and beaten for information all those years ago in the jungle.

Francesca couldn't have known what had happened to him—he'd never told her about it—but he hated her for her selfishness, for reminding him of what it felt like to be utterly helpless.

He was here to make her pay.

A noise on the stairs captured Francesca's attention before she'd recovered herself enough to speak. She took a step in that direction but was unable to halt the progress of the man who stumbled to a halt and stared at Marcos with barely disguised loathing.

"Please don't, Gilles," she said when the man looked ready to pounce on him. "It's not worth it."

The two exchanged a look and a different sort of rage blazed to life in Marcos's gut. The way this man looked at Francesca, the way they communicated without speaking another word. It was nothing to Marcos, and yet—

She turned back to him then. "Marcos—"

"Tell your lover who I am, Francesca. *What* I am to you."

There were two high spots of color in her cheeks. A moment later her expression hardened. "How dare you? You are *nothing* to me. Less than nothing."

"This is not what you said when you promised to love, honor, and obey me for the rest of our lives."

She didn't look at her lover, not once. She didn't have to. Marcos could tell the other man knew what their relationship had been. What manner of other things had she told him to get him to cooperate in stealing the necklace? Because Marcos knew this had been the man on the other end of the radio last night.

"We are *not* married, Marcos. Not any longer. You left, remember? And you did not contest the annulment."

He let his eyes move lazily down her body. Though she was dressed in a baggy black sweater and jeans, they did little to hide the lush curves underneath. Francesca d'Oro had not looked like this at eighteen. If she had, perhaps he'd have been unable to leave for Argentina so soon after their sham of a marriage had taken place.

She'd shed the baby fat that had once clung to her, rounding her face. The thick glasses were gone as well. Her hair had been blonde before, and cut in an unflattering bob that only made her face seem plumper.

Now, the golden-streaked mass was closer to brown than blonde and fell halfway down her back. Her eyes were hazel, he noted, more chocolate than green or gold, and her mouth was kissable in a way he hadn't remembered. Her lower lip was thicker than the upper, giving her an artless sexy pout.

He wanted to plunder that mouth, spend hours making love to it. The strength of the compulsion shocked him.

When he met her gaze again, he was almost amused

to see the hate in her eyes. If she thought she hated him before, she was certain to do so even more when he finished with her this time.

"I suggest you give me the Corazón del Diablo now, *querida*," he said coolly, twisting the endearment into an insult.

Her chin tilted up. "How did you find me so fast?"

He saw no reason to prevaricate. "You did not really think I would be so stupid as to trust that your family wouldn't pull a stunt such as this? There is a GPS transmitter attached to the necklace. These things are quite small now."

Her eyes closed briefly before snapping open to glare at him again. "It belongs to me, Marcos. You stole it on our wedding night."

"You gave it to me, *mi amor*. I remember this clearly."

"I would not have done so if I'd known you'd planned to abandon me."

"Ah yes, you thought I was bought and paid for, *sí*? That Daddy's money could bring anything your heart desired if only you begged him to buy it for you."

She flushed pink. "You're disgusting."

He shrugged casually, though anger scorched a path through his soul. Because he'd allowed himself to be bought, hadn't he? He'd wanted the Corazón del Diablo, had spent months attempting to purchase it from her father though he did not in truth have the money to do so.

But Massimo d'Oro was crafty. He'd given the jewel to his daughter. It was Marcos's fault for always paying attention to her. He'd believed she was a sweet girl, an ugly duckling who wilted in the shade of her more beautiful sister. Francesca had worn her innocence like a mantle, and he'd fallen for the act. He'd paid attention to her because she'd seemed to blossom when he did so. She smiled and came out of her shell and he only felt more protective.

Until the day her father had informed him that the only way to obtain the Corazón del Diablo—and his help in wresting control of Navarre Industries from Federico—was to marry Francesca. He'd realized then what he should have known all along: she was a d'Oro, vain, spoiled, and shallow, just like her mother and sister. Her gifts were not theirs; she hadn't been beautiful, so she'd had to use her other talents. And he'd fallen for it, just as they'd expected him to.

"You did not think I was so disgusting when you married me, *querida*." He sliced a hand through the air. What was done was done. "Enough of this reminiscing. You will bring me the Corazón del Diablo now or I will let my men tear this place apart looking for it. Decide."

Her answer was not what he expected, though perhaps he should have done so knowing what he did about her character.

"It's mine, Marcos. But I *will* sell it to you. For the right price."

Francesca wedged herself against the Bentley door and jerked the handle for the millionth time. She knew the result would be no different than before, but as furious as she was, she needed *something* to do.

Something besides launch herself at the man inside the car with her.

She'd already screamed until she was blue in the face. Marcos had threatened to gag her if she continued, so she'd stopped. In truth, her raw throat was relieved to have an excuse.

He had not reacted the way she'd expected. She hadn't really thought he would agree to pay her a dime, but she also hadn't believed he would kidnap her in broad daylight after he'd ordered his goons to search the store.

Furious tears pressed at the backs of her eyelids. Gilles had moved as if to prevent it from happening, but she'd begged him not to put himself in harm's way for her. He would have done so anyway, but one of Marcos's men pointed a gun at him and effectively ended the attempt. Gilles had stood by helplessly, fists clenching at his sides in impotent fury. She only hoped Jacques had slept through the raised voices and rhythmically slamming drawers.

What would happen when she was gone? How could Gilles keep the shop open and take care of Jacques too? Someone had to pick up Jacques's prescriptions, fix his favorite soup of clear broth and a little bit of egg noodles, and order the supplies for his bench. He didn't work often these days, but he still sculpted new creations out of wax when he felt up to it. When he finished a design, Gilles would cast it and start the rigorous polishing of the metal that was required before any gemstones could be set.

Oh, Jacques.

She crammed her fist against her mouth to stop the flood before it could break.

"Did you cry so prettily for me when we parted, Francesca?"

She swung her head around to look at him. "I'm not crying," she forced out between clenched teeth. The coolness on her cheeks betrayed the lie, but she refused to wipe the wetness away. She would not give him the satisfaction. "And I most definitely would never cry over you."

"Ah," he said. "How tragic for me then."

"Where are you taking me?"

His gaze grew sharp. "Buenos Aires, *mi amor.*"

Her heart began a staccato rhythm against her ribs. "What? You can't do that! This is my home, people need me—"

"I did warn you," he said, his voice deceptively mild and completely at odds with the fire in his gaze. She had the distinct impression he was enjoying himself.

"You don't want to do this."

"I do. Remember those words, Frankie?" He smoothed an imaginary wrinkle in his expensive sleeve.

"Stop toying with me, Marcos. And *don't* call me Frankie."

His dark eyes pierced her. "I thought you liked it. Is this your lover's pet name for you?"

Francesca wrapped her arms around her to ward off the chill creeping over her body. This man was nothing like the handsome young Argentinian who'd been so nice to her. But that had been a game, hadn't it? He'd only been nice to her in order to win her affection, to fool her into thinking he cared for her.

Once he'd gotten what he wanted, he'd left her to face the shame alone. He'd never even *kissed* her for God's sake! She'd been married to him for all of three hours and, aside from a peck on the cheek at the justice of the peace's office, they'd never shared a single kiss.

"You have to let me go," she said. "I can't be gone very long. Jacques needs me—"

"Ah yes, the man who owns the shop. Is he your lover too?"

She gaped at him, too shocked to summon outrage. "You went to all this trouble to find me, to find out who I was, and you didn't bother to learn that Jacques Fortier is seventy-five if he's a day, or that he'll die if I don't go back?" He looked so cold and unfeeling that a sob burst from her in spite of her best effort to prevent it. She stuffed the rest of them down deep before they could escape. "I need that necklace, Marcos. It's the only way to save Jacques. I need the money."

His mouth twisted. "A very likely story, Francesca. You forget that I know you, that I know what you are capable of. This Jacques may be sick, but he is simply the excuse you use to try and make me feel pity for you. You were always very good at that."

"No." She leaned toward him, tried to convey her sincerity, her desperation. "I'll go with you, I'll do whatever you want, I'll sign a paper saying I gave the necklace to you and that my mother and sister can have no claim to it. But you *must* help Jacques. Please."

He stared at her for so long she began to fear he hadn't heard her. "I have a better idea," he said, his voice so low she had to lean forward again. His gaze dropped and she realized that her baggy sweater was dipping perilously low, that he could see her bra and possibly the curve of her breasts.

As if her body could have any effect on him. No, she knew from experience that she did nothing for Marcos Navarre. She shifted position slightly, but only out of modesty. She could parade before him naked and he would not be affected.

"Anything," she said. "I'll do anything."

"Yes, I believe you would," he replied after another moment of letting his gaze wander.

Heat sizzled in the air between them. Her heart thumped, but she reminded herself it was only anger that charged the air, nothing more. What else could it be?

"You will come to Buenos Aires. Willingly, *querida*."

"I will," she replied quickly, though the thought filled her with dread. So long as he used his resources to help Jacques, she would dance naked on a tight rope if he demanded it. And yet she was curious. "Wouldn't a sworn statement to the authorities here be enough?"

"It might, but I prefer my solution. You will marry me—again—Francesca. Only this time, it will be a marriage in truth."

Her breath refused to fill her lungs properly. The blood rushed from her head, making her feel suddenly weightless. Of all the things she'd thought he would say, of all the things she would actually *do* to save Jacques, he'd chosen the one thing that would surely destroy her.

Marriage to him. Again.

"That's insane," she gasped. "I won't do it."

"Yet it is my price."

Francesca closed her eyes as she struggled to breathe normally. He had to be toying with her. This was part of his punishment for her, though she failed to see how it could possibly benefit him in any way. He was not attracted to her. Never had been. So what was the point?

Did he know about her ex-fiance? About her poor baby who'd been taken from her too soon? She hadn't been with a man since the miscarriage—was this his

way of tormenting her? Did he really mean to marry
her and bed her?

She'd said *anything* but she'd not considered this.
The one thing that terrified her more than any other.
She wasn't the naïve girl who'd once loved him, she
wasn't in danger of losing her heart, but to be forced
into intimacy with him when the act made her think of
what she'd lost? Of what she could never have? Of the
babies she would never, ever hold in her arms?

"You don't want me," she choked out. "You can't."

"Not permanently, no. I want you long enough to stop
any claims to the Corazón del Diablo that your family
might raise."

She had to find her center of calm, had to disconnect
from the swirling emotion and deal with this situation
as cold-bloodedly as he did. Her fingers shook as she
clasped them together in her lap. She'd learned how to
adapt, how to disconnect. She would do it here and now,
in spite of how he churned her emotions. "How long,
Marcos?"

He shrugged. "Three months, perhaps six."

Six months. Dear God.

She couldn't.

"I'll go with you. I'll sign papers stating the Corazón
del Diablo is irrevocably yours, and I'll stay in Buenos
Aires for three months if you'll help Jacques. But I can't
marry you. There's no reason for it."

"There is every reason," he said, his voice cracking
like a whip against her senses. "I will have no more
questions about who owns the stone. It is mine by right,
by birth. Any questions of ownership will be dead once
we marry."

She felt like someone was squeezing her, sucking

all the air from her space. "How do I know you'll keep your word, that you'll help Jacques?"

"I'll put it in writing."

He was boxing her in and the box was growing smaller by the second. How could she refuse? How could she deny Jacques the same care he'd given her when she'd needed it? Comfort, care, and love. Francesca closed her eyes, swallowed.

"There would be no need for a marriage in anything more than name," she said, the words like razor blades in her throat. "You can continue seeing other women. When the time is up, we can divorce and no one will be the wiser."

The scar scissoring from one corner of his mouth made him look so dangerous, so sensual. When he smiled it made him look more predatory, not less. He truly was a devil.

"Ah, but I would know, Francesca." He grasped her hand, pulling it to his mouth. His breath stole over her skin in the instant before his lips seared her.

Her body reacted. God help her, it reacted. Sensation spread outward from that one hot touch of his lips. Flooded her senses. Brought parts of her to life that she'd thought were permanently shut off.

No! This was precisely why she couldn't do this.

You have to, Francesca. You have no choice.

"Stop touching me," she managed, her heart fluttering like a moth trapped in a jar.

His smile was still so wolfish. "I am not willing to 'see' other women, as you put it. I intend to be true to our vows, for as long as we are married."

He was torturing her. There was no other explanation. He didn't really want her—couldn't want her. But if she didn't agree to his plan, he wouldn't help Jacques. Uniting d'Oro and Navarre once more would cement his possession of the Corazón del Diablo in the eyes of the world. He would be satisfied with nothing less.

Once he'd done that, perhaps he would lose interest in punishing her. Perhaps he'd let her go.

Francesca pulled her hand away. "I want the contracts drawn up first. I want to see it in writing."

Marcos took out his phone and punched in a number. Moments later, he was speaking in rapid-fire Spanish. When he finished, he put the phone away and smiled again. That devastatingly handsome smile that proclaimed his intention to win no matter the cost.

"The contracts will be ready when we arrive."

"I'd rather see them before I leave New York."

"This is too bad," he said. "My plane is prepared and the flight plan has been filed."

"Flight plans can be changed," she insisted.

Marcos's eyes were hard. "Not mine."

"You can't force me to go with you," she said, throwing one last desperate statement into the air between them.

"I will carry you onboard myself, Francesca, if you insist on acting like a child."

"I'll scream until someone notices—"

"And sentence your Jacques to certain death? I think not."

"I hate you," she whispered, turning to watch the city slide by before he could see a tear fall.

His voice, when he finally spoke, was as soft as satin, as hard as the Corazón del Diablo. "Then perhaps we understand one another after all."

Francesca closed her eyes. She understood all right. Understood that she'd just sold her soul to the devil. And deals with the devil never ended well…

CHAPTER THREE

THE FLIGHT TO Buenos Aires took more than ten hours. Though they'd traveled in luxury aboard Navarre Industries' corporate jet, Francesca was exhausted by the time they arrived. She hadn't slept well since the night before when she'd stolen into Marcos's hotel room and liberated the Corazón del Diablo.

Though it was dark when they landed, the city lights bathed the night sky in a pale pink glow. Francesca stumbled on the stairs leading from the jet, but Marcos caught her around the waist and kept her from tumbling down the gangway. His fingers burned into her back as he guided her the rest of the way down.

A sleek Mercedes waited for them nearby. Francesca sank into the interior and moved as far away from Marcos as she could get. He immediately took out his phone and made a call. She listened to the lyrical sound of his voice speaking Spanish as the car left the airport and headed into the city. She spoke tolerable French and German, could read Latin, but she'd never learned Spanish. She was certainly regretting that now.

Marcos eventually finished his call and they rode in silence. The city moved by at a quick pace, but a few things caught her attention.

The obelisk that looked like the Washington Monument, which sat at the center of the very wide street down which they'd been traveling, for instance. When she remarked on it, Marcos informed her it was called *El Obelisco* and had been built to commemorate the four-hundredth anniversary of the city.

"There are concerts held here from time to time," he said, and she realized there was actually a semi-circular swath of grass and concrete on one side of the monument that could accommodate many people.

In fact, though it was dark, there were people every-where, lingering around the obelisk or crossing the wide street. She even spotted a couple doing the tango. There was a crowd gathered to watch, but the scene slid by before she could see much of the dance.

In spite of her exhaustion, in spite of the reason she was here, the color and movement of the big city excited her. She'd traveled quite a bit as a child, but she'd never been to South America. Her mother had loved to fre-quent Paris, Rome, and the Med. While she and Livia fidgeted inside hotel suites with their tutors, her mother attended fashion shows and shopped like there was no tomorrow.

Perhaps her mother had been onto something, since most of her father's fortune died when he did. Penny Jameson d'Oro no longer took shopping trips abroad. A fact for which she firmly blamed Francesca.

"I don't believe I've ever seen a street so wide," she said in a rush, pushing away the ugly, depress-ing thoughts that came whenever she thought of her mother.

"No, you are not likely to do so either. This is the

Avenida 9 de Julio; it is the widest street in the world. There are twelve lanes of traffic."

"Fast traffic." Cars zipped along at Autobahn speed— or so it seemed.

"*Sí*, people are in a hurry to get where they are going."

"And where are we going? Is it much farther?" As much as she feared reaching their final destination, she also wanted to collapse on a bed and sleep for the next twelve hours.

"We are nearly there," he said. "My family home is in Recoleta."

"I thought we were in Buenos Aires. Have we left it behind?" It was entirely possible, she supposed. As tired as she was, they could have driven to another city and she wouldn't have really noticed.

"Recoleta is a *barrio*, a neighborhood."

"Did you grow up there?"

The corners of his mouth tightened, the scar whitening. "No. When my parents were taken, I was sent to live with relatives."

"Taken?" she said, zeroing in on that single word. Not *died*, not *left*, not *went away and never came back*. *Taken*.

"It is a long story, Francesca, and more appropriate for another night. Suffice it to say I have reclaimed the family home and moved back into it."

The car turned, and soon they were cruising along an avenue lined with ornate buildings that looked as if they'd been plucked from the streets of Paris and set down here. The architecture was ornate, beautiful, and decidedly French rather than Spanish. Soon they came to an iron gate that swung open on a mechanical

hinge, then passed through and halted before an imposing white façade.

A lush collection of palm trees and flowering grasses
grew in the little courtyard near the entrance. A man
in a uniform hurried out to greet them as they stepped
from the car.

"Señor Navarre, bienvenido."

"Thank you, Miguel. It's good to be home again."

A phalanx of men moved to the rear of the car and
began removing luggage. Marcos ushered Francesca
inside a grand entry hall with a giant crystal chandelier,
black and white marble floor tiles set on the diagonal,
and a huge Venetian mirror on one wall.

The elegance made her stomach flip. She hadn't been
inside surroundings such as these in years. The weight
of expectation threatened to crush her. Already she felt
the walls closing in. She'd left deportment behind, left
luxury and the expectation that went with it in the past.
This place made her feel small, insignificant.

How could she do this now? How could she survive it? She would make mistakes, would fail where
she should not. She wasn't cut out for this life, couldn't
possibly masquerade as his wife for a single day, much
less three—or six—months.

Marcos grasped her hand. Francesca uttered a little
cry of surprise, then shivered when he lifted her hand to
his lips and placed a kiss on the tender skin of her wrist.
They'd spent the last several hours barely speaking to
each other, and now this. It disconcerted her, flustered
her.

What was he up to?

He gazed down at her, his expression a mixture of
heat and hatred. It confused her, but not as much as his

touch did. Why did she react? Why did she feel as if every cell of her body was straining toward him, wanting more?

"Until morning, *mi amor.* Juanita will show you to your room."

A young woman in a starched uniform stood nearby. She curtsied when Francesca looked over at her. Francesca gave her a weary smile, hoping she didn't look too wild eyed, before turning back to Marcos.

"Please don't call me that," she said in a low voice. She had to keep a distance between them, had to keep him from addling her with his sleek words and expert touch. She was still far too vulnerable to him, and it shocked her. She'd thought she'd left that girl in the past.

One dark eyebrow arched. "You do not like it? You would prefer *Frankie* now?"

Francesca pulled her hand away the instant his grip lightened. "No, of course not. But I don't want you calling me *your love* either. We both know I am not."

"*Sí,* we do indeed. And yet there is an appearance to maintain. We are marrying soon."

Francesca's heart skipped a beat. Dear God, what had she agreed to? She hadn't truly realized it until she'd walked into this…this *palace.*

Jacques, she told herself, she was doing it for Jacques.

"There's no reason to pretend we care for one another," she replied. Getting through the next few months would be hard enough. Pretending to feel things for this man was beyond her ability. She'd built a wall after he'd abandoned her so brutally; she didn't want to breach it ever again.

His expression grew hard. "There is every reason,

Francesca. As my wife, there will be many public duties you must perform. I won't have my reputation suffer simply because you are too spoiled to play the part you've agreed to. While you are here, while we are married, you will be *happy* to be my wife. *Comprendes?*"

Public duties. She would never pull it off. They'd know she was a fraud the instant she entered the room. And Marcos would not help Jacques.

She swayed on her feet before she could lock her knees. It was simply weariness and shock—fear, perhaps—that nearly made her fall. Marcos caught her, sweeping her into his arms and against his chest.

"No, please, it's all right," she managed. "Put me down."

He said something in Spanish, something low and dark, then barked out an order to the room in general before striding toward the curving staircase.

"I'm just tired," she said, hot embarrassment—and something else that contained heat—washing over her at the contact with his body.

She hadn't been this close to him when they were married, hadn't felt the power of his arms around her. But oh how she'd wanted to. How she'd dreamed of him sweeping her up just like this and carrying her into their bedroom while she laid her head against his shoulder and breathed in the wonderful scent of his aftershave.

Then he would lower her to the bed, whispering those words *mi amor*, before stripping her and kissing her and making love to her all night long.

But that was when she'd been eighteen. Now it was a nightmare to be so close to him. And to feel things she hadn't felt for a man in almost four years.

He strode up the steps and down a long hall while she

clung to him. The maid, Juanita, hurried past him at a run and threw open a door. Marcos carried Francesca inside and over to a low settee that stood beneath a tall window.

She closed her eyes as he set her down, both grateful and disappointed that he was no longer touching her.

When she opened them, Marcos stared down at her. "If you are pregnant with your lover's child, you had better tell me now."

She gaped at him, a sharp pain slashing into her heart. She felt like screaming, or laughing, or maybe even crying at the irony of the accusation, but she would do none of those things. She simply bit down on her lip and shook her head. "I'm not," she finally managed to force out. "I'm exhausted. I need sleep, not an inquisition."

"Perhaps you would not mind having blood drawn then. To verify."

Oh how she hated him in that moment. She had half a mind to tell him no, to ask if he'd care to take other medical tests, but she decided it wasn't worth the effort. It was a terrible invasion of her privacy, not to mention a hot dagger in her soul, but she only had to think of Jacques in a hospital, getting the best care money could buy.

"Draw all the blood you like. I have nothing to hide."

"You are shaking," he said, his brows drawing down as he studied her.

"I'll stop if you go away."

The tightness at the edges of his sensual mouth was back. The scar was white, and she knew she must have angered him.

Too bad, because he'd angered her. And hurt her.

"Please just go, Marcos," she said, holding onto the edges of her composure by a thread. "I don't want you here."

He towered over her, six-foot four-inches of angry Latin male. "You may spend this evening alone, remembering your lover, but tomorrow we begin to act like a happy couple. *Buenas noches, señorita. Hasta mañana.*"

Before she could say a word in reply, he strode out of the door and closed it behind him. The maid arrived a few moments later and drew her a hot bath in spite of her protestations that she could do it herself.

She hadn't planned to take a bath, yet she discovered when she sank into the fragrant water that she welcomed the chance to scrub away the chill that hadn't left her since Marcos had asked if she was pregnant.

Francesca closed her eyes as she leaned back on the bath pillow Juanita had provided. Damn him!

He was arrogant and proud, far more so than she remembered. She used to be in love with him, but it was a naïve, girlish love. The woman in her couldn't love a man like that.

She could want him, unfortunately, but she could never love him. Francesca tried to forget the way her body reacted when he'd held her. She'd melted, in spite of her anger. She'd wanted, for those few minutes he carried her, to be in his arms naked. To wrap her legs around his waist and feel the power of his body moving inside hers.

Oh God.

It was shocking to feel physical desire when she'd thought she would never do so again.

Francesca ran cold water into the bath to cool her heated imaginings, then climbed from the tub and dried off before she could start thinking of him again. She picked up the grey silk pajamas Juanita had left out for her. Briefly, she considered digging into the suitcase she'd hastily packed in search of her favorite cotton T-shirt, but the silk felt cool and soft, and it was so much easier to put them on than to search through her things for something familiar.

In spite of her exhaustion, she lay awake for what seemed like hours, listening to the strange sounds of a strange house and wishing she were back home in her tiny loft. She was just drifting off when a noise woke her.

A harsh cry. She bolted up in bed, her heart pounding. Had she imagined it?

But no, there it was again. A man's voice, hard and harsh and full of anguish. She shoved the covers off and padded toward the door. Could no one else hear him? Should she get someone? What was going on?

Francesca pulled open the door and peered into the hallway. There was nothing there, nothing but silence and moonlight. Another sound came from behind the door across the hall and her pulse shot higher.

Slowly, she crept toward the entry, arguing with herself the whole way. Whoever was behind that door needed help, didn't he? But maybe he didn't. Maybe he would be angry with her for intruding.

She reached for the handle, twisted it. But the door was locked. The voice cried out again and any reservations she had evaporated. He sounded as if he was in pain. She pounded on the door, calling out to whoever was inside.

The noise stopped abruptly. Another minute and the door was wrenched open. Marcos stood in the opening, a sweat-soaked T-shirt clinging to his skin.

Francesca took a step backwards at the wild look in his eyes. "I heard something," she said. "I-I—"

"You are quite safe here," he said harshly. "You need not worry about intruders."

She blinked. Was he deliberately misunderstanding her?

"I thought someone was hurt."

"No one is hurt." He looked weary for a moment, but then the hard façade was back and he seemed angry. "Go back to bed."

The door slammed in her face. Francesca stood there in the silent hallway, wondering if she'd imagined the entire thing, wondering if she should knock again and make sure he was all right.

Finally, she returned to her room. It was a long time before she drifted into a restless sleep.

Marcos lay on the floor, unwilling to return to the soaked sheets of his bed. He could call someone to change them, but he knew from experience that he would sleep just as well on the floor as on the bed. The hard floor reminded him of what it was like to sleep in the jungle. Or on the street.

He hadn't had nightmares this bad in quite some time. Lately, however, he seemed to experience them more frequently. Being cuffed to the bed in the hotel hadn't helped, even if it had been of relatively short duration in comparison to his time in the enemy's prison.

Regardless, the experience brought back the flood of

memories and turned him once more into the kind of animal whose sole focus was survival.

He thought of Francesca standing in the hallway, of her wide eyes and tousled hair, and felt a mixture of hate and desire so strong it frightened him. When he'd jerked the door open, he'd wanted to haul her inside, strip her naked, and lose himself in her body for a few hours. It had taken all his willpower not to do so.

He'd also wanted to lash out, to bind her to him and make her pay for dredging up the memories of his past. Not for the first time, he wondered if bringing her here had been a mistake. Perhaps he should have simply taken the jewel and returned to Argentina. But she was here now, and he was committed to the course of action he'd chosen.

Marcos would allow nothing—and no one—to ruin all he'd worked for. And he would survive his nightmares. He always did.

"Spanish lessons? Is this necessary?" Francesca blinked at the calendar Marcos had handed to her. It was filled with appointments. Spanish lessons, culture lessons, tango lessons, shopping, hair, nails...

It was already late morning. After the night she'd had, she'd slept in far longer than usual. She'd showered and dressed in a pale blue peasant blouse and white jeans, one of the best outfits she owned these days. She'd wondered if Marcos would be here, or if he would be gone to an office for the day. She'd hoped he would be gone, because she didn't know what to say to him after last night.

She still didn't.

Marcos looked implacable as she met his gaze once

more. He also looked delicious, in spite of the restless night he must have had. His dark good looks were only enhanced by the white shirt and casual chinos he'd selected today. His shirtsleeves were rolled loosely, revealing his forearms. Powerful forearms.

One of them bore a crude tattoo of what she thought might be crossed swords. The ink bled at the edges, blurring the design. She didn't remember that from eight years ago, but had she ever seen him in short sleeves?

Possibly not.

"You do not speak Spanish," he said. "It is necessary."

Francesca tore her gaze from his tattoo. "But I'm not going to be here very long, so why bother?"

Marcos shrugged. "Why bother doing anything, Francesca? Why get up in the morning to watch a sunrise, why eat ice cream, why read a book, why take a walk on the beach? Because they are worth doing, that's why. Just as learning Spanish, for as long as you are here, is worth doing. Think of it as an adventure."

"I don't like adventures," she replied. "I like everything the way I expect it to be, and I like my life the way it is. *Was*."

"Yes, I seem to remember you were always a scared little rabbit."

Embarrassment wrapped a hand around her throat and squeezed. "I was shy."

He snorted in disbelief. "That's an old excuse. Don't try to hide behind it."

"I'm not hiding behind anything. And I know what I want. Don't try to analyze me, Marcos."

He shoved his hands in his pockets, his sleeve drop-

ping to cover the tattoo when he did so. "It is an obser-
vation, not an analysis."

"So why do you have that tattoo?" she asked. Anything to deflect the conversation away from herself.
Away from her shortcomings.

He lifted his arm until the sleeve fell away. She stared
at the green-blue ink, suddenly unsure she wanted the
answer. Especially if it had anything to do with the
sounds he had made last night.

"I did not choose it," he said. "But it was necessary.
Necessary to prove I was loyal."

"Loyal to what?"

His eyes burned into hers. "You don't want to
know."

She swallowed. "Maybe I do. Does it have anything
to do with your nightmares?"

If she'd expected a reaction, she didn't get it. Instead,
he closed the distance between them, reached out to tilt
her chin up with a finger. "Nice try, *querida*. But it won't
work. Your first Spanish lesson is in an hour."

Her skin sizzled where he touched. "Do you keep
it to remind you of something? Because they can laser
those off, you know."

His finger dropped away, his gaze shuttering. "It is
my own business, Francesca."

She stared at him for a moment before clearing her
throat and gazing at the calendar again. "Surely I don't
need to learn the tango."

"It is the national dance of Argentina."

"And two-stepping to country music is rather popular
in America. I don't remember you attempting to learn
this when we married before."

"The two-step is hardly a national dance, and you

are only half-American." His brow furrowed. "Come to think of it, I never saw you dance in all the months I knew you."

"I don't like to dance."

It wasn't true, but she'd always seemed to have two left feet when she'd gone to ballet classes. Livia flourished while Francesca stumbled. She'd been too fat to get her leg up on the bar, a fact which her mother took so seriously she ordered Francesca be fed a diet of lean chicken, fruit and rice until she could achieve the feat. It took two months, but she had got her foot on that bar. And she'd kept it there, even if she was graceless in every other way.

Marcos raked a hand through his hair. "Then you will learn. It is expected that my wife will be able to tango."

His wife. The words gave her chills. And another feeling she didn't dare analyze. "I don't seem to remember this was a requirement before. And I've yet to see a contract, so this talk of what I must do as your wife is rather moot at the moment."

"The contract will arrive soon. And *I* don't seem to remember having much of a say in anything to do with our marriage before." The look he gave her was loaded with suppressed fury.

Her ears burned hot. She'd been too young and starstruck to question her good fortune when they'd married. She'd thought it was real, fool that she was. "That's not my fault."

"Isn't it? I was nice to you, and you thought that gave you the right to have me for your own." He swore in Spanish. "You sent your daddy to buy me like I was a prized pony, Francesca. Don't pretend otherwise."

Sudden fury burned through her bones, leaving hot ash in its wake. She was tired of taking the blame for their sham of a marriage and the consequences it had wrought on so many lives. Suspicion went both ways, whether he realized it or not.

"*Why* were you nice to me, Marcos? Did you hope my father would agree to let you marry me? That the Corazón del Diablo would be yours because I was young and stupid and loved you blindly?"

He took a step toward her. "How dare you try to turn this around? *You* were spoiled, selfish, a d'Oro female accustomed to getting what she wanted. And you wanted me. Nothing could have stopped you—and I was fool enough to fall for your shy and innocent act."

He thought she was like her mother? Like Livia? She would laugh if it didn't hurt so much. He'd never known her at all. Everything she'd believed about him had been a lie. She'd known it for a long time now, but to have to relive it opened old wounds.

Francesca jabbed a finger into his chest. "There was no reason for a man like you to be nice to me. I was nothing, *less* than nothing to you. I wasn't capable of attracting a busboy's attention, let alone yours, so you were only nice to me for one reason. You *wanted* me to fall for you. It was part of your plan all along."

He made a sound in his throat very like a growl. "You did not possess the necklace when I first met you. Your father had it, though he would not admit it. And I was nice to you *then,* before you ever possessed it, because I felt sorry for you."

Francesca drew in a sharp breath. Of course she'd known he'd felt sorry for her. Of course.

So why did it hurt to hear him say it?

Because he'd ruined the fantasy, the slim hope she'd harbored that it was something about her, something he saw that no one else did. He felt sorry for her, nothing more. She turned away from him, more affected by the admission than she cared to admit. It was years ago. Over and done with. Why did it matter? She'd certainly dealt with far worse blows to her ego since then.

Far worse.

She drew in a fortifying breath and turned back to him. Her lip trembled; she bit down on it. "There was a lot to feel sorry for, wasn't there? Forty extra pounds of it."

His face was a thundercloud. "Weight is not important."

She laughed. "Oh yes, of course it's not. That woman in your hotel suite didn't have an ounce of extra fat, nor have the models and actresses you are usually photographed with. Well, rest assured Marcos, I will endeavor not to embarrass you by asking for second helpings at the dinner table."

"A woman's weight is only important to her," he said. "If she is comfortable in her skin, then weight is unimportant."

"God you're a hypocrite." Anger rolled through her in a fresh wave. "You never even kissed me. We were married and you never kissed me properly because I disgusted you."

"I never kissed you because I was angry." He took a step closer, looming over her. "I'm still angry. But I should have kissed you. I should have taken everything you offered."

Francesca took a step backward, her breath catching at the look in his eyes. She'd challenged him—and he wasn't about to back down. "I don't know what you're up to, but don't you dare kiss me now. It's too late for that."

"It's never too late," he said, yanking her close. Before she could process the million and one sensations of finding herself pressed to him so intimately, he dipped his head and claimed her mouth for his own.

CHAPTER FOUR

FRANCESCA TRIED TO pull out of his grip, but it was like trying to bend an iron bar. Her heart pounded so hard she thought surely he could feel it in his bones. One broad hand rested against the small of her spine, pressing her into his hard body. The other threaded into her hair, angling her head back to give him better access.

His tongue plunged between her lips. She'd meant to rebuff him. Meant to shove him away and refuse to engage in the kiss.

But being kissed by Marcos Navarre was a sensual bombardment. She could hardly remember her name, much less the fact that she was supposed to resist.

The kiss was thrilling. Arousing. Delicious.

She'd dreamed of kissing him when she was a girl. Dreamed of how sweet and tender it would be. Of how he would take her hand, look deeply into her eyes as he pulled her closer. Of how his head would dip, his eyes closing gently while her heart slammed into her ribs and she stretched up to meet him.

This kiss, however, was not sweet or tender. It was raw, untamed, and threatened to incinerate her from the inside out.

This was the kind of kiss a man gave a woman. The kind of kiss that said *I want you* and *You are mine*.

But why? Why would he kiss *her* like this? She wasn't the sort of woman he preferred, wasn't soft and gorgeous and oozing femininity. She'd desperately wanted to be when she was eighteen, yet she'd always known deep inside that he was not attracted to her. He could not be so now, either. It was a ploy, a means of subduing her.

And, God help her, it was working.

She'd pressed her hands to his chest to push him away, but now they lay against the soft cotton of his shirt, useless. Her body was softening in places she'd thought long dead. Melting. Liquefying.

When was the last time she'd felt sexual desire?

Over four years ago.

She'd had a few lovers over the years, and she'd enjoyed sex well enough. But after Robert abandoned her, after her baby was taken from her so tragically, she'd lost all desire for a man.

Until now.

Why, dear God, did it have to be this man?

Marcos's hand skimmed up her side, over the swell of her breast. She couldn't stop the little moan that escaped her when his thumb brushed her nipple. *So long since she'd felt pleasure…*

She leaned into him, on the verge of losing herself in his heat and maleness. Just once. Just this once, she wanted to feel alive again…

But what was she doing? If she allowed this, she was no different than the naïve girl she used to be, the girl who would have done *anything* to be what he desired. That girl was dead and buried, along with her innocent belief in unconditional love and all-consuming passion.

Francesca gripped his wrists, intending to push his hands away. But his body went rigid. He broke the kiss abruptly, jerking his arms from her hold so viciously that her fingers stung where he'd ripped her grip apart.

He was breathing hard, that haunted, wild look in his eyes again. The same look as last night.

"Marcos, what's wrong?"

He shook his head, shoved a hand through his hair as he put distance between them. "It's nothing. Forget it."

"It didn't feel like nothing." Was it because he'd realized who he was kissing? That he could no longer keep his disgust under control? She wrapped her arms around her chilled body. Of course that was it. She repulsed him.

And suddenly that angered her, especially after the way she'd responded to him. He made her feel things she'd thought forgotten—and she made him feel disgust.

"I told you not to kiss me. If you knew you would find the experience so repulsive, you shouldn't have done it."

"And I told you to forget it," he growled.

"I've been trying to forget for the past eight years," she said. "I was doing a pretty good job of it until you dragged me here."

He looked utterly furious. "Had you not tried to steal the Corazón del Diablo, you wouldn't be here. Do not blame me for your actions."

"You stole it first, Marcos. Or have you forgotten?"

"You have no idea what you are talking about,

Francesca," he bit out. "That gem was stolen from my family. It was never yours to begin with."

She clenched her fists at her side. "If you're saying that my father stole it—"

"No, my uncle did. And he used it to entice your father into business with him. But it wasn't his to give."

She stared at him, momentarily at a loss for words. She'd never heard this much of the story before. She'd only known that the Corazón del Diablo had once been in the Navarre family. She'd thought her father had bought it, like he'd bought so many other things he'd wanted. And when she'd married a Navarre, she'd thought he would be happy if she placed the necklace in his hands, if it became a symbol of their union. She hadn't expected him to take the jewel and discard her. The memory of her naïveté still stung.

"Why should I believe you?"

"I don't care if you believe me or not. This is the truth, and the jewel is mine. By right, by birth, by long-standing tradition. It is not and never has been yours."

She didn't want to believe him—and yet she remembered that her father had refused to use the courts to try and recover the necklace. She hadn't understood at the time. Nor had her mother, who'd raged and cried and blamed Francesca for their misfortune.

And then...

"My father shot himself over it," she said numbly. "His business interests were tangled with Navarre Industries, and when your uncle went down, he did too. Without the necklace, there was no way to save the business."

His expression changed. "I know, and I'm sorry for that, Francesca."

She dashed away a tear. "Yes, well, that helps so much." He couldn't miss the sarcasm in her voice—and she didn't care. Let him know what his selfishness had cost. What it still cost. She'd never been particularly close to her mother, but at least she'd had a mother. Now, she no longer had that relationship. Nor did she have one with her sister, who followed their mother's lead in everything.

Francesca had been alone since the moment her dad had pulled the trigger. Which he never would have done had she not been so blinded by love that she'd given the Corazón del Diablo to this man. This devil.

"It was an unfortunate tragedy," he said, "but the jewel would not have saved him. He would not have been able to sell it, Francesca. Legally, he had no right."

She hated thinking about that time, hated thinking about the desperation and despair her father must have felt in those moments before he'd pulled the trigger. How different would it have been if she'd never married Marcos? But, if he was right, when the business went sour, her father still would have been broke. The Corazón del Diablo would have been about as useful as a paperweight.

"Then why didn't you just take us to court over it? If your claim was so great, why didn't you get a lawyer and sue?"

"Because I couldn't afford it," he said. "I hoped your father would do the right thing and return it to me. Instead, he gave it to you and told me the only way to get it was to marry you."

She couldn't help the bubble of hysterical laughter that erupted from her throat. Her poor, misguided father.

Always trying to make her happy, to even out the inequality between her and Livia. "Oh yes, and you had no trouble doing that, did you? Marry the ugly duckling and seduce the necklace away. Except you forgot the seduction part."

"You weren't ugly," he said, his voice low and hard. "And you know it. Eight years later, and still you try to use that act on me. It does you no credit, Francesca, not now. You are a beautiful woman, not an awkward girl."

She gaped at him, her heart thudding for an entirely different reason now. But she would not fall for his smooth words, not ever again. He would say anything to make this process as smooth as possible for himself.

"Don't you dare say those things to me, not when you don't mean them. I'm here, and you have the stone. I've also agreed to marry you so you can rest easy at night that a collection of damn *rocks* is all yours. So save the sweet talk for your mistresses."

Marcos gave a snort of disgust as he picked up a briefcase from a chair. "*Dios*, why bother? I have work to do. I'll send someone for you when the contract arrives."

Francesca wanted to throw something at his departing back, but the only thing in her hand was the calendar. And that simply floated to the floor with an impotent sigh.

The contract was every bit as humiliating a document as she'd supposed it would be. It was thick, typed on expensive paper, and bound in a slim leather cover. Francesca read it carefully while Marcos's lawyers explained the clauses in detail.

They were in his office, a surprisingly bright room

with a mahogany desk, built-in bookshelves, and sleek contemporary furniture. She sat on one of the low couches, a lawyer beside her, while Marcos leaned against the wall, hands shoved in his pockets, resembling nothing so much as a dark cloud as he frowned over the procedure.

It was all spelled out in excruciating detail, as she'd known it would be. Marcos had not reached the pinnacle of success he currently enjoyed by leaving anything to chance. They would marry for a period of at least three months, possibly more. She would relinquish, on behalf of her family, all further claims on the Corazón del Diablo forever.

And good riddance, she thought. The fiery stone at the heart of the necklace truly was the devil's heart. It had caused her nothing but trouble from the moment she'd possessed it. She had no wish to do so ever again.

Money. Her heart stammered over the clause about money. She had to work to keep her eyes on the page instead of looking up at Marcos. Did he expect her to be grateful? Or perhaps he expected a protest that it wasn't enough.

At the conclusion of their marriage, he would endow her with ten million dollars. It was a small sum to him, she knew, and yet it was enough to keep Jacques comfortable for the rest of his life. No doubt Marcos did it to keep her from making larger claims on his fortune, but to her it was an incredible sum after these last several years.

She hadn't expected it, and she certainly didn't want it. But she had to take it for Jacques's sake. Indeed, if not for Jacques and the way this money would enable her to take care of him, she would refuse to accept even a dime from Marcos Navarre.

She flipped the page, scanning for the most important part. When she found it, relief surged through her. Jacques's medical expenses were covered one hundred percent, no matter the cost. Francesca's eyes flooded with tears. She blinked them back, scanning the legalese for a trick or a condition.

There was none, other than the agreement to wed and be Marcos's hostess, bedmate, and partner for the duration of the marriage. Her heart thumped at that, but it was the price she had to pay to take care of Jacques. She would not fail him.

"Give me a pen," she said, cutting off the man on her right in mid-explanation. He reached into his suit jacket, but Marcos was there first, handing her an expensive, custom-made pen. She touched it to the paper and smoothly signed her name.

Just like signing a deal with the devil.

Marcos took the folder, laid it on the desk and signed, then closed it and handed it to the waiting lawyers. The two men departed, and they were alone. Humiliation was a strong brew in her veins, but it was the price she had to pay—and at least it would be of short duration in the scheme of things.

"I'm glad that's over," she said, tilting her chin up. "It was clever of you to put that part in about the marriage being consummated. No one will ever question the validity of it now."

Marcos studied her with that peculiar mixture of heat and hate she was accustomed to. Though perhaps there was less hate this time? But, no, surely she only imagined it.

"And what if I intend to follow the contract to the letter?" he said, his voice as smooth and silky as polished glass.

Francesca managed to shrug, though her heart sped up at the thought. "Then I suppose I agreed to it."

"*Sí*, you did indeed."

She pushed to her feet. She wanted to get away from him, wanted to go into another room and try to forget the way he made her heart pound simply by looking at her. "If you are finished with me, I believe I have a tango lesson to attend."

"Not this afternoon. We have another matter to attend to."

"And what is so important it takes precedence over the tango?" she asked as sarcastically as possible.

His mouth curved in a smile. An impossibly devilish smile. Her sense of foreboding rocketed into high alert.

"Our wedding, *mi amor*."

CHAPTER FIVE

Marcos supposed he should be offended, and yet he found that he was mostly amused. He should still be angry, but everything was going his way and that pleased him.

Francesca clearly did not feel the same. She flashed him a look of pure loathing as he helped her from the limousine that had taken them to the Civil Registry Office. It was rather like a kitten trying to imitate a tiger. She simply couldn't pull it off, no matter how she tried.

And he found it amusing, though he wasn't quite certain why.

She smoothed the fabric of the peach silk dress she wore. When she'd come down the stairs in this garment that set off the tawny gold of her hair, he'd been glad she hadn't chosen to wear white. This color suited her so much more appropriately than white or cream would have done. The only problem was in the cut of the dress. It was shapeless, as if she feared to show her curves. He would need to make sure something was done about that, he decided.

"I'm surprised you didn't wear black," he murmured as she accepted his arm and they turned to walk into the building.

"I wanted to, but I somehow failed to pack a black dress in the fifteen minutes you gave me back in New York."

Marcos chuckled. "So prickly on your wedding day."

She did not join in his amusement. "It didn't work out the first time, Marcos. I'm not expecting a vastly different experience the second time. And how did you manage this so quickly? I had read there are no quickie marriages in Argentina."

"I have influence, *querida*. Money is a powerful motivator."

"Lucky me."

"Lucky you indeed," he said. "If not for my money, your Jacques would not be receiving the treatment he so badly needs."

Marcos still hadn't puzzled out why the old man meant so much to her. He'd asked for a report on her life since he'd last seen her on their wedding night eight years ago, but the information he'd received was sketchy. Shortly after her father had committed suicide, she'd left home for good. She'd gone to work for Jacques Fortier in his small jewelry shop and led an unremarkable life.

A life quite different from how she'd grown up. It made no sense to him, but he'd made enough odd choices of his own over the course of his thirty-four years not to question too deeply why others did the same.

Now she stopped inside the door and turned to him. Her hazel eyes were golden today, shining with moisture. Surprise rocked him. She was on the verge of tears? But for what? Jacques Fortier? Or the inevitability of this marriage?

"I am grateful for your help, Marcos. For Jacques. In

spite of your reasons, or this marriage, or anything else, I am grateful you've gotten the best treatment for him. It's more than I'd hoped, truly." She laughed, the sound nearly breaking on a sob. She pinched the bridge of her nose. "God, I wasn't going to do this. Not today."

The sound was so plaintive he felt his heart constrict in sympathy. He skimmed a knuckle along her cheek because he could not stifle the impulse to do so. "I am not as cruel as you believe me to be, Francesca. No one should die because they cannot afford medical treatment. Jacques is lucky to have you fighting for him."

"But if I hadn't taken the Corazón del Diablo, we wouldn't be here and—"

"These things happen for mysterious reasons." He'd learned that particular truth on the streets and in the jungle. Sometimes there was no explanation for why things occurred as they did. Why good people suffered. Why children died.

Dios. There were things he didn't want to remember either, not now.

She looked up at him. "Why do you have to be nice?"

Nice? He hadn't quite thought of it that way, but if she did, he wouldn't disabuse her of the notion. "I can cease this niceness if it pleases you."

"Oh no," she said, shaking her head slightly. "I want to see how long you can keep it up."

"All night if necessary."

She dropped her gaze, as if she were uncomfortable suddenly.

He tilted her chin up, forced her to look at him. "There is no need to pretend with me, Francesca."

Tears glittered on her lashes like diamonds. He had to stifle the urge to kiss them away.

"I'm not pretending anything, Marcos."

"Do you really expect me to believe you aren't aware of how lovely you are?"

Her eyes widened, her smooth skin flushing pink. For the first time, he began to wonder if he was wrong, if she truly did believe she was still the awkward girl she used to be. Or maybe she was just manipulating him, trying to make him feel sympathy.

"Don't," she managed, her voice thready.

"As you wish, *mi amor*." He dropped his hand away and she took a deep breath. Collected herself once more.

She'd grown tough in a way she'd not been when he'd first known her. It made him wonder what, besides her father's tragic death and her family's loss of status, had happened to make her this way.

Perhaps it was nothing. Perhaps she'd simply grown cynical with the passage of years.

"Will anyone from your family be here?" she asked.

"No. Magdalena and her husband are staying at their winery in Mendoza. They could not get away."

"Magdalena is your sister, right?"

"*Sí*, she is my younger sister. She has just had her third child and could not get away."

Francesca's eyes dropped and she swallowed. Her knuckles, he noticed, were white where she clasped her hands together. "I see."

"You will meet her soon enough. We must go to Mendoza for a visit now that the baby is here."

If he'd thought that statement would soothe her, he was surprised to see that it seemed to have the opposite effect. She seemed agitated. And she did everything in her power not to look at him again. Her throat worked, as if she were swallowing back tears.

"You are afraid to meet my sister?" he asked.

She looked up again. "No, not at all. But what's the point, Marcos? This marriage will be over soon. Why introduce me to your family, make them think this is real when we both know it's not?"

"It would be odd if I did not, Francesca. Surely you can get through a few hours with them. No one will become so attached to you that they will be devastated once we divorce. It's a simple visit. And Magdalena will be far more focused on her new baby than on us, I can assure you."

"Of course," she said, her head dipping, her voice flat and emotionless. "If that's what you want, I suppose I have no choice but to comply."

She was married. Again. The ritual had been quick, sterile. Say a few words, repeat in the appropriate places, and then Marcos slipped a ring on her finger and brushed his lips against her cheek.

The office staff offered their congratulations before Marcos ushered her from the building and back into the limousine.

Francesca stared at the three-carat rock on her finger and felt numb. It wasn't as large as she'd expected, yet it was the perfect size for her. She wouldn't have wanted anything bigger, and though Marcos hadn't asked her opinion, he'd still managed to pick the ideal ring for her.

Odd to think it wasn't real, this marriage. Or that the perfect ring was only temporary. A Band-Aid to shield a wound, nothing more.

The stone shot fire as the light reflected off its facets. The platinum band was inset with diamonds. The matching wedding band was also diamond-encrusted. Though Francesca wouldn't tell a soul, she loved beautiful things. Always had, which is why her inability to please her mother with her looks and minimal grace had hurt so much. Francesca had wanted the beautiful clothes that Livia wore so elegantly. She'd wanted the jewelry, the poise, and the grace to match.

Though she was older and far wiser now, she still felt like the awkward teenager beside Marcos's smooth elegance. She hadn't worried over her looks in years, had thought they were perfectly adequate for the life she led with Jacques—but Marcos's arrival in her life had turned everything upside down again. He'd said she was lovely. But did he really mean it?

She shoved the thought aside brutally. She did not care what Marcos Navarre thought of her. Not any longer. The girl who'd desperately wanted his approval was buried in the past.

Marcos sat beside her now, his voice musical in her ears as he conducted business on his cell phone while they rode back to his home in Recoleta. *Their home.*

No, as beautiful as the French-style mansion was, it would never be her home. She was a temporary resident only, and she would not grow attached to the beauty of the place, the serenity of the cool courtyards with their fountains and thick foliage. She had a home in New York, with Jacques, and she would return to it as soon as Marcos let her go.

She prayed it would be sooner rather than later, but she knew Marcos was determined to fulfill some agenda that only he knew. And so long as he held the keys to Jacques's treatment, she would remain.

The visit to his sister would surely test her in ways she dreaded. She'd not been around babies since she'd lost her own. She refused to hold them, to play with them, to spend time with them. It wasn't that she didn't love babies; it was simply that being around them made her ache for what could never be.

Once, long ago, she'd thought Marcos would be the father of her children. But even if they'd married for love this time, that was impossible.

How would she survive being around a woman with a newborn?

One day at a time, Francesca.

It's how life was lived, how she'd survived the worst of the dark days in her past. One damn day at a time.

"We are attending a reception tonight," Marcos said smoothly as he tucked his phone away.

Francesca struggled to concentrate on what he was saying. She felt like she was being ripped apart inside, and he was informing her about a social event?

God help her.

"You will wear the Corazón del Diablo," he continued.

"I'd rather not."

His expression grew chilly. "Reneging already, Francesca?"

"The necklace is yours, Marcos. I see little point in asking me to wear it."

The idea of donning the necklace now, after all it had cost her, seemed completely foreign. And unnecessary. She had no doubt he knew it. He simply wanted to prove his mastery of her.

"I don't believe I asked," he said, his voice as smooth as aged whiskey. "You will wear it because it is mine, because you are mine."

Francesca drew herself up, her emotions whipping higher. "You don't own me, Marcos. You bought my cooperation, not me."

"You are still very foolish, aren't you?" he said softly.

Francesca felt the burn of anger—and the heat of embarrassment—skating over her body in twin spirals.

Yet she wouldn't back down. He might own her cooperation, might own her promise to fulfill her end of the bargain. But she was adamant that he did not own her. No man did. If she'd learned anything in the past few years, it was that her life was her own.

For better or worse.

"I don't think so, no. Because I don't believe for an instant you would withdraw medical treatment from Jacques, not after what you said to me earlier. Unless it was a lie? Unless you only said what you thought I wanted to hear?"

He gazed at her steadily, his face a mask of detachment. Her heart thundered. Had she guessed wrong? Would he withdraw his financial support? Would he let Jacques die?

Had she gambled too much?

Marcos looked so cold, so remote and cruel that she wondered how she'd ever managed to be infatuated with him all those years ago. Why hadn't she sensed that he was so brutal beneath that layer of charm he wore like a blanket?

Why didn't she just wear the damn necklace and keep her mouth shut? Jacques's care meant more than the principle of the thing.

"No," he said, dark eyes flashing with an emotion she didn't understand, "I would not stop his treatment."

She stared at him, her breath shortening at the admission. It was the last thing she'd expected. Marcos Navarre had a human side. A side that cared for more than having things his way.

Francesca bowed her head to hide the strength of her emotional reaction. He didn't need to know how much his statement moved her. But she would give him something in return, would make sure he understood that she intended to honor the agreement. Francesca d'Oro—*Navarre*—did not go back on her word once it was given. She had integrity, no matter what he believed about her.

"If it's important to you, I will wear the Corazón del Diablo."

Disbelief crossed his handsome face. "You just stated you would not. Most adamantly."

Francesca shrugged as if it were nothing, when in fact it was everything. "If you had asked instead of ordered…"

"Why does this Jacques mean so much to you, Francesca?"

She met his gaze evenly. "He cared about me when no one else did. Jacques is the truest friend I have."

"And Gilles? He is your lover?"

Her pulse throbbed in her temples. He didn't deserve an answer to that, not after the blood test he'd forced her to endure, and yet…

"No. And he never has been."

Marcos looked puzzled. "You are a beautiful woman. I wonder why this is not so."

Heat flooded her cheeks. "Don't say things you don't mean, Marcos. I think we know where we stand with each other now, don't you? You married me for the necklace, and I married you for Jacques. Please don't try and prop up what you assume is my wounded vanity. I know I'm not pretty enough for a man like you. And I don't care. I'm me, and that's enough."

He suddenly seemed amused, which only served to irritate her. It wasn't the first time this afternoon and she still didn't understand how he could find humor in any part of this situation. She looked away from him, out of the window at the passing traffic, and tried to concentrate on what it would feel like to be one of those happy tourists strolling along the sidewalk.

"You are quite different from who you once were," he said. "I like that you fight back. Livia would not get the best of you any longer."

Her chest felt like someone had turned a vise. She shoved the feeling away. "You would probably have married *her* back then if not for the necklace."

Marcos laughed. "You underestimate me, *querida*. Your sister has never held any attraction for me."

She whirled around to face him. "Everybody thinks Livia is beautiful. And you can't tell me you don't agree."

"No, she is quite beautiful—or she was eight years ago. And she knew it too." He picked up her hand, traced his finger along the edge of her wedding band while tingles of pleasure radiated up her arm. "But you have something far better than beauty, Francesca. You seem to know who you are. I like that."

A pang of hurt throbbed to life inside her. "It's taken me long enough," she answered.

His eyes were hot as they moved over her face. "I believe you always knew to a certain extent. But yes, something has sharpened your sense of self-awareness. I wish to know what."

She pulled her hand away, folded it against her body. "Shall we trade secrets like gossiping old ladies, Marcos? I'd not have guessed that was your style."

"I think you will tell me before our time is up," he said. He pronounced it with so much certainty that she wanted very much to prove him wrong, to knock him down a few rungs.

"You have far too much confidence in yourself. Not every woman feels the urge to succumb to your charm."

"But you will, *querida*."

"Not a chance," she vowed, though her pulse jumped at the look on his face. Where was that hint of anger he always viewed her with? When it was missing, he reminded her of the old Marcos. The Marcos she'd fallen for because he was nice to her.

He arched one dark eyebrow. His scar made the gesture that much more wicked. "You should not have said that, Francesca."

"Why not? Someone needs to tell you that you aren't irresistible. Besides, have you ever considered it might be your money and not your sparkling personality that makes women fall at your feet?"

Marcos laughed. The sound was rich, uninhibited. She liked it, much to her dismay.

"*Dios*, you are stubborn. But I never could resist a challenge." He leaned in, cupped her jaw in one broad hand, and kissed her before she realized what he was about. "I will enjoy taking you to bed, Francesca. And I will learn all your secrets while we are there, I promise you…"

CHAPTER SIX

THE SUN HAD dropped beneath the horizon over an hour ago. The air coming in through the windows had the bite of early spring, but Francesca did not move to shut the pane. She liked the coolness rushing over her skin. Funny to think that in New York it was fall and the temperature was probably the same.

The heat in her body hadn't diminished since the moment Marcos had kissed her in the car. She'd even stood beneath a cool shower as she'd prepared for tonight. The second she'd gotten out and dried off, the warmth came back.

How could her body refuse to cooperate with her head? Her head knew that Marcos was bad news. Her heart knew it too.

Her body, however, stubbornly wanted to straddle his and fulfill all the fantasies she'd ever had about him.

Francesca studied her reflection in the mirror. Her cheekbones were barely visible in the roundness of her face. She'd lost forty pounds in the last eight years, but still her face was too full. And her hair. God. Her hair was thick and unruly and hadn't been touched by a real stylist in years. Once, she'd had artful blonde highlights and lowlights incorporated into her tresses. Now, they spilled over into natural waves that weren't colored. The blonde wasn't as strong as it had once been, and she was afraid her hair was too brown. Mousy.

The last time she'd had it cut was a year ago. Now, it hung down her back, a long mass of naturally curly spirals that were anything but elegant.

She eyed the black dress hanging nearby with longing. And fear. They'd stopped at a boutique on the way home, Marcos insisting she needed a proper gown for tonight. All her efforts to choose something that flowed over her body without clinging anywhere were thwarted as Marcos instructed the shop girl to dress her in something strapless and form fitting.

When she'd emerged in this dress, her breasts shoved into a push-up bra and her waist corseted so tight she'd never be able to bend over, he'd looked mildly surprised. And interested, in a way she'd have never thought possible. For the first time, she'd begun to believe that maybe he wasn't lying when he said he intended to bed her.

And that scared the hell out of her.

Because Marcos Navarre was still the sexiest man she'd ever known. Even his scar was sexy. The more she was with him, the more she wanted to kiss her way across his jaw, to feel the silvery zigzag beneath her lips before claiming his mouth in a kiss.

Stop.

Thoughts like those were dangerous. She couldn't really be vulnerable to him anymore. It was a long time ago, and she was an entirely different person. She was no longer naïve or innocent, no longer believed the best of people.

With one last look in the mirror, Francesca gathered a shawl and the tiny studded purse that matched the dress, and made her way down to the foyer. Marcos was talking with the majordomo. When he turned to her, the words he'd been speaking seemed to die away.

His gaze raked over her. She stood stiffly, more uncomfortable than she cared to admit in clothes that clung to, instead of masking, her faults. Why hadn't she insisted on the kind of garment she preferred?

Marcos came over and took her hand. When he lifted it to his lips, the shiver that slid down her body wasn't entirely surprising.

The force of it was.

"You look lovely, *mi esposa*."

"So do you," she said, and then cursed herself for the inanity when he chuckled.

But he was lovely. The tuxedo he wore had been custom fit to his powerful body. The shirt was as white and crisp as new snow, the jacket and pants as black as sin. Marcos was tall and imposing. He smelled expensive, and he looked absolutely edible.

Just as he had the night she'd broken into his room and held him at gunpoint.

He hadn't forgotten it either, if his expression was any indication. "Perhaps we can play cops and robbers later, yes?" he rumbled in her ear, his lips brushing her cheek as he withdrew. "Though I hope you won't mind if we only pretend there is a gun."

"I might need a real one," she said. "It helps get me in the mood."

Marcos laughed. The sound surprised her. Sent an answering grin to her lips. God, he was sexy.

She wiped the smile away as quickly as she was able. She did not need to be too friendly with him. She didn't really believe she was in danger of being charmed the way she'd once been, but she could take no chances. It was safer to keep her emotional distance from this man.

"You look far too serious, Francesca," he said. "It's a cocktail reception for a charity I support, not a guillotine we are going to."

"I haven't been to an event like this in years. I don't know what to do anymore." There was no sense hiding it from him; he would know soon enough when she tried to fade into the background.

"It will come back to you," he said with more confidence than she felt. "You've spent the last several years running a shop—how could you not be a natural at interacting with people?"

"That's different."

"I doubt that," he replied. His gaze skimmed over her once more. "You need something else."

He retrieved a long velvet box from the antique foyer table. Francesca's stomach flipped. The Corazón del Diablo. She'd promised to wear it.

But when he opened the box, it wasn't the necklace she'd expected. The jewels sparkling against the deep blue velvet were cool and green. Emeralds of the finest variety. Her practiced eye skimmed over them: they would have cost him a fortune.

Though of course he hadn't bought them for her, she reminded herself. No doubt he'd had them locked away and pulled them out for tonight. But why hadn't he brought the Corazón del Diablo? She gazed up at him as he took the necklace from the box.

"Another time, perhaps," he said. "This is better for tonight."

Francesca hesitated, then turned and held up her hair

while he laid the stones against her collarbone. One egg-shaped emerald dripped into the shadow of her cleavage. The stones were cool in their platinum settings, but she welcomed the shivery feeling.

His fingers brushed the back of her neck, sending prickles of heat up her spine, down her back. She couldn't stop the ripple of a chill.

Marcos's hands settled on her shoulders, pulling her back against him. His lips touched her ear. "You look beautiful, *querida*."

Her silly heart thrummed at the compliment. Her head told her not to believe it.

"I believe this time," he continued, "our wedding night will end as it should."

Marcos watched his new bride as she stood nearby, engaging in polite conversation with a group of ladies. She looked as elegant and polished as any of them, and if she were at all nervous or uncomfortable, she hid it well. Not that he'd expected anything different. She was, after all, a d'Oro female. She'd grown into a woman every bit as elegant as her mother and sister had been.

His eyes skimmed down her lush form. She'd protested over the dress, but she looked fabulous in it. How could she look in the mirror and not know how very enticing she was? And why did she insist on wearing shapeless clothes that hid her curves?

He sipped the glass of wine a waiter handed to him and studied the sleek lines of one leg as the side slit in her dress opened. He had a sudden urge to go to her, but he'd been caught in conversation with an elderly matron. The woman nattered on about something he ignored—until she began to speak of teaching proper manners to orphans.

Nothing else could have so effectively ruined his mood.

"Señora," he cut in suddenly—sharply if the startled look on her face was any indication, "the street children of Buenos Aires need more than etiquette lessons to improve their situation in life." He gave her a clipped bow. "If you will excuse me."

He didn't look back to see how the woman was taking his abrupt exit. *Dios.* One of the things that drove him insane about these kinds of events were the wrong-headed ideas people who'd never suffered from hunger a day in their lives had about the children he so desperately wanted to rescue.

No child should suffer the way he knew that many of them did. Manners were laughable when survival was the goal.

The crowd of elegantly clothed people fell away as he approached his wife. She looked up as Marcos arrived by her side. Her eyes clouded when she saw him. Surprisingly, a sharp pain pierced a spot right below his heart when she looked at him like that.

Like he was evil incarnate, a devil come to steal her soul.

He shoved the pain down deep and held out his hand. "Come, Francesca," he said. "I wish to dance."

He didn't really, but it was as good an excuse as any to hold her. He did not ask himself why he wanted to do so. He simply knew that he did.

"I—" Whatever she was about to say, she changed her mind. "Yes, of course." With a polite word to her companions, she put her hand in his and let him lead her to the dance floor.

The music was soft, slow, flowing around them as he drew her into his arms. She gazed up at him, her smile gone. In its place was a frown.

"Why do you smile for everyone but me?" he asked.

She seemed startled, but she quickly masked it. "That's not true. And I could ask why you look so severe. Did I do something wrong? Have I mixed the fish fork with the dessert spoon again? Seated the priest beside the prostitute?"

She was trying hard to be irreverent, but the catch in her voice surprised him. He worked to force away the dark clouds wreathing his mind. "It's nothing."

"You say that quite a lot, Marcos," she said, her gaze on the center of his chest as they moved.

"Do I?"

"You do. Last night, and this morning when I asked you about the tattoo."

Her eyes were troubled. He looked away, over her head at the sea of dancers. She almost seemed worried about him. He didn't like the way that made him feel. Like he wanted to share things with her, to make her understand.

She intrigued him like no on else, and he wasn't accustomed to it.

"There are things I don't wish to talk about, with you or anyone."

"Sometimes it helps to talk about the things that trouble us."

"Really? Do you intend to share your secrets with me? To tell me why you refuse to believe a man could want you, or why you love this Jacques Fortier so much that you would risk your life for him?"

"I never said a man couldn't want me. I said I wasn't the usual type of woman you were attracted to."

"Ah yes, you know so much about me. I had forgotten. And what about Jacques, Francesca?"

She refused to look up at him as they swirled across the floor. "I told you he took care of me when no one else would. I—I was very ill. He nursed me back to health."

He didn't like the way the thought of her being sick pierced the shield around his heart. "You are well now? It is nothing that will return?"

"I'm recovered, Marcos," she said, meeting his gaze with an evenness that somehow seemed contrived. "No lingering effects."

"You wished to return the favor, yes?"

"Absolutely. Jacques saved me, and I want to save him."

"Then you will be pleased to know I've had an update from the hospital. They believe he is a good candidate for an experimental treatment with a high success rate."

Her eyes filled with tears and she blinked rapidly to keep them from falling. "Really? They think they can save him?"

"There is no guarantee, Francesca. He is very sick. But they have hope."

"Why didn't you tell me earlier?"

"I have only just had the call since we've been here, *querida*. They needed my authorization to begin."

"Your authorization? Gilles is his next of kin."

"Yes, but I am paying. And this particular treatment does not come cheaply."

She fixed her gaze on his chest again. The tip of her nose was red, he noted. She was struggling not to cry. A pang of some emotion he couldn't name stabbed into him. What would it be like to have someone love you so much that your well-being was their first priority?

When she looked up again, her eyes were still shiny. But the tears seemed to be under control for the moment. "Why did you approve it, Marcos?"

He found he couldn't give her an easy answer. Why *had* he approved an expensive, experimental treatment for a man he didn't know when the usual treatments might also work, and at a lesser cost?

"Because it was the right thing to do," he said simply. "And because you would want me to."

He'd spent years being unable to care for anyone but himself. Now that he had money, how could he say that one life was worth less than another? That he could only do so much?

He couldn't.

"You surprise me," she said softly, her tongue darting out to tease her full lower lip.

His body grew hard. In spite of everything, he wanted to possess her. Now, tonight. He was still angry with her, but he was also damned by this need for her. He needed to prove his mastery over her, to exorcise the demons of his past in the body of a woman. This woman. The reprieve wouldn't last, he knew, but at least he could have a few hours of blissful silence in the echoing chambers of his mind.

He stopped moving to the music and drew her closer. She trembled in his arms, her breath catching when she came into contact with his blatant need for her. Her eyes grew wide as she blinked up at him.

"Sí," he whispered, "I want you."

His head dipped toward hers, her mouth parting—in surprise or need he did not know. The moment their lips touched, the moment the electricity sparked and sizzled between them, a woman cleared her throat beside them.

"Señor Navarre, we are ready for your speech now."

Francesca's heart rate refused to return to normal, even after Marcos escorted her back to their table and held out her chair for her. A fine sheen of sweat rose between her breasts, on her limbs, heating her from the inside out. Her feelings were tangled and torn.

She watched her husband mount the podium and stand there, waiting a few moments for everyone to reach their seats before he launched into his speech. A single light shone down on him, making him seem completely alone in this crowded room.

He was so much more than she'd thought, and yet he was dangerous as well. That he'd actually approved an expensive treatment for Jacques stunned her. She knew he had the money—that wasn't it at all—but the obligation? He had no reason, no incentive, to do so.

He said he'd done it for her. Even now, that thought had the power to shorten her breath. *Why would he do such a thing?*

Because he was decent. Because he wasn't as cold and cruel as she'd accused him of being. Another feeling rose in her breast, a feeling she didn't want to acknowledge but had to nonetheless.

Shame.

She was ashamed that she'd stolen the Corazón del Diablo from him, that she'd held him at gunpoint and cuffed him to the bed. If she'd gone to see him, perhaps he would have helped her after all.

You have no way of knowing, Francesca. You did what you had to do.

Yes, she'd done what she'd had to, and the result was far better than she perhaps deserved.

If she weren't careful, if she didn't keep her emotional distance, she was in as much danger of falling for Marcos Navarre as she'd ever been. And that was something she could not afford to do. No matter how compassionate he might be toward Jacques, no matter how he claimed to want her in his bed, this was a temporary arrangement and the only heart at stake, if she allowed herself to feel as she once had, was hers.

Soon, Marcos lifted his head and the crowd quieted. When he began to speak, his voice rolled over the Spanish words with authority. She wished she could understand what he said, but she would have to content herself with the crowd's reaction.

"I will translate for you." A woman dipped gracefully into the open seat beside Francesca. "Marcos has told me you do not speak Spanish yet, so I will tell you what he says."

Francesca thanked her even as she tried not to imagine how Marcos knew this elegant woman. It did not matter. Francesca was a contract wife, not a real wife. She wasn't in love with him. Nor would she be.

"He is speaking of the orphans," the woman said. "Of our duty and responsibility to provide for the poor children of Buenos Aires. It is his passion, his life's work to create opportunity and stability for them, to lift them from the circumstances in which..."

Francesca's heart contracted as the woman talked.

Fresh tears sprang to her eyes at the horror of Marcos's words. He told of children who stole food to survive, who ate garbage and hunted rats, of children who learned to be hard and angry. Who joined gangs and became menaces to society.

She could see the passion in his expression, hear it in his words, and understand it thanks to the woman translating for her. When he finished speaking, the room erupted in applause. He looked alone, angry, and perhaps even a bit lost. Francesca glanced at the others, wondering if they saw it too. But no one seemed to see anything more than a very powerful, very rich man who asked for their support.

And she saw what she did not want to see: a man with heart and soul.

"He is quite a man, your husband." The woman held out her hand. "I am Vina Aguilar, an old friend of the Navarre family. I went to school with Marcos's mother."

Francesca blinked as she took Vina's hand. Though this woman was old enough to be Marcos's mother, she didn't look a day over forty. She was tall, lean, and dressed in a Prada silk gown that showed her trim figure to perfection. Her face was unlined, except for a few crinkles around the eyes when she smiled.

"You are not what I expected," Vina said after they'd chatted for a few moments. "But I am pleased for Marcos. He deserves all the love and happiness he has never had. I am sure you will give it to him."

"Yes, he does." Francesca dropped her gaze, hoping Vina would take it as shyness instead of the confusion currently pounding through her.

"Are you filling my wife's head with tall tales, Vina?"

Francesca's gaze snapped to Marcos as the woman laughed. He seemed perfectly normal again. Had she imagined the pain and anguish in his demeanor? The loneliness?

"Darling, I have said not a word that wasn't true," Vina replied, rising and kissing him on both cheeks. "And I was just about to tell your lovely new wife that I hope you will take the time to have a few children of your own. We need more men like you, Marcos."

"*Gracias, señora,*" Marcos said while Francesca's head began to swim. He reached down and took her hand in his. If he noticed it was clammy, he did not react. "But we are taking time to get to know each other first. Perhaps later."

"Of course, of course." She suddenly waved at someone across the room. "Esteban needs me, darling. I'll write a check for the foundation, and I'll see you soon, yes? Bring your beautiful *esposa* to dinner."

Francesca couldn't look at him as he dropped into the chair Vina had vacated. Children? She'd wanted Marcos's children once. And tonight, hearing him speak so passionately about the lost children in the streets, she couldn't help but think that Vina was right. He did deserve children of his own.

Several people came by to speak with Marcos. Francesca sat there like a good wife, smiling and speaking with those who spoke to her, though her thoughts were far away. When Marcos eventually touched her shoulder, she jerked.

He frowned down at her. She hadn't even been aware he'd stood.

"If you are ready, we can leave," Marcos said.

"Yes, of course," she said, allowing him to help her up. "But shouldn't you stay to speak with the donors?"

He picked up her shawl and wrapped it around her. "The Foundation has a staff, *querida*. They are quite capable of handling the donations now that I've made the speech. And I've been speaking with people for the last half hour."

"How long have you been doing this, Marcos? I don't remember you ever speaking of this charity before."

He cupped her elbow and steered her toward the lobby. "The Reclaim Our Children Foundation is almost eight years old. I started it as soon as I regained Navarre Industries."

"How did you learn about these children?" she asked as they stopped under the portico to wait for their limousine. "I'm ashamed to say I had no idea this kind of thing went on in such a modern country."

He didn't speak at first and she wondered if he'd heard her. She looked up at him, surprised at the stark look on his face. He cared deeply for these children, she realized. And perhaps she was wrong to ask questions. Clearly, it was a painful subject for him.

"You don't have to—" she began.

"I learned about them firsthand, *querida*," he said, slicing her off in mid-sentence with his harsh words. "Because I was one of them."

CHAPTER SEVEN

WHY HAD HE told her what he'd never told anyone? His fiction had always been that he'd been sent to live with relatives. In the space of a moment, he'd told her the ugly truth.

Marcos poured a whiskey as soon as they were ensconced in the back seat of the limo and took a long drink. Francesca sat beside him, silent as the grave. She hadn't said anything since he'd spoken those ill-advised words. Not that she'd had any time. As soon as the words left his mouth, the car had arrived.

Now they were on their way, gliding down the drive and toward the street.

"I'm sorry," she said very softly. Marcos tilted the crystal tumbler back and drained it. Exactly what he did not want from anyone: pity.

"It was a long time ago," he bit out. "Forget it."

She let out an annoyed sigh. "That's your solution for everything, isn't it? Forget it."

"There is no point in dwelling on the past."

"But you can't forget it, obviously, or you wouldn't be so angry!"

He rounded on her, ready to lash her with words— except she'd finally let those tears fall. The ones she'd gulped back for Jacques Fortier were now sliding down her cheeks for him.

"Francesca," he said on a heavy sigh, "it's not important. The past is the past."

"But how did this happen, Marcos? What happened to your parents, and why didn't your uncle take care of you once they were gone?"

"Ah *Dios*," he breathed. What on earth had happened to his usual good sense in those few moments when he'd blurted out the truth? He didn't like talking about his past, yet he'd just told her one of the darkest secrets of his life. Not the darkest, certainly, but one of them.

He poured another drink and took a sip. Beside him, Francesca used the shawl to wipe away her tears. He handed her a cocktail napkin.

"My parents disappeared during the military *junta*. That was a time when people who were suspected of not supporting the government were quietly taken away and never seen again."

"You don't know what actually happened to them?"

He shook his head. He'd tried to find out, but the records from that time were not complete. The government had wanted no evidence of their crimes. "They were killed, Francesca, like so many thousands of others. And Magdalena and I were sent to an orphanage. When I was ten, I ran away. I lived on the streets for the next six years. Fortunately, she did not share my fate."

Her hand was cold where it grasped his. She squeezed hard, and though he did not want to accept her comfort, he found himself squeezing back.

"This is why you are so passionate about the children. It's very wonderful, what you do."

He shrugged. "Perhaps, but it can never be enough."

Though he'd set up the Reclaim Our Children Foundation, funded it when it was still in its infancy, made hundreds of speeches soliciting donations, and had the satisfaction of seeing children helped through the work his vision had created, it still affected him deeply each time he spoke as he had tonight.

He told himself he didn't care why wealthy people got involved, so long as they did. For some, it was the satisfaction of helping the less fortunate without actually doing anything themselves. For others, there was a true passion and desire to help the children have decent lives.

For him, it was the burning need to save every last child he could from his own experience on the streets. But he couldn't save them all, and that's why he felt so emotionally drained after these events.

"Marcos, my God," she said, straightening suddenly and leaning toward him with determination. "What you do is *important*. Never say it's not enough. You are making a difference in children's lives. Even if you can't help them all, saving just one from the fate you talked of earlier is extraordinary."

Marcos pressed the intercom button and spoke to the driver. Then he turned to Francesca. "I want to show you something."

She nodded, the emeralds at her throat winking in the streetlights. He reached out and touched the teardrop at the top of her cleavage. "I knew these would suit you. It's why I bought them, though perhaps you will think me quite shallow once you've seen what I am about to show you."

The pulse in her neck thrummed. He wanted to press his lips to it, but he did not.

Soon, the car slid into streets that weren't lit. Streets where garbage lined the sidewalks, graffiti covered the walls, and people scurried away like rats when the car crept through the alleys.

"This is where it happens, Francesca. Where they live."

Up ahead, another car was stopped and a youthful figured leaned against the window, talking to someone inside.

"That is either a drug deal, or someone looking for cheap sex," he said.

He could hear Francesca's breath catch. "Can't you put a stop to it?"

"No."

She turned to him, her eyes rimmed with tears again. "But you said—"

"This is what I meant," he replied, his voice harsher than he intended. "I cannot save them all. No matter how I try, there are those I cannot reach."

He tapped on the glass separating them from the driver, signaling the man it was time to go. The car accelerated and they were soon leaving the *barrio* behind and returning to the lit streets and vibrant life of the city.

"I know this shocks you," he said in the quiet stillness of the car.

"What shocks me," she replied in a hushed voice, "is that you are so much more amazing than I had ever realized."

Her words jolted him. In them, he glimpsed the eighteen year old with stars in her eyes. She'd wanted him for all the wrong reasons back then. He would not allow her to do so again. No matter how much he'd revealed to her, no matter that no other human being had ever learned as much about him as she, he would not lose sight of the fact that this was a temporary arrangement between them. There was nothing to build a future on. Nor did he want to.

Nothing was as she'd expected it to be. Francesca paced the confines of her room, her mind refusing to quiet and let her sleep. All her expectations and beliefs about Marcos had been turned upside down. Yes, she'd loved him blindly once, and only because he was handsome and paid attention to her when no one else did.

Those were not good reasons to love someone, of course.

Tonight, however, she'd been shown a side of Marcos Navarre that she'd never have guessed existed. After he'd left her eight years ago, taking the Corazón del Diablo with him, she'd believed he cared only for himself.

She'd blamed him for everything that had gone wrong in her life, yet in the space of a couple of days, she'd been forced to consider alternative views. First, that the Corazón del Diablo had always rightfully been his. That her father had killed himself not because of anything she'd done, but because he couldn't face what he had done.

And, most significantly, that Marcos had a heart beneath his hard exterior. He'd taken care of Jacques. He rescued children. And, dear God, he'd lived a life of hardship and deprivation on the streets of Buenos Aires.

She thought of the teen they'd seen leaning into the sleek car. Her mind couldn't help but wander toward another thought: had Marcos had to endure such things on the streets?

She'd told him he was amazing. Heat flamed through her at the memory. Had she learned nothing in the last eight years? Marcos might be more than she'd believed, but he didn't want her childish admiration any more than he ever had.

The way he'd ignored her the rest of the way home, and then excused himself once they'd arrived, was proof of that. It was their wedding night, and though she'd been afraid on so many levels of actually being intimate with him, she'd not expected he would go to bed alone. Especially not after she'd felt the proof of his arousal when he'd held her close on the dance floor tonight.

She did not kid herself about the strength of his reaction to her. He'd wanted her because she was available, because he'd married her and it was his right.

He'd slipped beneath her defenses tonight with his impassioned plea for those children, and with his shocking story of having been one of them. She didn't like the way it made her feel, the way she wanted to slip her arms around him and hold him tight. She should be relieved he'd gone to bed alone, and yet she was restless.

Francesca glanced at the bedside clock; the irony of the thought that this marriage had already lasted longer than their previous one came crashing through her. Yet she was as alone tonight as she had been that night so long ago.

With a growl of irritation, she yanked open the French doors fronting the veranda and stepped out into the cool night air. The thin cotton tank and sleep pants she wore were little protection from the chill, but her blood was so heated she didn't yet feel the cold.

"You wish to make yourself ill?"

Francesca spun toward the voice. Marcos emerged from the shadows, still clad in his tuxedo pants and white bespoke shirt. His tie was undone, and the shirt gaped open where he'd unbuttoned the first few studs.

"Not at all," she replied. "I couldn't sleep and wanted some fresh air."

"You should have put on a robe."

She wrapped her arms around her torso. "I'm not cold."

He moved closer. The shiny skin of his scar gleamed in the reflected light of the courtyard. He looked like a devil in the night. A very dark, very powerful, very sexy devil. Why oh why could he not be ugly and brutish? Why couldn't he be mean and cruel with no redeeming qualities whatsoever? Why couldn't she seem to keep her dislike of him wrapped tightly around her heart, like an impenetrable shield?

"You are shaking," he said softly, one finger reaching out to skim over her bare arm.

"It'll stop if you go away," she said. Let him figure that one out.

He tilted his head to one side. "You said that to me last night. But you aren't scared of me, Francesca. You might despise me, but you don't fear me."

She didn't know what to say to that. She wasn't even sure she despised him as much as she once had. Oh, she knew better than to believe she meant anything to him other than a means to an end—and that alone was reason enough to keep her heart locked up tight. But how could she despise him with the strength she'd had only yesterday?

She couldn't.

"What do you want from me, Marcos?"

"I want what men usually want, *querida*."

Her heart thrummed. "But why?"

"You really don't know, do you?" he said, his voice containing a kind of wonder.

"I know that I'm not the kind of woman you want. I've seen the photos of you from time to time. You date models, beauty queens, debutantes. I'm just a plain Jane, Marcos. I've always known it. I'm not polished or beautiful, and I'm not the kind of woman you would choose to marry of your own volition."

"You have always been lovely, Francesca. But I will admit that I have not always known it."

When he reached for her, she couldn't make herself move away, even though she knew she should do so. Her pulse was tripping and a sharp pain arced through her soul. *I have not always known it.*

She should put as much distance between herself and this devil as possible. Because he was bad for her heart, her soul. He was bad and dangerous and she trembled with excitement in spite of it.

Or perhaps because of it.

His body was big, solid. He caught her close and, instinctively, she brought her hands up to rest on his chest. Beneath the soft material of his shirt, his skin was hot. Her palms tingled.

Before she could speak, could think of a word to say in reply, his mouth claimed hers, hot and passionate—and perhaps even with an edge of desperation.

And she didn't care, because she felt something of that desperation too.

His hands slipped down her shoulders, over her waist, cupped her buttocks and brought her against the heat and hardness of his thighs. He was aroused, and her heart beat ratcheted up a level.

When his fingers slipped beneath her tank, she fought down a wave of panic. He would find her inadequate... he would change his mind and she would be humiliated again...

Slowly, he circled from her spine to her ribs and then up to cup the weight of one bare breast. A groan issued from his throat. The sound thrilled her. She'd forgotten what passion felt like, what those first moments of discovery in another's arms could be like. It was a drug—a heady, beautiful, natural drug.

His thumb whispered over the aching peak of one nipple. Francesca shuddered, but not from cold. Liquid heat blazed inside her.

He was the architect of her ruin, the instrument that had shattered all her girlish dreams, and her body didn't care.

She ached for want of him, for want of what she'd never had with him.

The kiss deepened, their mouths demanding more and more. Had she ever been kissed like this? Ever wanted a man as much as she wanted this one?

Francesca shoved the questions aside, torn between conflicting emotions. She hadn't been with a man in four years, hadn't wanted to be, and now she could think of nothing else but lying naked with Marcos, feeling the power of his body moving inside hers, watching the expression on his face as he found his release.

She wanted to wipe away the anguish and heartache she'd seen on his face earlier tonight. She wanted to be the one to make him forget, even if only for a little while.

Almost without conscious thought, she wrapped her arms around his neck, pulling herself closer, if that were possible.

She felt the heat and hardness of him, the rigid bulge of his arousal.

"I want you, Francesca," he said against her ear, tugging her shirt up to bare her breasts.

Too fast, too fast.

But she didn't want time to think, didn't want to realize she was making a mistake in letting herself be this close to him. Didn't want to know that to survive the experience, she needed to hide behind the wall around her heart.

When he stepped back to look at her, her arms dropped. She would have covered herself if he hadn't stopped her. Her shirt rested on the swells of her breasts, refusing to fall and hide her body from his greedy gaze. He lifted her arms out to the side, studying her.

"*Dios*, you are beautiful. How could you think any man would not find you so?"

"Marcos, you don't have to—"

He silenced her with a kiss, his hands threading into her hair. Then his mouth dropped down her neck, her collarbone. She knew what was coming, knew what he would do before he did it.

And she was powerless to stop him.

Powerless because she wanted it.

His lips fastened over one taut peak, teasing her, tormenting her.

Francesca gasped, her head falling back, heat spilling through her body as his tongue slid around and around her nipple. And then he sucked just hard enough to spike a shot of pure pleasure straight to her center.

The moan that escaped her was raw. Marcos made a sound of pleasure and repeated the motion.

And Francesca had to grasp his arms to keep from melting beneath his expert touch. Much more of that, and he could make her shatter simply from the pressure of his mouth on her breast.

It was exquisite, the pleasure. Surely she'd felt this kind of need before? Surely she had done so with Robert, with the man she'd nearly married before he'd walked out and left her to face the future alone?

Thoughts of Robert brought thoughts of her baby. Of the lifetime of loneliness she would lead because she could never have children of her own. Of the shattered fantasies she'd once harbored about having a family with Marcos Navarre.

Unbidden, a tear spilled down her cheek.

No, she would not cry.

But the tears didn't stop, sliding hotly down her face as he made such sweet love to her long-neglected flesh. She wanted more, and yet she cried.

Cried for her lost dreams and the barrenness that haunted her. She'd never believed that she had to have a child to be fulfilled as a woman, but having the choice taken away tormented her every single day.

A sob welled up in her throat. Desperate, she pushed him away and jerked her shirt down. Then she buried her face in her hands and let out the tears she'd been holding inside.

She thought Marcos would go, but instead he wrapped her in his arms and held her tight. The gesture was so surprising that she only cried harder.

"Come, you need to get back inside where it's warm."

"I'm f-f-fine," she said, trying to push him away again. Embarrassment was a sizzling wave of pain in her body. Why did she have to cry now? Why in front of him? How could she explain?

Marcos ushered her back into her room, then went into the bathroom and returned with a glass of water. "Drink this."

She took the glass, swiping furiously at her tears with the back of her hand. Marcos produced a box of tissues.

"I'm sorry," she said after a few moments.

"I would never force you into my bed," he said, his voice tight.

She blinked up at him. "That's what you think this is?"

He shrugged. He looked like a beautiful dark angel as he stared down at her. His snowy white shirt was open, revealing the v-neck undershirt that molded to his hard chest. She could see his pulse beat in his throat, see the tension in the set of his jaw and the vivid white relief of his scar. "What else?"

"It's complicated. But it's not you." Francesca gazed at the tissue in her hand, wadding it tighter and tighter. She thought of all he'd told her earlier, and suddenly she was too weary to hide her pain any longer. She wouldn't tell him all of it, of course. Some things were too private, too painful. "I was engaged. He left me and I haven't been with a man since."

She looked up, found Marcos watching her. The expression on his face said that he'd never considered she might have had a life after him. Perversely, that made her angry.

"I know it's a surprise, but yes, I actually had a fiancé that nobody bought for me."

"Francesca—"

"It's been four years, Marcos. And I find all of this here with you just a bit overwhelming."

He pinched the bridge of his nose sighing. "You must have loved him very much."

She bowed her head again and swallowed. She had thought she'd loved Robert for a time, but she'd quickly realized she'd confused companionship for love. "No. I was hurt, of course, but it wasn't the first time I'd had to deal with betrayal. I learned to be tough, thanks to you."

She should feel guilty saying that, since those events failed in comparison to the loss of her baby, but it was cathartic to accuse him of having had a hand in stripping away her naïveté. He had been a part of it, but not the biggest part.

"I'm sorry for your pain, Francesca, but life is not always fair. If it were, I'd have been raised in this house with two loving parents."

Shame flooded her. And the urge to tell him the truth. But then what? To do so would be engaging in a game of one-upmanship that was not fair to either of them. To try and top his pain with her own was wrong. It was not appropriate, not now.

"No, life is not fair," she agreed. "It simply is. And it could always be worse. Or that's what I tell myself anyway."

"Yes, it can always be worse." He seemed far away in that moment, his eyes unfocused and distant. But then he lasered in on her again. "Get some sleep. Tomorrow, we're flying to Mendoza."

* * *

She was awakened by a man yelling. Francesca bolted up in bed, her heart thundering. It had taken her a long time to fall asleep, especially after Marcos announced they were going to Mendoza where his fecund sister and her brood resided.

Now, she threw the covers back and headed across the hall. Marcos, whether he admitted it or not, suffered from nightmares. She could only imagine the things he dreamed about. Francesca tried the door handle. Amazingly, it ghosted open.

She hesitated for only a moment. Would Marcos be angry with her for invading his privacy? Probably, but she had to go to him. How could she let him suffer like this?

She crossed the threshold into the darkened room. Light from the courtyard shafted over the empty bed. Empty? Had she imagined she heard him crying out?

A groan sounded, and then a command in Spanish. It was definitely Marcos's voice, though grittier and harsher than she was accustomed to. She hurried toward the noise, then stopped short.

He lay in a tangle of blankets on the floor, his bare chest glistening with sweat. There was a scar across his abdomen. Shock rooted her feet to the spot. She'd never seen so much of his body before, had never thought he was anything but perfect. Had he been in an accident? She'd never asked him about the scar on his mouth. Perhaps he got them on the streets.

She shuddered to think about what he must have gone through.

He said something else in Spanish, his head twisting on the pillow. Francesca dropped to her knees beside him.

"Marcos," she said, touching his shoulder. "Marcos."

"No!" His hand flew up suddenly, as if he were about to strike her. Defensively, she grabbed his wrist. But he was strong, so strong, and the act of enclosing her fingers around his wrist only seemed to enrage him further. He shot up, his eyes snapping open, glaring wildly into the night.

Before she knew what was happening, he'd flipped her onto her back and stretched full-length on top of her. Both her arms were pinioned above her head, gripped in his strong hands that held her down so tightly.

"Marcos!" she cried. "For God's sake, it's me. Francesca!"

He seemed to hesitate. "Francesca?"

"Yes!"

"*Dios,*" he swore. "I could have killed you."

But still he did not let her go.

"I was only trying to wake you. I didn't mean to startle you."

"You should not have come in here."

"I couldn't let you suffer."

His laughter was broken. "Ah, if only that were true, *querida.*"

Her heart went out to him. "What can I do to help, Marcos? I can stay with you. Or I can get you something. Just tell me."

His eyes were hot, but whether from the inferno of his dreams or the way he was now looking at her, she wasn't certain. She didn't understand what was going on, yet she felt it was changing so fast she couldn't keep up.

"What if the thing I need from you is more personal?" He flexed his hips then, the rigid form of his erection pressing into the cradle of her hips. Igniting an answering ache in her body.

"Then I would give it to you." She said it without hesitation, which both shocked her and aroused her.

His gaze slid down her body. Her nipples peaked beneath the thin cotton shirt as she thought of what he'd done earlier. His eyes lingered there for a moment. Then he murmured, "God, I do admit I am tempted."

His head dropped, his lips sliding along the column of her throat. The floor at her back was hard, but she didn't care. The hardness of his body pressing into her, the heated, shivery feeling of his lips on her flesh, and the anticipation of something far more explosive made the ache between her legs sharper. She wanted him, and right now she didn't care about the consequences.

She arched against him, enjoying the hiss of his breath as she did so.

"Then do it, Marcos," she said. "I want you to do it."

His mouth fastened over her nipple. She gasped, wanting the wet cotton barrier to be gone, but he made no move to lift her shirt away. No, he simply teased her nipple through the cotton, driving her insane with the heat and pressure that weren't quite enough.

"Please, Marcos," she gasped.

But instead of ripping her shirt out of the way, his head lifted, his eyes searching hers.

"Please what?"

"Please."

"You can't say it, can you? You want to tell me to make love to you, but we both know that's not what this is."

He let her wrists go and pushed himself to a sitting

position, his back against the side of the bed, his eyes closed. She propped herself on her elbows, confused and disappointed all at once.

"This isn't what you want, Francesca, not when you've been waiting for four years." He speared her with glittering eyes. "I'm not capable of tenderness at the moment. What you would get would be raw, hard and meaningless."

Her heart hammered. "Maybe that's what I want too."

Once more, he laughed that rusty, broken laugh. "I doubt that."

She sat up and wrapped her arms around her knees, the intensity of his words scaring her more than she would admit. "What do you dream about, Marcos, that torments you so much?"

"Demons, *querida*. Many, many demons." He stood and held out his hand. She took it and he pulled her up. "And now it is time for you to go. Thank you for waking me."

She pulled from his grasp before they reached the door, whirled to face him. "Why do you keep this locked inside? Why won't you let me help you?"

His face was a cold mask in the darkness. "You can't help me, Francesca. No one can."

"No, it's that you won't accept help. No one has to suffer the way you do."

"What would you know of it, *mi gatita*?" he demanded.

"I know a lot more than you give me credit for, Marcos."

He pushed her against the closed door suddenly, then stepped in and trapped her with his body. "My control is on a thread. You really need to go before I do something we both regret in the morning."

He kissed her hard, his lips demanding surrender. She opened to him without hesitation. He groaned low in his throat, gripping her ribcage as he held her hard against him and kissed her like he was a dying man and she his only hope of salvation.

She kissed him back without fear, her body igniting, her hope soaring that he would actually take her to bed and give them both the release they wanted.

They were moving and he was reaching for something—

And then he pushed her into the hallway and shut the door before she'd even realized he'd stopped kissing her.

CHAPTER EIGHT

THEY FLEW ON one of Navarre Industries' corporate jets to the Cuyo province. Bordered on the west by the majestic snow-capped Andes, the region was the center of Argentina's wine production and boasted acres of vineyards that were fed by clean, cool melt-water from the mountains. Though the area was high desert, the plain around Mendoza was green with cultivation.

Francesca slipped on her sunglasses as she followed Marcos down the stairs that had been pushed up against the plane. She felt as if she could go back to bed and stay there for twelve hours straight. She hadn't exactly slept well last night.

Marcos, however, looked as if he'd slept the whole night through. He was fresh, alert, and she wondered how on earth he did it. Because it had been 3:00 a.m. when she'd left his room. When she'd stumbled into the breakfast room at nine, he was already there.

They hadn't spoken much, except for polite inanities. It was as if the fiery confrontation of last night had never happened. More than once she'd thought to broach the subject, to crack open the fragile egg of their silence on the matter, but she'd been unable to do it.

What was there left to say?

A car was waiting nearby. She thought they would drive straight to Magdalena's place, had been trying to prepare herself for it all morning, but when they pulled into a shopping district, she figured he wanted to pick up presents for the family. She folded her arms over her lap and leaned her head back to catch a few minutes of sleep while she waited.

"Come, Francesca," Marcos said.

"Why?"

She couldn't see his eyes behind the mirrored sunglasses he wore, but she could feel them moving down her body.

"You need clothes. I neglected to take you shopping before we left Buenos Aires."

"I have enough for a few days," she said. "Surely this can wait."

He removed the glasses. "What you have is not suitable."

Heat burned into her cheeks. "Why not? Are we attending a masked ball or something?"

"What you have is not suitable for you, *querida*." He waved his hand up and down her body. "These shapeless garments are not flattering."

She sat up straighter. She was wearing her favorite summer dress, a loose garment that flowed to her ankles. She thought it was feminine and pretty. "My wardrobe didn't seem to be a problem last night."

"Because we bought you a gown."

"I wasn't talking about that."

"Ah," he said. "Clothes, in that instance, are irrelevant. But you are beautiful, Francesca, and you need to wear clothes that show your gorgeous body."

"I like this dress," she said militantly.

"It belongs to someone two sizes larger."

She stared at him for a long minute. She'd had this dress for a few years—and she'd worn it when she was twenty pounds heavier. That he knew it was for someone bigger surprised her. And embarrassed her. She grabbed the handle and ripped open the door.

"Fine," she said. "Let's go. But we're only getting a few things."

He inclined his head. "As you wish."

Francesca marched into the first store, her dignity sorely bruised. But the shopping wasn't as excruciating as she expected. Marcos stayed out of it, mostly, but the shop girls refused to let her take a wrong turn. When she chose a garment that was a little too big or loose, they steered her toward something else. By the time they got back into the car, more than two hours had passed.

She hadn't selected much, but it seemed as if the boxes and bags had somehow multiplied on their way out to the car. She hadn't wanted to accept any more from him than she already had—the jewels last night still stunned her, but she knew that even if he'd bought them with her in mind, he had not bought them for her—yet she'd had to acknowledge she might feel more confident meeting his sister if she were dressed a bit more elegantly.

In spite of the new cream linen dress she'd changed into at the last store, Francesca began to panic as the car moved through the sycamore-studded landscape. They were getting closer and closer to meeting Magdalena and her new baby. When they finally turned in at a sprawling Spanish-style villa south of town, Francesca had to remind herself not to wipe her sweaty palms on her new dress.

As the car rolled down the drive, she braced herself for whatever would come next. She expected children to scamper out of the huge carved wooden double doors, a man and woman to linger with smiles on their faces and a baby in their arms as they welcomed Marcos to their home.

And her, of course. But what would his sister think of her? Especially if she couldn't look at the woman for fear of losing control of her rioting emotions?

She'd thought she'd put it behind her. The fear, the loss, the reality of what had been taken from her. She could not change the past, could not reclaim what had been stolen. There was only the future.

Yet the prospect of spending time with a happy family terrified her.

A happy family.

As the car came to a halt, Francesca watched the door to the villa, gathering her strength and preparing for the ordeal of meeting Marcos's family. No one emerged, and Marcos exited the car. The chauffeur came around and opened her door. She stepped out of the car, shading her eyes against the setting sun. The air was warmer than in Buenos Aires, and fragrant with the scent of an orchard nearby.

Plums perhaps?

Finally, the doors opened and a small man dressed in black pants and a white shirt hurried over to Marcos. The two exchanged words in Spanish, and then the man was grasping a suitcase and yelling instructions to the youngsters who came running from the interior.

Their luggage disappeared as Francesca stood there blinking at the scurrying children. Teenagers, actually.

"They work here," Marcos said, as if sensing her confusion. "For me."

"But I thought this was your sister's home…"

"Magdalena and her family have their own winery."

"This is your home?" She tilted her head back, taking in the Spanish portico, the stucco and wood beams, and felt a relief she hadn't expected flood her senses.

"*Sí*. This is the *Bodega Navarre*. We grow olives, plums, and grapes here. The children help make the oil, wine, and jellies. They sell it to tourists and…"

Francesca ceased listening. A buzzing started in her ears and wouldn't stop. Marcos employed the kids that he wanted to save from the streets. He'd said he didn't do enough, yet he did more than he'd told her. He'd talked of hiring the kids, teaching them a trade, giving them something meaningful to do while they were schooled properly. She thought he meant through the Foundation, not that he personally did this.

In his home, with his money.

Oh God.

Her heart wasn't going to survive this experience. She already knew he was decent, that he cared for people and used his money for good. She'd thought she was safe to like him again.

But this. *This.*

She couldn't forget why she was here. Marcos Navarre simply wanted her for the Corazón del Diablo. It didn't matter if he was kind to orphans, or if he took care of needy children, or if he had nightmares that she didn't understand.

This was about the necklace, and his ownership of it, nothing else. He might realize that she wore clothes that didn't fit, but that didn't mean he cared for her. She'd been in Argentina for three days and she was already questioning her beliefs. How on earth would she survive for three months?

"Francesca."

She shook herself when he repeated her name. "Yes, sorry, just thinking."

He held out his arm. "Come inside. Ingrid will have prepared an amazing meal, and you must surely be hungry by now."

She was surprised to realize that her stomach was growling. "I am, yes."

Marcos showed her to a room, left her to freshen up, and said he would meet her in fifteen minutes outside her door. After a quick brush of her hair and a swipe of fresh lip-gloss, she emerged to find Marcos waiting for her. Her heart tumbled into her toes, then soared to the top of her head. He looked delicious, of course. He wore faded jeans and he'd loosely rolled the sleeves of his white cotton shirt. He'd also exchanged his polished loafers for a pair of flip-flops.

She thought he would take her to the dining room, but instead he showed her outside, to the covered veranda, where a table had been set up with linens, crystal, silver and china. Instead of a single rose, a spray of wild flowers bloomed in a vase in the center of the table.

Beyond the veranda, the cobbled terrace gave way to a manicured lawn that flowed naturally into the vineyard beyond. Vines twisted along the fences that lined each row. The back of the house faced west, so that beyond the vines she could see the snowy peaks of the Andes.

"It's beautiful," she said.

"*Sí.*" Marcos pulled her chair out for her. "I love to come here, when I can get away."

Once they were seated, a young man arrived with a bottle of wine. Marcos tested the small splash he was given, then nodded and said something in Spanish. The boy grinned and poured a full measure into Marcos's glass before coming to pour for her.

When he was gone again, Marcos lifted the glass and held it up to the light. "It is a Malbec," he said. "The grapes originally came from France, but they like Argentina better."

He sipped and closed his eyes. She watched the slide of his throat as he swallowed. Her mouth was suddenly dry as she sipped her own wine. She closed her eyes too, more to block out the sight of Marcos drinking than because she thought it would add to the experience.

The wine was fruity and full-bodied: plummy, with flavors of spice, currant, and vanilla.

"It's delicious," she said. "Do you make this here?"

He nodded. "We have a vintner on staff. The wine is mostly for Navarre Industries, though we sell some to the tourists."

"Why did you say you don't do enough for the kids? I can't imagine that anyone could do more."

He shrugged, but she knew the gesture was anything but light. "You have seen what I am up against. There are more kids every day who find themselves in the streets, begging, doing drugs, selling their bodies. Many have families to return to at the end of the day, families who live in shacks and who need the income they produce. Others have nowhere to go. The Foundation has better luck with them, but we try to reach them all."

"I think you're doing a wonderful job, Marcos…"

The words died in her throat as a black haired toddler came running out of the nearest door on chubby legs, a girl chasing him as he giggled and screamed. Marcos was on his feet in an instant, scooping the child into his arms before he could get away. The girl, a golden blonde creature who looked no more than twelve, stood with her head bowed and her hands behind her back.

"Señor Navarre," a tall, blonde woman who must be the girl's mother said as she hurried out of the house, "please forgive me. I turned my back for two seconds, and he was gone. Isabelle was trying to catch him for me."

Marcos smiled at the toddler who was clinging to him and giggling. "It's not a problem, Ingrid. And who is this little one?"

The woman wiped her hands on an apron as she came forward. "He belongs to Ana Luis, one of the new girls here. His name is Armando."

"Ah, I see." Armando's eyes grew wide as the food began to arrive. He bounced up and down in Marcos's arms. Marcos laughed. "Perhaps he is hungry, yes?"

"I was just about to feed him, as soon as I finished frosting the cakes."

"Go finish. He can stay with us for a while."

"He will disrupt your lovely dinner, señor."

Marcos smiled, so at ease for a moment that Francesca had trouble believing this was the same man who had violent nightmares. "We will cope."

Ingrid nodded. "I'll send Isabelle back with his food."

"Bueno."

The woman and girl left, and Marcos sat down with Armando on his lap. Francesca's heart had stopped beating minutes ago. Now, it lurched forward painfully as the boy gabbled nonsense and reached for the hot plate a waiter had set in front of Marcos.

"No, little one," Marcos said. "Be patient."

Francesca tried to concentrate on the food as it was being delivered. The scent of the steaks was divine. Besides steaks—*bife di lomo*, served with a *chimichurri* sauce—there were steaming vegetables, fragrant rice, and hot empanadas.

Someone brought an extra fork. Marcos put a little bit of rice on it and, once he tested it for heat, fed it to the boy. Isabelle returned with a plate of cut up steak and vegetables and set it near Marcos.

"You are a natural with children," Francesca managed as she cut into her own steak, her heart throbbing so painfully it was a wonder she could still speak. The little boy in Marcos's lap was adorable, with silky black curls, a bow mouth, and the smoothest olive skin she'd ever seen. When he looked up at her, long eyelashes framed dark eyes that watched her so solemnly.

What would her baby have looked like? Her little girl. She dropped the fork and pressed a hand to her mouth. She'd only just found out her baby was a girl a couple of weeks before the robbery.

Marcos was watching her, his brows drawing low. "What is wrong, Francesca? Something does not agree with you?"

She shook her head, swallowed. Forced her shaking hand to pick up the fork and knife again. "It's nothing."

"I seem to recall you taking me to task for saying this very thing. Are you quite sure?"

She forced a smile. "I'm quite sure it's nothing I wish

to talk about." She nodded at the little boy. "Armando is hungry."

"Do you wish to feed him?"

Francesca shook her head. Her food was a lump of sawdust in her stomach. "Let's not disrupt him when he's so happy with you."

Marcos fed the child another bite of steak. "Do children frighten you?"

"A bit," she said. "I don't know a thing about babies."

"I think you would be a good mother, Francesca."

Her pulse throbbed. "What makes you say that?"

"Because you have a kind heart. When you love someone, you love with your whole being. If you would go to such lengths for an old man you care about, what would you not do for your own child?"

Francesca put her napkin on the table. It was as if Marcos could see into her soul—and she didn't like the feeling one bit. She felt raw, exposed, as if he knew more about her than anyone ever had. Coming here had been a mistake. Except she hadn't had a choice, had she? To save Jacques, she'd made a deal with the devil. She just hadn't expected the payment to be so brutal.

"I'm afraid I didn't sleep so well last night," she said, standing. "I feel a headache coming on, so I think I'll go lie down."

Marcos looked concerned. "But you have not eaten. Surely that will help."

"I'm not very hungry after all."

Francesca didn't wait for a reply as she turned away. She simply couldn't look at the man and child any longer, at how natural they looked together. Marcos was meant to be a father, but she was not the woman who could give that to him.

And that knowledge hurt far more now than it would have only a few days ago.

Francesca couldn't sleep. She'd spent the evening in her room, watching the small television, flipping through magazines, and trying to read a book. She'd been starving after a few hours, but just when she was ready to leave her room in search of food, a girl arrived with a tray. Sent by Señor Navarre, she'd said. Francesca had thanked her and taken the tray to her bed, where she finished everything on the plate and tried not to think about the fact that Marcos had been considerate enough to send her food.

Now, Francesca climbed from bed and pushed back the curtains. The waxing moon was in the gibbous phase, not quite full yet, slanting down over the vineyard and illuminating the rows. She dragged on a pair of jeans, a light sweater, and her tennis shoes. It was late, but a walk in the brisk air would do her a world of good right now.

The night was quiet as she emerged from the darkened house. A light burned in one window. Someone else couldn't sleep, or maybe they were afraid of the dark. She wondered about Armando, about his mother Ana Luis. Perhaps the little boy couldn't sleep, and Ana was trying to soothe him. He was truly an adorable child. He had the dark curls that she imagined a child of Marcos's might have. A pang of regret shafted through her at the thought.

Francesca walked down the manicured lawn and crossed the edge of the vineyard. The rows were straight, narrow, but not as filled with vegetation as they would be once the season progressed. The leaves were new, the vines still growing from the hardened, twisted stumps in the ground. It always amazed her to see a grapevine, to see how the roots were so gnarled and looked almost dead. But every year, faithfully, vines shot forth onto the wired rows meant to hold them. Without fail, beauty grew from the twisted, ugly stumps.

She walked deeper into the vineyard, emerging at a spot where the rows crossed into another direction. A lone tree stood at the center of the clearing. Another gnarled beast, she decided, recognizing it for an olive tree. But why a single tree in the center of the vineyard?

Something moved at the mouth of the row across from her. Her heart shot into her throat and she turned as if to run back toward the house.

"Who's there?" a voice said.

Relief cascaded through her. And heat. Always, always the heat. "It's me," she said, "Francesca."

She could make out the white of his shirt, the darkness of his jeans as he moved toward her.

"What are you doing out here?"

"I couldn't sleep," she said. "You?"

He stopped in front of her. Scraped a hand through his hair. "The same."

He smelled good, like spice and citrus and outdoors. The warmth of his body reached out and enveloped her. Comforted her.

"Do you often walk at night?" she asked.

"Not in Buenos Aires. But here, yes. I like the quiet stillness of the vineyard."

Her thoughts exactly. "Why is this tree here? It seems rather lonely."

"I'm not sure," he replied, turning his head toward the olive tree. "It was always here. It is very old, I believe. We have a grove, but this tree stands alone."

"Maybe it's a special tree."

"Perhaps." He took a step closer. "And how is your head? Are you feeling better?"

"A bit, thank you," she said. "Did Armando finish his dinner?"

She could see the flash of his teeth in the moonlight. "*Sí*, he ate everything. And then he had a small slice of cake."

"You were very good with him."

He shrugged. "He is a child. It's not hard to please them really."

"I'm surprised you haven't married and had tons of kids by now," she said. "I'd have thought that would be one of your priorities."

"And what made you think that?"

"The Navarre Dynasty, the Corazón del Diablo. Who will you leave all this to?"

"There is Magdalena and her children. The Foundation."

She could hardly believe what she was hearing. "So you don't want children then?"

"I didn't say that." He took another step toward her. "What is all this about, Francesca?"

She shrugged, pushing her hands into her jeans pockets. "Just curious, that's all."

"I'm curious about something, too. I'm curious about why your engagement didn't work out."

"Robert decided marriage wasn't for him." She shrugged again. *"C'est la vie."*

"And you have not been with a man since. I find this extraordinary."

"It's not, really. I've been busy, and I haven't been interested enough in anyone to take the next step."

He hooked a finger in her jeans pocket, tugging her closer. "You seem interested in me."

"We're married," she said, her breath catching as desire shot through her limbs. "And it's part of your damn contract."

"So you would make love with me because of the contract?"

"I didn't think I had a choice."

A finger twirled in her hair. "You always have a choice, Francesca. But I think you will choose me."

"You are far too confident in yourself." But her blood was humming and her body was beginning to ache with need.

"No, but I am confident in this feeling between us. There is something…"

His head dipped, his lips ghosting over hers.

"Something?" she asked a touch breathlessly.

His arms went around her, pulling her in close as she automatically put her own around his neck. "There is something about you, something I very much want to explore…"

"But last night—"

"Last night was wrong. Tonight—tonight is right."

She didn't ask why it was right. Last night *had* been different. And, she realized, it wasn't worth traveling old territory when what mattered was here and now. She ached to soothe him, to take away his pain and his nightmares, but she didn't know how to do it.

All she knew was that she was ready for this.

Amazingly, unbelievably—she wanted him. Without fear or regret. There would be consequences, she knew that, but she was so ready to push past her fear and insecurity and experience this with him. With the man she'd once loved more than any other.

With the man she could love again.

Francesca shuddered as their lips met. What was she getting herself into? But, oh God, how could she resist?

His mouth was magical, his kiss insistent and confident. Her limbs softened, her body turning liquid. She was jelly in his arms.

He pulled back. "Unless you wish to make love *al fresco*, we need to return to the house."

"I don't care, Marcos," she murmured, pressing her lips to the warm skin of his neck. He smelled so good, so vibrant and alive.

"I might not either, except that we have no blankets—and the night is chilly."

She acknowledged that could be a problem. That and she didn't know what kind of bugs crawled around in vineyards at night. "Then I'll race you back," she said before sprinting into the night.

CHAPTER NINE

MARCOS LET HER win the run to the house. She hesitated when she reached the threshold, but he grabbed her hand and led her toward her room. The one thing he never did was spend the entire night with his lovers. Usually, he took them to hotels or met them at their place, but he rarely took them home to his. And when he did, he bundled them off before daybreak.

He did not sleep with anyone. Ever.

Francesca was the first woman to catch him in the midst of his nightmares, but still he would not share his sleep with her. He would make love to her—was dying to do so, really—but he would return to his own room when they'd exhausted each other too much for more lovemaking.

When they reached her room, she seemed to grow suddenly shy. She moved away quickly, before he could take her in his arms again, and busied herself with tidying up a stack of magazines on the bedside table.

"You are having second thoughts?" he asked, because he was never willing to dance around the truth.

"N-no, not at all," she said with a toss of her glorious hair. She looked defiant. Like a scared little kitten trying to be brave.

Marcos smiled. "Ah, *mi gatita*," he said softly. "There is nothing to be frightened of. I will be gentle with you."

"Who said I was afraid? Really, Marcos, you think too much of yourself."

He laughed. Then he unbuttoned his shirt and cast it off. The blood pounded in his veins, urging him to take her now, but he would not do so. He intended to use the utmost control, to take it slow and thorough. To make up for eight years of wanting. Surprisingly, the wanting was as much his as it was hers. He hadn't considered consummating their relationship back then, but since he'd seen her again, he regretted not having done so. An odd feeling, to be sure, but there was no use questioning it.

He crossed to her, while she watched with wide eyes, and wound his hands in her mane of hair.

"So much hair," he said, "so beautiful. I do not know why you never wore it this way before."

Her gaze dropped. He could see the pulse beat in her throat. And in that moment, he found her more attractive than he could ever remember finding any woman. Francesca had that killer combination of wide-eyed innocence and a deep sensuality she seemed unaware she possessed. He wondered, only for a moment, if this was another act, a metamorphosis of her persona eight years ago.

But, no, he didn't believe that. The woman who'd fought him for the sake of an old man she loved did not need to resort to playing games now. What would be the point anyway? They were here, in this room, and he was going to strip her slowly and make love to her for as long as he was able.

And, *Dios*, he was going to enjoy it.

* * *

Francesca felt like she was viewing the scene from somewhere up above. Surely Marcos Navarre was not standing before her shirtless and tugging her toward him by gently winding her hair around his fist. Surely his eyes weren't ablaze with heat for her? The bulge in his jeans was not because of her.

But there was no one else in the room.

She slipped her arms around his naked waist, the heat of his skin sizzling into her like a brand. Then she tilted her head up and closed the distance between their mouths before he could do it. She was afraid that if she didn't, she would wake and discover this had only been a dream.

The kiss was far gentler than she'd thought it would be, gentler than the kiss in the vineyard had been. It was as if he was trying too hard to be careful with her.

"Marcos," she said against his lips, "I'm not going to break. *Kiss me.*"

"I am kissing you," he murmured.

"*Really* kiss me. Like you mean it."

"Oh, I mean it."

She gasped as he cupped her face in both hands, his mouth coming down on hers hotly. If she thought they'd shared a passionate kiss before now, she was mistaken. *This* kiss was so much more, so full of heat and passion and longing that she didn't know how they'd ever make it to the bed before they went up in flames.

His hands left her face, slipped beneath her sweater and pushed it upward. They broke the kiss long enough for him to rip it over her head, and then they were kissing again. Francesca reached for the fastening of his jeans while he unsnapped her bra and tugged it off her arms.

She wrapped her arms around him again, and then she was pressed against him, naked chest to naked chest. The sensation was exquisite, so full of heat and sensation that she wanted to moan with the pleasure of it.

But then Marcos swept her into his arms, never breaking the kiss, and she clung to him with heady anticipation. A moment later, he laid her on the bed, following her down. It felt wicked to be here like this, him on top of her, both still clad in jeans, their bodies grinding together through the barrier of fabric.

She was on fire. Absolutely on fire. Arcs of electricity shot through her core, tingling into her limbs. Marcos broke the kiss and sat up as he started to remove her jeans.

"We need to turn off the light," she blurted.

He stopped what he was doing. "I want to see you. All of you."

"No—Marcos, I can't."

His brows drew down. "Why not? Because you think I will disapprove of something? *Dios*, you are a naïve woman."

She crossed her arms over her bare chest and bit her lip. "I'm self-conscious, that's all."

"I know this. And I intend to prove to you how beautiful you are to me." He stripped her jeans and panties in a smooth motion, then stood and shoved his own pants down his hips. His penis sprang free, glorious, erect—and, wow, more than she'd expected. "Do I look as if I'm turned off by your body, *mi gatita*?"

Francesca shook her head, a hot feeling bubbling up inside her at the sight of him. He was truly magnificent. And she was a very lucky woman right this moment.

Marcos stretched out over top of her, his weight pressing her into the bed. Dizzily, she thought it must be the most erotic thing she'd ever experienced—because she wanted him so badly, had wanted him for years. And she was about to have him. The anticipation was excruciating, amazing…

Marcos slid down her body. "I've been wanting to do this…"

He cupped her breasts, pushing them together so that he could suckle each one in turn. He used his tongue and teeth, licking and nipping her ever so lightly while she squirmed beneath him, the pleasure so exquisite she thought would surely expire of it before much longer.

"Marcos—oh…"

"You are delicious, Francesca. Everything a man could want…" he said against her damp skin.

His mouth made a hot path to her belly button, and then he was moving lower, pressing a kiss to her hip, her abdomen.

Francesca gasped as he moved lower. She would never survive it. Never.

"Marcos, don't—"

He said something in Spanish then, something hot and dark that melted the words in her throat, melted her fear. And then he was parting her thighs, gazing at her.

She wanted to pant with the anticipation of it. It'd been so long, so damn long since she'd felt pleasure.

Marcos parted her with his thumbs, and then his mouth was there, licking and sucking that part of her that had been neglected for so many years. Francesca didn't have even a moment to build up to her release; she shattered immediately, the world turning into a bright white burst of feeling that wrung a sharp cry from her before it let her go.

"Madre de Dios," Marcos breathed. "You are incredibly sexy, Francesca. Never doubt this."

And then he was taking her over the edge again with his lips and tongue, before moving up her body and kissing her while she wrapped her legs around his waist.

He groaned low in his throat, halting his forward motion. "I had intended to go slower, but I find I cannot wait. You must tell me if it's too much, if I hurt you."

"I'm not a virgin," she said, threading her hand through his hair and arching up until her breasts were touching his chest. How much she'd wanted to do this with him so many years ago, before she even understood what it really entailed. To let him be the first—and only—man in her life.

"You might be tender after so long."

"I really don't care. I want you, Marcos." How freeing to say those words, openly, and know he felt the same. At least in this.

She tugged his head down, fusing her mouth to his. Marcos must have surrendered to the inevitable, because he slid into her body in one long glide that took her breath away.

Francesca tilted her hips up, then gasped at the lightning bolt of sensation streaking through her. Marcos tore his mouth from hers.

"Don't move," he said harshly, his eyes glazing. "For God's sake, don't move."

She did it again, her breath snagging in her chest, her body sizzling. "But it feels amazing…"

So amazing she wanted to cry with the wonder of it.

His jaw was granite. "*Sí*, but this will be over far too soon if you don't stop moving."

She caressed his cheek, joy welling inside her, making her giddy. "Oh, Marcos, why didn't you tell me you had premature issues?"

He swore. And then he laughed, though she knew he tried not to. "Why do you amuse me even now? Is this not serious to you?"

"Very."

"And to me," he growled. Then he flexed his hips. A shiver began at the top of her head and rolled to her toes. It was so unlike anything she'd ever experienced before. All thought of teasing him flew from her head. Raw need was a clarion blast in her soul.

"Marcos—"

When he rolled his hips forward again, she couldn't remember what she'd been about to say. Couldn't think. Could only *feel*.

"Oh yes, *mi gatita*," he said, somehow still capable of thought and speech, "it is *very* serious indeed."

When he withdrew and surged forward again, Francesca was lost to everything but what their bodies did. The way they rose and fell together, their breaths mingling, tongues tangling, the rhythm of their thrusts becoming more and more frenzied. It was as if they fought each other, and yet it wasn't a fight at all. It was a tango, a beautiful dance that required each partner to give everything to the other in pursuit of satisfaction.

The air in the room was charged, zinging with electricity, and she felt as if she were drawing all of it into her body, concentrating it in her core until it would inevitably burst forth and incinerate her in the process.

It seemed to last forever and not long enough. She had no warning before she was flung into space, gasping and shuddering, her body dissolving into nothingness. She heard Marcos's groan of satisfaction, felt the power of his final thrust, the tremors in his body as he found his release.

A few moments later, he propped himself up on his forearms so as not to crush her beneath him. And yet she missed the pressure of his body, the hard hot feel of him melting into her. God, she'd do it again right this instant if she had the energy.

And so would he, perhaps, if the fact he was as hard as ever was anything to go by.

Francesca stretched, still floating on a cloud of satisfaction and unwilling to come down off it to deal with reality anytime soon. There was plenty of time for that later.

"And how did that feel, *mi gatita*? Was it worth the wait?"

"Oh yes," she purred. "Very worth it."

He laughed, then kissed the skin beneath her ear while she sighed. "And you said I was too sure of myself."

"You are. But Marcos?"

"Mmm?"

"Why do you call me *mi gatita*? What is that?"

His smile was genuine. "I call you my kitten because you are so fierce, and so sweet at the same time."

No matter how she cautioned herself against reading too much into it, her heart cracked wide open. She was allowing him to get too close, allowing herself to feel too much. She turned her head away on the pillow, stared at the tiny bug that swirled around the lamp. Would it get too close to the heat?

Was she in danger of burning up in Marcos's white-hot flame?

"You are thinking about something," he said. "But I want you to think only of me."

Marcos flexed his hips, and her body answered with heat and want that wasn't diminished in the least by the release she'd already had.

"Think only of me," he repeated. "Of us."

And then he made it impossible for her to think of anything else.

He was sitting in a darkened room, on the floor because there was no furniture, and he could hear the scritch-scritch of small rodents behind the walls. His wrists were bound in manacles. They'd stopped stinging hours ago. Now they throbbed. Throbbed because they were swelling from the raw wounds he'd opened by trying to pull free.

He couldn't see what they'd chained him to. Couldn't see anything. Could only hear the rats and smell his own sweat and blood. How long had he been here? He'd lost track of time in the darkness and deprivation of the last few days.

Nearby, something hissed, sending his battered senses into high alert. Marcos struggled against the bindings, uncaring that his wrists felt as though they were being ripped open anew.

The hissing grew louder, the dry coiling of scales on

the floor more precise as the serpent moved. Marcos yelled, as much to scare the snake as to express his fear—

"Marcos!"

He blinked. The room was dark, but he was in a bed. And he wasn't alone.

"Marcos, it's okay," a woman's soft voice said. "You're with me. There's no one here but us…"

Her arms went around him, her face tucking into the crook of his neck. His first instinct was to push her away.

But he didn't want to. He wanted to hold her, to let her drive the dreams away.

"Francesca," he rasped.

"Yes, I'm here." She pushed away suddenly. "I'll get you some water. You're so hot."

He grabbed her arm. "Stay. Please."

She seemed to hesitate, but then she lay back down and curled into him again. Her body against his was comforting, soothing. He stared at the ceiling. How had he fallen asleep here with her? And why didn't he want to leave?

He should push himself up, should return to his own room, but he couldn't seem to do so.

"Would it help to talk about it?" she asked very quietly.

"It's an old dream," he said, though that's not what he'd intended to say. "There's a dark room, rats, and a snake."

"Is this something that happened when you were a child? When you lived on the streets?"

He swallowed. How could he tell her it was worse than that? "Something like that, yes."

Her hand slipped over his abdomen, tracing the scar he'd gotten from a close brush with an enemy machete. "Where did this come from, Marcos? Does this have anything to do with your dreams?"

"No more words," he said, rolling on top of her soft body. "I can think of better things than talking."

CHAPTER TEN

FRANCESCA DIDN'T EVER want to leave the bed again, not when Marcos was in it with her. But hunger finally won out. She slipped from the bed and took a quick shower, her body still aching in places it had not in a very long time. But it was a very pleasurable ache.

She almost hoped Marcos would wake and join her in the shower, but then it would be even longer before she got any breakfast. Frowning, she thought back to the last time they'd made love, when he'd woken from his nightmare. He'd been so intense, so driven. She wanted to take away his pain, and the only way she'd been able to do that was by giving him her body.

Yet she'd wanted more. She'd wanted him to talk to her, really talk to her, and she'd wanted to feel as if she were important to him as more than a bed partner. He'd called her his kitten, and her heart still throbbed when she remembered the way he'd said it, but she had to remind herself it meant nothing in the scheme of things.

This was a temporary arrangement, and she was leaving as soon as it was over. She had to remember that.

But her heart didn't want to think about it. Her heart, dismayingly, only wanted to think of Marcos.

When she emerged from the shower, she dressed in one of the new outfits, a flattering cream silk tank and pale yellow Capri pants. It surprised her, but she had to admit that Marcos had been right about her clothes. These were far more suitable than the older jeans and blousy tops she'd been wearing.

She felt good, but whether it was the clothes or the afterglow from last night, she wasn't quite sure. Perhaps a bit of both.

She returned to the bedroom, a little kick of disappointment hitting her in the breastbone when she discovered that Marcos had gone.

Probably, he'd returned to his own room to shower and dress. What would happen now that they'd been intimate? Would he expect her to move into his room? Would he move in here? Or would they keep separate rooms and spend their nights like illicit lovers rather than a married couple?

So many questions, and none she could really answer. Voices issued from the kitchen as she approached. Curious, she peeked inside. Armando sat in a high chair, banging the tray, and Ingrid was gesturing wildly as she spoke to another woman. They turned when they saw her.

"Señora Navarre," Ingrid said. "*Buenas tardes.* If you would like to go outside, I will serve breakfast there in a few moments."

"Of course," Francesca said, though it still jolted her to hear herself referred to as *Señora Navarre.* "But what's wrong? Is it something I can help with?"

Ingrid sighed and glanced at the other woman. "Ana Luis has run away. She met a boy, and has left to be with him."

Francesca glanced at Armando. He seemed oblivious to his mother's absence as he shoved cereal around on his tray. "She left her baby?"

"Yes," Ingrid said with a sigh.

"Does Marcos know?"

"Señor Navarre has just been informed. He has sent men to look for her, I believe."

"When did she go?"

"Sometime in the night. I found Armando alone in his crib when I arrived. Poor baby," she said, reaching over to tousle his hair. Armando giggled. Francesca's heart squeezed hard at the sound. He had no idea he'd been abandoned. No idea he wasn't wanted.

Why could people who didn't care about children have them when she couldn't?

Stop. It was no use traveling that road. She'd been down it before, and there were no answers. Only heartache and pain.

Ingrid put a palm to her temple. "I have so much to do today, and no idea how it will all get done when I must watch this little one here."

"Why don't I take him?" Francesca said, shocking both herself and Ingrid if the look on the other woman's face was any indication.

"Oh no, señora, I cannot ask you to do that. This is your honeymoon! You must have fun, spend time with your husband. A baby would be a distraction."

"Nonsense," Francesca said. Marcos had told people it was their honeymoon? Her heart leapt just a little at that, before she reminded herself it meant nothing. "It's not Armando's fault, and I'm not doing anything anyway."

"You're certain?"

Hell no, she wasn't certain, if the reckless pounding of her pulse was any indication. "Of course."

Ingrid grabbed a rag and wiped Armando's face, then lifted him from the chair and carried him over to her. For a moment, Francesca wondered if she'd made a mistake, if she knew what she was doing, but Armando smiled and spread his chubby little arms wide. She took him, tears springing to her eyes as he wrapped his arms around her neck.

He smelled like a baby. And like cereal and sunshine. She wanted to squeeze him close and kiss his little cheeks. Instead, she took him to the veranda and bounced him on her lap while she waited for breakfast to arrive.

Someone brought a play pen and popped it open. Francesca thanked the girl, though she was pretty certain by the frown on Armando's face that he didn't want to spend any time in it.

"It's okay, Armando," Francesca soothed. "You can sit right here with me if you're a good boy."

The baby burbled happily. Francesca gazed at him in wonder, her heart expanding so wide it hurt. Her own little girl would have been almost four. She'd stayed away from children because it hurt too much, but holding this little boy right now felt like the best thing she'd done in a long time. Besides making love with Marcos, of course.

As if thinking of him summoned him, he suddenly appeared in the doorway. The expression on his face, she noted, was thunderous. It cleared a little when he saw her, and he even managed a smile when Armando turned to look at him.

"Have you found her?" Francesca asked as he came over and pulled out a chair.

"No."

Armando reached for Marcos. Oddly, she felt a little reluctant to let him go, but Marcos took him and tickled his belly. The baby laughed uproariously while Marcos made faces.

A pang of longing pierced her soul. She wanted this life. Wanted Marcos and a baby. Wanted nights like the last night, and days that were perfect and stretched endlessly before her like a sea of happiness. She wanted what was, essentially, a beautiful illusion. And she wanted it to be real.

"What will happen if you can't find her?"

"Ah, *Dios*, I wish I knew."

"What about Armando?"

Marcos looked at the little boy in his arms. "He will be taken care of."

"By whom?"

"I don't know yet."

It pierced her to think of this baby without his mother, but what could she say? She and Marcos weren't in a real relationship, and thoughts of the two of them taking care of Armando if Ana didn't come back were a pipe dream. "I'm sorry, Marcos. I know it hurts you to have her leave like this."

His expression was controlled. "I told you I cannot save them all. And Ana has run away with a boy she met. She has not returned to the streets. Perhaps they will even marry."

"What usually happens with the teens you employ here?" she asked, wishing to distract him just a little bit. To get him to focus on the positive results of what he did.

"Some of them go to university," he said. "Others choose a trade."

"Do many of them choose college?"

"Many do, yes. Navarre Industries hires them once they graduate, should they desire to work for us."

What he did was amazing, and yet he beat himself up so badly over the ones he lost. She didn't understand it. "And what would happen to them if you did not do this, Marcos?"

He looked solemn. "Drugs, prostitution, gangs, death. Even war," he added, almost as an afterthought.

One word stood out. "War?"

"*Sí*. There is much unrest in parts of Latin America. Guerilla warfare against what one perceives to be society's oppressors can be an attractive option for some."

Her heart began to pound. "I had no idea." She thought of the scar on his abdomen, of the way he dreamed so violently. Could he have gotten scarred like that on the streets? Or was it a product of warfare? Suddenly, she had to know the truth. "Is that what happened to you?"

His eyes seemed so hard, so cold, as if his emotions had frozen solid. "Do you really wish to know? Do you think you can save me if only you know what drives me? That the love of a good woman will keep me from reliving the nightmare?"

He was so defensive that she knew she must be right. And it saddened her. Made her ache for the boy he'd been, the young man who'd suffered so much. He hid it away inside, and it was killing him.

But he couldn't see it.

"Yes, Marcos, I do want to know. But I imagine no one can save you except yourself."

The food arrived before he could reply. Marcos let Ingrid's daughter take the baby and put him in the play pen. His little eyes had begun to droop, and soon he was curled up asleep with his thumb in his mouth.

The moment was gone, so she didn't expect Marcus would answer her now. He surprised her when he did. He looked pensive, a bit lost, as if it wasn't quite his choice to speak but as though he couldn't stop himself.

"I am not accustomed to talking about this with any-one," Marcos said once Ingrid and Isabelle had gone. "But yes, I was a guerilla fighter, Francesca. I saw battle, I saw despair and evil and the worst a man can do to another man."

"I'm sure you did what you had to do," she said softly, trying not to let the tears mounding behind her eyes fall. He would not appreciate any show of pity.

He sighed and leaned back in his chair, his food un-touched. "I have always done what I thought I had to do to survive. I can't apologize for any of it, but I wish it had been different."

"I think I understand why you hated your uncle so much now. And why the Corazón del Diablo is so im-portant to you." She leaned forward suddenly, grabbed his wrist where it lay on the table. His reaction was im-mediate. He jerked his arm away so quickly she found herself grasping air and wondering what she'd done wrong.

"Don't ever do that," he ground out.

She sat back and folded her hands in her lap. She thought back to how he'd reacted so violently in Buenos

Aires when she'd gone to wake him and grabbed his
wrist before he could accidentally hit her in his sleep.
What was it about his wrists? She wanted to ask him,
but she did not. She'd already intruded enough on his
memories.

"I was just going to say that I think you are too hard
on yourself, that you push yourself too much and don't
take the time to realize all the good you've done. You
take the failures much harder than you celebrate the
successes."

Marcos shoved a hand through his hair, swearing softly.
She opened his wounds wide and didn't even know it.
And she cut so close to the truth that it threatened to
crumble all his defensive walls. He was accustomed to
success, maybe so much so that he took it for granted.

"You are right," he said carefully. "I do take the failures personally. Especially the kids. But when I fail
them, I lose more than money or prestige. I lose entire
lives."

"But you also save lives."

He picked up his cup of *café con leche* and took a
drink. *Dios*, he needed the caffeine. So much was changing, and so rapidly. He'd brought Francesca to Argentina
to punish her for taking the Corazón del Diablo, and to
cement his possession of it. He'd not brought her here
to let her worm her way beneath his defenses. She saw
through him, saw to the heart of him in a way no one
else seemed to do.

Why was that? Because she paid attention? Because
she was more perceptive than others? Or because she'd
known him in the past and had years to consider his
personality?

He did not know, but he didn't like it. Didn't like the way his perception of her was forced to undergo a shift from old beliefs to newer ones.

Yet he knew that if his choices were to put her on a plane this afternoon, or to have her in his bed later tonight, having her in his bed would win the battle. One night with her, and he was addicted to the rush he felt when he made love to her.

The feeling was temporary, he knew that from experience, but it was damned inconvenient as well. Still, he intended to make the most of it while this arrangement lasted.

Even if she did get under his skin with her too-sharp perception and pointed questions.

"Yes, the Foundation saves lives. I am happy with this, but I will be happier when we are no longer needed. I'm not sure we will ever see that day."

"No, perhaps not," she said. "But you will never cease working to make it so. Of that I'm certain."

He nodded, then glanced over at the sleeping child. "I will be happy if we can find and bring back Ana Luis. Her baby will miss her."

Francesca's eyes were shiny with unshed tears. "I don't understand how she can be happy without him. Perhaps she will miss him so much she'll come back on her own."

Marcos studied her. She looked...wistful. As if she longed for a child, no matter that she'd claimed to be afraid of them only yesterday. She'd looked happy enough when he'd found her holding Armando.

"You could be right," he said, "but I doubt it. She is a sixteen-year-old girl. A baby is probably a burden. She wants to be free, to have fun, and this little one is like a millstone around her neck, I imagine. She may love him, but she has probably convinced herself he is better off without her."

She blinked, as if she'd never considered such a possibility. "Or maybe her head was turned by this boy she met. Maybe she'll come to her senses."

"Is that what you did, *querida*?" he asked very softly.

"What do you mean?"

"With me. Did it take you very long to come to your senses? Or would you have followed where you thought your heart wanted to go? If I had taken you with me that night, eight years ago, would you have come?"

She looked away, toying with the half-eaten croissant on her plate. "I imagine I would have followed you to the ends of the earth, Marcos. Though I'm sure I'd have figured out the truth soon enough."

"The truth?"

"That you were only using me."

"As you were using me."

"You can continue to believe that if it makes you feel better," she said. Then she speared him with a glare. "But the truth is, if I had thought that asking my father to *buy* you for me would have worked, I probably would have done it. Because yes, I was that hopelessly in love. That deluded."

Her words pricked him more than he liked. *Deluded.* "How do you know that you did not ask him? You didn't have to say those exact words, after all."

"I never spoke with my father about you. I never spoke with any of them, because I was afraid of what they would say."

"And what did you think that would be?"

She thrust her chin up, a gesture he was beginning to recognize as a defense mechanism. It was her mantle of self-assurance settling into place, however tattered a mantle it may be.

"That I was delusional, that I wasn't pretty enough or smart enough, that you would never look at me twice. The list can get quite long if you want to hear it all."

Anger surged through him at the thought of her family saying such things to her. And they would have, he knew. At least her mother and sister would have. Her father had adored her, which was perhaps why her mother and sister had been so jealous.

"They would have been wrong, Francesca."

She snorted. "Of course. And you proved how wrong they were by leaving as soon as the ink was dry on the marriage license."

He leaned forward and caught her face between his hands, kissing her until she began to soften, until he could feel the blood rushing to his groin and feel the pounding of desire in his veins. "They could say none of those things now, and you know it," he said, leaning his forehead against hers. "Stop picking at old wounds. Life is about forward motion, not regrets."

She gently disentangled herself from his grasp. Her golden-green eyes were full of sadness as she searched his face. He felt like he'd been shoved beneath a microscope—and the scrutiny was becoming uncomfortable because it went so far beneath the surface.

"Then why don't you take your own advice, Marcos? Because from where I'm sitting, you're a man living so deeply in the past you can't even enjoy the present."

They had not found Ana and her boyfriend by nightfall. Francesca took turns with Ingrid and another of the women who worked there in playing with Armando. He was a sweet little boy, but he was beginning to get fussy the longer he went without his mother.

Surely, Ana must have done a few things right, or her son would not have bonded with her so strongly as to notice she'd been gone for a very long time. Francesca had just given the child back to Ingrid and decided to go for a walk in the vineyard when Marcos emerged from his office.

She'd not spoken with him since breakfast. Once they'd finished eating, he'd said he had business to attend to and shut himself away. He'd even had his lunch delivered and had eaten behind closed doors.

She'd thought he meant to ignore her completely after what she'd said to him this morning. Looking at him now, her heart contracted. "Have they found her?" she asked, hoping beyond hope that he'd found out something.

He shook his head. He looked so forlorn in that moment, so defeated. She wanted to go to him, wrap her arms around him. Tell him how she felt.

And just like that, the truth of what she was feeling slammed into her, stole her breath away. She loved him.

She loved Marcos Navarre. This time it was real, not the childish love of an infatuated teenager. He was far from the selfish, cruel bastard she'd thought him to be. He felt things deeply, and he acted with more dignity and morality than anyone she'd ever known.

Including her own family. Her mother was selfish beyond belief, her sister had always been concerned with herself and the way she looked, and her father indulged them all with bigger and better gifts and trips.

Not one of them had ever expressed concern over those less fortunate than they were. She didn't ever remember any talk about favorite charities or reasons other than tax deductions to give money away.

And she'd been just as bad, living in her shell and worrying about herself and her secret—or not so secret—crush on Marcos.

Yet, in spite of loss and pain and a difficult childhood, Marcos had dedicated himself to helping others.

And she loved him for it.

The thought sent a little shiver of heat and joy racing up her spine all at once. And fear.

Because he did not love her in return, nor was he likely to do so. This was a temporary marriage, based on his desire to reclaim his family birthright once and for all. At the end of their time together, he would stick her on a plane and say goodbye forever.

"How is Armando?" he asked her.

"He seems fine," she said. "Ingrid has taken him."

Marcos shoved a hand through his hair. "This has never happened before. I cannot allow that child to go to an orphanage," he finished fiercely.

Francesca finally conquered her paralysis. She went to him, slipped her arms around his waist and pressed in close, her head on his chest. He did not push her away. Instead, he squeezed her to him.

"Of course you can't," she said. "It won't come down to that."

"What a tiger you are," he murmured. "So fierce, so strong in your beliefs. I am thankful you've never been disillusioned."

She pushed back, tilted her head up to look at him.

"I've been disillusioned plenty, Marcos. But that doesn't mean I give up."

He threaded his fingers through her hair. "I do not give up either. Perhaps we are more alike than I thought."

Heat wound its way through her limbs, sizzling into her nerve endings. All he had to do was touch her—no, all he had to do was *look* at her—and she was on fire. She dropped her chin, certain he would see her heart in her eyes if she kept looking at him.

A baby's wail ricocheted through the house. Marcos stiffened, though she knew it wasn't out of annoyance or anger.

"We should go see what's happening," she said. "Maybe Armando will respond to one of us."

"Sí," Marcos replied, taking her hand and leading her toward the kitchen.

The scene they entered into was one of controlled chaos. Ingrid was extracting her hands from a pile of dough, her skin too covered in flour and gluten to quickly be free, and Isabelle was cleaning up an oozing pile of spaghetti that had spattered on the floor, the table, her, and Armando. A stoneware bowl also lay on the floor, shattered.

Baby Armando wailed at the top of his lungs in his high chair. Francesca hurried over to help Isabelle while Marcos grabbed a wet rag and wiped off Armando's face. Then he lifted the toddler out of the chair, uncaring of the tomato sauce that got on his shirt as he held Armando close and began to bounce him up and down.

Armando kept wailing.

"Give him to me," Francesca said when she'd helped Isabelle pick up the broken stoneware. Marcos handed him over, and though he continued to cry, he began calming down as she crooned a song to him. A song she'd sung to her unborn baby at night when her little girl would kick and keep her awake. It had often worked, or so she'd convinced herself.

It worked on Armando too. He lay his head on her shoulder and stuck his thumb in his mouth, though he still sniffled and hiccoughed.

"He likes you," Marcos said, shooting her a smile that melted her insides.

"Only this time. Later, it could be you he prefers."

Marcos's smiled didn't waver. "I doubt that, *mi gatita*. He knows he has found a soft heart in you."

She turned from her husband, certain her face was red. Ingrid gave her a smile and a wink. Francesca couldn't help but smile back. She carried Armando into the cavernous living area and sat down on one of the long couches there. Marcos was close behind, his hands in his jeans pockets, his shirt streaked with red sauce.

He'd never looked sexier to her. She could imagine him being so tender and good with his own child, and her heart ached. She loved him, and she could never give him that.

A pain throbbed in her breastbone. He didn't want that kind of life with her anyway. This was not a true marriage, and she was not a true wife. She'd been so incredibly stupid in not keeping an emotional distance from this man.

But how could she have done so? Each new thing she learned about him was like a nail in the coffin of her determination not to like him.

She'd failed, and she would pay the price when the time came.

Marcos perched on the thick wooden coffee table in front of the couch. "And you said you were scared of children."

"I'd never been around them, is all," she replied, stroking Armando's soft curls. Her eyes filled with tears. She tried to hold them back, but one spilled down her cheek regardless.

Marcos leaned forward, his brows drawing together as he caught a teardrop on his finger. "What is this, *querida*? You have told me to have faith. Do you not take your own advice?"

"It's not that," she whispered, suddenly overwhelmed with all she wanted to say. With all she wanted to share. "I-I was pregnant once."

Shock rocked him back. "Pregnant?"

She nodded, unable to look at him, her heart throbbing. "I lost the baby at six months. There was a robbery at the store, and I was beaten. They killed my baby."

"Francesca, my God—"

"She was a girl. Jacques cared for me when all I wanted to do was die as well. It wasn't just physical, either. He saved me from myself."

"Your mother? Your sister?"

She shook her head. "He called them, but they'd disowned me. Because of the Corazón del Diablo."

"Madre de Dios," he breathed, visibly shaken. "When did this happen? What did they do to the men who did this?"

"It was four years ago, soon after Robert and I split. The men were caught. One of them died in prison, but the other two are still there. There's one more thing." She drew in a deep breath. "I can never have children of my own. The doctors say the damage was too great."

CHAPTER ELEVEN

HE DIDN'T KNOW what to say. Shock, outrage—even despair—were the emotions crashing through him at the moment. He stared at his wife in disbelief. Francesca's head was bowed, her attention focused on the toddler sleeping so peacefully in her arms. She stroked his hair with a shaky hand.

She could never have children—no wonder she'd been so uncomfortable when Armando had first appeared. She'd told him she had a headache, that she needed to lie down. But what she'd needed, he realized now, was escape.

He wanted to destroy the men who had done this to her. Wanted to destroy the man who'd left her to face the future alone while she was pregnant with his child.

He shot to his feet, overwhelmed with hot emotion, ready to do battle for her and slay the demons of her past. Yet it was too late, as he well knew.

She gazed up at him. Tears slid freely down her cheeks now and she swiped them away with the backs of her fingers while she tried not to awaken Armando.

He was so gripped with feeling, with emotion he didn't understand. He needed to escape, at least for a few moments. He needed time to regain his perspective.

"It's okay," she said. "I understand."

He couldn't move. He wanted to go, but he couldn't. "Understand what?"

"You're angry, probably even horrified. And you're glad we have a contract, because we both know this is ending in three months. You aren't saddled with a barren wife for real."

As long as she lived, she would never forget the way he was looking at her right now. His expression was hard, angry. The scar on his face was white, and she didn't think he realized that his hands were clenched into fists at his side.

Perhaps she should have waited to see what he would have said, but the truth was she couldn't bear it. So she'd said it for him, because she was certain he would not. He would have told her how sorry he was, how sad, and then she would have been forced to murmur her thanks, all while holding this precious baby, who almost looked like he could belong to Marcos, in her arms.

She couldn't bear it, so she'd given him his out.

"Francesca, that's not at all what I was thinking."

She sniffed, and was furious with herself for doing so. Being weak was not how she'd survived those dark days, or how she'd gotten where she was now.

"It's all right, Marcos. You don't have to explain."

He sank down again, elbows on his knees, his hands steepled together. "I am angry, you are correct about this. Angry enough that I want to find these men and punish them for what they did to you. And I want to find this Robert too. I want them to bleed, Francesca. For you."

She sucked in a sharp breath. "That's not what I want," she managed, her heart zipping recklessly.

"I know this," he replied. "It's what I want."

She could see the warrior in him then. A man who said he'd seen the worst that one person could do to the other. He'd not only seen it, he knew how to do it. And she knew he was capable of it. A shiver washed down her spine at the thought.

"I will not do this," he continued. "But it's what I want to do."

"It's in the past, Marcos. Nothing will bring my little girl back now. If it would, I'd do it myself, believe me."

He was looking at her in a new way, she realized. Was it respect? Or pity? She couldn't tell, and she was too emotionally exhausted to figure it out.

"It is no wonder I didn't recognize you that night," he said. "You have changed, Francesca, and not only in a physical way. Don't you see how strong you are? How fierce and protective? How could you think that you are not unbelievably beautiful? You blind me with your beauty."

Armando stirred in her arms then, saving her from having to say something in return. Because, quite frankly, he'd stunned her. And given her hope. Was it possible he felt something more for her too? Was it silly to believe that maybe there could be something wonderful between them?

Marcos's cell phone rang. He answered it with a clipped, *"Sí."* And then, much quicker than she'd expected, he was finished. His eyes were dark with emotion. He reached out to stroke Armando's curls and shook his head, his jaw clenched tight.

"Marcos, what is it?" she asked. Deep inside, she knew it wasn't good. She could see it in his face, feel it in the air. Poor, poor Armando.

"They've found Ana."

"But that's good, right?" Hope beyond hope. *Please let this baby get his mother back...*

"She's not coming back, Francesca. Not ever. She and her boyfriend were drinking. There was an auto accident. They did not survive."

The house was in an uproar for several hours. Marcos went with one of the men to claim the body for burial. The teens seemed to come out of the woodwork now, their ability to concentrate on their tasks severely compromised. Ingrid rocked Isabelle, who cried endlessly. Though Ana hadn't lived at the winery for long, Isabelle had grown close to her in that short time.

Ana, it seemed, had been vibrant and fun, quick to laugh, a peacemaker and sweet girl who just wanted to be loved. It was that need to be loved that had led her to run away with a boy she'd thought adored her. No one knew who Armando's father had been, but they knew Ana had been in love with him once. He'd abandoned her and she'd ended up here, lonely and scared and still looking for love.

Armando was, thankfully, asleep in his crib. He'd begun to cry again when so many others were doing so, but Francesca got him to go back to sleep and he was currently bedded down in the room he'd shared with his mother.

By the time Marcos returned, it was late. Everyone had trickled back to their rooms by then. One of the young women had gone to stay in the room with

Armando. Francesca had thought about having him brought into her room, but he'd been asleep and she'd been afraid that moving him would only wake him.

When Marcos walked in, she could see the strain on his face. Her heart went out to him. How was it that this man, this wealthy man who controlled a vast empire, could be so broken up over one young girl whom he'd never even met?

She could explain it, because she knew Marcos, but there truly weren't enough words to do so. The way she'd fought for Jacques, the way she would have fought for her baby if she could have, this was the way he fought for these kids. With his whole heart, though she wasn't sure he realized that's what it was. He felt obligated, he'd said, because he'd been one of them.

But it was more than that. He could have turned out so cold and brutal after what had happened to him, but he wasn't.

He came over and caught her to him, sweeping her off her feet so quickly she gasped in surprise.

"No words, Francesca," he said. "I need you too much for words."

She didn't realize he'd carried her to his room until they were inside and he was whisking her shirt over her head. For some reason, the fact he'd taken her to *his* room caught at her heart and made hope blossom more strongly than before.

He stripped her urgently while she tore at his clothes in return. As soon as they were naked, they fell to the bed, mouths melding, limbs fusing, bodies straining for each other.

She was so turned on, so ready for him, that she didn't need any preliminaries. Wrapping her legs around his waist, she urged him inside her. When they were joined, she thought he would take her to the heights of pleasure very quickly, that his need was urgent.

Instead, he moved languidly, thoroughly, touching her so deeply that she could only gasp with each stroke. She'd never felt like this before, never felt her heart expanding so wide, the joy and pleasure of being with a man she loved so very much making the experience that much more intense.

What did Marcos feel when he was moving inside her like this? Did he feel the joy too? Or was it just the usual sort of pleasure a man felt in a woman's body?

He caught her face between his hands, forcing her to look at him as he made love to her. Her heart pounded in her chest, her temples, her throat. Surely he could see the way she felt shining in her eyes, hear it in the gasps and moans she couldn't help.

"You are beautiful, Francesca," he whispered. "Beautiful."

"Marcos, I—" She closed her eyes, swallowed. "I can't think...of anything...but you."

He kissed her—hot, wet, deep—stroking into her faster and faster until she finally shattered with a cry that felt like it had been ripped from her throat. The pleasure didn't stop there, however. Marcos slipped his hand between them and brought her to climax again, stroking her with his fingers and his body, this time following her over the edge when she went.

Soon, he rolled away, and though she mourned the loss of him, she welcomed the cool air rushing over her skin. He lay beside her, his chest rising and falling, his eyes closed. He was absolutely the sexiest thing she'd ever seen in her life. His body glistened with sweat, the hard muscles and smooth planes making her want to climb on top of him and repeat the experience.

To have all that to herself? To enjoy the power and beauty of a man like Marcos Navarre whenever she wanted? She was lucky, yes, but simply having sex with him wasn't enough. Would never be enough.

She'd never thought she would feel this way. After her baby died, part of her had died too. To feel love for someone, the kind of love that ripped you apart and sewed you back up again with every waking moment, was not something she'd been prepared for.

She studied his body without hesitation. He'd thrown an arm over his eyes. His hand lay against the pillow, his wrist turned out, the underside exposed. She leaned forward, studying the pale marks there. How had she not noticed this before? Marcos had very fine scars, so fine they weren't apparent until you were up close, in a band across his skin.

Carefully, she reached out and traced one finger along them. He flinched, but did not jerk away as he'd done in the past. Then she traced the scar on his abdomen. He dropped his arm, his eyes glittering as he watched her.

"You said you would make those men bleed for me, Marcos. And I would take the pain of these away, if I could."

"I know you would." He caught her fingers in his, kissed them. "I am sorry for what happened to you, Francesca. I can't help but think if I hadn't come into your life, it would have turned out differently."

"And if your uncle had never betrayed your parents and bartered the Corazón del Diablo to my father, perhaps my life would have been different. Or perhaps not."

"Have you always been so stoic?"

"Definitely not." She turned toward him, traced the line of his arm until she was at his wrist again. "Will you tell me what this is from?"

He closed his eyes, the pain on his features apparent. "I've never told anyone."

"Tell me."

"It's brutal, Francesca. Ugly."

"You mean ugly like being beaten so badly you lose your baby and can never have another one?"

He swore. She didn't think that was a good sign, but then he said, "I was captured by the enemy, chained in a dark room for days on end with no food, minimal water, and every incentive in the world to escape." He lifted his wrists, turned them out so she could see the fine markings on both. "I did not succeed, by the way."

Her heart was pounding for an entirely different reason now. She'd handcuffed him to a bed, for God's sake! She remembered the way he'd looked at her, the hatred in his eyes then. She'd humiliated him, forced him to recall his worst memories while she'd taken the Corazón del Diablo and disappeared into the night. No wonder he'd been so angry when he'd tracked her down.

"They beat me for information, but I did not give it to them. And they left me in the dark with rats and snakes coming in through the crumbling walls." He laughed, but there was no humor in it. "I spent one night with a python curled next to me for warmth. Why it didn't strangle me, I still don't know."

"Oh, Marcos," she breathed, tears pricking the backs of her eyes.

"I've seen too much ugliness, Francesca. And I suppose it's right you know, because you need to understand that I'm not capable of love, not really. I had it burned out of me in the hell of my life."

Pain wound around her heart, squeezed. "I don't believe that."

He pushed her back on the pillows, his handsome, tortured face hovering so close above hers. "Believe it, Francesca." His head dipped, his lips touching the hollow of her throat where her pulse beat hard and strong. "I am capable of this," he murmured, his tongue touching her pulse point, "of passion and sex. And I do want you. But I don't love you. I can't."

Though he was soon inside her again, taking her to the edge of pleasure and beyond with his skillful lovemaking, it didn't feel nearly as joyful as it had the last time.

Marcos bolted upright in bed, the dregs of the nightmare fading almost immediately as Francesca stirred beside him. She didn't wake, and he thought with some amazement that perhaps he hadn't cried out. Or maybe she was simply exhausted from their lovemaking. He'd taken much from her in his quest to drive the memory of tonight's events from his head.

Poor Ana Luis. Her body had been smashed almost beyond recognition in the single-car accident that claimed both her and the boy who was the son of a neighboring vintner. As horrible as those memories were, the image of Francesca rocking little Armando, who was now an orphan, and her quiet insistence on learning all of Marcos's deepest secrets with just a soft word and equally soft touch, were the primary things on his mind.

He'd told her everything. He had no secrets from this woman, and that alarmed him in some respects. How was it possible he'd told her those things?

But he had—and oddly enough, it made the burden somewhat lighter. Not much, but a little.

His heart still pounded from the dream, but not as fiercely as usual. For once, he couldn't even remember the specifics of the dream. He lay back down, curled around the warm woman next to him. Her back was to him, her beautiful naked buttocks thrust against his groin.

His cock stirred, but it was only out of proximity to her naked body and not because he wasn't satiated already. In fact, he didn't think he *could* make love again tonight. He wrapped his arms around her, happy in a way he'd not been in a long time to have a woman nestled against him. This woman.

He hadn't lied when he'd told her he was incapable of love, but he acknowledged that he did feel something for her. Something beyond what he usually felt for the women who shared his bed.

She was more of a kindred spirit, in some respects. He kissed her shoulder, drew in a breath scented with whatever flowery shampoo she used. Her hair was a gorgeous tumble of silk. He drew it aside, up and out of the way, and pressed his lips to the back of her neck. She stirred in her sleep, made a little mewling sound that made him hard when he'd thought it was probably impossible again tonight.

How had he missed the lush beauty of her figure

before? Even with forty extra pounds, she couldn't have hidden these curves away. But he'd been fooled by the baggy clothes and shyness, just as everyone else had been. Her sister must have known Francesca was the real beauty, that Francesca would someday outshine her, and she'd been evil because of it.

He'd always believed Francesca was as duplicitous in their first marriage as her family had been, but now he wasn't so sure. And, even if she was, she'd certainly paid enough for it, hadn't she?

It killed him to think she'd suffered so much. Because he'd taken the Corazón del Diablo and alienated her from her family. She'd have never been working in a jewelry store, never been in a position to be attacked so brutally, had her family kept their fortune and she remained a debutante.

But what choice had there been? The jewel was his, the symbol of his family and the touchstone of their memory. He'd have sold his soul to the devil to regain it.

Though, thinking about it, perhaps he already had.

Francesca turned in his arms then, her lips finding the sensitive spot beneath his ear, her tongue tracing the column of his neck and settling into the hollow of his throat. Marcos groaned as she rolled him onto his back and straddled his erect penis.

So much for being incapable again tonight.

Thank God.

The next day, when the house was still in mourning and arrangements to bury Ana were being made, Magdalena and her family came for a visit. Francesca instantly liked Marcos's sister. She was a sweet, sunny personality, and she expressed sympathy and horror over the news about Ana's death.

Francesca could tell she adored Marcos, who seemed to adore her equally. He'd said he wasn't capable of love, but clearly he was mistaken. He played with the children, held the baby, and gave everyone presents.

When Magdalena asked if Francesca wanted to hold her newborn, Marcos shot her a frown. In spite of her determination not to let her silly heart see hope where there was none, that gesture alone flooded her with warmth. He knew it might be hard on her and he was prepared to intervene with some excuse if she gave him reason.

"Of course I would," she said, taking little Amelia in her arms. The baby was red-faced and wide-eyed, and Francesca held her close, breathing in the scent of powder and newborn. It hurt to hold such a tiny baby— but maybe it hurt a little less than she'd thought it would only a few days before.

Cutting herself off from children until now had been necessary, but she felt as if she were ready to be around them again, as if the joy and love they brought weren't necessarily denied her forever.

As Marcos's involvement with his Foundation had brought home to her, there were still children who needed parents. She would never have her own child, but that didn't mean she had to be childless if she chose not to be.

Once Magdalena and her husband and children had gone again, Marcos returned to his office and left her to her own devices. She spent time with Armando and then went for a walk in the vineyard. Her emotions were so tangled and torn.

She loved Marcos, but he'd said he did not love her.

Could never love her. How could she manage the next three months this way?

How could she not?

There was no easy answer to that question. She wanted to spend every moment she could with him, wring every moment of happiness out of the situation, and hope for the best. And she wanted to escape at the same time, before she was crushed by the futility of loving a man who did not love her.

The rest of the week passed uneventfully enough, other than the sadness surrounding the funeral of a sixteen-year-old girl. Everyone from the winery turned out for the service. Ana was buried in a beautiful little cemetery near town. Marcos spared no expense, and the service was dignified and solemn. There would be no pauper's grave for the poor girl from the streets.

The funeral saddened Francesca and made her anxious. When she returned to the *bodega*, she called Gilles. He seemed surprised to hear from her, but the news he gave her was good. Jacques's doctors were pleased with his response to treatment thus far, though he was not out of the woods yet. He had a long road ahead, but everything seemed hopeful. Gilles had hired another jeweler, and a manager to run the business, and all was proceeding very well.

She hung up feeling both relieved and a bit wistful. The shop was doing great without her. After nearly eight years with Jacques, Gilles and a new crew could take the place over without her being missed at all. It was almost as if she'd had no imprint at all.

"What is wrong, *querida*?" Marcos asked.

Francesca had been so lost in thought that she hadn't realized he'd walked in. "I was just talking to Gilles.

He says Jacques is doing well, and the shop is running smoothly."

"And this is something to look worried about?"

"I was just thinking that they didn't need me. It was an odd feeling."

"You are needed here."

But he didn't mean it the way she wanted him to mean it. "Only for the next couple of months," she replied more crisply than she'd meant to.

Marcos either didn't notice or purposely ignored the dig. "We are retuning to Buenos Aires in the morning," he said. "I've been away from my business for too long as it is."

Her heart began to throb. "What about baby Armando? Will he come with us?"

Marcos shook his head, his hands shoved in the pockets of the crisp black trousers he'd worn to the funeral. "I am working on finding him a home, but for now I think it's best he stay here where he is familiar with everything."

Francesca gaped at him. "He's a toddler, Marcos. He's familiar with us. We could take care of him—"

"No," he cut in almost brutally. "Do not think we are taking this child, Francesca. He needs a permanent home, and he needs people who will not abandon him when he's come to love them."

She slapped a hand to her chest. "*I* wouldn't abandon him."

"Ah, but you will when our marriage contract is up."

CHAPTER TWELVE

BUENOS AIRES WAS a shock to the senses after the high desert beauty of Mendoza and the wine country. But even more of a shock was the reality of her situation with Marcos. They'd made love every night at the winery, they'd spent days walking in the vineyard, talking about Ana and the Foundation and the kids that it helped. They'd spent hours with Armando, playing with him, taking him for a sunny picnic once under the lone olive tree, and tucking him in at night.

In short, they'd played a happy family and she'd let herself be sucked in by the performance. No matter that he'd said he didn't love her, she'd thought surely he must love little Armando, that he would want her to stay and help him take care of the child.

Instead, he planned to let someone else adopt the boy.

Stupid, stupid, stupid. She'd been stupid to let herself believe, because when it came down to it, Marcos was not going to want to stay married to a woman who couldn't have his children.

And she didn't blame him, not really. He deserved children of his own, and she was not the woman who could ever give that to him. This was not a permanent marriage and would never be so. Marcos was under no delusions about the reality of it, while she kept trying to convince herself that he cared and that things could change given time.

As the day wore on, Francesca realized how much she missed little Armando. How could you fall in love with a child in a week? But she had, and while she didn't doubt that Marcos wanted the best for him too, she was sick to think that she'd never see the little boy again.

Marcos returned from his offices downtown sometime around eight that evening. Francesca had not heard from him since they'd touched down that morning and he'd gone to Navarre Industries' headquarters. She was watching television in the living area when he stalked in and tossed his briefcase and suit jacket on one of the couches.

Her heart always leapt at the sight of him, but now her joy was tinged with hurt and sadness. He picked up the remote and clicked the mute button.

"We are having a cocktail party here tomorrow evening," he said without preamble. "I need you to coordinate the menu with the chef. You will also need to choose a suitable dress since you will be wearing the Corazón del Diablo."

Francesca blinked. Anger began to build like a kettle on a low flame. "And what is this cocktail party for?"

"It's business—but there will be a couple attending who I've been told cannot conceive. They may be perfect for Armando."

"You certainly waste no time," she said crisply.

He looked puzzled. "You would be happier if this was not a top priority to find Armando a loving family?"

"I didn't say that. But you seem to think that choosing a family is rather like going to a store and picking out a new suit."

He shoved a hand through his hair. "I don't know what you expect from me, Francesca. I won't let just anyone adopt Armando. They are a possibility, not a definite choice."

What could she say? That she was angry and hurt because he wanted to find the child a loving home? What sense did that make?

None, of course. But it went deeper than that. It was about them as a couple, about the death knell of her dreams. It hurt to be faced with the reality of his feelings for her.

Marcos's expression changed. Grew softer, pitying even. "Francesca, I'm sorry if this hurts you. But I have to find a home for him. He is my responsibility. I know you grew close to him, but you will not always be in his life. Surely you can see how this is a problem?"

"Of course," she said, because there was nothing else to say.

Marcos nodded. "Good, I'm glad you agree."

But she did not. Instead, she hurt inside, hurt for all that would never be. For what she would never have.

And she realized, as the pain wrapped its tentacles around her heart, she couldn't do this. She couldn't stay here for the next couple of months, sharing Marcos's bed, hostessing his parties, living with him and loving him and knowing he did not feel the same. Would never feel the same.

Because she was damaged, and though she believed he was very sorry for what had happened to her, he would never be able to love her, to have her as his wife when she could not give him the children who would inherit his empire someday.

And she just couldn't live with that knowledge anymore. She had to leave, and she had to do it soon.

"I think I'll go to bed now," she said, standing.

Marcos's expression was carefully blank. "Goodnight, Francesca. We'll talk more in the morning."

She didn't trust herself to speak, so she inclined her head in reply. Then she turned her back and walked away.

Marcos didn't go to her bed that night, though he ached to do so. But she was angry with him, he knew, and it bothered him far too much that she was. He stayed away because he wanted to prove to himself he could do so, that Francesca had no real pull on him other than the desire that constantly pounded through his veins.

He wanted her, but he would be disciplined about it. Besides, a night alone would do them both good, would help to clear their heads about everything that had happened at the *Bodega Navarre*.

He'd loved spending time with her, and though their stay had been tinged by tragedy, there had been real joy in being there with her. She'd been a rock through the whole ordeal, and she'd helped to take care of the baby though it had surely made her think of the child she'd lost. He'd admired her very much then, and he'd even let himself consider what it would be like to tear up their contract and convince her to stay with him.

Because he enjoyed her company, craved her body,

and felt more at ease with her than he ever had with anyone. It was as if she understood him.

But on the day of the funeral, when they'd stood at the gravesite and watched the coffin being lowered into the ground, he'd realized he couldn't ask her to stay. She deserved better. She deserved a man who wasn't so damaged by life that he could never love her, and she deserved to have a home and, yes, even an adopted family if she chose.

He'd known, looking into her eyes that night, what she'd wanted from him. She'd wanted him to say they could keep Armando, could live as a family together, and though part of him strongly wanted to do so, he'd done what had to be done.

It was the right thing to do. Francesca would thank him someday.

The next morning, he breakfasted with her. She was aloof and distracted, he thought, but she was no doubt still hurt. She fidgeted with her food, pushing it around on the plate, before she finally speared him with golden-green eyes.

"I'm leaving, Marcos," she said.

He ignored the funny little flip his heart did. "Where are you going?"

"Back to New York."

He wanted to howl. "We have a contract, *querida.*"

"I know. And I also know you won't cease Jacques's care. That was my only incentive to stay, when I thought you would do so. But you're too good, Marcos. As angry as you might be with me, you won't hurt someone you can help."

"I might," he said, though it was an empty threat. "The Corazón del Diablo—"

"Is yours. I will write you a letter stating my family has no claim and never has. I didn't want it, Marcos. I only wanted the money to take care of Jacques. Now that I don't need it, I don't care."

"Will you at least tell me why?"

She dropped her gaze to her lap and swallowed. Then she looked at him again, her heart shining in her eyes. "Because I love you. Because I want you to have what makes you happy, Marcos, and I've realized that it's not me. And I can't stay here with you when I know it's hopeless. If you care for me at all, even just a little bit, you have to let me leave."

He felt as if someone was squeezing a giant vise around his chest. He didn't want to let her go, not yet. But how could he not? He'd upended her life once before when she'd thought she loved him. He could not in good conscience do so again. It was wrong, so very wrong to keep her here simply to suit his own needs.

No matter how much he wanted to.

"Very well," he said, the words scraping his throat like sandpaper. "I will make the arrangements."

Snow had come early to New York that year. The sidewalks were blanketed in a crisp layer of white, and everything looked magical and fresh.

Francesca was numb, but not from cold. She'd been back for three weeks and she hadn't heard from Marcos at all. She'd made it through that last day with him, hosted the cocktail party gowned in a gorgeous ruby red dress and wearing the Corazón del Diablo, and met the very sweet couple who would probably become Armando's parents.

Marcos had smiled and mingled as if nothing was wrong, and her heart had cracked every time she'd heard him laugh. He'd agreed so easily to her request. So easily that she knew she truly meant nothing to him. A part of her had harbored the hope that he would refuse, that he would be forced to realize she meant something to him after all.

He had not. The next morning, she hadn't even seen him before the car arrived and it was time to go. It was as if he'd cut her from his life completely once he'd agreed to her request.

Francesca walked down the street with her collar turned up and her eyes fixed on the sidewalk in front of her. Soon, the snow would turn black with dirt and footprints—which would certainly match her mood more accurately.

A pang of longing for the warmth of the high desert in Mendoza sliced through her. Worse, a pang of longing for the man who'd shared those glorious days with her rode hard on its heels. She thought about Armando, wondered if he was in his new home yet. She hoped he would be happy and healthy and have the kind of life his mother would have wanted for him.

Marcos had not called or sent any form of communication since she'd left Argentina. She had expected divorce papers, but it was still early. They could be delivered any day now.

At least there was a bright spot in her otherwise dreary life. Jacques's condition was improving tremendously. He was actually beginning to get color back into his cheeks. He was coming home in a few days, though he would have to return twice weekly for treatment.

A nurse would be accompanying him for around-the clock-care.

One more thing for which to be grateful to Marcos. Jacques wasn't out of the woods yet, but the doctors grew more optimistic each day.

Francesca took the steps up to her apartment and let herself in, unwinding her scarf and dropping it onto a chair. She shrugged out of her coat and hung it up, then went to the kitchen to check on the soup she'd left simmering at the back of the stove.

How easily she'd slipped back into her normal life— and how strange and empty it all seemed.

The buzzer to the downstairs door rang. She went to the intercom and, once she'd determined it was a deliveryman, let him inside. Dread pooled in the pit of her stomach as she stood on the landing. Could it be the divorce papers?

The man came up the steps with a small package clutched beneath one arm. He had her sign an electronic form, keyed in some information, and handed the parcel to her. Francesca thanked him, then went inside and took the package to the counter in the kitchen.

There was no return address, and she had no idea who might send her something express delivery.

Though perhaps it was something from the hospital. Something of Jacques's. She grabbed a pair of scissors from a drawer and sliced into the cardboard.

A velvet box lay nestled among the air packets. She lifted it out, puzzled. When she flipped open the lid, her heart skidded to a stop before it began to beat double time.

The fiery yellow glow of the gemstone winking at

her from a sea of white diamonds was unmistakable.
She snatched up the folded note that lay beneath the
Corazón del Diablo.

Come to the Four Seasons. There is a car waiting.
Marcos

CHAPTER THIRTEEN

MARCOS STOOD ON the fifty-first floor, gazing out of the window of this luxurious suite, and wondered if she would come.

Of course she will come.

He'd sent the necklace as a gesture of his surrender. But was it too subtle? Would she be so angry with him that she would not take the chance?

He scraped a hand through his hair and blew out a breath. He eyed the handcuffs he'd bought.

Could he really do what he planned to do?

Yes, because she will come.

Francesca had said she loved him, and he'd held onto those words for the past three weeks. They'd rung through his head every minute of every day. At first, he'd believed that letting her go was the right thing to do.

But nothing had been the same once she'd gone. He'd watched from a window as she'd climbed into the car, feeling numb. Then he'd made himself watch as the car pulled into the street and disappeared into traffic.

He'd stood there for a long time after, envisioning the journey to the airport, wondering what Francesca was thinking.

Was she hating him now? Congratulating herself on a lucky escape?

Or was she crying?

She was brave and tough, his little tiger kitten. The thought of her crying twisted his heart into a knot. He didn't want to make her cry.

He'd tried to push her from his mind as the days dragged by, tried to continue running his business and the Foundation.

But she'd left a hollow spot inside him with her absence. He'd thought it would fill up slowly, but it never did. The hole grew bigger with each passing day, until he realized what a fool he'd been.

He had to win her back. Determined, he turned and picked up the cuffs. She would come, and he would prove to her that he needed her, that he could be the man she deserved.

Francesca hadn't bothered to change out of her jeans and sweater before shoving the jewel box in her purse and bounding outside to the idling limo that waited at the curb. Now that she'd arrived, however, she was beginning to regret that she'd not taken time to make herself look a bit more presentable.

The grand foyer, with its rows of tall columns and gleaming surfaces, was understatedly elegant. And she was completely out of place. She'd hoped Marcos would meet her in the lobby, but instead she was pointed to the elevators and given an access key with a room number printed on it.

She rode the elevator up to the fifty-first floor. Thank goodness he'd not stayed here the first time, or she'd never have been able to get inside. When she entered the luxurious Presidential suite, it was quiet except for the hiss and crackle of the gas fireplace in the living room. Was he even here?

"Marcos?" she called.

"In here."

She followed his voice, emerging into a bedroom with spectacular views of Central Park and the night sky. But that wasn't what caught her attention.

Marcos was on the bed, fully clothed, leaning against the headboard. One arm was raised over his head. His wrist was cuffed to the bedpost.

"What are you doing?" she cried.

He smiled, though the scar at the corner of his mouth was white. "Therapy."

She hurried over to his side, dropping her purse on the floor. "Where is the key?"

"I'm not quite sure. I threw it out of reach before I closed the cuff. I did not wish to chicken out, as you Americans say."

"Marcos, that's insane!" She turned in a circle, looking for a slice of silver in the dim lamplight.

"Perhaps, but I had to do something."

She popped her hands on her hips and glared at him. "There are many things you could do about it, but this probably wasn't the best idea. What if I hadn't come?"

"I knew you would."

"What if I hadn't been home? What if I hadn't got the package tonight? They'd have taken it back to the warehouse and attempted redelivery tomorrow."

"I had faith."

Francesca rolled her eyes. "My God, Marcos, couldn't you have simply picked up the phone?"

He looked suddenly wary. "I was afraid you wouldn't listen."

"And this is designed to make me listen?" She turned away, intent on finding the key. Marcos didn't say anything, and she knew he was fighting with himself. Trying not to panic, she was certain.

Her heart pounded so hard. The blood rushed in her ears, drowning out sound. She had to find that key, had to free him. Knowing what she did, she couldn't stand to see him like this. He may think trial by fire was therapy—a typical alpha male way of approaching things—but it was killing her to know he was in pain.

Falling to her hands and knees, she patted the carpet. When she felt something small and cool, she snatched it up. Her hands shook as she inserted the key into the lock. Marcos leaned toward her, his face practically touching her breasts as she worked the catch. Desire flared to life inside her as he took a deep breath.

"You smell good, *mi gatita*."

The lock clicked and the cuff snapped open. Marcos put both arms around her before she could take a step away.

"I have missed you," he said.

She put her hands on his shoulders, pushing until his grip loosened. Then she pulled away and wrapped her arms around her middle.

"You are angry with me," he said.

"A bit." And hurt. And confused. And unsure she wanted to relive even a moment of pleasure with him if it was only going to lead to more heartbreak.

Because he did want her, she knew that. But it was a physical need, not an emotional one. Had he really called her here just to get in her panties again? After this stunt, she truly had no idea what he was capable of.

"You have every right to be," he said. "I understand this."

"Then why are you here? Do you feel guilty? Want to ease your troubled conscience?" She was surprised to find that anger was indeed the dominant emotion she felt at the moment. Because she really didn't know what he wanted. He'd dragged her here with the Corazón del Diablo and a note, but he'd not fallen to his knees and proclaimed his undying love, or said he needed her in his life, or anything else.

Instead, he'd chained himself to the bed and scared her half to death in the process.

"The nightmares are back," he said softly. He stood and shoved his hands in his pockets. "They are even worse now, in some ways."

"And you thought that chaining yourself to this bed and hoping I would come along might help?"

"Perhaps not the best plan, but I'm working on it."

She shook her head. "How is it possible the dreams are worse?"

"Because you are in them, and it is you I cannot save."

"I'm fine, I assure you."

"I can see that. But without you, I do not sleep well."

"And what is the solution to that? That I return to Argentina and sleep with you every night?"

"*Sí.*"

Francesca blinked. "For how long?"

He shrugged. "As long as it takes."

"No." Damn him! How dare he come along and entice

her with such a thing, and all because he slept better when she was there? "Ask some other woman."

He shoved a hand through his hair. "Clearly, I am doing this wrong."

"Clearly."

He caught her by the shoulders, gripping her too hard for her to get away easily but not so hard it hurt. "I need you, Francesca. I was a fool to let you go."

Her eyes filled with tears. It was what she wanted to hear—but after so much pain and heartbreak, how could she believe it? She'd believed in him before, and she'd been wrong.

"What changed your mind? Nightmares? Because I'm not sure that's enough, Marcos."

He let her go, walked over to the windows and gazed out at the nightlights of the city. His shoulders seemed to sag a little.

"I'm afraid, Francesca. Afraid because for the first time in my life, I actually care about someone else's happiness and well being more than my own." He turned to face her again. "I know I've not done this well, and I know you have reason not to trust me, but I'm trying to tell you that I love you. As deeply and as much as I am able."

A tear slid down her cheek and she dashed it away. "Why should that be so hard to say?" she asked, her throat aching.

"Because I know I'm not a good bargain. Part of me is ruined and broken. It's unfair to ask you to fix that, but you are the only one who can. Without you, I'm lost. And I know this is selfish of me, but I want you to come back."

Her legs refused to hold her upright any longer. She

sank onto the end of the bed and stared at him. "I love you, Marcos, but I'm scared too. Because I can never have children, and you are a man who deserves to have his own children. How do I know you won't resent me for it later? That you won't regret this once you feel like the damage of the past is repaired? Because it's not me who will repair it, but you. I really have nothing to do with it."

"You have *everything* to do with it. If you hadn't come into my life again, I wouldn't have understood that I have the strength to move beyond my past. You taught me that." He came over to her then, knelt before her and took her hands in his. His handsome face was so serious. "And you of all people should know that a family is built on love, not genetics. Is Jacques any less your family because you are not related? Do your mother and sister have a greater claim on your affections because they share your blood?"

She shook her head. The lump in her throat was too big to speak. She thought of her mother, her cold cruel mother in her drafty house with her mantle of blame, and knew what he said was right. Just because someone gave birth to you did not mean they were capable of loving you.

He squeezed her hands. "Do you know why I sent you the Corazón del Diablo?"

"No," she managed.

"Because possessing it has caused me nothing but sorrow. It *is* the devil's heart, and it exacts a great price. And I'm tired of being a prisoner to my past. I want to go forward, and I want to do this with you."

"How is giving me the necklace letting go of the past?"

"Because you are free to do with it what you wish. Donate it to a museum, give it to Jacques—I don't care. But when you've done what you want, all I ask is that you come home with me. I need you."

Hope was unfurling in her soul, the wind of his words catching it and fanning it higher. Could she really dare to believe? "It's your birthright, Marcos. You can't just give it up like that. It means too much. You've fought too hard for it."

"I have already let it go," he said, his eyes so serious as they searched hers. "It's yours. As am I. The symbolism is meaningless without you."

But she had to be sure. "You would give up the possibility of ever having a biological child? It's not something to be done lightly, Marcos. I didn't have a choice, but you do."

He kissed her hands, then cupped the back of her head and kissed her lips. "I love you, Francesca. You make my world brighter. Whether or not you are able to give me a child of my blood has nothing to do with how I feel about you."

She shook her head, so scared and so uncertain—and so hopeful. "You'll regret it. You'll resent me later—"

"No, I won't. I cannot resent you when you are my heart, my soul. You make me whole again. I need you. Armando needs you."

"Armando?"

"He's had quite an upheaval, but he needs a stable life. We can give that to him. I want us to be the ones who give it to him."

"But I thought you had found him a family."

"He already has a family. Us, Ingrid and Isabelle. The *bodega* and everyone there."

She squeezed her eyes shut. "It's not fair to try and bribe me this way."

"I don't care about fair, *mi amor*. I care about you. I want to spend every day with you, talking, arguing, making love, going for walks, taking care of Armando. I want to wake up each day knowing you will be there. And I want you to know that I love you, and that I've never said those words to anyone other than my mother. Not anyone, Francesca. Not ever."

Her heart was expanding with all she felt. With every word he said, she believed him. She touched his face, traced the scar at his mouth. He turned his head, and kissed her palm.

"Please, Francesca," he said urgently. "I can't do this without you. Say you will come home with me, that you will love me—"

"I already do love you. So much it scares me."

"Then say you will marry me and be my wife forever."

"Luckily, we're already married," she said with a watery smile.

He answered her with a sexy grin. "Then we can start immediately on the honeymoon. My favorite part."

"Mine too."

"*Bueno,*" he said, tugging her sweater up. "Because I have much I wish to do to you before this night is through…"

It was a very wonderful night, Francesca thought. But not until much, much later…

EPILOGUE

HE TRULY WAS THE luckiest man in the world. Marcos sat on the veranda of the *Bodega Navarre*, gazing out at the vineyards and the laughing little boy playing with Francesca. Little Armando was a dynamo at three years old. He was quick, smart, and as adorable as ever.

Marcos loved him with all his heart. Though it saddened him to think of how the boy had come into their lives, he was very happy they were the ones who'd adopted the child once his mother had died so tragically. Armando would have a good life as a Navarre. And, when he was old enough, he would know about his mother. Both Marcos and Francesca agreed that was important.

Ingrid came to take Armando for his bath, and Francesca collapsed into a chair.

"Wore you out, did he?"

"Lord yes," she said, taking a sip of the cool lemon ice water one of the girls had brought out. He watched her, felt a well of emotion as she set the glass down and gave him a funny little look. "What?"

"I love you, Francesca. You are the most beautiful woman in the world."

"You don't have to keep telling me I'm beautiful.

We've been married for almost two years now. I'm not worried you'll let another woman turn your head."

"But you are beautiful. Extraordinarily so. I tell you this because I mean it." He leaned over and kissed her. "If you would like to retire for a *siesta*, I could show you how beautiful you are to me. I am aching to do so."

Her smile turned wicked. "Marcos Navarre, are you trying to corrupt me?"

"Every chance I get," he vowed. He pulled her onto his lap and kissed her. She made a little sound of pleasure in her throat when she discovered he was already hard for her.

"Oh my," she said. "I'm looking forward to that *siesta*."

"Let's go then."

"Do you two ever stop?"

Francesca jumped up and went to hug the old man who'd hobbled onto the veranda. "Jacques, how are you feeling? Did you sleep well?"

"I'm fine, sweetheart," he said.

She helped him into a chair and poured a glass of wine for him. "And your sleep?"

He took an appreciative sip. "I slept like an old man of seventy-seven should sleep. Stop fussing, Francesca. Now you two go on and do whatever you were going to do, don't mind me. I'll just sit here and enjoy the view."

"Then we will enjoy it with you," Marcos said without hesitation. Francesca smiled at him, and he thought once more what a lucky man he was. Tonight, he would show her just how he felt. And every night for the rest of their lives.

PLEASURED IN THE PLAYBOY'S PENTHOUSE

NATALIE RIVERS

Natalie Rivers grew up in the Sussex countryside. As a child she always loved to lose herself in a good book, or in games that gave free rein to her imagination. She went to Sheffield University, where she met her husband in the first week of term. It was love at first sight and they have been together ever since, moving to London after graduating, getting married and having two wonderful children.

After university Natalie worked in a lab at a medical research charity and later retrained to be a primary school teacher. Now she is lucky enough to be able to combine her two favourite occupations—being a full-time mum and writing passionate romances.

For Soraya—you are so generous and supportive, always dropping everything to read in a rush and then getting back to me so quickly and so helpfully...and this one was some rush, wasn't it? I am really looking forward to repaying you in kind so very soon.

CHAPTER ONE

DID she want a 'sex machine' or a 'slow comfortable screw'? Choices, choices…and tonight Bella was struggling with decisions. The names were all such appalling puns, she didn't know if she'd be able to ask for one without blushing. Especially as she was sitting all alone in this bar—on a Friday night. The bartender would probably panic and think she was coming on to him. But as she looked at the gleaming glasses lined up behind the counter and the rows of bottles holding varying amounts of brightly coloured liquid, her taste buds were tickled. It had been a while since she'd had anything more indulgent than whatever was the cheapest red wine at the supermarket. Surely she was justified in having something fabulous to celebrate her day? And as this weekend had already burned one huge hole in her savings, she might as well make it a crater.

She looked back at the cocktail list, but barely read on. She'd waited all day for someone to say it. Someone. Anyone. It wasn't as if she expected a party—a cake, candles or even a card. It was a frantic time getting everything organised for Vita's wedding, Bella understood that. But surely even one of them could have remembered? Her father perhaps?

But no. She was just there, as usual, in the background, like the family cat. Present, accounted for, but blending in as if part of the furniture. It was only if she had some sort of catastrophe that they remembered her. And she was determined to avoid any catastrophes this weekend. This was Vita's special time. As uncomfortable as Bella felt, she was determined to help make the weekend as wonderful as it could be for her sister.

Volunteering to oversee the decorating had been her best idea. It had meant she'd been able to avoid most of the others. And honestly, she'd felt more at home with the waitresses and staff of the exclusive resort than with her own family and their friends.

When she'd paused at lunchtime she'd looked up and seen them out walking along the beach. The island of Waiheke looked as if it had been taken over by an accountancy convention. In truth it basically had. They were like clones. All wearing corporate casual. The men in fawn trousers and open-collared pale blue shirts. Tomorrow they'd be in fawn again only with white shirts for the wedding. Afterwards, they'd saunter on the sand in three-quarter 'casual' trousers, overly colourful Hawaiian shirts, with their pale feet sliding in leather 'mandals'. They all had crisp cut hair, and expensive sunglasses plastered across their faces. The women were using their even more expensive sunglasses to pin back their long, sleek hair. Her tall, glamorous cousins, her sister. They were all the same. All so incredibly successful—if you equated money, high-flying jobs and incredibly suitable partners with success.

She'd tried it once—to play it their way. She'd dated a guy who was more approved of by her own family than she was herself. What a disaster that had been. They still didn't believe that she'd been the one to end it. Of course, there were reasons for that. But none Bella felt like dwelling on now. Tomorrow was going to be bad enough.

After she'd finally hung all the ribbons on the white-shrouded chairs, she'd headed straight for the bar inside the main building of the hotel. She'd celebrate herself. Toast in another year. Raise a glass to the success of the last. Even if no one else was going to. Even if there wasn't that much success to toast.

There had been talk of a family dinner, but the preparations had run too late—drinks maybe. She was glad. She didn't want to face the all too inevitable questions about her career and her love-life, the looks of unwanted sympathy from her aunts. There'd be time enough for that the next day, when there was no way she could avoid them as much as she had today. For today was *her* day and she could spend the last of it however she wanted to.

Now, as she sat and waited to be served, she avoided looking around, pretending she was happy to be there alone. She pushed back the inadequacy with some mind games—she'd play a role and fake the confidence. She would do cosmopolitan woman—the woman who took on the world and played it her way. Who took no prisoners, had what she wanted and lived it to the max. It would be good practice for tomorrow when she'd be confronted by Rex and Celia. One of the fun things about being an actress—even a minor-league, bit-part player—was the pretending.

She read through the list again, muttering as she narrowed her choices. 'Do I want "sex on the beach" or a "screaming orgasm"?'

'Why do you have to choose?'

She turned her head sharply. There was a guy standing right beside her. One incredibly hot guy whom she knew she'd never seen before because she'd damn well remember if she had. Tall and dark and with the bluest of eyes capturing hers. While she was staring, he was talking some more.

'I would have thought a woman like you would always have both.'

Sex on the beach *and* a screaming orgasm? Looking up at him, she took a firmer grip on both the menu card and the sensation suddenly beating through her—the tantalising tempo of temptation.

He must be just about the only person here who wasn't involved in the wedding. Or maybe he was. He was probably one of her cousins' dates. For a split second disappointment washed through her. But then she looked him over again—he wasn't wearing an Armani suit and if he was one of their dates he'd definitely be in Armani. And he'd be hanging on his date's arm, not alone and possibly on the prowl in a bar. This guy was in jeans—the roughest fabric she'd seen in the place to date. They were wet around the ankles as if he'd been splashing in the water, and on his feet were a pair of ancient-looking boat shoes. A light grey long-sleeved tee shirt covered his top half. It had a slight vee at the neck, exposing the base of the tanned column that was his neck. It was such a relief to see someone doing truly casual—someone not flaunting evidence of their superb bank balance.

Those bright blue eyes smiled at her. Very brightly. And then they looked her up and down.

Suddenly she felt totally uncomfortable as she thought about her own appearance. Not for the first time she wished for the cool, glamorous gene that the rest of her family had inherited. Instead she was hot, mosquito bitten, with a stripe of cooked-lobster-red sunburn across one half of her chest where she'd missed with her 110 SPF sunscreen. Her white cotton blouse was more off-white than bright and the fire-engine-red ribbon of her floral skirt was starting to come loose—but that was what you got for wearing second-hand.

It was one of her more sedate outfits, an attempt to dress up a little, in deference to the 'family' and their expectations. She'd even used the hotel iron—a real concession given she usually got at least one burn when she went anywhere near the things. Today had been no different. There was a small, very red, very sore patch just below her elbow. And now, thanks to a day spent on her knees dressing chairs in white robes and yellow ribbons, she knew she looked a sight.

As she took in his beautifully chiselled jaw, she really wished she'd bothered to go to her room and check her face or something on the way. There'd been some mascara on her eyelashes this morning, a rub of lip balm. Both were undoubtedly long gone. She was hardly in a state to be drawing single guys to her across a bar. She darted a glance around. She was the only female in the room. And there were only a couple of other customers. Then she looked at her watch. It was early. He was just making small talk with the only woman about. He was probably a travelling salesman. Only he definitely didn't look the salesman type. And despite the suggestion in his talk he didn't come across as sleazy. There was a bit of a glint in those blue eyes—she'd like to think it was appreciation, but it was more of a dare. And there was more humour than anything. She could do with some humour.

The bartender came back down to where they were standing. And Bella took up the challenge. Cosmopolitan woman she would be. Summoning all her courage and telling her cheeks to remain free of excess colour, she ordered. 'A "sex on the beach" and a "screaming orgasm" please.'

She refused to look at him but she could sense his smile of approval—could hear it in his voice as he ordered too.

'I'll have two "screaming orgasms" and "sex on the beach".'

Bella studiously watched the bartender line up the five shot glasses. She didn't want to turn and look in his eyes again, not entirely sure she wouldn't be mesmerised completely. But peripheral vision was very handy. She was motionless, seemingly fixated on the bartender as he carefully poured in each ingredient, but in reality she was wholly focused on the guy next to her as he pulled out the bar stool next to hers and sat on it. His leg brushed against hers as he did. It was a very long leg, and it looked fine clad in the faded denim. She could feel the strength just from that one accidental touch.

Silently, shaking inside, she went to lift the first glass in the line-up. But then his hand covered hers, lightly pressing it down to the wood. Did he feel her fingers jerk beneath his? She snatched a moment to recover her self-possession before attempting to look at him with what she hoped was sophisticated query.

His bright blues were twinkling. 'Have the orgasm first.'

She could feel the heat as her blood beat its way to her cheeks.

The twinkles in his eyes burned brighter. 'After all, you can always have another one later.'

She stared at him as he released her. He'd turned on the widest, laziest, most sensual smile she'd ever seen. Spellbound wasn't the word. Almost without thinking, she moved her fingers, encircling the second shot.

'What about you?' Why had her voice suddenly gone whispery?

'A gentleman always lets the lady go first.'

So she picked up the orgasm, kind of amazed her hand wasn't visibly trembling. In a swift motion she knocked the contents back into her mouth and swallowed the lot. She took a moment before breathing—then it was a short, sharp breath as she absorbed the burning hit. Slowly she put the glass back down on the bar.

His smile was wicked now. He'd picked up the sex shot, pausing pointedly with it slightly raised, until she did the same. She met his eyes and lifted the glass to her lips. Simultaneously they tipped back and swallowed.

Slamming his on the bench, he picked up the next shot. Then he paused again, inclined his head towards the remaining orgasm.

'You know it's for you.' That smile twisted his mouth as he spoke and its teasing warmth reached out to her.

There was no way she could refuse. She couldn't actually speak for the fire in her throat. So she picked up the shot and again, eyes trained on him, drank. And he mirrored her, barely half a beat behind.

It was a long, deep breath she drew that time. And her recovery was much slower. She stared for a while at the five empty glasses in front of them. And then she looked back at him.

He wasn't smiling any more. At least, his mouth wasn't turned up. But his eyes searched hers while sending a message at the same time. And the warmth was all pervasive. The burning sensation rippled through her body, showing no sign of cooling. Instead her temperature was still rising. And she wasn't at all sure if it was from the alcohol or the fire in his gaze.

Wow. She tried to take another deep breath. But the cool of the air made her tingling lips sizzle more. His gaze dropped to her mouth as if he knew of her sensitivity. The sizzle didn't cease.

She blinked, pressed her lips together to try to stop the whisper of temptation they were screaming to her, resumed visual contemplation of the empty shot glasses. She should never have looked at him.

'Thank you,' she managed, studying him peripherally again.

He shrugged, mouth twitching, lightening the atmosphere and making her wonder if she'd overemphasised that supercharged moment. Of course there was no way he would be hitting on her. Now his eyes said it was all just a joke. As if he knew that if she thought he was really after her, she'd be running a mile. City slicker vixen-in-a-bar was so not her style. But she'd decided anything could be possible tonight. Anything she wanted could be hers. She was pretending, remember?

'So are we celebrating, or drowning sorrows?' He flashed that easy smile again. And it gave her the confidence that up until now she'd been faking.

'Celebrating.' She turned to face him.

His brows raised. She could understand his surprise. People didn't usually celebrate in a bar drinking *all by themselves*. So she elaborated.

'It's my birthday.'

'Oh? Which one?'

Did the man not know it was rude to ask? She nearly giggled. But he was so gorgeous she decided to forgive him immediately. Besides, she had the feeling his boldness was innate. It was simply him. It gave her another charge. 'My flirtieth.'

'I'm sorry?' She could see the corners of his mouth twitching again.

'My flirtieth.' So she was making an idiot of herself. What did she care? This night was hers and she could do as she wanted with it—and that might just include flirting with strangers.

'You're either lying or lisping. I think maybe both.' His lips quirked again. And the thing was, she didn't find it offensive.

So he was laughing at her. It was worth it just to see the way that smile reached right into his eyes.

'How many have you had?' he asked. 'You seem to be slurring.'

Not only that, she was still staring fixedly at him. She forced herself to blink again. It was so hard not to look at him. His was a face that captured attention and held it for ever. 'These were my first.'

'And last.' He called the bartender over and ordered. 'Sedate white wine spritzer, please.'

'Who wants sedate?' she argued, ignoring his further instructions to the waiter. 'The last thing I want is wine.' The urge for something stronger gripped her—something even more powerful, something to really take her breath away. She wanted the taste of fire to take away the lonely bitterness of disappointment.

'Not true. Come on, whine away. Why are you here, celebrating alone?'

He'd do. The blue in his eyes was all fire.

'I'm not alone. My family is here too—my sister is getting married tomorrow in the resort.'

His brows flashed upwards again. 'So why aren't they here now celebrating your birthday with you?'

She paused. A chink in her act was about to be revealed, but she answered honestly. 'They've forgotten.'

'Ah.' He looked at her, only a half-smile now. 'So the birthday girl has missed out on her party.'

She shrugged. 'Everyone's been busy with the wedding.'

The spritzer arrived, together with a bottle of wine for him and two tall glasses of water.

'Tell me about this wedding.' He said wedding as if it were a bad word.

'What's to tell? She's gorgeous. He's gorgeous. A successful, wealthy, nice guy.'

He inclined his head towards her. 'And you're a little jealous?'

'No!' She shook her head, but a little hurt stabbed inside. She wasn't jealous of Vita, surely she wasn't. She was truly pleased for her. And no way on this earth would she want Hamish. 'He's solid and dependable.' The truth came out. 'Square.'

'You don't like square?'

She thought about it. Hamish *was* a nice person. And he thought the world of Vita—you could see it in the way he looked at her. He adored her. That little hurt stabbed again. She toughed it out. 'I like a guy who can make me laugh.'

'Do you, now?' But he was the one who laughed. A low chuckle that made her want to smile too—if she weren't having a self-piteous moment. He sobered. 'What's your role in the wedding?'

'Chief bridesmaid,' she said mournfully.

His warm laughter rumbled again.

'It's all right for you,' she said indignantly. 'You've never been a bridesmaid.'

'And you have?'

She nodded. It was all too hideous. 'I know all about it. This is my fourth outing.'

And, yes, she knew what they said. Three times a bridesmaid and all that. Her aunts would be reminding her tomorrow. The only one of her siblings not perfectly paired off.

'What's the best man like?'

She couldn't hide the wince. Rex. How unfortunate that Hamish's best friend was the guy Bella had once picked in her weak moment of trying to be all that the family wanted.

'That bad, huh?'

'Worse.' Because after she'd broken up with him—and it had been her—he'd started dating her most perfect cousin of them all, Celia. And no one in the family could believe that Bella would dump such a catch as Rex and so it was that she earned even more sympathy—more shakes of the head. Not only could she not hold down a decent job, she couldn't hold onto a decent man. No wonder her father treated her like a child. She supposed, despite her Masters degree and her array of part-time jobs, she was. She still hadn't left home, was still dependent on the old man for the basics—like food.

'So.' Her charming companion at the bar speared her attention again with a laser-like look. 'Invite me.'

'I'm sorry?'

'You're the chief bridesmaid, aren't you? You've got to have a date for the wedding.'

'I'm not going to invite a total stranger to my sister's wedding.'

'Why not? It'll make it interesting.'

'How so?' she asked. 'Because you're really a psycho out to create mayhem?'

He laughed at that. 'Look, it's pretty clear you're not looking forward to it. They've forgotten your birthday. This isn't about them. This is about you doing something you want to. Do something you think is tempting.'

'You think you're tempting?' OK, so he was. He sure was. But *he* didn't need to be so sure about it.

He leaned forward. 'I think what tempts you is the thought of doing something unexpected.'

He was daring her. She very nearly smiled then. It would be too—totally unexpected. And the idea really appealed to her. It had been her motivation all evening—for most of her life, in fact. To be utterly unlike the staid, conservative perfectionists in her bean-counter family. And how wonderful it would be to turn up on the arm of the most handsome man she'd ever seen. Pure fantasy. Especially when she was the only one of the younger generation not to be in a happy couple and have a high-powered career.

And then, for once, she had a flash of her father's conservatism—of realism. 'I can't ask you. I barely know you.'

He leaned forward another inch. 'But you have all night to get to know me.'

CHAPTER TWO

ALL night? Now it was Bella's lips twitching.

His smile was wicked. 'Come on. Ask me anything.'

Holding his gaze was something she wasn't capable of any more. She ducked it, sat back and concentrated on the conversation.

'All right. Are you married?' She'd better establish the basics.

'Never have, never will.'

Uh-huh. 'Live-in lover?'

'Heaven forbid.'

She paused. He was letting her know exactly where he stood on the commitment front. Devilry danced in his eyes. She knew he meant every word, but she also knew he was challenging her to pull him up on it.

'Gay?' she asked blithely.

He looked smugly amused. 'Will you take my word for it or do you want proof?'

Now *there* was a challenge. And not one she was up for just yet.

'Diseases?' Tart this time.

His amusement deepened. 'I think there's diabetes on my father's side, but that doesn't seem to manifest until old age.'

She refused to smile, was determined to find some flaw. To get the better of him somehow. 'What do you do for a living?'

'I work with computers.'

Gee, she nearly snorted, that could mean anything. 'Computers? As in programming?'

His head angled and for the first time his gaze slid from hers. 'Sort of.'

'Ah-h-h.' She nodded, as if it all made perfect sense. Then she wrinkled her nose.

'Ah, what?' He sat up straighter. 'Why the disapproval?'

She hit him then, with everything she could think of. 'Did you know the people most likely to download porn are single, male computer nerds aged between twenty-five and thirty-five? You've probably got some warped perception of the female body now, right? And I bet you're into games—with those female characters with boobs bigger than bazookas and skinny hips and who can knock out five hit men in three seconds.' She stopped for breath, dared him to meet *her* challenge.

'Ah.' His smile widened while his eyes promised retribution. 'Well, actually, no, that's not me.'

'You think?' she asked innocently.

'I'm single, I'm male, I'm into computers and I'm aged between twenty-five and thirty-five. But I don't need porn because…' he leaned closer and whispered '…I'm not a nerd.'

She leaned a little closer, whispered right back. 'That's what you think.' Admittedly he didn't look much like one, but she could bluff.

But then he called her on it. Laughing aloud, he asked, 'Should I be wearing glasses and have long, lank, greasy hair?'

His hair was short and wind-spiked and his eyes were bright, perceptive and unadorned—and suddenly they flashed with glee.

'Do nerds have muscles like these?' He slapped his bicep with his hand. 'Go on, feel them.'

She could hardly refuse when she'd been the one to throw the insult. Tentatively she reached out a hand and poked gingerly at his upper arm with her finger. It was rock hard. Intrigued, she took a second shot. Spread her fingers wide, pressing down on the grey sleeve. Underneath was big, solid muscle. Really big. And she could feel the definition, was totally tempted to feel further...

But she pulled back, because there was a sudden fire streaming through her. She must be blushing something awful. She took a much-needed sip of her watered-down wine.

His told-you-so gaze teased her.

She sniffed. 'You're probably wearing a body suit under that shirt.' Completely clutching at straws.

'OK,' he said calmly, 'feel them now.' He took her hand, lifted the hem of his shirt and before she knew it her palm was pressed to his bare abs.

OK? Hell, yes, OK!

She froze. Her mind froze. Her whole body froze. But her hand didn't. The skin on his stomach was warm and beneath her fingers she could feel the light scratchiness of hair and then the rock-hard indents of muscles. This was no weedy-boy-who-spent-hours-in-front-of-a-computer physique. And this wasn't just big, strong male. This was fit. *Superfit.*

Her fingers badly wanted to stretch out some more and explore. If she moved her thumb a fraction she'd be able to stroke below his navel. She whipped her hand out while she still had it under control.

His smile was wicked as the heat in her cheeks became unbearable. 'And what about this tan, hmm?' He pushed up a sleeve and displayed a bronzed forearm as if it were some treasured museum exhibit. She stared at the length of it, lightly hair-dusted, muscle flexing, she could see the clear outline of a thick vein running down to the back of a very broad palm. Very real, very much alive—and strong. She was taken with his hand for some time.

Finally she got back the ability to speak. 'Is the tan all-over-body?'

'If you're lucky you might get to find out.'

The guy had some nerve. But he was laughing as he said it.

'So why are you single, then?' she said, trying to adopt an acidic tone. 'I mean, if you're such a catch, why haven't you been caught already?'

'You misunderstand the game, sweetheart,' he answered softly. 'I'm not the prey. I'm the predator.'

And if she could bring herself to admit it, she wanted him to pounce on her right now. But she was still working on defence and denial. 'Well, you're not that good, then, are you? Where's your catch tonight?'

The only answer was a quick lift of his brows and a wink.

She pressed her lips together, but couldn't quite stop them quirking upwards. 'You hunt often?'

He laughed outright at that, shaking his head. She wasn't sure if it was a negative to her question or simple disbelief at the conversation in general. 'I'm like a big-game animal—one hunt will last me some time.' His eyes caught hers again. 'And I only hunt when I see something really, really juicy.'

Juicy, huh? Her juices were running now and that voice in her head saying 'eat me' really should be shot.

His laughter resurfaced, though not as loud, and she knew he'd twigged her thoughts.

Still she refused to join in. 'But you don't keep your catches.'

'No.' He shook his head. 'Catch and release. That's the rule.'

Hmm. Bella wasn't so sure about the strategy. 'What if she doesn't want to be released?'

'Ah, but she does,' he corrected. 'Because she understands the rules of the game. And even if she doesn't, it won't take long until she wants out.'

Her mouth dropped. She couldn't imagine any woman wanting to get away from this guy's net. Flirting outrageously was too much fun—especially when the flirt had a body like this and eyes like those.

His smile sharpened round the edges. 'I have it on good authority that I'm *very* selfish.'

'Ah-h-h.' She was intrigued. That smacked of bitter-ex-girlfriend speak. Was he playing the field on the rebound? 'You've never wanted to catch and keep?'

He grimaced. 'No.'

'Why not?'

For the first time he looked serious. 'Nothing *keeps*. Things don't ever stay the same.' He paused, the glint resurfaced. 'The answer is to go for what you want, when you want it.'

'And after that?'

He didn't reply, merely shrugged his shoulders.

Bella took another sip of the spritzer and contemplated what she knew to be the ultimate temptation before her— defence and denial crumbling. 'After that' didn't matter really, did it? He had a beautiful body and a sense of humour—what more would a confident, cosmopolitan woman want for an evening? And wasn't that what she was—for tonight?

'So, now that you know something about me,' he said, 'tell me, what do *you* do?'

He might have told her some things, but strangely she felt as if she knew even less. But what she really wanted to know, he didn't need words for. She wanted to know if that tan was all-over-body, she wanted to know the heat and strength of those muscles—the feel of them. Everything of him. Cosmo woman here she was.

'I'm an actor,' she declared, chin high.

There was a pause. 'Ah-h-h.'

'Ah, what?' She didn't like the look of his exaggerated, knowing nod.

'I bet you're a very good one,' he sidestepped.

Her cosmo confidence ebbed. 'I could be.' Given the opportunity.

'Could?'

'Sure.' She just needed that lucky break.

Now he was looking way too amused. 'What else do you do?'

'What do you mean what else?' she snapped. 'I'm an actor.'

'I don't know of many actors who don't have some sort of day job.'

She sighed—totally theatrically, and then capitulated. 'I make really good coffee.'

He laughed again. 'Of course you do.'

Of course. She was the walking cliché. The family joke. The wannabe. And no way in hell was she telling him what else she did. Children's birthday party entertainer ranked as one of the lowest, most laughable occupations on the earth— her family gave her no end of grief about it. She didn't need to give him more reason to as well.

'And how is the life of a jobbing actor these days?' He was still looking a tad too cynically amused for her liking.

She sighed again—doubly theatrical. 'I have "the nose".'

'"The nose"?'

She turned her head, offered him a profile shot.

He studied it seriously for several seconds. Then, 'What's wrong with it?'

'A little long, a little straight.'

'I'd say it's majestic.'

She jumped when he ran his finger down it. The tip tingled as he tapped it.

'Quite,' she acknowledged, sitting back out of reach. 'It gives me character and that's what I am—a character actress.'

'I'm not convinced it's the nose that makes you so full of character,' he drawled.

'Quite.' She almost laughed—it was taking everything to ignore his irony. 'I've not the looks for the heroine. I'm the sidekick.'

She didn't mention it, but there was also the fact she was on the rounder side of skinny. A little short, a little curvy for anything like Hollywood. But Wellywood—more formally known as Wellington, New Zealand's own movie town? Maybe. She just needed to get the guts to move there.

'Oh, I wouldn't say—'

'Don't.' She raised her hand, stopped him mid-sentence. 'It's true. No leading-lady looks here, but it doesn't matter because the smart-ass sidekick gets all the best lines anyway.'

'But not the guy.'

She frowned. So true. And half the time she didn't get the sidekick part either. She got the walk-on-here, quick-exit-there parts. The no-name ones that never earned any money, fame or even notoriety.

She figured it was because she hadn't done the posh drama academy thing. Her father had put his foot down. She wasn't to waste her brain on that piffle—a hobby sure, but never a career. So she'd been packed off to university—like all her siblings. Only instead of brain-addling accountancy or law, she'd read English. And, to her father's horror, film studies. After a while he'd 'supposed she might go into teaching'.

He'd supposed wrong. She'd done evening classes in acting at the local high school. Read every method book in the library. Watched the classic films a million kazillion times. Only at all those agencies and casting calls it was almost always the same talent turning up and she couldn't help but be psyched out by the pros, by the natural talents who'd been onstage from the age of three and who had all the confidence and self-belief in the world.

Bella thought she had self-belief. But it fought a hard battle against the disbelief of her family. 'When are you going to settle into a real job?' they constantly asked. 'This drama thing is just a hobby. You don't want to be standing on your feet making coffee, or blowing up balloons for spoilt toddlers for the rest of your days…' And on and on and on.

'Well, who wants the guy anyway?' she asked grumpily. 'I don't want the saccharine love story. Give me adventure and snappy repartee any day.'

'Really?' he asked in total disbelief. 'You sure you don't want the big, fluffy princess part?'

'No, Prince Charming is boring.' And Prince Charming, the guy her family had adored, wouldn't let her be herself.

He leaned forward, took her chin in his hand and turned her to face him. 'I don't believe you're always this cynical.'

The comment struck another little stab into her. It twisted a little sharper when she saw he was totally serious.

'No,' she admitted honestly. 'Only when it's my birthday and no one has remembered and I'm stuck in wedding-of-the-century hell.'

'All weddings are hell.' His fingers left her face but his focus didn't.

Well, this one sure was. 'Here was me thinking it was going to be a barefoot-on-the-beach number with hardly anyone in attendance, but it's massive—ninety-nine per cent of the resort is booked out with all the guests!'

'Hmm.' He was silent a moment. Then he flicked her a sideways glance. 'How lucky for you that I'm in that remaining one per cent.'

Wordless, she stared at him, taking a second to believe the lazy arrogance in the comment he'd so dryly delivered. Then she saw the teasing, over-the-top wink.

Her face broke and the amusement burst forth.

'Finally!' He spoke above her giggles. 'She laughs. And when she laughs...'

The laughter passed between them, light and fresh, low and sweet. And her mood totally lifted.

'I am so sorry,' she apologised, shaking her head.

'That's OK. You're clearly having a trying day.'

'Something like that.' The thought of tomorrow hadn't made it any easier and she'd felt guilty for feeling so me-me-me that it had all compounded into a serious case of the grumps.

'Shall we start over?' His eyes were twinkling again and this time she didn't try to stop her answering smile.

'Please, that would be good.' And it would be good. Because it was quite clear that under his super-flirt exterior there was actually a nice guy. Not to mention, damn attractive.

'I'm Owen Hughes. Disease-free, single and straight.'

Owen. A player to be sure—but one that she knew would be a lot of fun.

'I'm Bella Cotton. Also disease-free, single and straight.'

'Bella,' he repeated, but didn't make the obvious 'beautiful' translation. He didn't need to—simply the way he said it made her feel its meaning. Then he made her smile some more. 'Any chance you're in need of a laugh?'

She nodded. 'Desperately. Light relief is what I need.'

'I can do that.' He grinned again and she found herself feeling happier than she had all day—all week even. He leaned towards her. 'Look, I've got an empty pit instead of a stomach right now. Have dinner with me—unless you've got some full-on rehearsal dinner to go to or something?'

She shook her head. 'Amazingly that's not the plan. I think some of the younger guests are just supposed to meet up later for drinks. The olds are doing their own thing.'

'Maybe they've organised a surprise birthday party for you.'

'As nice as that idea sounds—' and it did sound really nice '—they haven't. You can trust me on that.'

'OK. Then let's go find a table.'

She found herself standing and walking with him to the adjoining restaurant just like that. No hesitation, no second thought, just simplicity.

He grinned as they sat down. 'I really am starving.'

'So you haven't caught anything much lately, you big tiger, you,' she mocked.

He laughed. 'I'm confident I can make up for it.'

Bella met the message in his eyes. And was quite sure he could.

CHAPTER THREE

OWEN felt a ridiculous surge of pleasure at finally having made Bella see the funny side. And, just as he'd suspected, she had a killer of a smile and a deadly sweet giggle. Her full lips invited and her eyes crinkled at the corners. He couldn't decide if they were pale blue or grey, but he liked looking a lot while trying to work it out and he liked watching them widen the more he looked.

He'd been bluffing—if he really were some tiger in the jungle, he'd have died of starvation months ago. Sex was a recreational hobby for him, very recreational. But it had been a while. Way too much of a while. Maybe that was why he'd felt the irresistible pull of attraction when she'd walked into the bar. He'd been sitting at a table in the corner and almost without will had walked up to stand beside her at the bar. Just to get a closer look at her little hourglass figure. In the shirt and skirt he could see shapely legs and frankly bountiful breasts that had called to the most base of elements in him.

Then he'd noticed the droop to her lip that she'd been determinedly trying to lift as she'd read that menu. And he'd just had to make her smile.

The table he'd led her to was in the most isolated corner of the restaurant he could find. He didn't want her family interrupting any sooner than necessary. Wanted to keep jousting and joking with her. Wanted a whole lot more than that too and needed the time to make it happen.

'So,' she asked, suddenly perky, 'what sort of computers? You work for some software giant?'

'I work for myself.' For the last ten years he'd done nothing much other than work—pulling it together, thinking it through, organising the team and getting it done.

'Programming what—games? Banking software?'

'I work in security.'

'Oh, my.' She rolled her eyes. 'I bet you're one of them whiz-kids who broke into the FBI's files when you were fourteen, or created some nasty virus. Bad-boy hacker now crossed over to the good side or something—am I right?'

'No.' He chuckled. Truth was the actual programming stuff wasn't him—he had bona fide computer nerds working for him. He was the ideas guy—who'd thought up a way to make online payments more secure, and now to protect identity. 'I've never been in trouble with the law.'

'Oh. So…' She paused, clearly trying to think up the next big assault. 'Business good?'

'You could say that.' Inwardly he smiled. He now had employees scattered around the world. A truly international operation, but one that he preferred to direct from his inner-city bolt hole in Wellington. But he didn't want to talk about work—it was all consuming, even keeping his mind racing when he should be asleep. That was why he was on Waiheke, staying at his holiday home a few yards down the beach from the hotel. He was due for some R & R, a little distraction. And the ideal distraction seemed to have stepped right in front of him.

His banter before hadn't all been a lie, though. He did

believe in going for what he wanted and then moving right on. This little poppet was the perfect pastime for his weekend of unwind time. So he'd made sure she understood the way he played it. Spelt the rules out loud and clear. She'd got them, as he'd intended, and she was tempted. Now he just had to give her that extra little nudge.

She was studying the menu intently. And he studied her, taken by the stripe of sunburn that disappeared under her shirt. It seemed to be riding along to the crest of her breast and his fingers itched to follow its path.

When the waiter came she ordered with an almost reckless abandonment and he joined in. He *was* hungry. He'd splashed up the beach over an hour ago now. He hadn't been able to be bothered fixing something for himself, figured he'd get a meal to take away from the restaurant. Only now he'd found something better to take back with him.

'Oh, no.' The look on her face was comical.

'What?' he asked.

'Some of my family has arrived.'

'It's time for drinks, then, huh?' He turned his head in the direction she was staring. Inwardly cursing. Just when she was getting warmed up.

He saw the tall blonde looking over at them speculatively. When she saw them notice her, she strode over, long legs making short work of the distance.

'Bella. So sorry,' she clipped. 'It's your birthday and you're here all alone.'

What? thought Owen. Was he suddenly invisible?

'I can't believe you didn't remind us,' the blonde continued, still ignoring him.

'I didn't want to say anything.' For a second he saw the pain in Bella's eyes. A surge of anger hit him.

He realised what she'd done. She'd tested them. And they'd failed.

'Don't worry.' He spoke up. 'She's not alone. It's just that we wanted to have our own private celebration.'

The blonde looked at him then, frosty faced. 'And you are?'

'Owen,' he answered, as if that explained it all.

'Owen.' She glanced to Bella and then back to give him the once-over. He watched her coldness thaw to a sugary smile as she checked out his watch and his shoes. He knew she recognised the brands. Yes, darling, he thought, I'm loaded. And it was one thing Bella *hadn't* noticed. He found it refreshing.

'It seems you've been keeping a few things to yourself lately, Isabella.'

Owen looked at Bella. There was a plea in her eyes he couldn't ignore.

The silence deepened, becoming more awkward as he kept his focus on her. And a tinge of amusement tugged when finally the willowy blonde spoke, sounding disconcerted. 'I'll leave you to your meal, then.'

'Thank you,' Owen answered, not taking his gaze off Bella. He was never normally so rude, but he could do arrogance when necessary. And when he'd seen the hurt in Bella's eyes he'd known it was necessary. The irrational need to help her, to support her, had bitten him. Stupid. Because Owen wasn't the sort to do support. Ordinarily he did all he could to avoid any show of interest or involvement other than the purely physical, purely fun. He'd made that mistake before and been pushed too close to commitment as a result. His ex-girlfriend had wanted the ring, the ceremony, the works. He hadn't. But then she'd tried to force it in a way he totally resented her for. The experience had been so bad he was determined to make damn sure it didn't happen again. He no longer had relationships. He had flings.

But now he simply hoped that his brush-off would be reported back to the rest of the family and they'd all stay away for a bit.

The waiter arrived with the first plates, breaking the moment. Bella was busy picking up her fork, but he could see her struggling to hold back her smile.

He waited until she'd swallowed her first bite. 'Am I invited now?'

'If I do, your job is to entertain me, right?' Her smile was freed. 'No eyeing up my beautiful cousins.'

He didn't need anyone else to eye up. And he'd entertain her all night and then some if she wanted. But he played the tease some more. 'How beautiful are they?'

She stared down her majestic nose at him. 'You just met one of them.'

'Her?' he asked, putting on surprise. 'She's not beautiful.'

Her expression of disbelief was magic.

He laughed. 'She's not. So she's tall and blonde. So what? They're a dime a dozen. I'd far rather spend time with someone interesting.' He'd done tall and blonde many times over in his past. These days he was searching for something a little different.

She ignored him. 'No getting wildly drunk and embarrassing me. That isn't why you want to go, is it? The free booze?'

'No.'

'Then why?'

The truth slipped out. 'I want to see you have a really good time. A really, really good time.'

He did too. And he knew he could give it to her, and how. There was a baseline sizzle between them that was intense and undeniable. He'd seen the recognition, the jolt of awareness in her expression the moment their gazes had first locked. It was what she needed; it was what he needed. And he'd happily spend the weekend at her dull family wedding to get it. He'd put up with a lot more to get it if he had to.

On top of that primary, physical attraction, she was funny. Smart. Definitely a little bitter. And he liked her smile. He liked to make her smile.

As their dinner progressed it was nice to forget about everything for a moment as he concentrated wholly on her. He pulled his mobile out of his pocket and flicked it to Vibrate, pushing work from his mind. He was supposed to be having a couple of hours off after all. Like forty-eight.

He saw her glance into the main body of the restaurant as it filled. Saw her attention turn from him to whatever the deal was about tomorrow.

'It's going to be a massive wedding,' she said gloomily. 'The whole family and extended family and friends and everyone.'

'All that fuss for nothing.' He just couldn't see the point of it. Nor could he see why it was such a problem for her.

'All that money for just one day.' She shook her head. Her hair feathered out; shoulder length, it was a light wavy brown. He wanted to lean over and feel it fly over his face.

'Do you know how much she's spent on the dress?'

So money was some of it. 'I hate to think.' His drollery seemed to pass her by.

'And I've got the most hideous bridesmaid's dress. Hideous.'

'You'll look gorgeous.' She was such a cute package she could wear anything and look good.

'You don't understand,' she said mournfully. 'It's a cast of thousands. Celia—the gorgeous cousin—is one too. And there are others.' The little frown was back.

Her every emotion seemed to play out on her face—she was highly readable. If she could control it, learn to manipulate it, then she'd make a very good actress.

'The dress suits all of them, of course.'

'Of course.' And she was worried about what she looked like—what woman wasn't? He'd be happy to reassure her, spend some time emphasising her most favourable assets.

She looked up at him balefully. 'They're all five-seven or more and svelte.'

Whereas she was maybe five-four and all curves. He'd have her over ten tall blonde Celias any day.

'Did they go with a gift list?' He played along.

'Yes.' She ground out the answer. 'The cheapest item was just under a hundred bucks—and you had to buy a pair.'

Money was definitely an issue. He supposed it must be— fledgling actresses and café staff didn't exactly earn lots. And this resort was one of the most exclusive and expensive in the country. To be having a wedding here meant someone had some serious dosh. Was she worried about not keeping up with the family success?

He laughed, wanting to keep the mood light. 'Lists are such a waste of time. They'd be better off leaving it to chance and getting two coffee plungers. That way when they split up they can have one each.'

Surprise flashed on her face. 'Oh, and you call *me* cynical.'

'Marriage isn't worth the paper it's written on.' He'd been witness to that one all right—hit on the head with a sledge-hammer. It was all a sham.

'You think?'

'Come on, how many people make it to ten years these days, seven even? What's the point?' Because at some point, *always*, it ended. Owen figured it was better to walk before the boredom or the bitterness set in—and it would set in. The feelings never lasted—he'd seen that, he'd felt it himself. Now he knew it was better not to get tied into something you didn't want—and certainly not to drag the lives of innocents into it either. He wasn't running the risk of that happening ever again. No live-in lover, no wife, no kids.

Bella sat back and thought. She had to give him that—one of her older cousins had separated only last month, a marriage of three and a half years over already. But other marriages worked out, didn't they? She had high hopes for Vita and Hamish. She had faint hopes for herself—if she was lucky.

She frowned at him. 'Yes, we already know it's not on your agenda.' He couldn't commit to marriage—the monogamy bit would get him. He was too buff to be limited to one woman. Smorgasbord was his style. Well, that was fine. She was hardly at a 'settle down' point in life. She was still working on the *'get'* a life bit.

'That's right.' He grinned. 'But I'm not averse to helping others celebrate their folly.'

'So you can flirt with all the bridesmaids?' A little dig.

'Not all of them. Just one.'

The shorter, darker-haired, dumpier one with the long straight nose? He was just being nice because he hadn't actually *seen* all the others yet. When he did, it would be all over. She looked up from her cleared plate and encountered his stare again. The glint was back and notch by notch making her smoulder.

His stare didn't waver. And the message grew stronger.

Pure want.

She curled her fingers around her chilled wine glass. She felt flushed all over and had the almost desperate thought that she needed to cool down. Her fingers tightened. Then his hand covered hers, holding the glass to the table.

'I think you've had enough.'

She narrowed her eyes, unsure of his meaning.

He lifted his hands, spread his fingers as he shrugged loosely. 'I'm not suggesting you're drunk. Far from it.' His smile flashed, and it was all wicked. 'But the more you drink, the duller your senses become and I wouldn't want you to lose any sensation. Not tonight.'

'I'm going to need my senses?' She was mesmerised.

'All of them.'

OK.

He inclined his head to the large bi-folding doors that opened out to the deck. A small jazz ensemble was playing. She hadn't even noticed them set up. Too focused on her companion—the most casual customer in the place yet the one who commanded all her attention.

'Dance with me.' He stood. 'We can see how well we move together. Make sure we've got it right for the big day tomorrow.'

Why did she take everything he said and think he was really meaning something else?

He grinned, seeming to understand her problem exactly, and silently telling her that she was absolutely right. He held out his hand.

For a split second she looked at it. The broad palm, the long fingers, the invitation. The instant she placed her hand on top, he locked it into his. There was no going back now.

They walked out the doors together, to the part of the deck by the band where people were dancing. The waves were gently washing the beach. The evening was warm and for Bella the night seemed to exude magic.

'I like this old music,' he muttered, curling one arm around her waist while holding her hand to his chest with the other. 'Made for my kind of dancing.'

'Your kind?'

'Where you actually touch.' His hand was wide and firm across the small of her back as he pulled her towards him, and she went to him because she couldn't not. Because in reality she wanted to get closer still. Her head barely reached above his shoulders, but it didn't matter because she couldn't focus much further than on the material right in front of her anyway, and on the inviting, warm strength beneath it.

His fingers feathered over her back, skin to skin. She trembled at the sensation, nearly stumbled with the need that rose deep within her. She masked the craziness of her response with some sarcasm. 'I said yes to dancing, not having your hands up my shirt.'

'I thought up your shirt might be quite good.' His low reply in her ear made her need heighten to almost painful intensity.

Good was an understatement. He pressed her that little bit closer, so her breasts were only a millimetre from the hard wall that was his chest. Not quite close enough to touch, but she could almost, almost feel him and her nipples were tight.

She dragged in a burning breath. 'Owen, I—'

'Shh,' he said. 'Your family is watching.'

He danced her away from the others and into the farthest corner of the deck, where the darkness of night lurked, encroaching on the lights and loud conviviality of the restaurant. Gently he swayed them both to the languid music, talking to her in low tones, telling her just to dance with him. Was it one song, was it three, or five? Time seemed suspended. He muttered her name, his breath stirring her hair, then nothing. And as she moved to his lead she fell deeper into his web.

When the band took a break, she took a moment in the bathroom to try to recover her aplomb—cooling her wrists under the rush of water from the cold tap. She shouldn't have had those shots. She'd barely drunk a drop since, but she felt giddy. And as she looked at her reflection—at her large eyes, and the heightened colour in her cheeks and lips—she knew she didn't want to recover her aplomb at all. She wanted to follow this madness to its natural conclusion. Nothing else seemed to matter any more—nothing but being with Owen. Just for while she was on this fantasy island.

She stepped out of the bathroom and saw him straighten from where he'd been leaning against the wall, eyes trained on her door. She walked over to meet him, but her path was intercepted by Vita, her sister.

'Bella, where have you been all night? More to the point, who is that guy you're dancing with?' Vita looked astounded.

'Owen is an old friend.'

'How old?' The disbelief on her sister's face was mortifying.

'Well, not that old.' Bella looked up to where he stood now looming large and close, right behind Vita, his eyes keen. She just kept slim control of her voice and the hysterical giggle out of it. 'You were born what, about thirty years ago, weren't you?'

'Somewhere thereabouts.' He took the last couple of steps so he stood beside her, circling his arm around her waist as naturally as if he'd done it a thousand times.

Then he smiled at her, a glowing, deeply intimate smile that had Bella blinking as much as Vita. His fingers pressed her slightly closer to him and inside she shook. He held her even more firmly.

When he turned his head to Vita, the smile lost its intimacy but was no less potent. 'You must be Bella's sister, the beautiful bride. Congratulations.'

Vita blinked and took more than a second to recover her manners. 'Thank you…er…Owen. Will we be seeing you tomorrow? You're more than welcome.'

'Well…' he glanced back to Bella and she saw the laughter dancing in his eyes '…I'd love to be there, but Bella wasn't sure…'

'Oh, if you're a friend of Bella's, of course you're welcome.'

Bella turned sharply, narrowed her gaze on Vita. Did she stress the 'if'?

'Thank you.' Owen closed off the conversation smoothly. And with a nod drew Bella back outside and threaded them through the dancing couples.

Bella went into his arms hardly thinking about what she was doing. Melancholy had struck. Vita had seemed stunned that Bella might actually have a gorgeous guy wanting to be with her. They were probably all watching agog—amazed at the development. Oh, why did she have to be here with her perfect sister and her perfect family—when she was so obviously the odd one out?

He must have read her thoughts because he pulled her close and looked right in her eyes. 'She's not that perfect.'

She didn't believe him. Her little sister, by a year, had always been the one to do things how they were supposed to—the way her father wanted.

'She didn't wish you a happy birthday,' he said softly.

Bella sighed. 'She's preoccupied.' And she was. This wedding was a mammoth operation.

Owen frowned, clearly thinking that it wasn't a good enough excuse. Warmth flooded her. He was so damn attractive.

'So how many candles should you be blowing out tonight, Bella?'

'Twenty-four.' She hadn't the energy for joking any more—she was too focused on her feelings for him. And all of a sudden the giddiness took over—she couldn't slow the speed of her heartbeat; her breath was knocked from her lungs. She stumbled.

His hands tightened on her arms. 'You're tired.'

Tired was the last thing she was feeling.

But he stepped back, breaking their physical contact. 'I'll walk you to your room.'

Disappointment flooded her. She'd been having a wonderful night and she didn't want it to come to an end. But it had—with Vita's interruption the fantasy had been shattered. And Owen was already moving them across the deck, towards the stairs that led to the sandy beach.

She glanced up into his face, hoping for a sign of that glint, only to find it shuttered. Blandly unreadable. The sense of disappointment swelled.

As they reached the steps, Celia stepped in front of them.

'You're not leaving already?' she asked, full of vivaciousness.

'It's a big day tomorrow. Bella needs to turn in now,' Owen answered before she had the chance.

Celia turned her stunning gaze from him to Bella and the glance became stabbing. 'You'd better put some cream on that sunburn or you'll look like a zebra tomorrow.'

Oh, she just had to get that jibe in, didn't she? Bella smarted.

Owen turned slightly. Slowly, carefully, he gave Bella such an intense once-over that she could feel the impact as if he were really touching her, a bold caress. But it was his eyes that kissed—from the tip of her nose all the way to her toes. And then he did touch her. Lifting his hand, with a firm finger, he stroked the red stripe on her chest—from the top of it near her collarbone, down the angled line to where it disappeared into her blouse. His eyes followed the path, and then went lower, seeming to be able to see everything, regardless of the material.

'Don't worry.' He spoke slowly. 'I'll make sure she takes care of it.'

Bella stared up at him, fascinated by the flare in his eyes. The flare that had been there from that moment when she'd turned her head to his voice as she'd sat at the bar. It had flashed now and then as they'd talked and laughed their way through dinner. But now it was back and bigger than before and she couldn't help her response. Every muscle, every fibre, every cell tightened within her. As he looked at her like that, his hunger was obvious to anyone. She'd never felt more wanted than she did in that moment and she was utterly seduced. The whole of his attention was on her and the whole of her responded. But she wasn't just willing, she was wanting.

She dimly heard a cough, but when she finally managed to tear her gaze from his, Celia had already walked off. Bella managed a vague smile after her general direction, but then, compelled by the pull between them, she walked with Owen—barely aware of her cousin's and her sister's gazes following her. She no longer cared. She was too focused on the burn of her skin where his finger had touched, and the excitement burgeoning now as he held her hand and matched her step for step.

CHAPTER FOUR

DOWN on the sand the breeze lifted and the drop in temperature checked Bella.

'Where are you staying?' Owen asked, his voice oddly gentle.

'One of the studios round the back.' She wasn't in one of the luxury villas, but a tiny unit in a building with several other tiny units. It was still nice. It didn't quite have the view and door opening directly onto the beach that the villas did, but it didn't have the price tag either.

'Show me.' Still gentle.

But her mind teased her with what it was that he wanted her to show him. It took only a minute or so to wind around the back of the building, to where the units were. At her door she stopped. She gazed at the frame of it, suddenly shy of wanting to look him in the eye. 'Thank you for seeing me through that.'

'No problem.' He loomed beside her. 'It was fun.'

Fun. Disappointment wafted over her again. Stupid, when he'd given her a victory she'd mentally relive time and time again, but there was something else she wanted now. Something she sensed would be much, much better.

He gestured towards the door. 'Are you alone in there? Not twin sharing with your great-aunt Amelia or anyone awful?'

'All alone. Just me.' She chanced a look up at him then, saw the hint of the smile, the gleam of teeth flashing white in the darkness.

'Want me to come in and make sure there are no monsters in the wardrobe?'

Confidence trickled back through her. She stepped a little closer. 'Quite the gentleman, aren't you? Are you going to turn down my sheet as well?'

'If you like.' He matched her move, stepped closer still. 'Would you like, Bella?'

Such a simple question. It needed only the simplest of answers. And she already knew what he was asking and what her answer would be. There was no way she could ever say no to him. Probably no one had ever said no to him and she didn't blame any of them.

'Yes.'

His head bent. His smile was no wider, but somehow stronger. 'Good.'

His first kiss was soft, just a gentle press of lips on lips. No other contact. Then he pulled away—just a fraction, for just a moment. Then he was back. Another butterfly-light kiss that had her reaching after him when he pulled back again. And as she moved forward he swept her into his arms. Strong and tight they held her and the next kiss changed completely. Deep, then deeper again. The awareness that had sizzled between them all night was unleashed. Her hands threaded through his hair, his hands moulded over her curves. Together they strained closer, lips hungry, tongues tasting. Bella was lost. He felt better than she'd imagined—broad, lean, hard. Her eyes closed as his lips left hers, roving down to her jaw, down her throat, hot and hungry. The fire in her belly roared.

And then he was kissing her sunburn stripe, undoing the top few buttons on her blouse, pulling it open so he could follow the path of reddened skin with lush wet kisses that did anything but soothe. The red stopped on the curve of her breast—where her bikini cup had been. But he didn't stop. He pulled the lace of her bra down until her nipple popped up over it. And then he took that in his mouth too.

She arched back as sensations spasmed deep inside. His other arm took her weight, pulling her pelvis into the heat of his hips, and she could feel his hardness through his jeans. She gasped at the impact—and at the pleasure ricocheting through her system. He lifted his head, his hunger showing in the strain on his face and in his body. The air was cool on her bared skin but she was still steaming up.

Breathless, she pulled back, her blouse hanging half open, breast spilling over her bra. 'I think I better get the door unlocked now.'

'I think you better had,' he teased, but her confidence surged higher when she heard his equal breathlessness. 'Because the thing about sex on the beach,' he added, 'is the sand.'

Giggling, she slipped her hand in her pocket, closed her fingers around the key. Turning, she fumbled to get it into the lock. He stood behind her, ran his hands over her hips and then pressed so close she could feel everything he had to offer. Her hand lurched off course completely. He put his fingers over hers and guided the key safely home.

Pressing even harder against her, he spoke in her ear, hot and full of sexy humour. 'We are having screaming orgasms though, OK?'

'OK.' She just got the door open and the answer out before he spun her around and his mouth came down on hers again. He backed her in, kicking the door shut behind them with his foot. He kept backing her, but angled her direction so after only a couple of paces she was up against the wall. Relief flooded her as she felt it behind her and she half sagged against it. She didn't think her legs were strong enough to hold her up all on their own any more. When the man kissed, all she could think of was a bed, and her desperation to be on it and exploring and feeling and being kissed like that everywhere.

His hands held her face up to his, warm fingers stroked down her neck, but he stood back so his body didn't touch hers. She wanted it to touch again—all of it against her. The kisses grew deeper as she opened more to him—inviting him in with the sighs of pleasure she let escape and the way she sought him with her tongue.

But her confidence came in waves—ebbing again as his caresses became more intimate, as he undid the last buttons and hooks. Shyness overcame her as her blouse and her bra slipped away completely.

He looked down at her, sensing her stillness. 'You're sure?'

She nodded, but explained. 'It's been a while.'

'Me too.'

She didn't believe that for a second. But it was nice of him to say it.

Then her shyness melted as he whisked his shirt over his head and she saw the beauty of his body beneath.

Her hands lifted instinctively, and she spread her fingers on his shoulder, slowly letting them trace down the impressive breadth of his chest and then lower, over the taut upper abs down to where his jeans were fastened. He lifted his head at that, grinning wickedly. 'Stop that, sweetness. It'll all be over all too soon. As it is it's going to be a close one.'

'Very close,' she agreed, letting her fingers walk some more.

'Stop that.' His smile only widened.

'I can't. You feel fantastic. You really do have muscles.' She marvelled at it. How the hell did a computer geek grow muscles like these?

But then her own actions slowed as she became acutely aware of his—of the kisses dulling her sense of initiative. He was taking the lead and increasingly all she could do was follow. Slowly, so slowly, he was stripping the skirt off her. Dropping to his knees, he eased it down, pressing kisses to her thighs and legs.

Then he stood again, him still clad in jeans, her in nothing but knickers. Their shoes had been kicked off somewhere outside the door. He took her face in his hands again, searching her eyes and then smiling. Then kissing. And with every moment of the kiss her need grew. Until, pressing her shoulders against the wall for support, she pushed her hips forward towards him—aching for closeness.

'Something you want?' he asked.

'You know.'

He slid his hands from her shoulders all the way down until he curled his fingers round hers. Then he lifted them, swinging her arms up above her head, pinning them back to the wall with his hands. The movement lifted her breasts, her hard nipples strained straight up to him.

He paused and took advantage of the view. Looking into his eyes, she saw the passion and simply melted more—shivering as she did. Swiftly he kissed her and transferred the possession of both her hands to only one of his. He glided his other hand down her throat, then lower. Cupping her breast, he stroked the taut nipple with his thumb. She whimpered into his mouth. His hand moved again, fingers sliding down her stomach, and then they slipped inside her panties, right down, curving into her, feeling the extent of the warm wetness there as she moaned.

'Mmm.' He lifted his mouth from hers, looked into her eyes as another moan escaped her. And any embarrassment dissolved as she took in his pleased expression.

'That's what I want,' he muttered, kissing her eyes closed, one and then the other. Gentle. His fingers started to work. So slowly, gently. And his mouth pressed to hers again, his tongue exploring, just as his fingers were. Slow and gentle and tormenting. Insistent. And the giddiness was back. She kept her eyes closed, lost in the feeling, utterly at his mercy, until she was writhing and arching and wanting harder and faster. But still he kept it slow, teasing her. And then she was panting, pleading in the scarce moments when he lifted his head to let her take breath.

And he listened, watched, altered his actions. Not so gentle. Faster and deeper. Passionate kisses that bruised her lips and then roved hard over her face and then down. His mouth was hot as he nuzzled his way down the side of her throat, to her breast and back to her starving mouth.

He lifted his head to watch as her panting grew shallower, faster, louder. She started to shake, was begging for him not to stop, for him to give her more.

His eyes gleamed with satisfaction. 'Screaming, remember?'

But he didn't need to tell her. She couldn't stop it anyway, the cry that came as she came—hard and loud.

His fingers loosened on her wrists, her arms dropped down to her sides and he braced his hands on the wall either side of her. He brushed a gentle kiss on her nose.

She shook her head. 'I can't stand any more.'

'Yes, you can.'

'No, I mean literally. I can't stand any more.' And her feet began to slip out in front of her, a slow slither to the floor.

He scooped her straight up.

'Oh, thanks. My legs just didn't want to be upright any more.'

'What do they want?' He chuckled.

'To be wrapped round you. Like this.' She hooked them round his waist and felt her desire for him surge back stronger than before.

'Mmm.' He nodded. 'Feels good to me.'

'Does this feel good?' She slid one hand down his chest, eager to feel his muscles respond.

His arms tightened. 'Thought I told you to quit it.'

'Afraid you can't handle it?'

'Sure am.' His teeth flashed white and she knew he didn't mean it. This guy could handle anything—especially her.

The bed was unmissable and in four paces he had her on it, following immediately. She opened her arms, her mouth, her legs. Ready for everything.

He groaned as he pressed close. 'Condoms?'

She shook her head.

'You don't have any?' He paused and she shook her head again. Then he grinned. 'I do.'

Of course he did. She lay still beneath him as he pulled his wallet out of his back pocket, pulled a small square from inside that and then put it beside her.

'Quite the Boy Scout.'

He met her snark with an unapologetic look. 'Accidents are best avoided, don't you think?'

She nodded. She knew he was right to be prepared—to protect both of them. And then, as he kissed her, she decided his experience was something to celebrate—because nobody had kissed her like this before. No one had known how to turn her on like this. She'd never known such raw lust, or had such an ache for physical fulfilment.

He worked his way down her body, peeling her panties

from her, stoking the fire within with caresses and whispers and kisses. Her hands grappled with the fastening of his jeans—she could wait no longer. But he took over, rolling to his back, tearing the denim from his body and quickly sorting the condom. Then he was back, settling over her, and the level of her anticipation almost had her hyperventilating.

He held back for a second, humour twinkling in the dark desire. 'Happy birthday, Bella.'

She closed her eyes. The first person to actually say it today. And now he was—*oh*! She gasped. Opened her eyes again—wide.

'Birthday girls deserve big presents.' He was watching her closely. 'That OK?'

'Oh, yes.' She squealed as he moved closer and a smile stretched his mouth. Air rushed out from her lungs in jagged segments as her body adjusted to his—to the glorious delight of it.

And then, when she was able to revel in the feel of him, he moved, rolling her over, lifting her so she was sitting astride him while at the same time arching up into her so the connection wasn't lost.

'Let me see how beautiful you are, Bella.'

She looked down at him, marvelling that she was astride such magnificence. His chest tabled out before her and she spread her hands over it, leaning forward so she could slide up his length—and back down. Her eyes closed as she slowly hit his hilt again. And then again and again.

Shuddering, she opened her eyes to see him watching, with his head on the big pillows, appreciation apparent as he roved over her body, taking in her reaction. His hands spread wide, sliding up her thighs, lifting to cup her breasts and then take them in a ripe handful.

'Beautiful Bella,' he muttered, thumbs stroking. His heat fired her to go faster. And then he moved to match her.

'Oh, God,' she gasped. 'You really are a tiger.'

He growled in response.

Her giggle was lost in another gasp as he moved more, encouraging her to take more. And the sensations grew—overwhelming everything. Until there was nothing left in her mind—no thought, no humour, recognition of nothing but this wild passion that was all-consuming. Tension seared through her, until it could tighten no more, making her body rigid as she was thrust to the brink of madness.

His arms encircled her as he surged up with more force and depth than ever, and his hands clenched, supporting her as her orgasm tore through her, taking her strength with it. But he held her hard, making her face the intensity of it, squeezing every last sensation from her until she screamed with the exquisite pleasure of it.

She collapsed forward onto him, his shout still reverberating in her ears. Every muscle quivered—hot and bubbling, seeming to sing and so sensitive she could hardly believe it. She'd never felt anything like it.

'In about half an hour or so,' he murmured as her lids lowered, 'we're going to do that again.'

'And more,' she mumbled. She had plans for him, oh, yes, she had plans…in about half an hour…

There was a strange buzzing sound. As if an oversized bumblebee had made its way in and was trapped inside. Her warm pillow jerked up. Startled, she rolled away, and he quickly slid from the bed. Blinking rapidly so her eyes adjusted, feeling cold, she watched as he found his jeans. He swore crudely as he struggled to find the right pocket in the dark. The screen cast a cold blue glow on his face. He studied it for a moment, then his fingers pressed buttons, fast, frantic.

He glanced up, distance reflected in his eyes. 'What a nightmare.'

She wasn't sure what he was referring to—the message, or the situation. After another minute or so the phone buzzed again. He read the message.

'I have to go,' he said, pushing more buttons.

It wasn't light yet. Not even close. And this was summer in New Zealand when it got light near five a.m. Hell, he was running out in the middle of the night.

'It's so early.'

He had his jeans on and was still pressing buttons. 'In New York, it's nine a.m. and my client needs help right now.'

'But it's Saturday.' He wouldn't even look at her.

'No such thing as Saturdays, not for me. I have to get back right away.'

But what about the wedding? Devastated, she envisaged the hours to come. But she wasn't going to remind him. He'd probably had too much to drink to even remember. The idea of him being her date had only ever been a joke. Except her family knew. Everyone knew. She was on the train to humiliation central.

She drew her knees up. Face it, she was already there. Mortification spread over her skin and she was glad it was dark and her blush hidden. He could hardly wait to leave her. Silently, quickly, he found his top, pulling it over his head. His mind had already left the building.

Frowning at the screen, he spoke. 'Give me your number.'

He was taking the control—not giving her his details, but trying to make her feel better. As if he'd ever call.

'Bella.' He spoke sharply. 'Tell me your number.'

She recited it, with a cold heart and a determined mind.

He nodded, still pressing buttons. 'I'll call you.'

He made it sound sincere. But she knew for a fact he wouldn't.

Thirteen hours and no sleep later, Bella watched Vita and Hamish walk around the beach wearing their cheesy flip-flops that left 'Just Married' imprinted in the sand. She really wished she had a hangover. That way she could blame the whole escapade on booze. Say she'd been blind drunk and shrug the thing off with the insouciance of an ingénue.

But while she was aching, the pain wasn't in her head—it was deep inside her chest and she tried to tell herself it wasn't really that bad. Fact was, she'd never had a one-night stand before. She'd had boyfriends that hadn't lasted long—OK, so all three of her ex-boyfriends would fall into that category. But she'd never had a fling that lasted less than ten hours. And she'd gone and done it in front of her entire family—who thought she was a hopeless case already. What had she been thinking?

And there was Celia, hanging on the arm of Rex, flashing victorious glances her way at every opportunity. Thank goodness he hadn't arrived until this morning and hadn't been witness to last night too. And now everyone was thinking she couldn't hang onto anyone—not the fabulously suitable accountancy star that was Rex or the laid-back, coolly casual sex god that was Owen. Thank heavens her father had spent the night talking business with his brothers—hopefully he wouldn't have heard a thing about it.

She felt a prickle inside as she saw the sheer joy on her sister's face. Maybe Owen had been right—she was a little jealous. But who wouldn't want to be loved like that? And little sister Vita seemed to have it all—she'd been the one to embrace the family profession—as all four of their elder brothers had. Vita had been the one able to do everything the way the family wanted. Even down to marrying one of the partners in the firm. She'd worked really hard to get her degree and her charter. And to cap it off, she was nice. She deserved to be happy.

But Bella worked hard too. Damn hard. Didn't she deserve to be happy? Didn't she deserve some respect too?

She *was* jealous. How nice it would be to have someone look at her the way Hamish looked at Vita. To have the career and the lover. But she'd yet to *get* the job she wanted, and she couldn't even have a one-night stand last the whole night.

As if Owen had really had to get up and go to work at three in the damn morning? On a *Saturday*. He'd probably programmed his phone to buzz then and the talk of the client in New York was just for believability. It was probably his standard modus operandi—enabling him to make that quick escape and avoid the awkward morning-after scene.

The morning after had been unbearably awkward for Bella. And it wasn't just because of the questioning looks of the younger members of the family—the ones who'd been in the restaurant last night. She'd gone to Reception and asked which room 'Owen' was staying in—only to be told there was no Owen staying at all. And no Owen had checked out recently either. Then she'd asked to check her tab, bracing herself for a huge bill from the bar. But she found it had been paid in full, including the accommodation cost. She'd asked whose name was on the card—but apparently whoever it was had paid in cash.

It had been him—she was sure of it. What was he doing—paying for services rendered?

She stood, brushed the sand from the horrendous dress. She wasn't going to sit around and be the object of mockery or pity any more—and certainly not her own self-pity either. It was time for action. Things were going to have to change.

CHAPTER FIVE

A LOT could happen in three weeks and a day. Life-changing decisions could be made and the resulting plans put into action. And it was too late for regrets now. Bella had finally pushed herself out of the nest—and it was time to see if she could fly. Thus far, she was succeeding *barely* on a day-by-day basis.

The minute she'd got back from that hellish weekend she'd moved out of her father's home in Auckland and down to Wellington. Movies were made there. There were theatres. It was the arts hub. She'd found a tiny flat quite easily. Above another flat where a couple lived. It was in the shade of a hill and was a little damp, but it would do. She hadn't wanted to flat-share. She was going independent—all the way.

Because she'd finally had the shove she needed. And it wasn't ambition. It was one humiliation too many. If she ever saw Owen again she'd have to thank him. His was the boot that had got her moving. The smug sideways glances of Celia, the questions in her perfect sister's eyes at the reception. Bella had explained that he'd had to leave for work. It had sounded lame even to her. When they'd asked what he did, where he worked, she'd only been able to parrot the vague answers that he'd given her.

She didn't want to run the risk of bumping into him ever

again. It would have been just her luck that he'd have come into the café where she'd worked in central Auckland.

So now she worked at a café in central Wellington. The manager of that branch of the chain had jumped at the chance to hire someone already trained, and with so much experience she could step in as deputy manager any time he needed. And she'd started children's party entertaining here too. She'd had a couple of recommendations from contacts in Auckland and today's supreme effort had ensured a booking for her second party already. Several other parents had asked for her card at the end of it too. It wasn't exactly glam work, but she was good at it.

But then there was the lecherous uncle. There was always one. The younger brother of the mother, or the cousin of the father, who fancied a woman in a fairy dress. He'd cornered her as she was packing up her gear.

'Make *my* wish come true. Have dinner with me.'

As if she hadn't heard that one before. Then he'd touched her, an attempt at playfulness. He'd run his fingers down her arm and they'd felt reptilian. She'd made a quick exit—smiling politely at the hosts. Once out the door she'd bolted, because she'd seen him coming down the hall after her. She'd been in such a hurry to get into the car and away she'd pulled hard on her dress as she'd sat and one of the cute capped sleeves had just ripped right off, meaning that side of the top was in imminent danger of slipping south too. Well, the dress had been slightly tight. She'd been eating a little more choco-late than usual these last three weeks. Like a couple of king-size cakes a day to get her through the move. Now she needed to top up on essential supplies. And so it was that she pulled into the supermarket car park—fully costumed up and half falling out of it.

Ordinarily she'd never stop and shop while in character, but this wasn't an ordinary day. She was tired and ever so slightly depressed. She picked up a basket on her way in and ignored the looks from the other customers. Didn't they often see fully grown women wearing silver fairy dresses and wings, an eyeload of make-up and an entire tube of glitter gel?

She'd blow her last fifteen dollars on some serious comfort food. She loaded in her favourite chocolate. The best ice cream—she could just afford the two-litre pack so long as she could find a five-dollar bottle of wine. In this, one of the posher supermarkets, she might be pushing her luck. As it was her luck was always limited.

She headed to the wine aisle and searched for the bright yellow 'on special' tags. She'd just selected one particularly dodgy-looking one when the voice in her ear startled her.

'And you told me you didn't want the fluffy princess part.'

Her fingers were around the wine, taking the weight, but at the sound of that smooth drawl they instinctively flexed.

The bottle smashed all over the floor—wine splattered everywhere, punctuated by large shards of green glass.

Oh, great. It would have to happen to her. Right this very second. She looked hard at the rapidly spreading red puddle on the floor so she wouldn't have to face the stares of the gazillion other customers, especially not… Was it really him?

'Sorry, I didn't mean to give you such a fright.'

She couldn't avoid it any longer. She looked up at—yes, it was him. Right there. Right in front of her. And utterly devastating.

'Oh, no.' The words were out before she thought better of it. 'What are *you* doing here? I thought you lived in—' She broke off. Actually she had no idea where he lived. She'd thought Auckland, but there was no real reason for her to have done so. They hadn't really talked details much—not about anything that really mattered.

After a disturbingly stern appraisal, he bent, picked up the fragment of wine bottle and read the smeared label. It reminded her where they were and the mess she'd just made. She glanced down the aisle and saw a uniform-clad spotty teenager headed their way with a bucket and mop.

'No, no, no and no again.' Owen, if that indeed was his name, was shaking his head.

'It's for cooking. A casserole.' Ultra defensive, she invented wildly.

He drew back up to full height and looked in her basket. Both brows flipped. 'Some casserole.'

'It is actually,' she breezed, determined to ignore the heat in her cheeks. 'Pretty extraordinary.'

'Ultra extraordinary,' he said, still looking at her with a sharpness that was making her feel guilty somehow. It maddened her—he was the one who'd skipped out that crazy night. Don't think about it. Do *not* think about it!

But suddenly it was all back in a rush—all she could see was him naked, her body remembering the warmth of his, the thrill. And all she could hear was his low laughter and how seductive it had been.

The heat in her cheeks went from merely hot to scorching. And he stood still and watched its progression—degree, by slow degree.

Then his gaze dropped, flared and only then did she remember the state of her dress. Quickly she tugged the low sagging neckline up and kept her fist curled round the material just below her shoulder.

His eyes seemed to stroke her skin. 'Your sunburn has faded.'

It didn't feel as if it had now—it felt more on fire than it had weeks ago when it had been almost raw.

'I'm sorry about this.' He gestured to the mess. 'I'll pay for it.'

And then she remembered how he'd left her.

'No, thanks,' she said briskly. 'You don't have to—'

He wasn't listening. He'd turned, studying the shelves of wine. After a moment he picked one out and put it in her basket. 'I think this one will serve you better.'

She caught a glimpse of a white tag—not a yellow 'on special' one—and winced. No way could she afford that bottle of wine. But she couldn't put it back in front of him.

Then he took her basket off her. 'Is that everything you need for your casserole?' he asked blandly.

'Oh, er, sure.'

He turned away from her and headed towards the checkout. She paused, staring after him, panic rising. More humiliation was imminent. She'd chopped up her credit card—not wanting to get into debt—so all she had was that fifteen dollars in her pocket. While she had the cheque from the birthday party she'd just done, it was Sunday and she couldn't cash it.

And no way was she letting him pay her bill—not *again*.

But he put both lots of shopping on the conveyor belt. His was all connoisseur—prime beef steak, a bag of baby spinach, two bottles of hellishly expensive red wine. She couldn't help wondering if he was cooking for a date. Then, as she helplessly watched, he paid for it all—hers as well as his—with a couple of crisp hundred-dollar bills.

Cash. Of course. But as he put the change back in his wallet, she saw the array of cards in there too—exclusive, private banking ones—and she really started to seethe.

* * *

Owen didn't glance her way once during the transaction. He tried to focus on getting the shopping sorted, but all the while his mind was screening the sight of her spilling out of that unbelievable dress.

Bella Cotton. The woman who'd haunted his dreams every night for the last three weeks. He was mad with her. Madder with himself for not being able to shake her from his head.

And now here she was—real and in the beautifully round flesh he couldn't help but remember. She didn't exactly seem thrilled to see him. In fact she looked extremely uncomfortable. Well, so she should, after fobbing him off with a false number like that.

But her embarrassment only made him that bit madder. Made him feel perverse enough to drag out their bumping into each other even longer. Made him all the more determined to interfere and help her out because she so clearly didn't want him to. How awful for her to have to suffer his company for a few more minutes. He very nearly ground his teeth.

Well, he hadn't wanted her to take up as much of his brain space as she had these last few weeks either. Night after night, restless, he'd thought of her—suffered cold showers because of her. During the day too—at those quiet moments when he should have been thinking of important things. He'd even got so distracted one day he'd actually searched for her on the Internet like some sad jilted lover.

So he'd known she was in Wellington, but he hadn't known where or why or for how long. He certainly hadn't expected to see her in his local supermarket. And he sure as hell hadn't expected her to be wearing the most ridiculous get-up—or half wearing it. And he most definitely hadn't expected to feel that rush of desire again—because he was mad with her, wasn't he? He *was* that jilted lover. He really wanted to know why she'd done it—why when even now, for a few moments, he'd seen that passionate rush reflected in her eyes.

So while the rational part of him was telling him to hand over her shopping and walk away asap, the wounded-male-pride bit was making him hold onto it. The flick of desire was making sure his grip was tight.

He was walking out of the supermarket already. Hadn't looked at her once while at the checkout—not even to ask whether it was OK with her. He'd just paid for the lot, ensured their goods were separately bagged and then picked them up. Now he was carrying both sets of shopping out to the car park. She had no option but to follow behind him—her temper spiking higher with every step. And seeing him still looking so hot, casual in jeans and tee again, made every 'take me' hormone start jiggling inside. She stopped them with an iron-hard clench of her teeth and her tummy muscles. She was angry with him. He'd done a runner and insulted her with his payment choices.

But she could hardly wrench the bag off him. Not in front of everyone—she was already causing a big enough scene.

Her car was parked in the first row. She stopped beside it and sent a quick look in his direction to assess his reaction. He was looking at it with his bland-man expression. It only made her even more defensive.

'She's called Bubbles. The kids like it.'

'Kids?'

'I'm a children's party entertainer. The fairy.' People usually laughed. It wasn't exactly seen as the ultimate work and as a result her credibility—especially with her family—was low. They thought it was the biggest waste of her time ever.

He nodded slowly. 'Hence the wings.'

'And the frock.'

There was a silence. 'Do you do adult parties?'

'That's the third time I've been asked that today,' she snapped. 'You're about to get the non-polite answer.'

His grin flashed for the first time. And she was almost floored once more. Or she would have been if she weren't feeling so cross with him—Mr I'll-Pay-For-Everything-Including-You.

Her ancient Bambini was painted baby-blue and had bright-coloured spots all over it. She quickly unlocked it, glancing pointedly at the bag he was carrying, not looking higher than his hand.

Silently he handed it over. 'Thanks.' She aimed for blitheness over bitterness but wasn't entirely sure of her success. 'Nice to see you again.' Saccharine all over. She got in the car before she lost it, ending the conversation, and hitting the ignition.

Nothing.

She tried again. Willed the car to start. Start before she made even more of an idiot of herself.

The engine choked. Her heart sank. Had the long drive down from Auckland finally done the old darling in? She tried the ignition once more. It choked again.

He knocked on the window. Reluctantly she wound it down.

'Having trouble?'

She wasn't looking at him. She was looking at the fuel gauge. The arrow was on the wrong side of E. Totally on the wrong side. It was beyond the red bit and into the nothing. As in NOTHING. No petrol. Nada. Zip.

Man, she was an idiot. But relief trickled through her all the same. She had real affection for the car she'd had for years and had painted herself.

She took a deep breath. She could fake it, right? At least

try to get through the next two minutes with a scrap of dignity? She got out of the car.

'Problem?'

Did he have to be so smooth? So calm, so damn well in control? Didn't he do dumb things on occasion?

'I forgot something,' she answered briefly. Now she remembered the warning light had been on—when was that? Yesterday? The day before? But it had gone off. She'd thought it was OK, that it had been a warning and then changed its mind. She mentally gave herself a clunk in the head—as if it had found some more petrol in its back pocket?

Clearly not. It had completely run out of juice. And the nearest garage was... Where was it exactly? The only one she could think of was the one near her flat—the one she should have filled up at this morning, had she had the funds.

'What?' he asked—dry, almost bored-sounding.

But she was extremely conscious that he hadn't taken his eyes off her. And she was doing everything not to have to look into them, because they were that brilliant blue and she knew how well they could mesmerise her.

She tugged her top up again. 'Petrol.'

'Oh.' He looked away from her then, seeming to take an age looking at the other cars. She realised he was barely holding in his amusement. Finally he spoke. 'The nearest service station is just—'

'Uh, no, thanks,' she interrupted. 'I'll go home first.'

There was no way she was having him beside her when she put five dollars into a jerry can so she could cough and splutter the car home and leave it there until her cheque cleared. After this final splurge it was going to be a tin of baked beans and stale bread for a couple of days. No bad thing given the way she was spilling out the top of the fairy frock.

'How far away is home?'

'Not far.' A twenty-minute walk. Make that thirty in her sequined, patent leather slippers.

There was a silence. She felt his gaze rake her from head to toes—lingering around the middle before settling back up on her face. Heat filled her and she just knew he was enjoying watching her blush deepen. She stared fixedly at the seam on the neckline of his tee shirt and refused to think of anything but how much she was going to appreciate her ice cream when she got the chance.

And then he asked, 'Can I give you a ride?' Mockery twisted his lips, coloured the question and vexed her all the more.

Get a ride with him? Oh, no. She'd already had one ride of sorts and that was plenty, right? She could cope with this just fine on her own.

She'd call the breakdown service. But then she remembered it was her father's account and she refused to lean on him again. Independence was her new mantra. They wouldn't take her seriously until she got herself sorted. Until she proved she was completely capable of succeeding alone. She frowned; she'd have to walk.

'You trusted me enough to sleep with me, I think you can trust me to run you home safely.'

She looked straight at him then, taken by his soft words. With unwavering intensity, he regarded her. She'd known she'd be stunned if she looked into his eyes—brilliant, blue and beautiful. Good grief, he was gorgeous. So gorgeous and all she could think about was how great he'd felt up close and every cell suddenly yearned for the impact.

Her own eyes widened as she read his deepening expression—was there actually a touch of chagrin there? Why?

'Thanks.' It was a whisper. It wasn't what she'd meant to say at all.

* * *

His car sat low to the ground, gleaming black and ultra expensive. The little badge on the bonnet told her that with its yellow background and rearing black horse. He unlocked it, opened the door. She started as the door and seemingly half the roof swung up into the air.

She sent a sarcastic look in his direction. 'That's ridiculous.'

'No, Bella, *that's* ridiculous,' he said, pointing back to her Bambini.

She bent low and managed to slide in without popping right out of her top. The interior was polished and smooth and impeccably tidy and also surprisingly spartan. She tried to convince herself the seat wasn't that much more comfortable than the one in her own old banger. But it was—sleek and moulding to her body.

Owen took the driver's seat, started the engine—a low growl. 'He's called Enzo.'

'I'd have thought it would be more plush.'

He shook his head. 'It's the closest thing to a Formula One racing car you can drive on conventional streets.'

'Oh.' Like that was fabulous?

Her feigned lack of interest didn't stop him. 'I like things that go fast.'

She looked at him sharply. He was staring straight ahead, but his grin was sly and it was widening with every second.

Coolly as she could, she gave him her address. The sooner she got home and away from him, the sooner she could forget about it all and get on with her new life.

The fire vehicle outside her house should have warned her—nothing ever went smoothly for Bella. There was always some weird catastrophe that occurred—the kind of thing that was so outrageous it would never happen to other normal people.

Like being caught in a ripped fairy dress in the supermarket by her only one-night stand—the guy who'd given her the best sexual experience of her life.

'Looks like there might be some kind of trouble.' He stated the obvious calmly as he parked the car.

She stared at the big red appliance with an impending sense of doom intuitively knowing it was something to do with her. She'd have done something stupid. But behind the truck, the house still stood. She released the breath she'd been holding.

'I'm sure whatever's happened isn't that major.'

So he figured it had something to do with her too. She might as well walk around with a neon sign saying 'danger, accident-prone idiot approaching'. But her embarrassment over every-thing to do with him faded into the background as she got out of the car and focused on whatever had gone wrong now.

As she walked up the path, one seriously bad smell hit her. The couple from the downstairs flat were standing in the middle of the lawn. A few firemen were standing next to them talking. Silence descended as she approached, but they weren't even trying to hide their grins. It was a moment before she remembered her fairy dress and quickly put her hand to her chest. Wow, what an entrance.

'You left something on the hob.' The head fire guy stepped forward.

She'd what?

'I think you were hard-boiling some eggs.'

Oh, hell—she had been, the rest of the box because they'd been getting dangerously close to their use-by date and she hadn't wanted to waste any. She'd decided to cook them up and have them ready for the next day, and then in the rush to get to the café and pack all her party gear, she'd forgotten all about them.

Isla, her neighbour, piped up, 'They had to break down the door—we didn't have a key.'

The doors to both flats were narrow and side by side. Only now hers was smashed—splinters of wood lay on the ground, and the remainder of the door was half off its hinges.

'I'm so sorry,' she mumbled.

She trudged up the stairs and almost had a heart attack when she saw the damage to the door up there too. The whole thing would have to be replaced as well as the one downstairs. Bye bye bond money. And she'd probably be working extra hours at the café to make up the rest of it.

She stared around at the little room she'd called home for a grand total of two weeks. Her first independent, solely occupied home. There was almost no furniture—a beanbag she liked to curl into and read a book or watch telly. But it had been hers. Now it was tainted by the most horrendous smell imaginable and she couldn't imagine it ever being a welcome sanctuary again. She'd spoilt things—again—with her own stupidity.

'You can't stay here.'

She nearly jumped out of her skin when Owen spoke.

'No.' For one thing the smell was too awful. For another it was no longer secure with both doors broken like that. She wouldn't sleep a wink.

She saw him looking around, figured he must be thinking how austere it was. When his gaze came to rest on her again, concern was evident in his eyes. She didn't much like that look. She wasn't some dippy puppy that needed to be taken care of.

'Can I drop you somewhere else?'

Her heart sank even lower into her shiny slippers. The last thing she wanted to do was call on the family. Having finally broken out she wanted to manage—for more than a month at least. If she phoned them now she'd never get any credibility. The two months' deposit on the flat had taken out her savings, but she didn't care. She'd wanted to be alone, to be independent, and she'd really wanted it to work this time. She could check into a hostel, but she had no money. She had no-where to go. She'd have to stay here, put a peg on her nose and her ear on the door.

He took a step in her direction. 'I have a spare room at my place.'

She looked at him—this stranger whom she knew so intimately, yet barely knew at all.

'Grab a bag and we'll get out of here. Leave it and come back tomorrow.' He spoke lightly. 'It won't be nearly so bad then.'

She knew it was a good idea but she felt sickened. It was the last straw on a hellish day and her slim control snapped. Anger surged as she stared at him. Irrationally she felt as if he were to blame for everything. 'Is your name really Owen?'

He looked astonished. 'Of course. Why do you ask?'

'I asked at the hotel reception for you.' She was too stewed to care about what that admission might reveal. 'They had no record of any Owen staying there.'

He paused, looked a touch uncomfortable. 'I wasn't staying at the resort.'

She stared at him in disbelief.

'I have a holiday house just down from it.'

A holiday house—in one of the most exclusive stretches of beach on Waiheke Island? Who the hell was he?

He looked away, walked to the window. 'No strings, Bella,' he said carelessly, returning to her present predicament. 'All

I'm offering is a place to stay for a couple of days until this
mess gets cleaned up.'

Bella pushed the memories out and internally debated. She
didn't have much in the way of personal possessions—nothing
of any great value anyway. The most important stuff was her
kit for the parties and that was in her car. It wouldn't take five
minutes to chuck a few things into a bag. And maybe, if she
took up his offer, she could keep this latest catastrophe to
herself? Her family need never know.

Slowly, she swallowed her remaining smidge of pride. 'Are
you sure?'

'Of course.' He shrugged, as if it was nothing. It probably
was nothing to him. 'I work all hours. I'll hardly notice you're
there.'

She knew she could trust him; he certainly didn't seem as
if he was about to pounce. He'd gone running away in the
night, hadn't he? Humiliation washed over her again. But she
had little choice—her family or him. She picked him—she'd
lost all dignity as far as he was concerned already. Maybe she
could keep the scrap she had left for her father. 'OK.'

Owen failed to hide his smile, so turned quickly, heading
down the stairs to deal with the fire crew. He fixed the bottom
door enough to make it look as all right as possible from the
outside and gave a half-guilty mutter of thanks for her misfortune. He wasn't afraid to take advantage of this situation—
not when she'd so coolly cut him loose that night. Because
that flick of desire had blown to full-on inferno again—from
a mere five minutes in her company. And now he had the
perfect opportunity to have even more of her company—one
night, maybe two. Enough to find out what had gone wrong,
and then to finish what had started.

Bella stuffed a few clothes into a bag—not many—while dwelling on the glimpse of that wide, wicked, Waiheke smile he'd just flashed. It would only be one night. Two, tops.

Not taking sexy black lingerie. *Not* taking sexy black lingerie. Somehow it ended up stuffed at the bottom of the bag.

CHAPTER SIX

THINGS came in threes, right? And Bella had had her three—her dress, the wine and now her flat. Surely nothing else could go wrong with this day?

'Is there anyone you should call?' Owen asked, opening the car door for her.

She shook her head. 'I'll take care of it later.'

'Then let's go.'

She sat back and tried to relax as he turned the car round and headed back towards the centre of town. He slowed as they hit what had once been the industrial district with lots of warehouses for storing the goods that came in on the harbour. Only now most of the warehouses had been converted—restaurants, upmarket shops and residential conversions in the upper storeys. It was the ultimate in inner-city living with theatres around the corner, Te Papa the national museum, the best film house in the country and shops, shops, shops. All less than a five-minute walk away.

He pulled in front of one warehouse. On one side of it was a restaurant, the other a funky design store. But there was nothing in the ground floor of this one. The windows were darkened. His car window slid down and he reached out to press numbers of the security pad that stood on a stand in front. The wide door opened up and he drove the car in. In the dim light she saw a big empty space—save for a mountain bike and some assorted gym equipment. It immediately reminded her of his muscles. She looked away. There was a lift to the side and a steep flight of stairs heading up in a straight line. He stepped forward, tackling the stairs.

'My apartment is on the top floor.'

Of course it was. On the third level there was another security pad, another pin number. The guy was clearly security conscious. Once inside she blinked—her eyes taking a second to cope with the transition from gloomy stairwell to bright room. It was huge. At first glance all she saw were wooden floors, bricks, steel beams. Half the roof had been ripped off and replaced with skylights—flooding the place in fresh, natural light. There was a huge table in the centre, surrounded by an assortment of chairs, but it was the long workbench that ran the length of one wall that caught her attention.

'Is your computer screen big enough?' She stared in amazement at the display of technology lined up on it. 'Have you got enough of them?'

He grinned. 'Actually most of them are in the office on the second floor.'

'So what, these are just for fun?'

He gave her a whisker of a wink, a faint fingerprint of the humour he'd had that night on Waiheke. Then it was gone. He walked ahead of her, leading her to the kitchen area, and she watched awkwardly as he put items into the fridge and freezer.

'Most of the apartment has yet to be done. After getting my room and the kitchen done I just ran out of—'

'Money?' she interpolated hopefully. Surely she couldn't have been so far wrong about this guy.

'Time,' he corrected, smiling faintly. 'Business has been

busy.' He looked about. 'The basic design is there but I haven't had the chance to get the last bits done yet.' He glanced at her. 'I'll show you to your room.'

It was on the far side of the living area. There were more rooms heading down the corridor next to it, but through their open doors she could see that they were empty. In the room he stopped at, there was just a bed and a chest of drawers.

'Sorry it's so bare.'

She shook her head. 'I'm used to less.'

'I'll make up the bed.'

'I can do it.' She didn't want him in the room any more than necessary.

She took a look out the window—it overlooked the street; she could see all the shoppers. There was a seriously yummy smell wafting up from the Malaysian restaurant next door. 'You must eat out all the time.'

He answered from the doorway. 'They do me take-out packages. But I try to cook a few nights a week. The downside is the rubbish collection—before six o'clock every morning all the bottles from the night before get tipped into the recy-cling truck. Makes a hell of a din.'

'I'd have thought you'd be well up by then anyway.' She shot him a look. *'Working.'*

That hint of humour resurged, warming her. It was then she fully recognised the danger—she was still hopelessly attracted to him. If he turned on the smile charm again she'd be his in a heartbeat.

She kicked herself. He wasn't offering anything but a room, remember? And she didn't want his sort of gratitude. Tiredness swamped her and the fairy dress slipped lower. She desperately needed a shower. Desperately needed to get dressed in some-thing far more concealing. 'Do you mind if I use the bathroom?'

The amusement in his eyes became unholy. 'Sure. Follow me.'

He led her back into the main space, and across it. Her footsteps slowed as she spied what was through the doorway he was headed to—a very big bed with most definitely masculine-coloured coverings.

'We'll have to share the bathroom—is that OK?'

'Um…sure,' she mumbled. 'That's fine.'

She was in his bedroom. Her skin was prickling with heat.

'The bathroom is one of the things yet to be finished.' He was talking again. 'There's a loo near the kitchen, but the only shower and bath at the moment are the ones in the en suite for the master bedroom.'

The master bedroom—his bedroom—*this* bedroom. Oh, life couldn't be so cruel.

He was watching her with that wicked twinkle faintly sparking in his eyes. 'It's a really nice shower.'

She was quite sure it would be. She wanted to ask if there was a lock on the door, but thought better of being so rude. She hurriedly looked away from him, only to get an eyeful of his walk-in wardrobe space—and all the suits that were hanging there.

Suits.

Completely thrown, she followed where he'd wandered into the bathroom. It was her turn to stop in the doorway.

He stood in the centre of the room. He turned towards her, his smile satisfied. 'It's something, isn't it?'

She nodded. It was all she could manage.

'When I get the chance I'll get the rest of place up to standard too.'

It was beautiful. A huge wet play area that oozed with refined elegance. All the fittings were obviously expensive. The colourings were muted—dark grey, black with sparse splashes of red. A shower space with ample room for two and the biggest bath she'd ever seen.

She railed against her own appreciation of it. Materialistic was not her—there were other, more important things in life. And yet there was no way she couldn't indulge in such classical luxury. No way she couldn't stop thinking of him in there too.

'Take as long as you want,' he said, passing her so closely she shivered. 'You'll find everything you need in here.'

She sagged against the door after he closed it behind him. What she wanted and needed had just walked out.

The kitten heels of her slippers echoed on the wooden floors as she walked back through to the kitchen. She could smell the most delicious smell. So good it wiped the final traces of the rank burnt-egg odour from her senses.

He was barefoot and looking like that careless, gorgeous hunk of a guy she'd met that wild night. Again she was transported back to the moments when she'd felt the firmness of his denim-wrapped thighs between hers. When he'd pulled her close on the dance floor, even closer in her room... Somewhere inside she softened...and immediately she sought to firm up again.

This was the guy who'd been so keen to get away he'd sneaked out in the crazy hours.

This was the guy who wasn't anything like she'd thought, who'd totally misled her—hadn't he?

Now he was standing in his designer kitchen stirring something in a wok with a quick hand. She hovered near the edge of the bench and watched as he added the now diced beef into the mix. Another pot was on the hob and, judging from the steam rising, was on rapid boil.

He glanced up at her. 'You must be hungry.'

Yes, her mouth was definitely watering. And it wasn't the only part of her growing damper. She shifted further away from him. 'How many?'

'How many what?'

'How many are coming to dinner? You could feed an army with a steak that size.'

'Just me.' He laughed. 'And now you.'

'You really are a tiger,' she murmured, turning to look at the living area again, not really meaning for him to hear. 'So your office is on the level downstairs?' She tried to go for some safe conversation.

'Yeah,' he answered. 'I'm not sure what I want to do with the ground-floor level yet. Not a restaurant, that's for sure. Maybe retail?' He shrugged.

He could afford to leave it untenanted? Inner-city space like this would be worth a fortune. *He* must be worth a fortune. Her heart sank lower.

How could she have been so wrong? Stupid. Most women would be thrilled to discover someone was actually a kazillionaire. But it just emphasised to Bella her lack of judgment—and the fact she was so out of place here. She'd never be the girl for anyone as successful as this; she was too much of a liability, too much of a joke. Moodily she stared at the dream space again.

But like a bee to honey she was drawn to look back, watching as he poured in an unlabelled jar of the something that smelt heavenly. Intrigued, she couldn't not ask. 'What's that?'

His wicked look was back. 'The restaurant down the road gives it to me on the sly.'

'It smells incredible.'

'And that's nothing on how it tastes.' He nodded to a

slimline drawer. 'You'll find cutlery in there. Put some on that tray, will you?'

She was glad for something to do. It meant she had to turn her back on him and not watch the impressive cook on display.

'So how long have you been living in that flat?' he called to her above the sizzling sound of the searing meat.

'Two weeks.'

'Really?' He'd moved so he could see her and she could see the lift of his brows.

'I've only just moved to Wellington.'

'Why the shift?'

'To further my career.' The wedding had been the catalyst. The last push she'd needed to finally get out of there and turn her dreams to reality. Only, already it was falling apart.

'Oh?'

'There are good theatres here. The movie industry is based here.'

'There are good cafés here,' he added, full of irony.

She tossed her head. 'There are.'

'So why now?' He was putting food on plates and she was so hungry she could hardly concentrate on what she was saying.

'It needed to happen.'

'You've got work already?'

She nodded and admitted it. 'I've got a job at one of those good cafés. And I'm going to hit the audition circuit.' She'd already scoped the talent agencies. Knew which ones she was going to target. Hopefully they'd take her on. And then it was a matter of keeping trying and hoping for Lady Luck to smile on her.

He lifted the plates onto the tray. Noodles with wilted spinach and slices of seared beef. Her mouth watered. She hadn't had a meal as good as this in weeks.

'Wine?'

She hadn't noticed the bottle of red standing on the bench. 'Thanks.'

He added the bottle to the tray, glanced at her, all irony again. 'Can you manage the glasses?'

'I think so,' she answered coolly.

She followed him up the stairs she hadn't even noticed earlier. They literally climbed to the roof—to a door that took them right out onto it.

The air outside was warm and not too windy. Most of the roof was bare, but there was a collection of plants in pots lined up close together. As he led her around them she saw they created a hedge. On the sheltered side a small table stood, with a couple of chairs, and a collection of smaller pots holding herbs, a couple holding cherry-tomato bushes. It wasn't a huge garden, but it was well cared for. And the view took in the vibrant part of the city, gave them a soundtrack that was full of life.

He balanced the tray on the edge of the table, unloaded the plates with such ease she knew he'd done it countless times before. Just how many women had dined on his roof? It was, she speculated, the perfect scene for seduction.

Well, not hers. Not again.

But she sat when he gestured and he sat too. He seemed bigger than she recalled. His legs were close under the table and it would be nothing to stretch out and brush hers against his. She felt the flush rise in her cheeks and took a sip of the wine so she could hide behind the glass.

'I've organised for your car to be taken to my local garage. I'll get them to check the tyres too. A couple looked a little bald.'

Bella's nerves jangled. The wine tasted sharper. She swallowed it down hard. She couldn't afford new tyres and the last thing she wanted to be was even more indebted to him. A night in his spare room she could deal with. But nothing more. And fixing up her car was well beyond her at the moment. She didn't want to be dependent on anyone. Certainly didn't want to be beholden to him.

'I'd really prefer that you didn't,' she said with as much dignity as she could muster. 'I can take care of it myself.'

And she would. She was over having people interfering and trying to organise her life for her, as if they all thought she couldn't. As if they thought the decisions she made were ill judged.

He didn't reply immediately—coolly having a sip of his wine and seeming to savour it while studying her expression. 'At least let me arrange to have it brought here. It'll be a sitting duck left in a supermarket car park like that.'

She bit the inside of her lip. He was right. It was the ideal target for teenage joyriders—irresistible, in fact. And she loved Bubbles, would hate to see her wrecked, which she would be if any boy racers decided to have a laugh in her. Besides, she suddenly remembered all her party gear was in the back. She certainly couldn't afford to replace all that in a hurry. She knew that once again she couldn't refuse him.

'OK,' she capitulated in a low voice. 'Thanks.'

She sampled some of her dinner. He was right, the sauce was divine—and so was the way he'd cooked the meat in it. But she couldn't enjoy it as much as she ought—the day's events were catching up with her and she realised just what the small fire in her flat had meant. The silence grew and while she knew she should make the attempt she couldn't think what to say. It was like the white elephant in the room—that subject she was determined to avoid. How did people play this sort of thing? How would some sophisticate handle it? How did she pretend bumping into the guy she'd had the hottest sex of her life with was no big deal? But it was a big deal.

Because she wanted it again—badly. Only he'd walked away so quickly, so easily and seemingly without thought to where it had left her.

And now, seeing him in his home environment, she knew he was nothing like the guy she'd pegged him as. He was way out of her league and, judging by the blandly polite way he was dealing with her, he was no longer interested anyway.

He rested his fork on his plate and looked at her. 'So tell me about the wedding.'

She lowered her fork too. So he did remember about that— did he remember he'd offered to be her date too? She shrugged the question off. 'What's to tell?'

Owen lifted his fork again and determinedly focused on his food. It was just like that night on Waiheke—one glance and all he wanted to do was take her to bed. For that time in the bar he couldn't have cared less about work and the commitments he knew were burdening him. Not until he'd had her. But then those commitments had pulled. He'd cursed it at the time, mentally swearing as he'd worked through the early hours answering the questions his client had been struggling with.

He'd walked from her. He'd had to work—that was his first priority. It was the one thing he knew he could be relied on to do, and all the while he'd been doing it he'd been thinking of her—of the most spectacular sex of his life. But then, only a few hours later, he'd tried her number, wanting to apologise for letting her down about the wedding and for walking out so fast, but found it rang to someone who'd never heard of her.

Stung, he'd decided it was for the best—a one-off, as most

of his encounters were. It was the way he liked it—simple, uncomplicated, with no threat of someone wanting something more from him, emotionally or financially. He'd been appalled to discover years ago that he didn't have the 'more' emotionally to give. When Liz had tried to force a commitment, he'd realised damn quick how much he didn't want the burden of it. He couldn't meet high needs, high maintenance, high anything. He didn't want the responsibility of family and forever and all that. Casual, brief, fun. That was all he offered and all he wanted.

But it still niggled. She'd cut at his pride. Tony's Lawn Mowing Service. He wouldn't forget that low point in a hurry.

'Was it fun?' He wanted to see if she'd refer to it. Would she even apologise? But instead she was looking at him as if he were the one who had something to be sorry about. Well, he didn't think so.

But he didn't want to challenge her—not yet. He'd bide his time—see if the sizzle was still there for her as it was for him. Because if it was, and he was pretty sure it was, then he wanted to rouse it. He wanted her wanting him again—and not hiding it. That would be the moment to strike. And once he'd heard her reason, had her apology, he'd have her.

He figured it couldn't be as good again—it had been a unique set of circumstances leading to that explosion between them on Waiheke. Sex that good definitely wasn't possible a second time—it would be fun, but it would be finished. Maybe then he'd get some sleep again.

'The wedding was nice.' She spoke in a resigned voice. 'Beautiful food, fabulous setting.'

And a beautiful bridesmaid—he knew that for a fact. 'And the company?'

Her smile was filled with rue. 'Was as expected.'

'You didn't enjoy it.'

She screwed up her face. 'Not parts of it, no. But some things were great.'

'Your family approves of the groom?' He got the impression family approval was something of a major in Bella's life.

'Oh, yes.' The answer came quickly. 'Hamish is a nice guy. He loves Vita. He makes her happy. But that's not why Dad was so happy to have him marry her.'

'No?' He couldn't stop the questions, found he was more and more intrigued as her face grew even more expressive.

She rolled her eyes. 'Money. It all comes down to doing the maths and in the spreadsheet Hamish has it all. He has the right job and went to the right school. Drives the right car, lives in the right suburb. That's the measure. Visible, measurable success.'

Success, huh? He thought of her tiny unfurnished flat, her barely road-safe car, the bad budget wine she'd been about to buy. He felt a twinge of sympathy for her father. 'Maybe he just wants security for her.'

'What sort of security?' she scoffed. 'It wouldn't matter to him if he was a complete jerk, so long as he could check the right boxes he'd be happy.'

He sensed the hurt in her again. Figured he knew its source. 'Let me guess—you had a boyfriend who didn't measure up.'

'Actually, no. He was exactly what my father wanted.'

A crazy spurt of competition flared through him. 'How so?'

'He had it all.' She ticked off her fingers. 'An accountant. Very successful. Has the car, the apartment. Really good at team sports, the works. The whole family loved him.'

'So what went wrong?'

'He wanted me to wear something more conservative.'

Owen stared at her, only just holding back the burst of laughter. He couldn't imagine Bella allowing that in a million years. Not this woman who was currently wearing some huge flowing blouse and a skirt that was so long it practically dragged on the ground. And he was spending far too long mentally pushing the whole ugly lot off her.

She stared at him, all defiance. 'Nobody tells me what I should or shouldn't wear.'

'That was it?' he asked.

'That was just the start.' She stabbed another bite of meat. 'I'm not interested in someone who wants to change me. Or who wants me to be something I'm not.'

Fair enough point. And he was pleased he'd been right. The guy must have been blind to not see how expression of her individuality was a cornerstone for Bella. 'So what happened to him?'

'He was the best man.'

His mouth dropped. 'At the wedding?'

She nodded. 'He's Hamish's best friend. But it's OK.' She smiled saccharine sweet. 'He's still part of the family. Probably will be part of the family because now he's dating Celia.'

'Cousin Celia?' Owen felt the cold chill ripple through him. Was that why Bella had played so wildly with him? Because she'd wanted to show them all she didn't need them? Just wanted a hot date to throw in their faces? He'd known at the time that that was part of it and he'd enjoyed playing along. But once they'd been behind closed doors there'd been a genuine, raw passion in her—an intensity that he hadn't expected. And he'd found an answering need rising in him. A hunger that had been extreme and that hadn't been fully fed. He'd wanted more and had thought she did too.

Now he knew better. So that wildness had purely been

driven by rebound and pride? No wonder she hadn't wanted to know him after and had given him a false number. He'd just been a convenient tool for the evening. His fingers curled tighter round his cutlery. Maybe he wasn't going to bide his time after all. Maybe he would have a go for the way she'd treated him that night—right about now.

But Bella was still talking. 'They're all so pleased, because he is such a great guy,' she continued. 'But of course, they do feel for me. I mean, it must be so hard, seeing him with my cousin like that. After he broke my heart and all. But he just fell in love with Celia, you see. And she really is his perfect match.'

Owen stared at her for a second, not sure if she was being sarcastic or not. Then he caught the glint in her eye. And he started to laugh. Couldn't help it, and the knot of tension loosened again.

Bella smiled too. 'I can see the funny side. I can. But they all think he broke up with me. They just can't believe that I'd have ditched him. It's beyond their comprehension that someone like me would have thrown away a catch like him.'

It soothed him no end to hear she'd been the one to dump the jerk. 'Does what they think really matter so much?'

'Maybe it shouldn't.' She looked at her clear plate. 'But it does.'

'Why?'

'I just want them to respect me.' She pushed back her chair and stood. 'I want them to respect what I do.'

Owen stood, picked up his plate and headed after her. He could see some of the problem. It might be hard, for the conservative type her family seemed to be, to respect someone who wore a Walt Disney dress and drove a car called Bubbles.

He followed her back inside, down the stairs, struggling with the fact his desire for her wasn't abating at all. How was he going to manoeuvre this the way he wanted? Could he really do patience?

'So what was the best bit of the day?' He put his plate on the bench, near where she now stood, filling the sink with hot water and detergent. 'Assuming there was a best bit.'

She turned and smiled then, a brilliant, genuine smile that made him snatch a quick breath.

'Seeing my sister so happy.'

Bella could see she'd surprised him. She rinsed the plates and pots and stacked them in the dishwasher. She felt a bit embarrassed about all she'd just unloaded—but once she'd started babbling she couldn't stop and it meant there weren't those heavy silences. The last thing she'd wanted was to sound like some little girl whining about her family not taking her seriously. She was hard to take seriously because she did tend to make stupid mistakes. But that didn't mean that what she did contribute wasn't worthwhile.

She certainly hadn't meant to harp on about Rex. Celia could have him. She honestly didn't want him. He wasn't her type at all. And based on what she could see around she was determined to think Owen wasn't either. People who had this kind of success were conservative, weren't they? They worked hard, played safe, climbed to the top—from the looks of things Owen was definitely at the top. And conservative people just didn't 'get' Bella. No wonder he'd skipped out as soon as he could. No wonder he was Mr Reluctant now. She refused to embarrass him by throwing herself at him. She would be nice, polite, not make a fool of herself—any more than she already had. But she couldn't help appreciating his closeness as he sorted out the dishwasher and switched it on.

'I'm really tired,' she said. 'It's been quite a day.'

'Sure has,' he agreed—those soft, gentle tones again like on the beach as they'd headed to her studio.

Heart thudding, she turned, quickly, awkwardly, to head to her room. But just as she was about to leave it hit her how kind he'd been. He hadn't lectured her about her many mishaps of the day, hadn't teased her mercilessly as her family and friends would have. He'd just accepted it. Dealt with it. Helped her.

And she really appreciated it.

She turned back, still feeling completely awkward. 'Owen, thank you,' she began formally.

He walked up to her then and, now she'd looked up at him, he captured her gaze with his—with the vivid intensity of it. He put a finger on her lips and she was held fast.

'Leave it. It's not a problem.'

Like a statue she stood, mesmerised once more, filled with the memory of how well they'd fitted together. How wonderful his body had felt. How much she'd like to feel it again.

His focus dropped, flickered over her face and then lower. His finger followed, leaving her mouth to touch the hollow just below her collarbone, brushing back her blouse to reveal the skin. 'Is this new?'

What? Oh, the unicorn, the fake tattoo she always wore for parties. She put one on all the kids too. It was part of the fairy ritual.

'It's temporary,' she whispered. She didn't know why she was whispering, it was just that her voice wouldn't go any louder as his thumb smoothly stroked the small spot.

And at her words a touch of seriousness dulled the gleam in his eyes. A half-smile curved one side of his mouth, but it wasn't one of tease or wicked intent. He stepped back. 'Sleep well.'

Disappointment wafted through her. So he wasn't inter-ested. It had been a night of craziness for him and not one he wanted to repeat. For now she was back in his life but only, like her tattoo, temporary.

What had happened today might not be a problem for him. But it was for her.

CHAPTER SEVEN

OWEN sat back in his chair, letting the debate wash over him as two of his young design team warred over the best way to progress a new program they were working on. They had a meeting with the client in just an hour's time and they had to decide before then. He watched disinterestedly as they both tried to secure his vote with impassioned speeches aimed in his direction. He wasn't really listening.

He hadn't seen Bella leave this morning. Figured she must be on an early shift at the café she was working at. The fairy dress that had haunted him all night was slung over one of the chairs so he knew she hadn't skipped out on him already. Although he suspected she wanted to. He studied the fabric, saw her in it in his mind's eye. The outfit was demure, no parents would object, and yet she looked so damn sexy, so edible. Like a silver-wrapped bon bon—one that he wanted to unpeel and devour in one big bite. No wonder she was asked if she did adult parties. He'd been awake all hours, still seeing her in it—and the curve of her breast almost *not* in it.

She had this whole slightly incompetent thing going—she had a car that looked as if it had a bad case of multicoloured measles and tyres so bald you could practically see your reflection in them. As for the hard-boiled eggs... He could still feel the mortification that had emanated from her in great waves. It hadn't been hard not to laugh. Unlike her neighbours and the firefighters, he'd seen under the blushes to the hurt beneath, and the fear. The clarity of it all surprised him. He wasn't usually one to tune into the deep feelings of others, but with her it had been so acute he'd almost felt it himself. And crazily he didn't want her to feel alone. He didn't want her to *be* alone. Alarming, when being alone was the one thing he liked best.

But she'd been faced with a situation where she'd been feeling desperate—desperate enough to come home with him, because he knew she hadn't wanted to. And that, despite those occasional signs pointing the other way, made him keep the brakes on.

She hadn't wanted to see him again—had deliberately given him the wrong number—and then had been forced to accept his assistance. Assistance he'd been careful to offer casually—knowing instinctively that if he'd come on strong she'd refuse and he hadn't wanted that. Because he was certain there was still a strong attraction there—she might not like it, but the chemical reaction between them was undeniable.

Now, somehow, he was going to find out why she didn't like it, and then he was going to get rid of it.

It slowly dawned on him that the room had descended into silence. They were all looking his way. And then he saw that the attention of his team wasn't on him or the lack of conversation. They were all fixated on a spot over his shoulder.

He heard slightly laboured breathing and turned to look behind him. And he was glad he was sitting down. Because the zip on his trousers was instantly pulled really tight. If he were to stand it would be obvious to all the world what this woman did to him. As it was he might have given it away with his mouth hanging open for the last—how long was it already?

She was standing only a few paces into the room, the door to her bedroom open behind her. She was wearing an old, thin, white tee shirt. It was oversized, the sleeves coming to her elbows, the hem only just covering the tops of her thighs. Good thing it reached even that far because that, it seemed, was it. Her only other adornment was a thin white cord coming from each ear, in her hand the tiny MP3 player. Even from this distance, in the silence of his colleagues, he could hear the faint strains of the music playing in her ears.

He clawed back the ability to move and glanced at the table, catching the surreptitious smiles between his workers and saw Billy openly staring at her. He couldn't blame him. He swung his face back towards her himself, unable to look away for long.

Her mouth had opened. She might have apologised but it wasn't audible. He saw her take in another deep shuddering breath. And then she turned, and walked back into the bedroom. As she'd moved her breasts had moved too, making it more than clear that there was no bra on under there.

'Excuse me.' Her voice was louder that time, her profile fiery as she darted back into the bedroom.

Owen stared after her. She had surprisingly long legs for someone who really wasn't that tall. He remembered them around his waist and wanted to wrap them there again— preferably *now*.

Instead he turned his head back to his team.

'One sec, guys,' he managed to mutter. He swivelled his chair right around before standing so his back was to them as he rose. Gritting his teeth and praying for self-control, he headed after her.

She was across the other side of the room, but turned back to the door as he entered. He glanced about for a moment to buy some more control time before looking at her again. The glance took in her rumpled bed. It didn't help his focus.

'I'm so sorry,' she mumbled, cheeks still stop-sign red. 'I was listening to my music and didn't hear you all out there.'

'I should have warned you, but I thought you'd gone. We have meetings up here every so often.'

All he wanted to do was slide his fingers under the hem of that ratty old shirt and find out for sure if her bottom truly was as bare as her legs were. Looking down, he could see the outline of her nipples. Her glorious, soft warm breasts that he longed to cup in his hands and kiss as he had that magical night on Waiheke.

He was twisting up inside with the effort of trying to control his want, knowing he had to get back to that meeting when all he wanted was to back her up against the bed and take her. The way he was feeling right now it wouldn't take long. Just a few minutes. Fast and furious.

But he knew it wouldn't be enough. He needed longer with her—he needed a whole night.

'I'll be on my way in a moment.' She was still mumbling.

He looked into her face then and the hunger in it jolted him. She was staring—as if she hadn't seen him before, her silvery blue eyes wide. He wondered if she knew how transparent they were. The desire shone in them, the dazed surprise as she looked him over. But at the back of them he could also see hesitation. And that was the bit he didn't understand. What had happened that night? And how could he right it? Nothing could happen until he did. He wanted her as willing and as wild as she'd been at the beginning.

So with sheer force of will he turned away, and, acting as normally as he could, went back to his incredibly boring meeting.

When she emerged from the bedroom the next time she

was clothed in the black trousers and shirt he figured was her work attire. He rose and walked her to the door, shielding her from the overly curious stares of his colleagues. He bet they'd be curious. They'd never seen a woman here before. He was glad she'd emerged from one of the spare rooms. He knew he had a reputation for short term, and that was a reputation and a reality that he wanted to keep. It was a good way of keeping gold-diggers at bay. But he wasn't glad about the way Billy was still eyeing her up.

'Are you going to the café?' Of course she was, but he wanted to have some sort of conversation with her, wanted to hold her there for just a fraction longer.

She nodded, still not looking at him, clearly eager to escape.

'But you haven't had breakfast.'

'I'll have something at work.'

She'd slipped out the door before he could think of anything else stupid to say.

He usually worked most of the day up in his apartment, liking the light and the space to think freely—away from the phones and noise of his employees. But today, after the meeting, he stayed down on the second floor with them. Keeping away from the sight of that damn dress and the scent of her.

He was going to have to win her over again. How? Make her laugh? Do something nice for her? He had the suspicion he needed to be careful about that—she'd got huffy over his offer to take care of her car. So what, then?

Annoyed with himself for spending so long thinking about her, he forced himself to work longer and harder. And when that failed he went out and got physical.

Bella had had a long day. She was well used to working in a café but was more tired than usual from standing and smiling for so many hours. She'd spent the whole time seeing Owen looking the ultimate stud in that suit. Devastating, distracting, delicious—and totally beyond her reach.

Now she was sitting at his big table, desperately trying to sew the sleeve back onto the offending fairy dress. She'd had a call from one of the parents who'd been at yesterday's party. She had a four-year-old niece who was having a party this weekend and would she be able to attend? Of course she would. She needed the money too badly to say no. She needed to get out of Owen's apartment before she threw herself at him desperate-wench style.

Sighing, she tried to thread the needle again. She was having more luck with her party entertaining than she was with her serious acting. She'd phoned up one of the theatres and had felt totally psyched out when the artistic director started asking about what training she'd had and so on. She'd stumbled, like the amateur she was. He'd said they had nothing now but to keep an eye out in the paper for the next auditions call. She didn't know what else she'd expected, but it was disheartening all the same.

Then Owen got home. She stared as he gave her a brief grin and headed to the kitchen. He'd been to the gym or for a run or something because he was in shorts and a light tee and trainers and there was bare brown skin on show. He was filmed in sweat and breathing hard. She was fascinated. Her own pulse skipped faster, forcing her to take in air quicker too.

He reached into the fridge and pulled out a bottle of water. Seeing him swigging deeply like that, Bella totally lost her stitch. She struggled once more to rethread the needle.

He wandered closer, staring just as hard back at her with an expression she couldn't define. The thread slipped again.

'Repairs not going so well?'

Major understatement. She'd scrubbed so hard at the hem to get the wine stains out and had only partially succeeded. She was gutted because it was a one-in-a-million dress and if she didn't get it sorted she wouldn't be able to work. She couldn't afford a new one and she couldn't afford to get this one fixed. She was going to have to do it herself. She squared her shoulders. Determined to do it, refusing to send an SOS to her father, refusing to give up.

'Let me have a go.' He went back to the kitchen, washed his hands, dried them and then reached for the fabric.

Stunned, she handed it over. 'You really were some sort of Boy Scout?'

He glanced at her then, his eyes full of awareness, and she kicked herself for bringing the memory of that night out into the open. She flushed.

He looked back to the needle, lips twitching. 'Actually, no, but I figure I can't do as bad a job as you are.'

'Thanks very much.'

He sat in the chair next to hers. Suddenly antsy, she moved and took a quick walk around the room before returning to stand over him. He'd been out running for over an hour. She could see the '68' minutes frozen on his stopwatch where he'd recorded his time. Yet his breathing was now normal. Fit guy. But then she knew that already. She could feel the heat from him and all it did was make her uncomfortably hot and her breath came shorter and faster still—as if she were the one out marathon training.

He didn't look too competent with the needle, though.

'Damn.'

Sure enough he'd pricked his finger.

She felt mightily glad to see he was a little useless at something.

He looked up at her, his eyes suddenly all puppy-dog apologetic. 'Sorry,' he said. 'Tell you what, I'll get my dry-cleaner to take it—they do mending as well.'

'No.' She shook her head.

'Bella, I have to. I've smeared blood on it now. I owe you.'

She looked at the dress; sure enough, there was a big spot right on the cute capped sleeve.

'Oh.' Her heart lurched.

'It's the least I can do.' He really did look sorry. 'I'm sure they'll be able to fix it.'

She hadn't got the wine stains out. She'd have no luck getting the blood mark either. Damn it, he'd put her in the position of having to accept his help again. 'OK.'

He slung the dress back over the chair. 'They'll have it back in twenty-four hours.'

Just as he turned away she caught sight of his wicked grin and the suspicion that he'd done it deliberately flew at her. She opened her mouth to protest, but the words died on her tongue as she thought about it. She loved that dress. She *needed* that dress. She could pay him back after the party, couldn't she? She really had no option.

'I'm starving.' He stretched. 'Let's do pizza.'

Take-out pizza she could handle. It was cheap; it was yummy. Her sense of independence surged. Hell, she could even buy it.

'Just give me a couple of minutes to shower and change,' he called as he headed to his room.

She was opening all the kitchen cupboards and drawers when he got back.

'Looking for something?'

'Phonebook,' she muttered.

He stared at her quizzically for a moment. 'Ever heard of the Internet? Anyway, we're not ordering in, we're going out.'

'We are?' Nonplussed, she stared at him. Since when? But he was halfway to the door already.

She called after him as he sped down the stairs. 'Going out where?'

He grinned up at her as she descended the last few hundred steps. 'My favourite.'

It was a colourful Italian restaurant about five doors down from his warehouse. Not quite the cheap and cheerful she'd imagined. More refined than relaxed, but they didn't seem to mind his casual jeans and shirt and her charity shop special skirt.

Bella had kittens as she read the menu—and saw the prices. Owen seemed to read her mind. 'My treat. A further apology.'

That was the point where she finally baulked. 'No.' She was not going to have him call all the shots like this, and certainly not have him *pay* for everything. It made the situation sticky.

'Pardon?' He looked at her. The air almost crackled.

'No, thank you,' she enunciated clearly. 'You've already done far too much for me, Owen.'

He'd frozen. Clearly he didn't hear the word no very often. She was going to have to remedy that. 'You don't have any brothers or sisters, do you?' she asked.

'No,' he said, surprised. 'How did you figure that?'

'You're too used to getting your own way.'

He stared at her; she met the scrutiny with a determined lift to her chin. 'You think?' He suddenly stood. 'Let's get out of here, then. We'll do your precious takeaway.'

'*I'm* paying.' Assertiveness plus, that was the way.

'Fine.' His lips were twitching again.

The rooftop was as warm and seductive as the night before and Bella soon realised she would have been far safer in the overpriced restaurant. Desperately she went for small talk—anything to distract her from how hot he looked, how hot she felt. And to stop her from making a fool of herself. 'Where are your parents?'

'Mum's in Auckland, Dad's in Australia.'

So they'd split up. Somehow it didn't surprise her. 'Were you very old when they busted up?'

He looked cynically amused, as if he knew how she was analysing him. 'I was nineteen.'

'Really?'

Owen smiled at her surprise. 'Twenty-three years of marriage gone. Just like that.'

'Did one of them have an affair?'

'No,' he answered. Not to his knowledge. But that was the point, wasn't it? He hadn't known about any of it. He'd been so obtuse. Maybe it would have been easier if one of them had. 'They just grew apart.'

She was frowning. 'So what, they just woke up one day and decided to call it quits?'

That was how it had seemed to him at first. A bolt from the blue. Utterly unexpected, unforeseen. But if he'd had an ounce of awareness, he would have known. It still pained him that two of the most important people in his life had been slowly imploding and he hadn't even noticed. He'd been too preoccupied with himself and his work and all his great plans.

'They were unhappy for a long time. I never knew. I was too busy with school and sport and socialising to notice. But they agreed to stick together until I was through school and then separate. In those teen years it seemed every other mate's parents were busting up. I thought mine were the shining example of success. Turns out they just wanted to protect me— stop me going off the rails like so many of those mates then did.'

He didn't want to know that level of ignorance again. Part of him was angry with them for not being honest with him sooner, part of him respected them for the way they'd loved him. More of him was angry with himself for being so blind. And he couldn't be sure that he wouldn't be that blind again, so he wasn't up for that kind of risk.

She'd stopped eating her pizza and was staring at him with such expressive eyes, it jabbed him inside to look into them. He stared at the box between them instead and kept on talking to cover it.

'I think they got bored with each other. They had different interests. The only thing holding them together was me.' Together forever just wasn't a reality—not for anyone. If his parents couldn't make it, no one could. He cleared his throat. 'It wasn't acrimonious or anything. Don't think it left me scarred or anything. We can all get together and do dinner. They were both totally supportive when I decided to quit university to concentrate on developing my company.'

Not scarred? Bella doubted that. This was the man who swore never to marry. Who said it wasn't worth the paper it was written on. While many men could claim commitment-phobia, his seemed more vehement than most. If that wasn't scarred she didn't know what was. But maybe there was more to it. Her newly assertive, independent persona took a bite of pizza and went for it.

'And so you've just been working on your company ever since? No serious girlfriend?'

'What is this?' Irritation flashed. 'The Spanish Inquisition?'

So there was someone. 'Just answer.' She pointed her pizza at him. 'Has there really been no one serious in your life?'

'All right.' He took a huge bite of pizza and answered out the side of his mouth. 'I had a girlfriend. A long time ago.' Then he shut his lips and chomped hard.

'What happened?'

He shrugged, eventually swallowed. 'Nothing much.'

'Did you live together?' Why did she need all the details? She couldn't help but want all the details.

'For a while.'

The niggle of jealousy was bigger than she expected. 'What happened?'

'She met someone else. They're married now. Has a kid— two maybe.'

She stared at him, shocked. 'She *left* you?'

He looked levelly at her. 'I'm not a good companion, Bella.'

'What makes you say that?' Good grief, the guy was gorgeous.

'When I'm working on a project, that's my world, that's all there is. For those weeks, months, whatever, other things pass me by.'

She frowned. 'Are you working on something now?'

'Yes.'

Yet it seemed to her that nothing much passed him by. 'You don't think you're being a little hard on yourself?'

'I didn't notice my folks falling apart. I didn't notice her falling apart.' His face hardened. 'I'm selfish, Bella, remember?'

She stared, her mental picture elsewhere, thinking. From what she'd seen of him, it didn't quite ring true—yes, he did what he wanted, but he did what others wanted too. But he'd totally closed over now, moodily staring at the half-eaten pizza.

She wanted to lighten the mood. 'So what, you just lock yourself away and do geeky boy hacker things?'

His blue eyes met hers and sparked again. 'I have programmers who build the software, Bella. Then I use the programs to do the work that needs doing.'

'I'm surprised you need the programmers, Owen,' she

teased, pleased to have his humour back. 'Why don't you get all your precious computers to do it all for you?'

He chuckled. 'There's one thing that computers can't do. Something that I can do really, really well.'

'What's that?'

'Imagine,' he answered softly. 'I have a really, *really* good imagination, Bella.'

She stared at him, reading everything she wanted to read in his expression—heat. She was a dreamer—her father had told her off for it. That she wouldn't get anywhere sitting in a daydream all day...

'Someone has to dream it up.'

Someone like him. He was so enticing. Did he know what she was imagining right now? She suspected he might because that look in his eye was back.

Confusion made her run for deflection. 'I could never sit at a computer all day.'

'I could never stand on my feet slaving after people all day in a ton of noise.'

'I like the noise of the café. I like watching the customers as they sit and people-watch. I like the face-to-face contact.'

'I like face to face.'

'Really?' She didn't quite believe him. She had the feeling he holed himself away in that big apartment and thought up things her brain wasn't even capable of comprehending. And then he sold them. She'd been wrong—he was more entrepreneur than anything.

His grin turned wicked. 'And body to body.' He leaned closer, his voice lower, his eyes more intense. 'Skin to skin.'

Owen grinned as he saw the change in her eyes again. The sparkle went sultry. When he stepped close to her, when he spoke low to her, she coloured, flustered. But he wanted her more than flustered, he wanted her hot—and wild. And now he saw the way to that was so much simpler than he'd thought. All he had to do was get close to her. And she wanted to know about him? He'd tell her about him.

'A couple of years ago I sold the business to a conglomerate for many millions of dollars.' He was upfront, knowing money wasn't something that rang her bell. She seemed to take a strange joy in being broke; it was almost as if she deliberately mucked up—as if it was some sort of 'screw you' signal to her dad.

'So what did you do with all your millions?' she asked, her tone utterly astringent.

There, see? He'd known it would go down like the proverbial lead balloon. 'What do you think I did with it?'

'Bought yourself a Ferrari,' she snapped, 'and a few other boy toys. A plush pad in the centre of the city. An easy, playboy lifestyle.' Her eyes were like poisoned arrows pointing straight at him.

He batted them away. 'Yes to the Ferrari—it was my one big indulgence. But not so many other toys. As you've already seen the plush pad in the city isn't so plush—half of it still has to be plushed up.'

He paused, took in her focused attention. Good, it was time his little fairy saw things the way they actually were.

'I put half into a charitable trust and built a think tank with the other. The people you saw in that meeting yesterday have some of the brightest and best minds you'll find anywhere. Total computer geeks.' He winked at her. 'I get them together and they work through problems, building new programs.'

'That you can sell and make lots of money with.'

'That's right. We take the money, give half away and get

on with the next idea. I like ideas, Bella. I like to think them up and get them working and then I like to move on to the next big one.'

'You don't want to see them all the way through?'

He frowned. 'I don't like to get bored.' He didn't like to be complacent. He didn't like to be around long enough to 'miss' anything. It was better for him to keep his mind moving. 'As for the easy, playboy lifestyle—sure, occasionally. But for the most part I work very long, very hard.'

'Why? When you're wealthy enough to retire tomorrow?'

'Because I like it.' Because he couldn't not. Because he needed something to occupy his mind and his time. Because he was driven. Because he couldn't face the void inside him that he knew couldn't be filled. Because he was missing something that everyone else had—the compassion, the consideration, the plain awareness and empathy towards others. His relationship with Liz had made him feel claustrophobic. The family she'd threatened him with had proved to him he wasn't built for it and he had bitterly resented her for trying to force him into it. He would not allow that pressure to be put on him again. But he'd have a woman the way he wanted—he'd have Bella the way he wanted.

'For all that *success*—' he underlined the word, knowing the concept annoyed her '—I'm still the guy who made you laugh that night.' He tossed the pizza crust into the box and stood. 'I'm still the guy who made your legs so weak you couldn't stand.' He took a step back, determined to walk away now. He spoke softer. 'I'm still the guy who made you alternately sigh then scream with pleasure.' He paused. He'd leave her knowing exactly what his intentions were—plain and simple. He spoke softer still. 'And I'm the guy who's going to do it all again.'

CHAPTER EIGHT

BELLA stayed in her room until well after nine the next morning, sure that by then Owen would be downstairs overseeing his group of geeks, coming up with some program to bring about world peace or something. Last night had been the most frustrating night of her life—even more frustrating than after he'd left her bed on Waiheke, and she hadn't thought *anything* could top that.

After his outrageous comments, he'd gone. With a smile that had promised everything and threatened nothing he'd walked downstairs—presumably to his room. The door had been closed when she'd summoned the courage to leave the roof. What had she been supposed to do—follow him?

She'd badly, *badly* wanted to. But she didn't, of course, because her legs had lost all strength again—just with his words.

Now, as she moved quietly across the warehouse, she saw his bedroom door was closed. She knocked gently, just to be certain. When there was no reply she opened it and walked on in. Halfway to the bathroom door on the other side she realised that the big lump of bedding on the edge of his bed was moving; it actually had a lump in it—him. He sat up—all brown chest on white sheets, hair sticking up in all directions and wide sleepy grin. 'Good morning.'

She froze, halfway across the floor. 'I thought you'd be at work already.'

'No.' He yawned. 'I didn't get much sleep last night.'

She felt the colour flood into her face.

'I had a call from New York that went on for a while.'

Her colour continued to heighten. She started to back out of the room. At least she was wearing trackies now under the tee shirt. After the embarrassment of yesterday she wasn't running the risk of encountering all those people when she was half starkers again.

'No, don't worry,' he said, swinging his legs out of the bed and reaching for a shirt on the floor. 'Use the bathroom. I'm going for a run.'

She stopped in the doorway. He'd stood up from the bed. Naked except for the shirt he was holding to his lower belly. He was magnificent. Rippling muscles and indents and abs you wouldn't see anywhere other than the Olympic arena. He yawned again, stretched his free arm, showing his body off to complete perfection.

He was doing it deliberately. He had to be. She swallowed—once. Took a breath. Blinked. Swallowed again. Still couldn't seem to move her legs.

'Bella?'

She turned and walked then, straight back to her bedroom. Where she threw herself down and buried her burning face in the cool of the sheets.

Damn it, Owen. If you're going to do it, *do* it.

Half an hour later she figured he'd gone and be out for another hour at least. So she headed to the kitchen—she needed a long, very cold drink. As she downed the icy water she heard the door slam.

She turned, and there he was wearing loose shorts and a light tee. He was puffing, sweating a little. He stalked towards her. Straight towards her and he didn't seem to be stopping.

'You're back already,' she blurted.

'Yeah,' he muttered. To her acute disappointment he veered off course, halting and reaching into the fridge. 'It was short but intense.'

She held onto her glass, leaned back against the sink and stared.

'I ran up and down the stairs for twenty minutes.'

She quickly lowered her glass to the bench. He stood facing her, strong and fit, and she was breathing harder than he. It was early morning, broad daylight, she was stone-cold sober, and she wanted him more than she'd ever wanted anything.

He leaned back, resting on the bench opposite her. 'What are you thinking?'

'N-nothing.'

There was a silence where he looked at her with such amused disbelief and she wanted to squirm away from the knowledge in his eyes.

'Come here.'

She hesitated.

'Here.'

She walked, one whole step, aiming for nonchalant, before stopping, stupidly wishing she weren't still wearing her loose, ugly trackies and old tee shirt.

'Come right here.'

'What?' she asked as she moved fractionally closer, her mind tickled with an alternative meaning to his words, and a delicious mix of anticipation and alarm rose when he straightened. She took another tiny step.

'Why don't you do the "nothing" you've been thinking

about for the last five minutes?' He smiled then, took a step to meet her when she stopped short. 'Or is it longer that you've been thinking about "nothing"?'

Her mouth opened but nothing came out.

His gaze dropped to it; she could almost feel him roving over the curves and contours of her lips. She desperately wanted him to. His eyes flicked, coming back to snare hers. There was that warmth in them, the glow was back—the light that had seduced her so completely on Waiheke. And she couldn't walk away from it.

She knew he was waiting. But she was frozen. And then it seemed that words might not be necessary.

His breathing was more rapid now too—faster than when he'd first got back from his run. And the glow in his gaze had become a burn that was steadily gaining in intensity.

A shrill, tuneless series of beeps shattered the silence.

He didn't step away. 'Someone's trying to call you.'

She shook her head, unable to tear her gaze from his. 'It's just my phone telling me it's almost out of battery.'

'Recharge it.'

'I can't,' she confessed. 'I left the power cord at my flat.'

A smile stole into his eyes. The phone whistled the ugly tune again.

He reached forward, slipping his hand into her pocket and pulling out the phone. She thought, hoped, he was going to throw it away. But then he looked away from her, flipped it open and stared at it. Frowned. Pushed a couple of buttons.

'What's wrong? Is it not working?'

His head jerked in negation. 'I have a cord that should work with this,' he muttered, but his mind had clearly moved to something else. Suddenly she wanted her phone back. She reached, but he held it up high, still pressing buttons.

'What are you looking for?' she asked.

'Tony's Lawn Mowing Service.'

'What?'

'That was the number you gave me.' He gave her a hard look. 'That was why I couldn't get through to you. The phone number you gave me was completely wrong.'

Oh. Hell. 'Was it?' Her voice sounded weak, even to her.

He shot an even harder look. 'Accidentally on purpose.'

Her face fired up. The tension between them burst through her defences. 'You were in such a hurry to leave. I didn't want to be sitting around half hoping for you to call. Better to knock it out there and then.'

He moved, tossing the phone to the side, taking the last step forward so he was smack in front of her, blocking her exit. 'Only *half* hoping?' His smile teased but his eyes were laser sharp.

Her blush deepened and inside she wanted to beat her head against a wall—so he *had* tried. Now she felt more defensive than ever. 'Well, you didn't bother to give me your number,' she said miserably. 'Or even tell the truth about where you were staying.'

'That was irrelevant. At the time I was focused on making sure I could contact you. I knew there was no point giving you my number. You never would have called me. Would you?'

Her blush deepened. No. She never would. She'd been too mortified at the way he'd slunk off into the night. 'You just up and left me.' Even she heard it—how much her words betrayed her.

His smile twitched. 'I can see I have some work to do.'

'What sort of work?'

'Convincing you how much I want you. How much I wanted to stay that night.'

'If you'd wanted to stay, you could have.' A little petulant, still unforgiving.

He shook his head. 'Responsibilities, Bella. People were relying on me.'

'Priorities. Choices.' She'd been relying on him. Unfair of her perhaps, but she'd fallen—just like that. And she'd wanted him by her side. She'd enjoyed having him as a buffer between her and her family. But even more, she'd just wanted him at her side again—*in*side.

'I had every intention of calling you. I tried to call you.' He paused. 'You were the one who made the choice to stop that from happening.'

Humiliation at her exposure rose. Yes, she'd deliberately sabotaged any chance he might make contact because she'd been so sure he wouldn't and she didn't want to keep on hoping for ever that he would. Because she would have hoped—hoped and hoped and gone on hoping for evermore. And at the same time she'd been so sure he wouldn't. She didn't want to be that much of a loser any more.

His fingers were gentle but quite firm on her jaw as he turned her face back to him. He spoke very clearly. 'What you have yet to learn, Bella, is that I let very little stand in the way of what I want.'

'And what do you want?'

'You.'

She was melting inside, every bone liquefying.

'And the thing is…' he inched closer '…I get the distinct impression that you want me too.'

She was about to puddle at his feet. 'Owen—'

'Now why don't you do what you've been thinking about? Because that's exactly what I'm going to do.'

Her breathing skittered as he stepped closer again.

'I'm going to touch you and kiss you and feel you and watch you.'

She'd forgotten to blink and her eyes felt huge and dry.

'I want to watch you, Bella.' He was so close now. If she moved less than a millimetre, she'd be touching him.

'Do you know how expressive you are? How wide your eyes go when you want something? How pink your cheeks and your lips go?' His voice dropped as he whispered in her ear. 'How wet you get?'

She sucked in a breath. Shaken and very, very stirred. Did he know how wet she was now?

'Do it, Bella,' he urged in that low, sexy whisper. 'Do it.'

Her hand lifted and she spoke without thinking. A whisper, softer than his. 'Take your shirt off.'

For a moment their eyes met and she trembled at the flare of passion in the blue of his.

His hands moved to his top and with a fast movement he whipped it off, tossing it in a direction similar to her phone. He glanced down. The sweat had tracked down, slightly matting the fine layer of hair.

'I should shower.' The first hint of self-consciousness she'd ever seen in him.

'Not yet.' She placed the hand she'd raised on his chest, spreading her fingers on the heat, liking the dampness. She leant forward, licking the hollow at the base of his throat, tasting the salt. She liked him like this—raw, his body already primed for action. The run had just been the warm-up.

His breath hissed out.

Glancing down, she saw just how much he did want this—how much he wanted her. She looked back up and saw he'd seen her checking him out, and his smile had gone sinful.

His hands slipped down, pushing the old tracksuit pants

from her waist and down. She kicked them off as he unclasped her bra, then he pulled each strap down her arms so it fell from her. Underneath the tee shirt her breasts were now free.

'Tell me, the other day when you barged in on my meeting wearing this gorgeous old tee shirt, were you wearing panties beneath it?'

Bella hesitated. A smile slowly curving her mouth. 'What do you think?'

His smile grew too. 'I'm thinking no.'

'I think you might be right.'

'We'd better get them off, then.'

He dropped to his haunches, slipped his fingers to her hips and found the elastic of her undies. He tugged and she wiggled—just a fraction—so they slid down. As she stepped out of them she stepped closer to him. He stayed down, looking back up at her.

'Perfect.'

His fingers moved slowly over her thighs, his broad palms warm and smooth as they stroked.

He stood. 'I've been dreaming of you in this shirt ever since ten twenty-five yesterday morning.' Then he kissed her—his mouth moving over hers, his tongue invading with hungry surges, until she was breathless and giddy and he groaned.

'I am having that shower,' he said, taking her hand and leading her to his bedroom. 'Stay there, I'll be two minutes.' He kissed her again. 'Make that one.'

But now that Bella had taken the step, she wasn't letting him get away. She followed him into the bathroom, laughing as he grabbed the shower gel. Sobering as she watched him lather it in his hands, slap it onto his body, and seeing again how truly magnificent he was.

'Bella, if you keep looking at me like that I—'

'I haven't showered either.' She cut him off. Tee shirt and all, she followed him into the steam.

The water ran over her, making the cotton of the tee shirt thick and heavy. It clung to her. He cupped her breast through the sodden fabric, thumb stroking the taut nipple. She rubbed the soapy bubbles over his skin, starting with his shoulders, his chest and then lower.

'Bella…' There was definite warning in his tone. And then he growled, yanked her into his arms and kissed her hard, his hands keeping her close.

The elation ran through her as she tasted his desire, thrilled with the knowledge that it matched her own.

He kissed her until her knees went weak and standing was becoming a major issue. She clung to his shoulders, not wanting to break the bliss of the kiss.

Slowly he peeled the wet tee shirt up and off her body. It landed on the bathroom floor with a loud smack. He flipped the lever and shut off the water. The sudden silence was broken by the occasional drip. But the steam kept rising.

He took a step towards her, and with an impish smile, she took a step back. His eyes lit up so she took another, and another, and then with a giggle she turned and ran, exhilarated as she sensed his speed behind her. It was only a second or two and he'd caught her, dragging them both the last half-metre to the bed, and there they tumbled and rolled.

He rose above her, on all fours, trapping her between his legs, her hands in his. For a moment they paused, both enthralled and excited by the chase—and her surrender.

She deliberately relaxed, parted her legs, and sent him the invitation. He didn't need it. He was already taking—mastering her body by using the magic of his. His hands caressed, his lips kissed and his eyes promised. And within moments she was arching, her hips up high, the tension ready to burst. He kissed her again, so intimately, his mouth fastening onto her clitoris while his fingers played deep within.

Her hands clenched in the thickness of his hair as, oh, so quickly she was there, on the brink and over, her body shaking, twisting beneath his.

'Again,' he demanded, slipping up her body fast, his hand still between her legs. '*Again.*' He kissed her hard while his fingers were unrelenting. Slipping and sliding and teasing as he kissed her she felt the sensation inside bridge. His tongue thrust into her mouth and she shook with the need to have that other part of him deep inside her, plunging hard and fast— stirring her to an even greater ecstasy.

She broke free of his kiss as the breath expelled harshly from her lungs and her hips bucked. 'Yes!' she cried, incredulous as one orgasm moved into another, longer, more intense one. And he watched, a fiendishly satisfied grin lighting him as she shuddered beneath him.

And then, instead of that weightless, warm, replete feeling that usually came after ecstasy, she was filled with a ravenous void, the need for completion. It was an overpowering hunger. An intense ache that angered her and drove her to take in a way she'd never done before.

She spoke to him. Short, harsh words while her hands reached out, greedily touching him, and then her mouth too. And the look of smug arrogance and amusement left his features. Concentration took over, and suddenly he was as exposed as she, his hunger revealed as her words stripped him of his control.

She watched as his breathing became laboured, revelled in his haste to sheath himself with the condom. He swore when it took too long. Swore louder when she took over and teased it down on him cruelly slow, all the while whispering in a way that was clearly driving him to distraction, pausing now and then to press passionate, open kisses across his chest. Her hands worked over his body, pulling him to her. She wriggled beneath him, rocking against him, rotating, telling him not just with her words but with her body how hot she was for him. How badly she wanted him and was wanting him more with every passing moment.

'Now, now, now!' she cried, desperate for the fullness that only he could give. And with a raw growl he responded, thrusting deep.

'Har— Oh, yes! Like that. Like that.' She didn't need to say it. He was already doing it exactly how she wanted. Hard and fast, surging into her, and she worked to meet him, stroke for stroke, her fingers curling into his strong hips.

She was transported into a magical realm where her wickedest, wildest fantasy became raw reality and much, much better—and she told him. What he was doing to her, how he was doing it so incredibly and how much more she wanted.

Until the words would no longer come because her mind could no longer think and it was squeals and sighs and moans that escaped—she couldn't control anything any more. Her hunger, her desire, her response to the pleasure his body brought her. The tension mounted—nothing before had ever been so extreme as this. Until it snapped and spasms ravaged through her, the sensations heightened by his fierce growl and the power he plunged into her.

He rolled to the side, pulling her over so her head rested on his rapidly rising chest. He chuckled then. A warm, contented sound. 'I have never been so turned on in all my life as when you were beneath me begging like that.'

Embarrassment curled into her. She'd behaved like some sex-starved animal. She'd used words she never *thought,* let alone voiced. Bella instantly felt the need to retain even some sense of the upper hand. 'I wasn't begging.'

'No?'

'I was ordering,' she declared. 'Demanding, in fact.'

He yanked gently on her hair, tipping her face up so she could see his smile.

'Do it any time. I don't mind.' It was a light, teasing smile. 'I didn't think sex could get better than that night on Waiheke. Now I know different. That was fantastic.' He kissed her then. A slow, sweet kiss. One kiss turned into another. When his hand brushed between her thighs, she flinched.

He broke the kiss immediately, a concerned look in his eyes. 'You OK?'

'Just a bit sensitive.' She flushed. So much pleasure had brought her body to the point of pain.

He kissed her again. Gentle, relaxing kisses that soothed the intense over-sensitivity in her body—changing it to warm softness.

'We'll go slow this time.'

Bella had the feeling it was too late to be going slow at anything.

CHAPTER NINE

'I HAVE to get to the café.' Bella was on another late shift today. 'Shouldn't you be in a meeting or something?'

'Or something,' Owen muttered drowsily.

Bella moved, trying to slide from the bed, but his big heavy arm tightened, penning her in. 'I have to go,' she protested weakly. 'I can't be late.'

He groaned. But his arm relaxed.

She showered quickly, dressed. He was asleep when she went to leave. She spent a second or two by the bed, simply appreciating his tousled sexiness—even in sleep he was all consuming, all powerful—taking up most of the mattress.

And the flame of delight—of disbelief—glowed brighter in her heart. He'd tried to call her. He still wanted her. Relief, joy, satisfaction—she couldn't wipe the smile from her face. For once it seemed she was going to get something she really wanted. Maybe Lady Luck had finally turned her way.

She was halfway through her shift when she checked her mobile. It had been ominously quiet—despite Owen recharging it for her. Of course it was quiet—she'd accidentally switched it off. She put it back on and cleared the messages. There were three from her landlord. She listened, wincing at his increasingly irate tones, then drew breath and dialled his number.

Less than three minutes later he was no longer her land-lord. Her lease was terminated with immediate effect. He was keeping her deposit as payment for the door and inconvenience. She had the next day to remove the rest of her belongings.

In her break she went to the nearest ATM and got an account balance. She didn't really need to—she already knew the situation was dire. She had to save everything for a couple of weeks to get the bond for a new place. That meant she either had to stay with Owen or hit her family for another loan.

She knew what she wanted to do. But was it wise? Two weeks was a little longer than two days. They hadn't talked about anything remotely heavy like what, if any, future they had. She didn't want to—she already knew. Owen had told her right from the start that he didn't do commitment.

She'd swallow her pride and ask her father. It was inevitable anyway; she was as incompetent as he'd always said. Couldn't even manage a month on her own without stuffing up somehow and needing help.

When she got home later in the evening, Owen was waiting for her, music playing on the seriously fancy stereo, dinner keeping warm in the oven.

'What's up?' he asked the instant he saw her.

Was she that transparent?

'I've been turfed out of the flat. The landlord is keeping my bond. I'm going to—'

'Don't worry about it,' he interrupted carelessly, putting plates on the tray. 'You can stay here, long as you need to.'

Her spirits lifted and sank in the one moment. She hadn't wanted to call on her father, but she didn't particularly want to be in Owen's debt either—no more than she already was. Besides, he didn't do live-in lovers.

'Heaven forbid.'

He turned a startled gaze on her. 'What do you mean "heaven forbid"?'

She grinned, hoping to come across light but inside kind of terrified about his response. 'That's what you said at the bar on Waiheke when I asked if you had a live-in lover.'

He lifted a large iron casserole dish out of the oven, using a couple of tea towels to cover his hands. He carefully placed it on a protective mat on the bench. Only then did he answer—equally light in tone. 'Bella, we were in a bar flirting and being flippant.'

He began ladling the steaming contents of the dish onto their plates. 'I never knew you remembered everything I said so perfectly.'

Everything he'd ever said she'd committed to memory. If only she could learn her lines with the same skill.

'Anyway, you're only staying here till you sort out a new place of your own, right?' *Not* as his live-in lover, but a temporary guest. He was making the point subtly, but nonetheless still making it. Fair enough.

'Absolutely,' she agreed. They were just confirming everything—mainly because she felt the need for well-defined boundaries.

'So,' he added, 'we don't need the labels, right? You're a friend staying here.'

'Sleeping with you.' There was that small point.

'Till you've got your new place sorted,' he continued, ignoring her comment, starting to sort eating utensils.

'Is that when we stop sleeping together?' She held her breath.

He stopped fussing in the cutlery drawer and looked at her. 'We stop sleeping together when one or other of us says the word.' He fished out another fork, put it by the plates and caught her eyes with his own once more—not that it was hard; she couldn't seem to stop staring at him. 'And says the word *gently,* right?'

Right.

He left the tray and put his hands around her waist instead. 'Rules established?' he asked softly.

'I think so.' Better late than never, she figured.

Bed buddies. An indefinite series of one-night stands. Except if she thought about it she'd wonder whether this might be more to her than a one-night stand. She might not be that old or that experienced, but even she could see this could lead to trouble—for her at any rate. So she vowed to keep that limit on it—two weeks. She'd have as much of him as she wanted—and she really wanted—then she'd move out and end it all. Before her heart as well as her body got entwined.

Early the next morning she went to the flat and cleared out the last of her belongings. Gave the whole place a final clean, but even so the burnt-egg smell lingered. Back at Owen's warehouse she ran a bath, sank into it for the best part of an hour and appreciated the beauty of the room. The dark colour scheme could be austere, but it wasn't. The flashes of red here and there hinted at a touch of passion—the fire she knew burned inside him. He was full of vitality, ambition, discipline, drive. The bathroom designer had got a good handle on him. It was very, very masculine. It screamed bachelor—for life. And yet, there were twin hand-basins, side-by-side mirrors— one for him and one for the lady currently in his life, huh? The overnight guest.

All his toiletries were in the drawer beneath the basin, leaving the bench space clear and uncluttered. Minimalist.

With a spurt of defiance she lined up her bubble bath, shower gel, shampoo and assorted moisturisers in pump bottles. So she wasn't his live-in lover? She was just a friend staying? Fine, but she was quite determined to make her mark.

He was working at the computer when she got home from the café late in the evening.

'You'll get square eyes,' she teased.

'You're not even into the Internet?' He spun on the chair to face her. 'What about the social pages?'

'I have no interest in communicating with the people I went to school with when I was five.' Not when they'd all be wealthy lawyers or doctors or married to some famous person, or anything like that, when she was just a waitress.

'But it's a necessity in today's market. You need computer skills to work.'

'I'm not saying I don't have skills. I can point and click as well as anyone, I'm just not interested. Why would I want to stare at a screen all day?'

'What about online shopping?'

'I'd really rather go to the movies.'

'And that's not staring at a screen?' He looked sardonic.

'OK, show me, then,' she challenged. 'One thing that's really interesting.'

He grinned. 'Did you know your sister has put photos of the wedding up on her chat page?'

'No.' Bella froze. 'Has she?'

'There's a really cute one of you with the stripe.'

'No!' she shrieked.

'Yep, up there for anyone and everyone to see.' He spun back to the computer, clicked a few times.

The picture was huge on the big screen. Her skin crawled

with embarrassment at the line-up of tall blonde brides-maids…and her.

'We were supposed to look like daffodils,' she said. 'Only, there's me, the lemon on the end.'

'I'd rather have a lemon any day. So much more flavour.'

She was too aghast at the pictures to feel flattered. 'Anyone can see these? *Anyone?*'

He nodded. 'I really liked this one myself.'

Another picture flashed up onto the screen. She was in the background, behind Vita and Hamish. He pressed a couple of buttons and zoomed in on her. The wind had blown the fabric tight against her chest and in the cool breeze she had the biggest case of erect nipples ever seen—you could see the outline of everything.

She felt heat rise into her cheeks, then actually felt the hardness in her nipples as he looked away from the screen, back to her, desire in his eyes.

Embarrassed, she let sarcasm mask it. 'You really are into computer porn.'

He laughed. 'Search my hard drive. There's nothing there. But I'll admit to studying this one closely for some time. It was all I had until I found out where you were.'

'Where I was?' She frowned.

'You might not have much of a presence on the web, but your sister certainly does and she gives regular updates on her and her family's activities.'

Bella was appalled. 'She's supposed to be on honeymoon. She's not supposed to be sticking things up on…' She broke off, thinking about what he'd implied. 'You *knew* I was in Wellington?'

He nodded. 'She mentions in her blog how she missed your family farewell dinner.'

'So you were in the supermarket on purpose?' Oh, my, that was sneaky.

'No,' he laughed. 'That was the Fates being kind.'

'But you knew I'd moved down here.'

He nodded.

'Were you going to keep looking for me?' Her silly heart was skipping like crazy.

'I was thinking about it.' Casually he clicked the picture away. 'Why?'

'Why do you think?' He stood, walked away from the computer and towards her. 'I told you, Bella. I tend to get what I want.'

'But you were so frosty.'

'You'd blown me off, remember? With Tony's Lawn Mowing Service.'

'Only because *you* blew *me* off,' she defended, 'and I didn't know it was Tony or anyone.' And without hesitation she went into his arms. 'Do you always *know* what you want?'

'Generally.' He didn't have to think about the answer long. 'Do you?'

Rarely. She knew what she *didn't* want, but she didn't necessarily want the opposite of that. And for once, right now, she knew exactly what she wanted.

As his arms tightened she knew what he wanted too.

'I haven't forgiven you for leaving that night,' she confessed.

'I know you haven't.'

'But do you know why?'

'You didn't want to be alone at the wedding.'

'No,' she whispered, able to admit now that that wasn't it at all. 'There were things I had planned for you.'

'Yes,' his matching whisper mocked. 'We still have unfinished business, don't we?' His hands teased. 'Now wouldn't it have been so much easier for me to find you if you had a website? I could have typed in your name and discovered you're a sexy children's party fairy—booked up all your weekends.'

She rolled her eyes. The fairy thing wasn't something she was that proud of. She didn't want all those old school friends knowing that was all her ambition had amounted to.

'I'm going to build you one,' he murmured just before pressing a kiss to her neck.

'Hmm?' Fast losing track of the conversation as his mouth took a path downwards.

'A website. For your party business. It'll take a couple of hours max.'

She stopped tufting his hair with her fingers. 'Owen, you've already done enough for me.'

'Bella, please, let me indulge my geek side.' He chuckled, his breath warming her skin. 'More to the point, let me indulge my trainee's geek side.'

But at that she chilled completely. 'You can't get your employees to build me a website.'

He lifted his head and looked unconcerned. 'Why not?'

'I can't afford to pay you.' She couldn't take more *things* from him.

He placed his forehead on hers, literally closely watching her. 'It would be a good practice job for the student placement kid. I need something to occupy his time when the team is busy on strategic stuff.'

Owen really enjoyed the challenge of getting her to agree to his help. She was always so determined to say no and he liked nothing more than hearing 'yes' from her—although more often than not it was a soft 'OK'. Pricking his finger and staining the fairy dress had been a masterstroke in solving that problem. Building her a website was more of a difficult one. He could see the argument in her eyes. But it was really no biggie and it might be a bit of a confidence boost—make her see herself as the small businesswoman she was. If she took herself seriously, others might too.

'You'd be doing me a favour.' He knew she didn't really believe him. She knew, as well as he, it was a weak argument. But Owen liked to win, it didn't matter how minor the game— and this was minor, wasn't it? Maybe not, because he decided the end justified the means in this case. So he used his best weapon. And as he kissed her the hint of her refusal drowned beneath the rising desire.

The week slipped by. He refused to let her cook—saying he knew what she did to eggs and he wasn't letting her do that kind of damage to anything else. Instead he cooked, enjoying the creativity. He never normally bothered. But night after night he had it ready for when she got home. They ate and then snuggled on the sofa while she gave him a crash course in the great movie classics, starting with *Casablanca*. He hadn't spent so much time quietly relaxing in ages. And then, through the night, they hardly relaxed at all. Voracious—the more he had, the more he wanted. The passion ran unabated and it only seemed to get better every time.

The question of her staying with him had caused a fleeting awkwardness, but he thought he'd got through it smoothly. This was still a purely temporary situation, right? But he'd suffered a sharp twinge when she'd asked about them stopping sleeping together—he definitely wasn't ready for that yet. A few more days—several more nights. It wasn't done between them.

When he went for his run one morning she went with

him—riding his bike. She didn't talk too much. Just a word here and there, and he found it companionable. When he walked into the bathroom after, the scent of her shampoo hung in the steam and disappointment surged when he saw she'd finished already. By the time he got out she was dressed and heading to the door.

'What's the hurry? I thought you were on late shift again.'

'I have an audition.' Her hair hung in a wet rope down her back.

He looked her over. 'You want me to iron that shirt for you?'

'Do you iron, Owen?'

'Not usually.' He ignored her chill. 'I have a service. But I can do it for you if you want.'

Her cool look grew even frostier. 'The only thing I iron is my hair.'

Right, yet she hadn't even bothered with that.

'It wouldn't take a second.' It was a lovely shirt, but the crease down one side didn't exactly give her the professional look.

'I'm running late as it is.'

It was his turn to frown. It was her second audition of the week—and she'd been late to that one too, had said it had gone badly, that she'd fluffed the lines completely.

But she looked so on edge now he stepped aside, letting her go.

Friday night she was on another late shift. Only he didn't feel like staying home and cooking. For once the apartment felt too big, too quiet, too lonely. He raided the fridge, found some not-too-ancient leftovers—enough to satisfy the hunger of his stomach for a while. Then he left—needing to satisfy his other hunger.

She was behind the counter, the one taking the orders, not actually making the coffee. He walked straight up to her, registering with pleasure the surprise in her eyes, the pink in her cheeks, her widening smile. The rush of warmth inside rose so fast it threw him, made him awkward. It wasn't the heat of lust; while that simmered in the background, this was different. This was a buzz, a thrill of delight caused by something else—affection, maybe? Amusement? He couldn't think what else. He took a step back, sat at the long counter facing the window so he wasn't staring straight at her. He pretended to leaf through one of the glossy magazines in the stack, but all the while he was attuned to her sing-song voice as she served the customers.

'Would you like whipped cream with that?' The teasing question had him irresistibly turning to look at her.

She was smiling—it turned sinful as she glanced at him—and everything inside suffered an electrical jolt. She could tempt a hunger striker to a four-course banquet if she asked like that. *He'd* say yes to her like a shot. His discomfort level increased when he realised it—he already *was* saying yes to her, all the damn time.

Back at Owen's house, after her shift, Bella thought how her sense of their boundaries was becoming blurry. One day he was spelling out the terms of their relationship as if it were some business transaction, the next he was incredibly sweet and telling her about his geek-boy attempt to track her down. She couldn't help but wonder if the magnetism between them was made of something stronger than just a few nights of fun.

And he was so good at getting her to agree to everything, she wanted to wrest back some of the power. Wanted to gain that independence she'd been seeking for so long. But more than that, she wanted him to be as sunk in her as she was in him—because she'd fallen for him completely now. He was beautiful, bright and bold and she wanted to keep him.

She didn't have a hope. She wasn't the sort of woman for him—if he ever wanted to commit it would be to someone super successful, beautiful, articulate. Someone who could stand beside him in any situation and do him proud. Someone like Vita. Whereas Bella would be an embarrassment—she'd be the one inadvertently wearing half her dinner on her shirt at a posh restaurant; she'd be the one falling on her face down a flight of stairs at a charity ball. She was always the one making the stupid slip-ups somehow.

But she *could* be the best sex of his life. She smothered the chuckle at the lack of loftiness in her ambition. Oh, yes, for whatever reason he wanted her body, and maybe, if she could keep him wanting her, she could keep this affair burning for longer. She wanted longer. All she had to do was trap him in some kind of sensual net—where *he* couldn't say no, where *he* couldn't get enough.

Now, in his bed, she slowly crawled down his body, towards his legs. The view he'd be getting was one she'd never be brave enough to give anyone else. But with Owen, it was different. He made no secret of how much he liked to look at her. How much just looking at her turned him on. And she wanted to turn him on really, really hard because that was what he did to her. He'd been right the other day—she had been begging—and she was determined to make him suffer to the same degree. To make him want her so much he'd never be the one to utter the words that would end it. He made her feel capable of anything—of making her most secret fantasies a reality.

Dangerous—because right now *he* was her secret fantasy.

He muttered something unintelligible. His hands came up,

moulded round the contours of her bottom, then a finger traversed through her slick heat.

'You want me to stop?' she gasped.

'Oh, no. Please, no.'

She wriggled her hips pointedly and to her mixed relief and regret his hands slipped away. At least now she could try to focus.

'Come on,' he urged. 'You're killing me.'

She nuzzled into him, her hair teasing and twisting round his erection.

'Bella…'

'Roar.'

'Tigress.' His laugh sounded half strangled.

She turned around, so she was facing him as she straddled his legs, bending so her breasts were either side of his penis. 'Watch.'

'Oh, I am.'

She took him into her mouth and twirled her tongue on the tip of him.

His hands were fisted by his sides. Every muscle in his body tensed. 'Bella, stop. Please. I want you. I want all of you.'

'I don't mind…'

He shook his head. 'I want to be inside you.'

She slid the condom down slowly.

'Bella.' His lips barely moved, jaw locked, teeth clenched.

She slid herself down even slower.

His head fell back on the bed and the sound of his groan almost made her come. She bit her lip, the tiny pain keeping her sanity for her, stopping her from falling into an almost unconscious state of bliss. She wanted to remember this look of his forever. She wanted to savour the moment.

Heavy lidded, he looked at her body and then back to her face. She knew that right now he was incapable of speech.

She'd never felt more beautiful. More admired. More wanted. And she felt the power surge into her. She moved, slowly, tilting her head so her hair fell, twisting her hips so she rode him, watching him imprisoned by passion beneath her.

But then her attempt to keep in control failed and animal instinct took over. She moved, keeping the feel of him so delicious, and the tension drove her, making her work harder, faster until she suddenly stopped, locked into sensation. He took over, gripping her hips, moving only that little bit more to knock them both over the edge, to those timeless moments of brilliant darkness where muscles jerked and pleasure pulsed through every part of her.

His arms held her close. With supreme effort she lifted her head and looked at him—saw the lazy mix of satisfaction and humour, and madly her desire lurched into life again. She couldn't stop herself seeking his kiss. And with a sinking heart she knew the only person she'd succeeded in trapping was herself.

CHAPTER TEN

THE next day Bella left Owen's arms again, using all her will power. 'I have a party on this afternoon. I have to get ready.'

She showered quickly, towel-dried her hair and then slipped into her underwear. She plugged in her hair curler.

'A fairy always needs her wand.' She grinned at Owen, who was still lying in bed but watching through the open doorway. She took a length of her hair and wound it round the rod. A few seconds later she released it and there was a bouncy curl. She did a few more, and then tied long sparkly ribbons into it.

'You really go the whole hog.' He'd rolled to his side, rested his head on his hand and was watching her every move.

She tilted her head, frowning at her reflection. 'I'm in character. I have to look the part, fulfil the fantasy for the child.'

'The perfect party princess.'

'Oh, no,' she corrected. 'I'm not the princess. The princess is the little girl whose birthday it is. I'm the fairy godmother, there to grant the wishes.'

She started work on her face. 'That's why I'm not in pink—that's their colour. I'm in silver and blue. I have pink wings for the girls, pink wands, tiaras. They get a unicorn tattoo and some glitter gel and then become part of the fairy princess network. I'm just there to help them tap into their imaginations.' She paused. 'Most of them don't even need me really.' Smoothing the glitter down her cheekbone, she paused. 'But there's always one. The shy one, the self-conscious one, the one who feels like she doesn't fit in.'

'So how do you get her to fit in?'

'That's always the challenge.' She smiled. 'Take it easy, gently. It can be hard when, for the others, you need to be effervescent. But I want to try to do it because I just know that inside she really wants to be up there and part of it all.'

'How do you know?'

She turned from the mirror. 'Because that was me,' she said simply. 'I was the self-conscious one.'

His eyes said, Yeah, right. So did his voice. 'I can't believe you were ever self-conscious.'

She smiled in triumph then. 'And that's how I know I'll make it as an actress.' One day. 'I'm good at pretending.'

She turned back to her pots of powder and paint. 'At the end of the day you just want them to have fun.'

'All I ever wanted was the food.' He burrowed back down in the bed.

'Figures.' She concentrated on her eyes, worked in silence for several minutes.

'Do you do boys' parties?' he asked.

At that she slanted him a look, saw the mischief in his face.

He tried to deny it, raising his hands all innocent-like. 'I'm serious. You're missing out on half your market.'

'I do. But admittedly it's more girls' parties than boys'. But there are often boys there—especially the preschooler ones. I have a pirate queen routine that I do for them.'

'You're a pirate?' He was back up on his elbows.

'I make a really good balloon sword.'

'You do?'

She giggled.

'The depth of your talent never ceases to amaze me,' he drawled, then watched her majestic nose wrinkle.

'Yeah right.'

She stood in front of the mirror, clad only in bra and panties, and he was having a hard time concentrating on stringing more than two words together.

'Where is the unicorn going today?'

'Where do you think it should go?' She grinned.

He knew exactly where it should go. On the slope of one of those creamy breasts, where it would peek out from the ruffles of the silver-and-blue dress, drawing the eye to the treasure beneath—not that his eyes needed any more pointers.

She glanced at the clock and gave a little squeal of horror. 'Stop distracting me. Lie there and be quiet. I can't be late.'

He didn't stay lying down but he did stay quiet. He stood, wrapped a towel round his hips to try to be a little decent, and then came right up behind her to watch more closely while she finished her make-up. Silently he studied her as she fixed the tattoo with a damp flannel, as she smoothed glitter gel across her shoulders and chest.

Her eyes met his in the mirror for a moment, then they skittered away, then back once more. He felt his tension—his everything—rising. He needed to know it was the same for her, this crazy, unfettered lust. He drew a breath and blew lightly over her shoulder, down onto the spot below her collarbone where the unicorn tattoo was drying. She shivered. He watched her nipples poke harder against the lace of her bra and he was about to pounce. But speedily she turned, left his space, went into the wardrobe where her dress was hanging. All too soon it was on and zipped and she was walking away.

'Right.' Her voice was high-pitched. 'See you later, then.'

He said nothing, just walked beside her all the way to the door, barely curbing his frustration.

As she reached to open it he reached for her—slid his hand round the nape of her neck, fingers wide so they caught in the curls of her hair. He pulled her to him for a hard, brief, melting kiss that didn't relieve him one iota.

'Later.' He basically growled.

He prowled around the apartment like a caged animal. Wished like hell he'd had her before she went to the damn party. But she'd been insistent on getting there on time. Now, three hours later, he was at bursting point. He'd never known a passion as intense as this. Never known a woman who could take up so much of his brain space either. He thought of her all the damn time. Thought up things he could do for her. Crazy stuff, silly stuff, irresistible stuff. He didn't much like it. Wanted to burn it out—blow it out with one big, hard puff.

Finally he heard the slam of the door downstairs. He went to the top of the stairs and waited. She was trotting up them, the silver fairy dress floating up towards him. His body tightened harder with her every step closer. He was filled with the urge to reach out and grab, to hold onto her in complete caveman style. He wanted to possess. He wanted to brand.

She got to the top and raised her brows as she saw him standing there. He watched the smokiness enter her eyes as she got his unspoken message. He watched as her breathing didn't ease at all—accelerated, in fact.

He took her arm and pulled her inside. The door shut behind them but he hardly heard it because by then he'd got his mouth on hers and he was asking for everything. She opened for him immediately and the rush of need overwhelmed him. He had to have her right now; he couldn't reclaim anything until he did.

He got them as far as the big table, pushed her against it, kissing her deeply while yanking up her dress. He pulled her panties out of the way while with his other hand he undid his jeans.

Her hands were in his hair and she leaned back, kissing him, taking him with her. He broke the seal of their lips briefly, to breathe and to thrust and then he was there and she was wet and hot and moving beneath him, full of life and heat and making him so welcome with a sigh and a murmur of delight. And then there was nothing because he kissed her again—hard and long and fierce while he possessed her with his body, pressing her against the hard wood. Trapping her, claiming her as the passion he had for her trapped and claimed him. He wanted to fight it, but pushed harder against her, into her. Harder and harder until suddenly there was everything bursting through him—colour and light and heat and the taste of her pleasure.

And then there was nothing.

He lifted his head, looked down at her and felt the tinge of embarrassment and guilt as he saw her bruised lips and the dazed look in her eyes. He'd just taken her rough and ready on his table, she still had her dress on, they were still joined and already he was tightening with anticipation about their next encounter.

He still wanted her. *How* he wanted her. He couldn't get enough.

Irritation, self-disgust, flared. Just sex. That was all this could be.

But just now had been more intense than anything. And here he was doing things, wanting things, thinking things… and it was madness because he knew, ultimately, he couldn't see this through. He didn't *want* complicated. He didn't want to be committed.

Her gaze ducked from his. She pushed gently at his shoulders. He left the warm embrace and instantly felt cold.

'The party was good, thanks.' She'd pulled up her knickers and was walking to the kitchen.

He grunted then, unable to stop the spurt of laughter bubbling through his annoyance.

'I think I've got another booking.'

He leaned on the table and tried to get his breath back, watching her as she moved around, completely at home in his kitchen. He needed to back out of this, but instead he walked over to her, ran a gentle hand down her arm. Quelled the urge to pull her back into his embrace. 'Are you OK?' he asked. Self-conscious wasn't really him. But it was flushing through, heating his cheeks now.

She looked surprised.

'I'm sorry, that was a little—'

'Barbarian?' she suggested.

He smiled again, still a little uncertain.

She put her glass down and a naughty twinkle lit her face. 'You can ravish me any time, Owen, you know that.'

He did know it. She welcomed him any time, every time. That didn't mean he should take advantage of her. Not any more. Guilt ripped through him. It trebled when he saw the tinge of vulnerability suddenly shadow her eyes. He'd got himself into a mess.

This was why he didn't do live-in anything. This was why he was better off alone. He just didn't have it in him to be the kind of guy a woman like Bella needed—any woman needed. He couldn't promise that he'd be there through thick and thin, or that he'd even *see* the thin patches. He sure as hell hadn't with his parents.

He didn't want to become bored and careless, as he had

with Liz. He didn't want to wake one day and see the lust in Bella's eyes had been replaced with disappointment and bitterness. And he definitely didn't want to be there to see her turn from his arms to someone else's.

His whole body clenched. It was time to push away. It was way beyond time, because it'd hurt—until now he hadn't realised it would. But better now than further along when it would only hurt more.

Then he thought of something else. Something so painful it twisted inside, becoming bitter anger. 'Bella, I didn't use anything just then. I didn't have a condom on.'

He'd just lost it. Seen her. Kissed her. Taken her as fast as possible. And now—what if? He could hardly bear to look at her. He already knew he'd make a lousy father.

Bella carefully kept her weight back against the bench; her legs still weren't working properly and at the expression in his eyes they were going even weaker. But it wasn't from lust. It was from fear. Because it was fear she could read in his eyes. Fear and regret.

'I know.' She'd had the thought in her head for a split second, but it had gone as she'd been swept away in the chaos and bliss of the moment.

'You didn't stop me.' His eyes had narrowed.

'You didn't stop yourself,' she reminded him. She'd wanted it as much as he had—and he had *wanted* it. She'd never seen that expression on his face before—that naked need. The desire that he could scarcely seem to control. It had turned her on—for a moment she'd felt nothing but power and then she too had been totally lost. But he still wasn't willing to recognise the strength of it. Right now he looked as if he wanted to run.

'Is there a chance you might…' He didn't even seem able to say it.

'Have a baby?' She wanted to use the b-word. Not just say pregnant. She wanted to see how he'd react to the mental image of a tiny little life—real. A child that shared their blood, that breathed because of them.

The loss of colour in his cheeks was almost imperceptible, but she was watching closely.

His 'Yeah' was drawn out and low.

'There's a chance.' It was a slim chance, very slim as her period was due in only a day or two. But she wasn't ready to let him off the hook just yet. She was hurt from that look, the dread and fear in it. And she wanted to know what it was he was going to say.

He exhaled. 'Whatever happens, you know I'll support you.' His gaze slid from hers. 'Whatever you decide.'

Whatever *she* decided? So it would be her choice and hers alone. He wanted no part in anything that might be? She squeezed her fingers hard on the bench behind her. Still said nothing, but only because her heart was ripping.

'Whatever you want to do,' he was mumbling now. 'I don't...'

What, he didn't—mind? *Care?*

She'd known, hadn't she? He'd told her that very first night. And, no matter what she fantasised, the reality was exactly as he'd told it. She'd been warned.

But she hadn't paid attention—had just had the bit between her teeth and gone along for the ride. And the consequences were going to be more serious than she'd ever thought possible.

She'd never had her heart broken before.

So much for independence. She'd gone and got herself totally dependent on someone who could never offer her anything like all that she wanted. She wished he'd go away and she could lick her wounds in private. Regroup. Gather up her shredded pride. But at that her pride came racing back, fully armed.

She crossed the room, picked up the little bag she'd dropped by the door and thanked the heavens that the family today had paid her in cash. She opened the envelope and flung the dollar notes down on the bench next to Owen.

'What's that for?' He looked at it, distaste all over his face.

'That's the money for rent, for the four new tyres that Bubbles has—don't think I haven't noticed them—for the petrol, for the groceries, for all the dinners, the wine, for the website and for the hotel bill in Waiheke.' She stopped for breath. It wasn't nearly enough to cover all that, but it sure felt good to say it.

'I don't want it,' he said flatly.

'I won't have you paying for things for me.' She tossed her head. 'It makes me feel like a who—'

'Don't you dare!' he shouted then, his step closer shutting her up. Anger flushed his cheeks and flashed in his eyes. 'I have *never* paid for sex, Bella, and I don't intend to start now.'

'Really?' she said scornfully, sounding a whole lot braver than she felt. 'But isn't that what's happening here?'

'You know damn well it isn't.' He spoke through his teeth. 'It's just money. It's meaningless.'

Like the sex? Not to her, it wasn't.

He seemed to read her face and growled. 'Why are you so damn keen to label everything?'

'Why are you so keen to deny everything?' The attraction between them wasn't anything ordinary—surely he could sense that?

'This is just sex, Bella.' His words came like the cracks of a whip. 'I like it. You like it. That's all there is to it.'

Bella blinked. Bit the inside of her cheek as she absorbed

the shock of what he'd said and the depth of his scowl. Humiliation started to seep into her very core.

'Why did you pay for that night in the hotel?' She winced. Did he hear that slight cry in her voice?

'I don't know,' he answered irritably, stepping away. 'It was just a spur-of-the-moment thing. I knew you were tight for money. I just wanted to help you out.'

'Well, I don't want your help.' She spoke quickly, marched to the bedroom, unzipping her dress and walking right out of it, leaving it on the floor. She'd never be able to wear it again without thinking of this moment—the time when he'd taken her so passionately and then turned on her.

'Don't you?' He was right behind her. 'Well, you're certainly not helping yourself.'

'What does that mean?' Furious with the way she felt tears close by, she picked a skirt and pulled on the nearest top she could find.

'You won't let me help you. You won't let anyone help you.'

'That's right, Owen. I won't.' She grabbed a flannel and scrubbed her face hard, blocking the sight and sound of him with water from the tap, stopping any stupid tears from even starting.

When her face was bare and reddened, but masked once more, she turned and headed for the door.

'Where are you going?'

'I have an audition.'

'Now?'

She sent him a glare while slipping into her sandals. 'Yes, now.'

'And you're going like that?'

'Yes.' She walked.

He swore. 'You deliberately sabotage yourself.'

After a minuscule pause she kept walking.

'You do,' he said, seemingly just getting into the swing of getting at her. 'You spend over an hour getting ready for one of your parties and less than five minutes getting ready for an audition that could change your life. It's like you don't really want it.'

She whirled to face him. 'Of course I want it.'

'No, you don't! You're never late to work at the café and yet you're late almost every time to a casting call. Tell me,' he said snidely. 'What do you believe in, Bella? Fairies?' He bent to pick up her dress from the floor, his acidity eating an even bigger hole in her heart. 'Do you really think you've got some fairy godmother who's going to make it all happen for you?'

'Of course not.' She turned back and started walking to the door again.

'Then what do you believe in?'

She said nothing, kept walking. It didn't seem like the moment to mention luck.

'Why don't you try believing in yourself?' he called after her. 'If *you* don't believe in your abilities, why should anyone else?'

She couldn't not face that. He was in the middle of the room, shaking his head at her. 'Instead you blame anything you can. Your family isn't supportive, you haven't had formal acting training, you haven't had that "lucky" break. But it's not about luck, it's about making the decision to do it and then persevering, putting in that hard work.'

Her anger rose another notch. 'I work damn hard.'

'I know, but not at—'

'But nothing,' she snapped. 'You don't know the first thing about acting, about going to casting call after casting call. It's not about learning the lines and spouting them automaton fashion. There *is* luck involved. Who's your competition?

What look are they after? You have to be in the right place at the right time with the right product. I haven't yet.'

'Then you keep going,' he lectured, her dress hanging from his hands. 'You research. You find out what they want and you give it to them as professionally as you can. You believe and work and eventually it'll happen.'

'You make it all sound so easy,' she said bitterly. 'Like it's some computer program.'

'I know it's not easy. But you have to believe in yourself. You have to have the passion for it.'

'I do have the passion!' She was yelling now. 'God, Owen, what do you want?'

'This isn't about what I want!' he yelled back. 'This is about you and you're not the person you can be yet. You're floating along the edges too scared to dive right in. I don't think you even know what it is you *do* want. It's much easier to skate along and blame it all on everyone or anything else.'

'Well, what about you?' The viciousness of his attack forced her into fight mode. Red-hot anger ran through her veins, releasing the words from her. 'You're not exactly living life to the full either, are you, Mr Workaholic? And as for this Mr Don't-Get-Near-Me-Because-I'm-Selfish routine… What sort of a rubbish excuse is that, Owen? You're not selfish. Doling out money *proves* you're not selfish,' she shouted, losing her grip entirely. 'What you are is scared!'

His face whitened, his jaw locked, but she hardly noticed. She was on way too much of a roll now.

'You say you don't want labels, but you're the one trying to squeeze us into the smallest compartment possible. Sex is all it is, huh? Well, how convenient for you. You can just keep your distance and don't have to invest anything remotely risky like emotion or take responsibility. What is it you're afraid of,

Owen?' Scathing, she flung him the answer. 'Failing at something for once in your life? Hell, I fail at things all the time, but at least I have the guts to get back up and give it another go.'

She spat her fury and hurt. 'So don't you dare lecture me about hovering on life's edges. You're the one not facing up to what's really going on here. You're the coward!'

Breathless, she stopped, realising what she'd said and all she'd revealed—the degree to which she was involved, how much she wanted more, how she wanted him to accept that there *was* more…but, oh, my Lord, maybe there really wasn't anything more in this for him? Of course there wasn't—she wasn't anything like the kind of woman he'd really want. She turned, more desperate to get out of there than ever before.

'Who's the coward now?' he roared after her. 'Who's the one throwing the accusations and then walking out without giving me a chance to respond?'

She whirled back, bleeding inside. 'Well, what's the point in my staying just to hear you deny everything and say nothing?' Bitterly, she glared at him.

His hands were fisted in her dress, rumpling it so bad it would have to go back to the dry-cleaners again. His face was still pale and a picture of savage tension. He met her glare with one of his own—just as bitter, just as furious. But his jaw was clamped and as she stared she could see his muscles flex down tighter.

He had no answer to that and she didn't want to hear it anyway. She stalked out of the apartment and slammed the door as hard as she could. It was all so easy for him. He was nothing but killer instinct. Nothing but what he wanted now, now, now. All 'I want that, I'm going to do that…' and off he went and had and did with no regard to consequences. It would serve him right to suffer the consequences for once.

Because she was. She couldn't compartmentalise this the way he wanted to—this *thing* was all too big, for her anyway.

She fumed all the way to the audition and barely noticed the competition. She was too busy stewing over the argument. Too busy trying to stay mad and not recognise the extent of the break in her heart.

They had to call her name twice.

CHAPTER ELEVEN

BELLA spent that night alone in the spare room, most of it
awake, plotting her way out of there. She was mortified at
what Owen had said and what she'd said—and spent hours
deciding on the truth of it all. This was just sex for him, and
his efforts to help her out—the dress, the website, the way he
cooked her dinner—was simply him. He'd stop and help an
old lady cross the street—that didn't mean he was on his way
to falling in love with her.

She was such a fool. And that was the point, wasn't it? She
was such a klutz he couldn't help himself trying to help her.
Because that was the kind of guy he was. And now she'd humiliated herself completely by insisting that there was more
to it. Of course he hadn't been able to reply—he hadn't
wanted to hurt her, and he'd already spelt it out as plainly as
he could: sex, that was all there was to it.

'How'd it go?'

Damn. She'd hoped he'd have gone downstairs to work
already this morning. Instead he was sitting at the table. She
felt her cheeks warm at the sight of it. Truthfully, she'd forgotten about the audition the minute she'd walked out of it. Somehow the lines had come to her. She must have come across like
an automaton. Ah, well, chalk another one up to experience.

'Don't ask.'

He looked moody. 'I'm sorry I was so grumpy.'

'I'm sorry I was so ungrateful.' She inched closer. 'I really appreciate everything you've done for me, Owen.' Oh, God, this was awkward.

'It's nothing.' He shook his head. 'No trouble.'

That was right—not for him. 'Please let me pay back what I owe you.'

His expression tightened more. 'It's just money, Bella. It doesn't matter.'

'It matters to me.' She hated being in his debt like this. Hated that all she had to offer in return was her heart, and he'd never want that.

'OK.' He paused, stared hard at the table. 'But only if you stay. I'd like you to stay.' He paused. 'Just until you get yourself sorted.'

There it was, the caveat. She'd been right—he couldn't hold back the offer of assistance, but nor could he offer anything else. Now she felt too awkward to say yes, too awkward to say no.

'OK.' Her reply came out on a heavy sigh. She couldn't see that getting herself sorted was going to happen any time soon, but she'd be out of here regardless. She took a deep breath and tackled the most awkward bit of all. 'I'll tell you as soon as I know.' A few days to be certain, then she'd leave. She refused to think about what would happen if she was pregnant—that was altogether too scary.

He looked back at her, looking as sombre as she'd sounded. She knew he knew what she was referring to. And she knew how badly he didn't want it.

The next two days dragged for Owen. He'd wanted to back off, but only seemed to be digging himself in deeper. He kept reliving that argument. She'd touched a nerve and he'd flared up at her, but he hadn't said anything that wasn't true—had he? He couldn't help the sickening feeling that he'd thrown something precious away before he'd even realised he had it.

Worse, he had the feeling she'd been the one hitting truth on the head at the end there. He couldn't face it—couldn't face her, until he knew whether she was pregnant or not. He couldn't *think* until he knew. It was like waiting for a jury to return its verdict—were they going to get a life sentence? Either way there'd be guilt and bitterness. And it was worse than Liz—this time he was to blame. It hadn't been Bella's fault at all. The sooner it was all over, the better.

And yet he missed her. How he missed her. He practically had to lock himself into his bedroom to stop from going into hers. His arms ached with emptiness. Sleep was utterly elusive—and so was she. She worked long hours at the café and hid in her room the rest of the time. He spent more time in the offices downstairs to give them both some space.

But truly finding space was impossible while she was staying with him. And he wasn't ready to ask her to leave yet. He still wanted her with a passion that was tearing him up inside and, more than that, he wanted to make things *right*. He decided a trip away was the answer. Just a couple of days. Regain perspective and work out what the hell he was going to do if she was pregnant.

She hadn't mentioned it again. Whereas by now Liz had chosen names and been practically putting the baby on the list for the most exclusive schools. Bella was making no demands—making a point of it, in fact. She'd backed right off and had shut down her expressive face. He hated that too—he wished he knew what she was thinking and wanted to know if she was OK.

* * *

Owen had withdrawn from her. He was working later, not coming into the café any more. Bella munched on her small bowl of muesli and watched him pack his laptop into his case.

'How long are you gone for?'

'I'm not sure yet. Couple of days maybe, I don't know.'

She nodded.

'You've got the security code?'

She nodded again. She'd take the opportunity to find herself a new flat. She could move into a flat-share with some students. There'd be plenty of cheap ones out in the suburbs. That was her plan. This was the end of the end. She knew it. He knew it.

He glanced into the contents of her bowl and his cheeky smile appeared. She hadn't seen it for a while and it made her heart ache.

'You're supposed to eat that stuff in the morning, you know.'

She managed a wry grin back. 'Better late than never.'

Both their grins faded.

Owen listened to the flight announcements, took another sip of his coffee, gripped his bag that little bit tighter. He should have checked in by now. If he didn't check in within the next minute or so he'd miss his flight. He looked into his cup—he still had half of it to go. It would be a shame to throw away good airport coffee.

Bella hadn't said anything. She'd known he was running away—he could see the reflection of his eyes in hers and knew she saw the truth of it there. But still she was making no demands.

And wasn't that what he thought he always wanted? No demands? For fear he wouldn't be able to meet them? Because he wasn't willing to provide the emotional support someone else needed? Damn it, Bella didn't seem to want *any* kind of support. And suddenly it was all he wanted to do. He wanted to know if she was OK, if she was scared or secretly excited or desperately unhappy. He wanted to help her deal with however she was feeling. And he wanted her to help *him* too.

His heart jerked. Maybe she didn't demand because she simply didn't care. He knew that for a lie. He saw it in her eyes. Every time she'd taken him into her she'd been loving him. Just sex? What a joke.

This time, he couldn't walk away. This time, he didn't want to.

The taxi seemed to take for ever. Driving alongside the water, the lights reflected on it. The aeroplanes looked as if they were going to end up in the sea if they didn't slam the brakes on damn fast. Was that him? Headed for a drowning if he didn't skid to a halt soon?

The apartment was in darkness and for an awful moment he thought she'd gone. Then he saw the large lump on the floor. He flicked on the lights. She was huddled in her beanbag. He took in her pale face, her eyes large and bruised and startled.

'I'm sorry, I didn't mean to scare you.' He put his bag on the table.

She blinked, clearly gathering her wits. 'What happened?'

'Last-minute change of plan.' He paused, inventing a non-excuse. 'I managed to get out of it.'

'Oh.'

He could see her biting back other questions and felt bad because of it. He wanted to answer her, wanted to communicate—a little at least.

He stripped off his jacket, wondering why the hell he was so buttoned up in a suit. It had all been for the show of it. He went to the bench in search of wine.

'I'm not pregnant.' Her voice was low, matter-of-fact. It took a few moments to register what she'd actually told him.

Not pregnant. No baby.

He was glad he was against the bench because he needed its strength for a second. He'd never expected to feel it as a blow. Never expected to feel *disappointment*. Only now was he seeing it in his mind, her body rounded with a baby, and then holding a child, his child. The ache that opened up in him was terrifying.

'When did you find out?' He managed to sound almost normal as he poured a large glass of red.

'Just tonight.'

He nodded, took a big sip. 'You're feeling OK?'

'Oh, sure. Fine.' She mirrored his nod.

He searched her pale features again and knew she was faking it. She looked miserable. He saw the half-eaten cake of chocolate beside her. For a mad moment he wanted to sweep her into his arms and tell her not to be sad, that they'd make babies together any time she wanted to. She just had to say the word.

But he didn't. He took a breath, another sip of wine and a long minute to regain sanity. He still felt lousy. Why—when this was what he wanted, right? No encumbrances.

'Want to watch a movie?' He walked over to her, touched her shoulder gently. Instantly felt a bit better. 'You can choose.'

'I already have.'

Then he noticed the blinking of the screen—black and white. *Casablanca*. Again.

'Need anything else—ice cream? Wine?'

'Yes, please.'

* * *

What she really wanted was a hug. What she really wanted was to know his reaction. At least he wasn't doing back-flips and saying, 'Thank God, what a relief.' She didn't know if she could handle that. Because even though she'd been fighting for independence for so long, the thought of a baby had intrigued her—because it would be his. She'd even lain awake and wondered whether their child would have his brilliant blue eyes or her pale ones. But he wasn't giving anything away.

She decided to find out. She took the wine he offered, and was surprised to see her hand wasn't shaking. 'With your attitude to marriage there's no need to ask. I know you're relieved.'

'I…'

'It's OK, Owen. You don't have to hide it.'

He looked away from her, as if what she'd said had hurt. 'I haven't got what they need.' His voice was low. 'Children deserve more than an emotionally absent father.'

She frowned. Emotionally absent? Owen wasn't absent— he was more real, more vital than anyone she'd ever met. She could see the trouble inside him on his face—something was stirring in him and she didn't think it was altogether because of her. But what? And she remembered what he'd said—what his ex had said—that he was selfish. Why had the woman thought that? What had happened? When it was obvious he was generous, not just financially but in more ways than he'd admit. Suddenly Bella wanted him to see that.

'Who waters your garden, Owen?'

He frowned.

'Your plants upstairs,' she explained.

'What's that got to do with anything?'

'Everything.' She smiled. 'That's noticing, that's remembering, that's caring.' She paused. 'That's all that children need.'

He was shaking his head. 'No,' he said. 'They also need to be wanted.'

Her suspicions solidified as she heard his desolate hollowness. And even though the thought of the answer terrified her, she couldn't stop from asking the question. 'Have you been through this before, Owen?'

Owen owed her honesty. Then she'd see the person he really was, and this whole ending thing wouldn't be nearly so bad—she'd be out of his place in no time. Because no woman would understand the way he'd reacted—especially not one who liked kids so much she actually worked with them. It would be over, and he could move on. 'You know I had that girlfriend, right?'

'The one who said you were selfish.'

'Right.' He grinned without mirth. 'Around the time I was selling the company she told me she was pregnant.'

Bella nodded.

He looked away from her, not coping with the hint of sympathy he saw in her eyes. 'I wasn't remotely keen. I felt nothing. I felt worse than nothing.' He took a breath and said it. 'I didn't want it. How terrible is that? Not to want your own flesh and blood?' He'd felt trapped. He still felt guilty about that.

'She was dreaming up names and was all excited and hanging out for a ring and I didn't want to know a thing about it.' He'd withdrawn and gone remote on her rather than admitting how he felt. Certainly hadn't dropped down on one knee instantly as she'd seemed to expect he would. 'It was a crazy time. I was working all hours negotiating this deal...' That was no excuse; he should have been just a little more interested. But the fact was he'd been wanting out of the relationship for a while already. He just hadn't got round to breaking off with her—too busy to be bothered. And he was still too busy to be able to think it through properly—he'd just avoided the issue for a while. Tried to pretend it wasn't real, tried to swallow the guilt that came with that.

'What happened?'

'She was mistaken. There was no baby.' She'd been late, that was all. When she'd told him, with red-rimmed eyes and a catch in her throat, he'd been so relieved and he hadn't been able to hide it from her. That was when she'd lost it—screamed at him about how selfish he was, how unsupportive, that his heart only beat for his business. And she'd been right. He hadn't wanted her or the baby or any of it. It had got really ugly then, and in the course of the argument Liz had slipped up.

It wasn't that she'd been late at all. She'd made it up—there had never been the possibility of a pregnancy. She'd tried to manipulate him—cornering him just as he was about to come into vast wealth. And she'd done it in such a low fashion—because even though he'd known it probably wouldn't work, his integrity would have insisted that he try. He'd have married her and she knew it. It was just that he hadn't come to the party soon enough for her to get away with it. Whether she'd wanted him or the money he didn't know—he suspected the latter.

He'd been viciously angry then and vowed never to be put in the same position again. No woman would wield that threat over him. He didn't want it—marriage, babies—not ever.

'She met someone else not long after.' He dragged out a cynical smile, feeling sorry for the poor bastard she'd netted. 'She married him, has a kid or two. She's happy.' She'd got what she'd wanted.

And he was happy too, right? Happy with his choices and with his freedom to focus on his work and on fun.

The silence was long. Bella was looking at him, expression

clouded. He felt bad—the bitterness that Liz had left him with wasn't for her. This hadn't been her fault—it had been his irresponsibility. He'd broken his own rules, he hadn't played safe—and he should have stopped fooling with her a week ago.

'I'm sorry, Bella.' He met her gaze squarely. 'I should never have put you in danger.' He didn't want to treat her badly, and he probably would have.

'I put myself there too, remember?' She looked away, stood. 'I think I'll go to bed. I'm a bit tired.'

He stood too. 'You OK? Comfortable? Need a painkiller or anything?'

She shook her head, a sad smile twisting her lips. He knew what she was wondering—if he felt the same about this baby-that-wasn't, if he had the same antipathy towards the idea. But he couldn't answer her, couldn't bear to think on it because it was hurting him more than he'd ever thought it could. And what hurt more was the realisation that she'd been right. He was a coward.

He watched her go. For the first time feeling as if he'd missed out on everything.

It had started out as the party from hell. The house had been tiny. The wind had meant there was no way they could be outside. The stereo system had failed. And there had been the most hideous boyfriend of one of the mothers who'd hit on Bella before she'd even got all the way up the path.

She'd worked hard to turn it around for the poor kid. Wished the audience of adults would just go away so she could have some fairy fun with the wee ones. In the end it had been good old-fashioned bubbles that had saved it—as she'd made big ones they'd spotted the rainbows in them. And then she'd read them the tale of the unicorn and the temporary tattoos had come out and the face paints and the magic of make-believe.

Bella parked Bubbles in the garage and braced herself. The week had gone quickly and she still hadn't moved out. Still hadn't the strength to leave the man she ached to love.

Now, with the payment from this party, she had no more excuses. She could give him at least some of the money she owed and get out. She'd phone her father for the rest to start afresh. It was best, because now she'd thought about it, she knew she wanted the whole marriage and kids bit. She couldn't live with less. So she needed to get away and over him.

He wasn't waiting to pounce on her the minute she walked back in. Instead he lifted his head from the paper he was reading in his big chair, took one look and frowned at her.

'Didn't it go so good?'

She sighed. 'It was OK. But the house was tiny—and I mean tiny. And they'd invited twelve kids and all their parents were there.'

It made her skin itchy just thinking about it—all that close contact with complete strangers. The kids were OK. It was the adults who grossed her out. And she simply couldn't perform to her best in an environment like that.

He shoved his paper to the floor and stood. 'Actually I've been thinking about you and your parties.' He paused, then words seemed to tumble from him. 'Why don't you use some of the space downstairs? You could do it up and get all the kids to come here. It would save you from lecher-ous uncles.'

Bella stared at him. 'You're kidding, right?' He'd never want that—would he?

'No. It might as well be used for something. It'll get other prospective tenants off my back and it'll only be used part of the time. During the week when my guys are in upstairs it'll be quiet.'

'Isn't it a waste of your resource?'

'It's mine to waste.' He shrugged. 'And it'll only be part of it. Still room for a restaurant if I ever want one.'

Oh, my, she thought as he winked. That sparkle was back and his expression was lighter and Bella felt herself falling once more, mesmerised by his vibrancy.

'I'd have to decorate it,' she said, half dazed. 'I don't have the money.'

'I'll loan you. Start-up costs. You can pay me back once you're up and running. You'll make it back in no time.'

She shook her head, stopped thinking completely. This was crazy.

'Bella.' He stepped near her. 'This is what you're good at. This is what you love. Every time you do a party you come home with bookings for at least one or two more. You're a wonderful entertainer. This is what you're meant to do.'

The idea was so tempting. Her own party space. She'd never even thought of it before. And she'd have such fun designing the venue… Unstoppable ideas swirled through her head.

He was grinning at her, as if he knew.

She inhaled deeply, shook her head. 'Owen, I can't.'

'Why not?'

Because things were complicated between them. She didn't want this to be his latest idea that he'd set up and then skip on to the next. They weren't together any more—were they? She really needed to get over him and on with her life. 'I need to get out and find a new flat. I can't stay here for ever.'

There was another non-committal shrug. 'Maybe, but there's plenty of time for that. Why not focus on building a business first? You could do the food too, couldn't you?'

Of course she could—standing on her head. More ideas teased her—of menus and fun things and dreams and fantasies.

'Tell you what.' He kept talking. 'Why don't you just take a segment downstairs and paint it? See what you think. It might not be right as there isn't an outdoor area. It might not work out at all.'

But it would work out. No outdoors didn't matter, not if she created a grotto indoors. And she knew she could do that. And if they built a pirate ship the kids could climb up it and hunt for treasure and…and…

She looked at him. He was acting so casually about this. And yet, in his own way, he was pushing it. Batting away her arguments with a shrug and his usual 'of course you can' attitude. What was his real agenda? Was there anything more to this than a simple offer of help?

Her mind—and heart—leapt to the most blissful conclusion. Was this his way of keeping her in his life? On the terms that he could handle?

Probably not, she scoffed at herself. This was just his latest obsession. And once it was set up he'd be onto something else. She was looking everywhere for anything. But the little bubble of hope wouldn't be popped. She'd keep on hoping, keep on dreaming. Maybe, just maybe, he'd wake up to the fact that there was more between them than either of them could have imagined. Or was it just her imagination going overtime again?

'Come on, let's go look at it now.' He took her arm, half dragging her down the stairs. The space was huge.

'We could partition it off.' He stood, arms stretched out marking imaginary walls.

'I'd have to get consents.' Her trailing footsteps echoed. 'There'd be building work to be done. I'd have to buy so much stuff.'

'Yeah, but wouldn't it be great?' His eyes were shining so damn attractively. No wonder he was successful—he could make anyone believe in anything. Passionate, enthusiastic, energetic.

'Look—' he dragged her over to one corner '—you could have a little shop next door here selling things—like the fairy dresses and the tattoos and glittery stuff. And you could paint a mural—throw in a few tigers.'

She was amazed. 'You've really thought about this.'

'Sure.'

She could have different themed parties—art, beading, pirates, jungles, teddy bears' picnics—the list was endless. His enthusiasm infected her—bubbling through her veins.

'Owen.' She was shaking her head, but she couldn't stop the smile.

He smiled back at her. And then he stepped closer, his hands on her arms. She only needed to take a step forward to touch him—and she wanted to touch him so much.

'Think about it,' he said softly.

She was. She read the offer deep within him. On a plate he was handing her everything she could ever want—anything material. But what she really wanted wasn't a tangible thing. And he didn't think he had it to give. But he did—and so badly she wanted him to give it to *her*. She was a fool, such a fool, but his blue eyes shone even more brilliantly and she couldn't ever say no—not when he looked at her like that.

He whispered again. 'I'm going to kiss you, Bella. So if you don't want me to, you better speak up now.'

Pure, deep, hopeless longing overcame her, rendering her silent, waiting and so willing for whatever he wanted.

But it wasn't the fiercely passionate kiss she expected. It was soft and sweet and so gentle. He stepped closer, his hands lifting to frame her face—so tender. She felt her eyes prickle. She closed them quickly and the bliss simply increased. It rushed from both her toes and the tip of her head—meeting in the middle of her, expanding, taking over the beating of her heart.

Suddenly, somehow, they were on the floor and he'd rolled, pulling her on top, protecting her from the cold, dusty concrete.

'This is bad,' she breathed. 'This is where the kids will be playing.'

'No kids here now. Only a couple of adults. Consenting.'

'Oh, yes.'

CHAPTER TWELVE

BELLA was dusting the shelves at the café the next morning, mentally choosing paint colours, when she heard the beep of her mobile. She pulled it from her pocket. Didn't recognise the number. She didn't recognise the voice either—fortunately the woman said she was calling from Take One Agency....

Oh, God. The audition. Just over a week ago and frankly she'd forgotten it. It had been the day she'd had that massive argument with Owen.

'I'm pleased to be able to offer you the part of...'

Bella tuned out—entering shock. She was being offered a part on a national touring show.

'Rehearsals start in Christchurch next week...'

She'd be paid. A full-time job as an actress—in a musical theatre production. Excitement flooded through her. She couldn't believe it. Couldn't wait to get home and tell Owen.

Owen.

She pulled up short. Owen—who was probably designing her a pirate ship this very minute. Owen—who was probably the reason why she'd got the job in the first place. Owen—who had made her so mad she'd gone into that audition all guns blazing and uncaring of the consequences. Owen—who had never made fun of her parties, but who made everything matter.

She had to leave him. Leave the business—while it was still a seed, just a fragment of a dream. For one wild moment she wanted to turn down the part. Pretend it hadn't happened. But as she listened to the woman warble on about the details she knew she couldn't. This was it, her shot at the big time. Do well in this and she could springboard to other, bigger, better shows.

Sydney, London, New York... Her imagination ballooned.

But there was Owen. And she wanted Owen. And she'd thought if she had a little more time, she might show Owen how much he had to offer—and not just in the money sense. But it probably was for the best, because that was the fantasy, wasn't it? Her winning him. She'd soon know anyway. She'd tell him about the part, see how he reacted. Then she'd know for sure if this was still just sex or something else entirely. She spent the afternoon totally excited, totally nervous, totally torn.

She raced home, but he wasn't there and she paced round the big space. Not sure how to tell him. How to act. But when he finally appeared the thrill, the disbelief, the pride all bubbled out of her.

'I got the part, I got the part!' She ran to him, her smile and arms wide.

He caught her, sweeping them both into the embrace, lifting and spinning her, grinning hugely.

'What part?' he asked when her toes touched the floor again.

'On the show.'

'What show?' He laughed.

'It's not the lead or anything,' she clarified. 'But it is a minor character. Well, quite a major minor character actually. And I do understudy the lead, which means in some matinees I'll be the lead.'

He was still laughing. 'This is fantastic. Which theatre? When?'

Her smile suddenly felt a little stiff. 'It's a travelling show.'

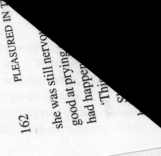

'Travelling?' His hand

She took her full weigh
behind her ear and blu
Christchurch. The show sta
Zealand tour is successful,

'Wow.' He was still grinn

He went straight to the fri
calls for a celebration, right?

The cork fired right across .... frothed. She watched as he poured, staring at the label. Good grief, she'd only ever seen that sort of champagne in the pages of posh magazines.

'Yeah,' she said slowly. Had he known a celebration was in order?

He handed her a glass. 'When do you go?'

'Later this week.'

'How long do you rehearse for?'

'Almost six weeks, I think. Then the tour starts. I don't know how long that'll be ultimately.'

He was all questions; she had no time to think of anything but the answers. It was a good twenty minutes before they quietened.

'You did it,' he said softly, smiling.

'I did.' She still couldn't believe it—any of it. Especially that she'd be leaving, right when things were getting interesting. She finally broached the subject. 'I'm really sorry about not using the space downstairs.'

'Oh. Don't worry about it. It was just an idea. I have lots of them.' He grinned.

Her heart ached. He really didn't mind.

'You'll have to phone and tell your family.'

She paused. 'Not yet.' She'd see how it went first—make sure it was a complete success that she could be proud of. And

...s about contacting Vita. Her sister was too
... and she'd want to do a post-mortem over what
...ed on Waiheke.

...s is great,' he said. 'This is really good.'

...ne supposed it was. An easy, clean finish for him. She'd
been the one building dream castles. Seeing them shatter, hurt.

Owen could see the shadows entering her eyes and steeled
himself not to give in. His heart was breaking—just as he'd
found he had one. But he could not do it. He could see the
question in her face and he refused to answer it. He was not
going to give her the out. He was not going to hold onto her
only to have her resent him for it in—what?—six months or
a year's time. He was not going to ruin it for her.

She had to go. And she had to go utterly free of him. So
he talked it up, went on about how exciting it was, how wonderful. She was finally going to realise her dreams. And not
once did he mention how it was tearing him apart inside. Not
once did he mention how much he wanted her to stay—to
choose him. He gave her no choice. Because he knew that
right now, inside, she cared for him. But she deserved to have
her chance. For a moment there he'd thought they could have
it all, but fate had decided it for both of them. The champagne
tasted bitter. He'd put it in the fridge to celebrate something
else entirely. He'd been going to cast off the coward label and
embrace the risk—of emotion and responsibility—just as
she'd challenged. Only now he was forced into a far more
brave action—letting her go. The irony of it all really sucked.

Bella didn't take time off work. Nor did Owen. In some ways
it was a relief. She worked the last two days at the café totally
on auto. They had pizza one night, Thai the next. Before she knew

it, it was the last night. She was flying. He'd insisted. Reckoned he'd got a cheap deal on the Internet. She'd let him. It beat the ferry and bus option. She was always sick on the ferry.

They'd talked and teased and joked their way through sex. And it had always been wonderful and fun. But this was no joke. She was making love to him for the last time and then she was leaving.

There was nothing she could say. There was no way of changing it—there was no time.

And so for the first time she caressed him in complete silence. Kissing and kissing and kissing so there was no chance to voice the secrets lodged in her heart. That she'd fallen in love with him. Wanted to be with him. Wanted to stay.

As he moved down her body she couldn't stop thinking. Couldn't quite give herself over to the lust. Couldn't enjoy it the way she really wanted to. He couldn't and wouldn't give her what she wanted. And what she wanted was taking her away. Acting was what she wanted most, right?

This was their last time—she had to make the most of it. But all she could think was that it *was* the last time. And that was ruining everything. She wanted to stop. She didn't want there to be a last time.

He must have known because he stopped nuzzling her breasts. Instead he lifted his head and looked in her eyes, framed her face with his hands—so gently. And then *he* kissed *her.* He kissed and kissed until she could no longer think. Until there was no room in her head for doubt or pain. Only touch.

And then, when her mind was gone and she was all sensation, he stroked the rest of her, leaning close so he could follow the path of his fingers with his eyes. He stroked and kissed and gently blew on her hot skin. Moving with such powerful gentleness it was almost her undoing. But he too was silent.

She closed her eyes against the message she so badly wanted to read in his and just let him play with her until the need for the ultimate satisfaction grew too strong for both of them.

When he entered her this time she held her breath, tightening around him, closing him into her embrace with her arms and legs and everything. In her head words had returned and she was chanting: not going to let you go, not going to let you go.

But she was the one going. And she didn't know if she really had the strength to follow through on it.

But later, as she dressed, alone in his bedroom, she knew she had to leave. It was to protect herself. She owed herself the chance of meeting her dreams. And she couldn't stay with a man who didn't want long term—not when she did. Marriage and babies were on her wish-list and she couldn't change that—just as she couldn't change him.

She tried to make the goodbye as quick as she could. It didn't dim the pain at all. She wouldn't look him in the face— couldn't. He wanted to take her to the airport, was insistent. It tore her up inside as he objected.

Finally she looked at him, unable to hide the ache. 'Please, Owen. Let me do this myself.'

He stopped then, a shadow passing over his face. 'You don't have to do everything yourself, Bella. It's OK to have help from people when you need it. Remember that, won't you?'

Yes, it was OK, but not all the time. And she had to do this alone; it was the only way she could.

The taxi was there in minutes and she turned to him feeling as if she had sawdust in her eyes and sandpaper in her throat. He lifted her bag into the boot.

'I'll call you,' he said.

'Actually—' she cleared her throat '—I'd rather you didn't.'

He stared at her.

She didn't want to be half hoping—*wholly* hoping—for the next however many months or years it was going to take to get over him. She needed it to end now. It was the perfect opportunity. Clean, final. Just how he'd like it. She didn't want him to pretend to offer anything else.

'You don't want me to contact you at all?'

She forced her head to move, slowly, side to side.

He stared at her for a long moment, ignoring the driver waiting patiently in the car.

'OK,' he said quietly. 'If that's what you want.'

She nodded then and looked down, not wanting to misread anything more in his face. Wanting to kill all her hope now. She didn't trust her voice at all.

There was a moment of silence. She knew she should move—the driver was waiting, the meter was ticking already. But all that moved were her lashes as she lifted her eyes, unable to resist one last long look at him. His eyes were still a brilliant blue, but charged with a variety of emotions—confusion? Regret?

She couldn't take any more and turned, got the door open. But as she did his hand was on her upper arm and it wasn't gentle as he grasped and swung her back to face him. The door slammed shut again, she had only a fraction of a second to see the blue ablaze and then he was so close and she shut her eyes. The kiss wasn't gentle either. It was hard and demanding and hurt.

But, as always, she softened for him, opened for him, couldn't say no to him. He could have her and take from her as much as he wanted. And then he softened too, his tongue caressing where moments before his mouth had pressed so fiercely, his fingers lightened on her arm and his lips soothed.

And at last she had the strength—she knew not from where—to twist away from him. He couldn't have everything from her when he wouldn't offer the same. It wasn't fair.

She turned, blindly groping for the door handle again, wrenching it open and scrambling into the seat.

'Drive.' It was sort of a bark but it ended as a broken sob. 'Please just drive.'

CHAPTER THIRTEEN

OWEN threw himself into work. He worked and worked and worked. And every minute of the day he thought about Bella. Missed her. Wondered what the hell she was doing—where she was, who she was with, whether she was happy, whether *she* was missing him. And then he worked some more.

He hadn't thought he had it in him to be so aware of another person. To be driven to meet their needs—to put someone before himself. He'd been so ignorant of his parents' situation, so wrapped up in himself and his ideals and ideas. Only now he saw how they and Liz had tainted his view of marriage and children.

He hadn't been in love with Liz. He'd never been in love with anyone until now. So of course back then he hadn't been ready for a child. The baby-that-wasn't hadn't ever seemed real to him, it had simply been the symbol of a burden he hadn't wanted then and thought he'd never want.

Now he knew that if Bella's child had been real he would have loved it—because now he knew what it was to love and how uncontrollable love could be.

When Liz had turned on him and told him how lonely he'd end up, he hadn't believed her. He'd never felt lonely. Too busy with his work. Too busy out partying when the need for physical company bit. He'd thought he had it all sussed.

Until now. Now he felt as lonely as it was possible to feel. And it hurt so badly he didn't know if he'd ever recover—he could only try to get used to it somehow.

He supposed it served him right. That the woman he'd found he was able to love wasn't one who needed it. The timing was all wrong. Her career was just starting. She was finally getting to where she'd wanted to be for so long. And he refused to ruin it for her. He didn't want her to resent him.

It was so ironic that when he finally found someone he wanted to care about, to love and cherish, help and protect, she was someone who was determined not to need those things. Bella didn't want help; she didn't want his money. She wanted independence. She'd said it, at the end there, that she needed to do this by herself. She was looking for respect. Trying to fight her family for it, fight him, every step of the way. But couldn't she see there was a balance? He couldn't stand back and watch her futile efforts when there were ways in which he could help. Maybe the way it had ended was all for the best.

Like hell it was.

As the days progressed, so his anger rose. Screw this true hero thing. It was a con. There was no happiness in nobility— not this sort. He should never have let her go, at least, not without him. She'd tipped his world upside down and then walked out, leaving him in a hell of a mess. Damn it, his wanting to help her wasn't because he thought she was incapable; it was about him simply wanting to support her. No one was truly independent—not even him.

And there he'd been worried he'd get bored with one person for life. He laughed, a bitter, self-mocking laugh. What an arrogant jerk. No one could ever be bored around Bella.

She was full of life—a little kooky perhaps, most definitely a touch accident-prone. But she was also true and sweet and generous and funny. He wanted the warmth she had to offer. And he didn't want to ever give it up.

He couldn't stop the emotion from flowering in him. She was his own magic fairy—she'd brought back his humanity, his humility, his hope. And he wanted to keep her by his side for ever. He chuckled. So he was still selfish. He was about to make his most selfish move ever.

The rehearsal weeks flew by. Bella had never worked so hard in all her life. They rehearsed all day and halfway through the evening. After that she collapsed into her little single bed in the tiny overcrowded flat that she was sharing with three other cast members and tried to sleep. Tried not to feel cold and lonely. But it was only when she closed her eyes tight and imagined herself in his big warm bed that she managed to drift off to sleep. In that blissful moment just on waking she'd still think she was there with him, but then she'd open her eyes and remember.

The work was full on but fun. She was glad she'd done all those years of dancing as a kid. Costumes were made, the set was designed, affairs were begun, gossip was spread. It was the mad, bad, bitchy world of musical theatre. She kept her distance from the worst of it. She learnt her part, understudied the other and developed an unhealthy obsession with the Internet. There was a lot on him—had she known she'd have looked sooner. But there was his website and a ton of articles about the savvy young entrepreneur. One of them had an accompanying picture of him in jeans and tee, totally looking like the relaxed guy she'd met that first night.

She couldn't indulge in her usual fix of chocolate, ice

cream and red wine without thinking of him, couldn't eat her muesli at odd times of the day, couldn't even have a coffee. Everywhere she turned, everything she did, she thought of him. But worst of all were the nights. When in her lonely, little bed she lay restless, remembering every moment, every move, every touch, every tease.

She worked harder, longer, not wanting her silly heart to ruin this time for her.

There was nothing, no contact from him, just as she'd requested. And she forced that stupid, still sparking hope inside to shrink—day by day.

Opening night was upon her before she knew it. Nerves threatened to swamp her. But as she put on her make-up the security guy came and delivered the most beautiful bunch of flowers to her. There was no note other than her name. No hint of who they might have come from. The speed of her pulse quadrupled. Were they from him? She got through the show on a buzz of adrenalin and bubbling hope. Was he out there—in the audience?

Afterwards she joined in the laughter and excitement of the others, then scurried back to her dressing room, changing into her opening-night party outfit. There was a knock at the door. Heart thundering, she opened it.

'Dad! Vita!' Her jaw dropped. 'It's you.'

'We wouldn't miss it for the world.' Vita threw her arms around her.

'I didn't think you even knew.' Bella emerged from the hug and looked from her father to her sister.

'Well, we wouldn't have if it was down to you.' Vita gave her a sharp look.

She hadn't thought they'd be that interested. Not that she was about to admit that to them.

'Did you get the flowers?' her father asked almost shyly.

'They were from you?' she asked in the wobbliest voice ever.

Her father nodded. 'Vita chose them.'

Her sister smiled at her.

Bella smiled back. She shouldn't feel disappointed. It was wonderful of them to have sent them. It was even more wonderful that they'd been here for her. But she'd wanted to believe they'd been from Owen. Crushed, she forced out a smile. Her best acting job of the night was required *after* the performance.

'We're coming again when you get to Auckland,' her father said unexpectedly.

Vita nodded enthusiastically. 'To a matinee when you're playing the lead. All the brothers are coming too. We've booked out a whole block of seats.'

Bella failed on the smile front then, bent her head to hide the sudden tears that were stinging her eyes. She blinked a few times. 'How did you know about that?'

'Someone sent us the details.' Her father spoke.

'Oh?'

'Owen sent an email to the whole family,' Vita said.

'What?' But there was no time for a repeat—now that her father had started talking, it seemed he couldn't stop.

'You were great up there, honey. I was so proud.' He beamed. 'Your mother would have loved it.'

She couldn't hide the tears then, and her father awkwardly put his arm around her, offering her a comfort she hadn't had in years.

Vita and Bella sat while their dad went up to the counter to get drinks at the after show party.

'You know, I've always been a bit jealous of you.' Vita smiled. 'Now I'm a lot.'

Nonplussed, Bella just stared at her for a moment. 'You want to be onstage?'

Vita laughed. 'No!' She shook her head. 'All that make-up would play havoc with my skin,' she joked. 'No, it was because you always seemed so confident. You didn't give a damn about what the rest of us were doing, or what Dad thought you should do. You just knew what you wanted and went for it. You've got such determination.'

'You've got to be kidding me.' Bella nearly choked. 'It's not like that at all.'

'But you've always known what you wanted,' Vita said. 'I've never known. I only did commerce because it was what everyone else had done and they seemed to do OK.'

Yes, but the fantasy of what Bella had wanted and the reality weren't panning out to be quite the same thing. 'Is it OK?' she asked her sister.

'Yeah, but I'm not exactly passionate about it.' Vita winked. 'Spreadsheets and tax returns aren't exactly something you live for.' She laughed. 'Whereas you have a job you love. I'm envious of that. But—' she leant forward '—I've got a secret. I'm quitting accountancy and I'm opening my own café.'

'You're what?' Bella was astounded. 'Vita, do you know how hard it is to work in a café?'

'Sure.'

'What does Hamish say?'

Vita's eyes glowed. 'He's really supportive. It's because of him that I'm finally going to do it. I'm doing a catering course and then I'm opening up. He's keeping an eye out for a good location now. He's such a great guy, Bella.'

'I know.' Bella nodded. 'Wow. That's really cool. Good for you.'

'I'd never have had the guts if I didn't have you as an example, though.'

Bella nearly laughed. If only her sister knew. It had only been because of Owen that she'd got the part. He'd made her so mad. Worst of all he'd been right. But she couldn't think of him any more. 'Thanks so much for coming to the show. And for bringing Dad. I really appreciate it.'

'It was Owen who organised it. What's happening with him anyway?'

'Oh, nothing,' Bella answered shortly, really not wanting to dwell on him. 'We're just friends.'

Vita giggled. 'As if. The two of you the night before my wedding? My God, you had the place steaming up so bad there was practically water running down the walls.'

Bella felt her cheeks blaze.

'He's very good-looking,' Vita said. 'And very successful.'

'What do you know about him?' She couldn't stop her curiosity.

'Bella—' Vita shook her head '—if you were remotely clued in to the real world like the rest of us you'd know too. He made squillions when he sold his web stuff to that multimedia conglomerate.' She looked sly. 'How did the two of you meet anyway?'

Bella shook her head. She sure didn't want to go there. 'It was nothing. It's over. This was just him being nice.'

'I don't think a guy like Owen would be organising your family for you if it was over—he wouldn't want us getting the wrong idea.'

'I haven't spoken to him in weeks. Trust me, it's over.' This last gesture was just the way he worked, charming to the end, still helping her out. Only now she was trying even harder to forget the heat in that final kiss, trying to stop wondering what might have happened if she hadn't got the part, if she hadn't left town.

Thankfully her father was heading to the table carrying a tray laden with glasses and nibbles. Talk returned to the show and the tour.

She got to the theatre early as usual the next day.

'This parcel arrived for you last night too—sorry I didn't get it to you sooner.' The security guy at the theatre door collared her as she made her way in.

'Oh, that's fine,' she answered, heart hammering as she recognised the handwriting on the packet, trying not to snatch the thing out of his hands. She hurried to her dressing room, ripped the end of the bag and tipped the contents out.

A soft toy tiger bounced onto the table. She picked up the plush creature. There was a small card on a ribbon around his neck. She read it. 'Break a leg.'

She didn't need her leg breaking as well, thanks very much. She already had a broken heart. That was more than enough. She tipped the bag upside down and shook it again. Nothing else. No other message. It wasn't even signed. There was no return address on the back.

Bastard. She tossed the tiger across the room. She'd asked him not to contact her, all the while been hoping he would and now he had and with what—a damn toy? For the child he thought she was? She'd wanted more—she'd wanted so much more. This almost felt worse than nothing.

Almost. She frowned at the tiger. Why had she thought that he'd taken her seriously? But for about five minutes there he'd really seemed to want to believe in her and her party business. Hell, he'd even offered to help her paint a jungle mural on his warehouse wall, for heaven's sake.

So what did he mean by this? She was too scared to try to figure it out and too stupid not to start hoping some more.

The tiger seemed to be looking at her reproachfully. She rolled her eyes. It was a toy, for goodness' sake. Inanimate. *Stuffed*. The reproachful look deepened.

'Oh, all right, then.' She stomped over to it. 'Stop making me feel so guilty.' She picked him up, fingers automatically smoothing his fur. 'Don't think you're sleeping in my bed, though.'

The nights started to blur together. After the excitement of the opening, the thrill of the first reviews, they settled into the performances, tried not to get stale. And the reality of her new life hit her.

She was lonely. The show lasted nearly two hours. The applause lasted maybe ten minutes at the most. There was no real contact or interaction with the audience. The cast and crew were fabulous, fun. They were a kind of family. But she couldn't quite get into it. Why was it that things were never quite how you imagined they would be?

Early in the mornings that followed, she snuggled deeper into her bed, hugged Tiger that little bit closer, and dreamed.

CHAPTER FOURTEEN

IT WAS the matinee performance and Bella was taking the lead for the first time. She swallowed her nerves, but found they got stuck in her throat. So she stood in the wings and remembered the fierce look on Owen's face when he'd told her she had to believe in herself.

Believe. Believe. Believe.

As the opening music started she closed her eyes, whispered it to herself one more time and then stepped onto the stage. Looking on it afterwards, the whole thing was a blur. But backstage everyone was effusive in their congratulations and support. Even the director was pleased and told her that if she kept up like that she'd be getting bigger parts very soon. Bittersweet success flavoured her mood as she tripped down the corridor to the dressing rooms.

She stopped. Owen was leaning against the wall outside her door.

She stared. Looked him up and down and up and down and again. Put a hand out to balance herself against the wall because her legs had gone lifeless.

At her dumbfounded appraisal his grin was boyish. 'My mother taught me to dress for the theatre.'

'Even the eleven a.m. matinee show with all the audience aged either under ten or over sixty?'

'It's still the theatre,' he said smoothly.

She took a step closer. The tuxedo was devastating. The jacket fitting so well across his broad shoulders and tapering into his lean hips it just had to have been tailor-made.

Finally her heart started beating again—loud, painful thumping. 'What are you doing here?' She couldn't believe it.

'You were great.' He'd lost the grin and was now serious and not quite meeting her eyes.

'What are you doing here?' She strained to focus. She had to know.

'You really were amazing on that stage.'

He spoke so softly, she almost wondered if he was talking to her or just himself.

'Are you listening to me?' What the hell was going on?

'You have a real gift.'

She couldn't handle any more of this madness.

'I'm getting changed.' She stalked straight past him, into the dressing room, and shut the door. She whipped off her costume, climbed into her usual skirt and top, and wiped off as much of the make-up as she could in thirty seconds. Then she stared at her reflection in the mirror. Had she just imagined that encounter? Was she finally going nuts?

Taking a deep, supposedly stabilising breath, she opened the door. He was leaning against the jamb right in front of her. The tux was no less magnificent. Her brain went fuzzy.

He straightened. 'Can we go somewhere to talk?'

She searched his features, wanting him to meet her gaze. 'Why are you here?'

He looked at her then, blue eyes blazing. 'Why do you think?'

She expelled a sharp breath as everything inside quivered.

She fought the sensation, tensing up—that *look* wasn't enough. She wanted to hear it. Wanted to *know*—because what he was here for might not be enough for her. Anger and uncertainty and fear ripped through the delight in seeing him. 'Are you ready to define us yet, Owen? Or are we still not applying labels?'

He glanced away, down the corridor, and she realised he too was tense all over. 'Just give me a minute, Bella.'

'You're kidding,' she snapped. 'How much time do you need?'

'Listen to you.' His sharp smile flashed. 'You really have got your act together.'

'Don't you patronise me.' Frustration trammelled through her. She was ready to slam the door again—in his face.

But in a swift movement he put his hands on her hips and jerked her out of the doorway towards him. 'Never.'

One arm snaked hard around her waist, pulling her home, while his other hand lifted, holding her head up to his as his mouth descended. Her body thudded into his as their lips connected and just like that her fight against him was gone, overtaken completely by desire and ultimately by love.

She was holding her head up all by herself and his hands were all over her, pressing, pulling her closer to his heat and strength. And still it wasn't close enough. Shaking, she threaded her fingers through his hair, holding him, clutching at him, reaching up on tiptoe as her mouth clung to his—giving, seeking, taking, wanting more and more. Pure energy, electricity, sent sparks through her where they touched. She moaned into his mouth, feeling his response—harder, fiercer, deeper. The madness was back and she wanted it to last for ever.

He was the one who eased them out of it. His large hands taking her wrists, lowering them as he slowly lifted his head.

For a second she strained up to follow. And then she heard it—the cacophony, the riot. She glanced to the side.

Oh, God, the entire cast and crew were in the corridor, watching them, catcalling and wolf-whistling and cheering.

She turned back and tried to tug free from his grip. She knew her cheeks were scarlet.

'I did ask you to give me a minute.' He grinned at her, but his hands were still tight, keeping her close. 'To get us some privacy. But now I'm not letting go.'

'My flat,' she muttered. 'It's only a few minutes away.'

He guided her out of the theatre, holding her hand firmly. Still flushed, she could hardly summon a smile for her colleagues as they called goodbye, wished her well and made the odd laughingly crude comment.

'And there was me thinking you liked an audience,' Owen said dryly as they got outside. He opened the door to the waiting taxi. She didn't question, just got in and gave the driver the address. Owen slid in the back seat beside her, reclaimed her hand and passed the time chatting to the taxi driver about the rugby.

But he said nothing as, trembling, she unlocked the door and led the way in. And when she turned in the tiny room and saw him behind her, looking at her with those brilliant eyes, the loneliness and heartache that she'd tried so hard to bury resurfaced in a crashing wave, crushing her. She couldn't believe that he was here. And what if he still couldn't give her everything she wanted? She couldn't settle for less, but she had no choice. She was so bound to him, had such need for him, it terrified her. She blinked as her eyes stung, but still the world went blurry.

'Ah, Bella.' Husky, he reached for her, took her into his arms, wrapping them around her—strong and secure. 'I'm sorry.'

She burrowed her face into his broad chest, gripped his lapels, a bundle of tension and fearful need.

But he said nothing more. For long moments he just cradled her gently, stroking his hand down her rigid back in a long, slow rhythm, until at last she felt her warmth returning, and could relax into him. His arms tightened.

And then she was the one who spoke. 'Vita and my dad came to the show.'

'I know.'

'Opening night.'

'I know.'

'They're coming again, when I'm the lead in Auckland.'

'I know.'

More tears leaked from her eyes. It had all been him. 'It means a lot to me.'

'I know.'

She took in a deep breath, shuddered with it. 'Thank you.' It was muffled, into his shoulder.

His fingers slid up, into her hair. His mouth moved on the top of her head. 'They loved it. They love you.'

'I know.'

'He just wants you to be happy.'

'Yeah.'

'He thought that what made them happy would be the same thing to make you happy. But you're different, Bella. You're you. And you had to work it out for yourself.'

She nodded. 'But what I thought would make me happy hasn't.'

He lifted her chin, frowning at her tear-stained face. 'You're not happy?'

She shook her head. 'Owen, I'm such a mess.' Another tear spilt. 'I thought I wanted all this, but I don't.'

He looked deep into her eyes. 'What do you want?'

You. She was sure he could read her answer. But she refused to say it; it sounded so pathetic. And he wasn't all she wanted. She still wanted everything. 'I'm not going to do the Australian leg of the tour. I'll do New Zealand, but that's it. It's not what I want to do.'

His frown returned, bigger than before. 'But, Bella—'

'I miss the kids,' she interrupted, wanting to explain before she lost the nerve. 'I miss the direct contact. It's make-up on, bright lights, but I can hardly see the audience. It's a big theatre but it seems lonely. They applaud, they leave. By the time I'm scrubbed and changed, there's no one there. There's no interaction.' She lifted her chin, determined to take pride in her decision. 'I know being a children's entertainer isn't exactly the most highly rated job there is, but I'm good with them. I enjoy it. I'm going to go ahead and find my own venue and set up a business like you suggested. It was a good idea.'

He smiled then, a warm, encouraging smile. 'Bella, that's wonderful.'

Pleasure washed through her as she heard and saw his support. He believed in her and how she loved him for it and suddenly nothing else mattered. She'd take whatever he had, for however long, it would be enough—because she loved him.

'Don't look at me like that,' he suddenly begged. 'I'm not kissing you again until I've said what I have to say.'

She leaned that little closer into him and he groaned.

'I'm coming on tour with you.' He blurted the words out.

'What?' She jerked upright again.

'I'm coming with you. Sorry if that's not what you want, but that's what's happening.' He spoke even faster. 'I'm not spending another night apart from you.' He bent his head. 'Ever.'

She gasped at the rush of exhilaration. This kiss was even

hungrier and more desperate than the one at the theatre. They clung, fierce, fevered. But again slowly, reluctantly, he drew back. He gripped her hands, stopping their frantic exploration, making her listen.

'I can work with my laptop and mobile. I'll have to fly to meetings every now and then, but I'll be back for the night. Every night.'

She couldn't stop the smile spreading as the glow inside grew stronger, becoming a solid flame of joy. 'OK.'

'And another thing,' he continued after another crazy kiss, his hands failing to stop their own exploration this time, 'the next family wedding you're going to is your own.'

'I thought you didn't believe in marriage.' She gaped. 'That it wasn't worth the paper it was written on.'

'You remember every stupid thing I've ever said, don't you?' he asked ruefully.

'Some of it wasn't so stupid.' He'd changed her life, made her see everything so much clearer. And now her whole body seemed to be singing.

'I want to marry you,' he said softly. 'I'll never want anyone but you. But I need you to tell me if you're not happy and I've not noticed.'

'You'll notice,' she assured him. 'You notice more about me than I do myself.'

'But if I'm buried in work…' He stopped, then almost whispered, 'I don't want to fail you.'

'You won't.' She raised her hand to his cheek, gently smiling. 'And if you do, I can always send you an email.'

'You'd do that?' He chuckled. 'For me?'

'I'd do anything for you,' she quietly admitted, knowing he already knew that.

His arms tightened. 'I never thought I could love anyone

the way I love you.' At last she saw the vulnerability in his eyes as he wholly opened up. 'I want to be everything for you.'

'You already are.'

He shook his head. 'I want to do everything with you. I want to give you everything.' He drew in a shaky breath. 'I want you to have our children, Bella. I want your children.'

At that she closed her burning eyes tight, pressed them hard against his jacket again. 'Me too,' she said, and then drew a deep breath. 'But maybe not for a while? I want to make the business work first.' And she wanted to have some time just with him, to broaden their foundations before they had their family.

'OK. You just say the word. When you're ready, I'll be ready.'

He was going to be there for her, for everything.

She reached up, pulled him down for her kiss and walked backwards, leading him to her tiny bedroom. He glanced around and she melted at the mix of relief and desire in his face. Her legs stumbled and he scooped her up.

'Do me a favour.' He lifted his mouth from hers for a moment.

'Anything.' She pulled it back to her.

'When we get home, can you put on that bridesmaid's dress?'

She paused then. 'It's hideous.'

He shook his head. 'It's beautiful.'

She undid his tie. 'Your eyesight is dodgy from all that staring at screens.'

'You have no idea the number of fantasies I've had involving that dress. All these long, lonely nights where I've had nothing but those pictures.' He stole another quick kiss. 'You have no idea how much I regret missing that wedding. I totally fell for you the minute I saw you in that bar—it was like nothing else. I should have held onto you then and there. Never let you go.'

She melted more. 'It happened right. You were right. I needed to stand up and try. To discover what it was I wanted.'

'And so did I.' He turned and leaned back, landing them both on her bed. But he didn't kiss her; instead he reached behind him, sliding his hand under the sheet and pulling out... Tiger.

Owen's whole expression softened, the lights in his eyes warming, mouth twitching. 'So you got him.'

She nodded. 'He usually comes to the theatre with me but the others were joking about him and I was worried he'd go wandering.'

'Well, sorry, tiger, there's no room in here any more.' He bent his arm back, about to throw him.

'Don't you dare!' Bella scolded, taking the toy from him. 'He's been a good friend to me these past few days.'

'Have you been cuddling him?'

'Maybe.' She tried to play it cool.

He grinned and took the toy from her. 'What a good little tiger, keeping her arms occupied and scaring off any interlopers.'

'As if I'd do that.'

'It wasn't you I was worried about,' he teased. 'It was all these showbiz boys and crew and groupies. They'll all be panting after you.'

'Half of them are gay.'

'And half of them aren't. I wanted tiger here to be the only thing in your arms. And you did a good job, didn't you, boy? Well, I'm back now and you can go sleep somewhere else.'

He stood up and put the tiger on an armchair, facing away from the bed, slung her cardigan over him.

'Happy now?' His eyes were twinkling.

'No,' she answered—all tragedy—but she couldn't hide the happiness any more. It burst out of her. 'Not until you're back here.'

He vaulted onto the bed, kissed her and their passion, too long denied, erupted. As he rose, his strong body braced over hers, she spread her fingers wide across his chest and marvelled. She simply couldn't believe she was going to have it all.

'How did I get so lucky?'

'It isn't luck, Bella,' he muttered as he pushed home. 'It's what you deserve.' He drew closer still. 'You deserve everything.'

She arched, reaching to meet him, wanting to give him as much as he was giving her, so that together they would have it all. And, as his murmurs of love melded to her moans, and the feeling of bliss between their bodies grew, she knew.

She'd succeeded.

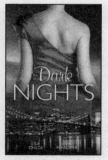

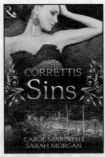

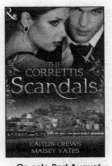

Where will *you* read
this summer?

#TeamShade

Join your team this summer.

www.millsandboon.co.uk/sunvshade

SUNSHADEb